BY THE POWERS OF SWORD AND SPELL. . . .

Torn between the callings of swordswoman and sorceress, a young woman must learn whether either talent holds true in a terrifying, late-night encounter with a band of trolls. . . .

Her apprentice stolen, can a healer stand alone against the evils of wizard and demon?

She was a sword singer facing her greatest test—to mend the flaw in the warlord's sword, a flaw so dangerous it could devastate the entire kingdom!

It was a warrior's quest straight out of legend—to reclaim her people's jewel of power from the mightiest of death wizards, the master of the Void!

These are but a few of the battles to be fought, the challenges to be answered in this all new collection of magical tales of—

SWORD AND SORCERESS

SWORD AND SORCERESS V

AN ANTHOLOGY
OF HEROIC FANTASY

Edited by
Marion Zimmer Bradley

DAW BOOKS, INC.
DONALD A. WOLLHEIM, PUBLISHER

1633 Broadway, New York, NY 10019

DAW Book Collectors No. 753.

First Printing, August 1988

1 2 3 4 5 6 7 8 9

PRINTED IN THE U.S.A.

TABLE OF CONTENTS

INTRODUCTION
OR SOMETHING

It gets harder every year to reject stories—though I have a pretty good idea of what I *don't* want. It gets harder and harder every year to think up a good reason for rejections. So if I've rejected your story and you still believe it's a good story, bear in mind that I do not speak from Mount Sinai on tablets of stone. If I reject your story for what seems not to be a good reason, it's just the way it struck me when I read it—or maybe I am just thinking "what can I say to this talented person which will make her (more likely than him) realize that while I can't buy this story because I already have too many stories like it, I might buy the next one?"

And when I am reading every year I have to read the same stories over and over; if I didn't buy *your* dragon or unicorn story—and you probably sent me one—everybody did, I think—please remember how many I've read already this year.

Nothing is ever settled, is it? Every year someone writes to me protesting my policy of *not* buying a story where someone says, "But this isn't women's work." My strong feeling is that anything is women's (or, for that matter, men's) work if they are strong enough for it and want to do it. I sometimes thank heaven that I was not made to climb utility poles, but if women want to, why they shouldn't is a mystery to me. So I don't buy stories where women are told, usually by the men in their life, that so and so—climbing utility poles, herding dragons,

7

or more often, swordplay or sorcery—isn't women's work. Yes, I know that battle, in real life, hasn't been won yet; I know that women do get told in real life that they can't herd dragons, climb utility poles or what have you—but it doesn't make a good story. We women have to know that in fiction we *won't* get told that; in the fiction I edit, *no* one gets told they can't herd dragons. Though why they want to is still a mystery to me. What's wrong with wearing pretty clothes anyhow? A child of the Depression, I'd have loved some! (This refers, of course, to the place in THE FEMALE MAN where somebody says that men get to do this or that and women get to wear pretty clothes.) I didn't—and I'd have loved to.

Be that as it may, I do not see fantasy as a way of fighting battles that should have been won long since, so don't re-invent the wheel in your story. It may need saying—that women can and do herd (or fight) dragons—but not in fiction, *except by their doing it.* And they do. And will continue to do so.

At least in my fiction for this anthology.

—M.Z.B.

SORCERER'S PET
by Margaret L. Carter

Every year, the first story I buy cuts off a dozen other choices. Reviewers sometimes say that I am fonder of "sword" stories than of those which deal with magic; but here is a story which deals with both. It is a "typical" story in a way because it deals with a mercenary, and is thus an "average" story insofar as any fantasy can be average; but this one has a lot of other things too, including both shapeshifting and sorcery.

So we open another anthology with this story by Margaret Carter, who has also sold to one of the Darkover anthologies.

The tall, lean, russet-haired young woman started up from her doze beside the campfire's embers. Her hand flew to her dagger hilt. She scanned the trees from which proceeded the rustling that had roused her. Twilight shadows were slanting through the dark green and bluish purple leaves. The underbrush near her stirred, and an animal emerged—a shaggy, fanged beast whose gray pelt was splotched with irregular patches the shade of old wine. It carried the carcass of a lopear in its jaws.

The woman relaxed, removing her hand from her belt. "Of all the irresponsible—"

The beast dropped the plump, long-eared animal it carried and swished its tail at her. Its brilliant turquoise

9

eyes held a pleading expression. The animal shape wavered like a reflection on water and dissolved into a column of grayish maroon smoke. It was replaced by the nude body of a boy in his late teens. Sandy-haired and slim, he was as tall as the woman but not filled out to man's bulk. The blue eyes, unchanged, met her violet ones with a mocking gleam. "Thought you might want fresh meat for supper, instead of those tough dried strips."

"Crawling Chaos, Bronn! I doze off for a few minutes, expecting you to keep watch, and you pull a trick like this! I don't know why I brought you."

Grinning, the boy squatted beside his knapsack to pull out his trousers and tunic. "Because even a mighty warrior like you can't pull off a task like this single-handed."

"Oh, shut your face and build up the fire while I get this thing skinned. It should be a tender one, but still not worth wasting a change on. When I tell Mother and Father how you've behaved—"

"Come on, Laenie, what do you expect they'll do? I'm a little old to be sent to bed without supper. Relax, I still have two changes left." Buttoning up his pants, he poked at the fire, his tunic still hanging open. Having just finished his shapeshifting apprenticeship, he was inordinately proud of the one form he'd mastered—the hoarfang—and missed no chance to show off.

"To last you until tomorrow's dawn," she reminded him, slashing viciously at the lopear's belly. "This is the only job I've had more exciting than bodyguarding travelers too lazy or inept to defend themselves. I won't let you foul it up."

Bronn gave her a sly smile. "I know what Master Osswen would say about you working for Mistress Moraya. Didn't he always say she was corrupt?"

Laenie disemboweled the lopear with a single twist of the blade. "What does Master Osswen know of the world? He spends his life in that mansion two hours' travel from the nearest village. Half the time he's scrying for lords and princes and well-off merchants like Father; the other half, he's buried in Gate experiments to plumb the secrets of the great Beyond or something. He doesn't understand people like us, who have our living to earn."

"You were interested enough in the great Beyond for awhile."

Laenie had spent not quite a year apprenticed to Master Osswen before deciding that sorcery was too remote from real life to hold her attention. She remained fond of the old man, her father's blood brother from childhood, but she didn't regret having changed to the warrior's profession. "Master Osswen said I had a sharp mind and quick memory, but I lacked the depth of purpose for a sorceress. And if 'depth' means understanding the philosophy of magic, he was right."

Preparing the lopear for the spit, she recalled hundreds of hours listening to Osswen drone on about magical ethics. She'd drowsed at his feet while he propounded endless moral problems, among whose manifold solutions she could glimpse not a hair's worth of difference. What did numbering the planes of existence or mapping the nodes where the Shadow Realm intersected the material world have to do with "good" and "evil?" Osswen had promised she would understand when she'd imbibed enough knowledge, but she hadn't had the patience to wait. She therefore took his ominous remarks about Mistress Moraya with scepticism. To Osswen, "corrupt" could simply mean the woman altered the words of some immemorial spell or used reptile's blood instead of bird's in her scrying bowl.

Moraya had chosen Laenie for this task because of her brief study with Osswen. "You know just enough about magic to be wary of it," the sorceress had said, "but not enough to fool around and alert your target. Unlike most warriors I've met, you probably have sense enough not to let your sword hand run away with your brains."

Though she liked her employer personally no more than Osswen did, Laenie had let the slur on warriors pass. A job was a job. According to Moraya, her former partner, Gelvon, had quarreled with her and, instead of splitting their assets honorably, had absconded with Moraya's most valued possession. "You are looking for a cage. It holds a—a pet I'm very fond of." Laenie had concealed her inward sneer behind a bland smile. Did Moraya really assume a former sorcerer's apprentice could be so naive as not to equate "pet" with "familiar?" True, familiar-using female mages were rare, that kind of sorcery being more masculine in style, but the phenomenon wasn't unheard of. Laenie suspected this Gelvon had an equal or greater right to the "pet," but it wasn't Laenie's place to judge the rights of an occult property dispute. She was loyal to the employer who paid her.

Bronn inquired about her plans as they dismembered the hot, dripping meat. "As soon as dark falls," said Laenie, "we'll move down the ridge, closer to Gelvon's house." Like most of his profession, Gelvon preferred to live away from other dwellings, to protect both his privacy from invasion and his neighbors from his experiments. "You'll take hoarfang shape and reconnoiter. I want to know where he keeps the cage, if possible, before I go barging in. And no clowning around this time."

"Yes, Sister," said Bronn with mock meekness.

About an hour after twilight Laenie judged that the shadows had deepened enough to let Bronn, in his four-legged form, creep up to the house unnoticed. After watching him transform and lope down the hill, she concealed herself among the trees until he returned. It seemed too long before she heard his panting as he trotted up to her. Whatever his faults, their parents would never forgive her if she let him get seriously hurt.

He flowed back into human shape. "It's there, all right. His workshop is the big room just beyond the antechamber, and the cage is in the center of the largest table. I couldn't get a good look at it. It—it glows somehow, hurts my eyes."

"Probably a glamour on it, a side effect of some magical protection," said Laenie. "But you did see enough?"

"Yes, just the way you said Moraya described it—a lattice-weave sphere a little larger than a man's head."

"Made of polished bone, with a white crystal at each of the intersections of the network," Laenie recalled. "And she said it's very fragile, so we have to be careful if we fight Gelvon in that room."

When full dark closed in, they moved within sight of the sorcerer's cottage. It was just that, not a mansion the size of Osswen's. Laenie's former master, though, needed the space for students; perhaps Gelvon took none. From what Laenie had heard of him in the nearest town, Gelvon was even more reclusive than the average member of his calling. One window showed a gleam through the shutters. It was just as well, thought Laenie, that Gelvon was awake and at work, for she didn't anticipate breaking in. Surrounded by magical wards—the reason Moraya hadn't simply used her own powers to recover the cage—the house would be guarded against the arts of an ordinary thief, as well. The application of tools to door or window would raise the alarm just as surely as the smell of magic would. Laenie hoped to trick the owner into opening the door.

She'd decided to play the role of a benighted traveler pursued by a ravenous beast. In the likely event that Gelvon had no compassion on youth in distress, she hoped curiosity would impel him to investigate the tumult. Or, if nothing else, anger at having his spells disturbed might bring him out. Bronn's shapeshifting would not stir Gelvon's occult awareness. Bronn's change was not true magic, but an inborn talent (signaled by his blue eyes) that had only needed developing.

Laenie realized she was mentally revolving the plan in nervous reluctance to get started. She signaled Bronn to change form. When he was ready, she descended the slope to the front door of the cottage. Approaching within easy hearing range, she set up a shriek as bloodcurdling as any tragedy player's. She ran at the door and pounded on it with both fists. Bronn played his role with zest, nipping at her heels and slavering almost too realistically.

Her throat was hoarse when the door was finally flung open. "Unspeakable Name! What is this idiocy?"

For an instant she was thrown off balance by the mage's appearance. She had expected a graybeard like Osswen. Gelvon proved to be a lean-muscled man in the prime of middle age, his face unlined except for creases etched around the eyes by long study. He wore a knee-length, sleeveless robe belted at the waist. Laenie recovered her wits at once. She fell to her knees and clutched one of his ankles in a simulation of mindless panic. Actually her legs were poised beneath her to spring up.

Gelvon tried to tug away from her, still annoyed rather than alarmed. "Let go, you stupid girl."

Bronn, as hoarfang, launched himself in a smooth arc

at the sorcerer's chest. Gelvon fell flat on his back.
Bronn sprinted past him into the house. Laenie leaped
up and followed before the mage could catch his breath.
She got a bare glimpse of the small entryway as she
dashed through it—empty except for the conventional
pool, stocked with miniature flash-fins, in one corner.
She heard Gelvon's soft-shod feet pursuing as she emerged
into the workroom.

It was equipped much as Osswen's or any other magician's laboratory. Several rough wood tables and chairs
stood around in no particular pattern, shelves lined the
walls, and a cacophony of smells, musty, pungent, and
sweet, permeated the air. On the center table sat the
"cage," just as Bronn had described it. More accustomed
to magic than Bronn was, Laenie could see the object
better than he had. The sphere was filled with an iridescent pink substance, like flesh set alight by an inner
flame. No, not quite flesh, for the longer she stared, the
less solid it seemed. It undulated like a glop of jelly
animated by a whimsical apprentice. It wasn't amusing,
though; its coiling made her head ache.

She needed only seconds to take in this image and
realize what the substance was. It was no glamour to
conceal the occupant of the sphere. Laenie had expected
the "pet" to be a reptile or rodent trained to serve the
sorcerer. Rather, this rippling jelly was itself the pet, a
life-form like no animal in nature.

She and Bronn whirled to face the furious Gelvon.
Weaponless, the mage headed for a table where a thin-
bladed ritual dagger lay. Bronn intercepted him. Gelvon
managed to snatch up the knife just as the hoarfang was
upon him. Bronn lunged at Gelvon but was halted by the
blade flailing near his eyes. The plan called for Bronn to
knock down and immobilize the sorcerer so that Laenie
could bind him. The flashing of Gelvon's knife, though,
restricted the animal to worrying at his legs, trying to trip
him. Gelvon kept his feet with more agility than Laenie
would have expected of his type.

He was concentrating on slashing at the hoarfang's
eyes. Eyes—it was only a matter of minutes before Gelvon
got a good look at them. Laenie noticed his start of

recognition. No true beast had blue eyes. Gelvon knew Bronn for a human being transformed.

To Laenie's surprise, Gelvon dropped the knife and crooked his fingers, clawlike. From his throat spewed a burst of unintelligible words. The guttural sound made the air crackle as with the foretaste of a thunderstorm. The spell took instant effect; Bronn stood before his opponent as a naked boy.

"Bronn, you dolt!" Laenie cried. "Change back!" He cast her a miserable look. She remembered that he had used his three changes for the day and had none left.

As a beast, Bronn was formidable. As a human male, he'd had no more combat training than the average young person his age. He flicked a glance toward the open door. Instead of fleeing, though, he raised his arms in an amateurish fighting pose and advanced on Gelvon. Laenie moved closer, dagger drawn, in search of an opening where she could attack without hurting her brother.

Gelvon was no frail scholar. He aimed a high kick at Bronn's groin. Bronn fell for the feint by dodging and bending double. Gelvon spun around and slammed the side of his hand into the boy's neck. Bronn crumpled to the floor, hitting his head on a table on the way down.

With a cry of rage Laenie threw herself at Gelvon. He ejaculated another deep-pitched magical phrase. Numbing cold instantaneously flooded her limbs. Her fingers opened, dropping the weapon, and her legs buckled. Gelvon shoved her immobile body into a chair and bound her, hands behind her back, ankles tied to the chair legs. He tied Bronn, still unconscious, hand and foot where he lay.

Gelvon took a few deep breaths and addressed Laenie for the first time. "Who are you, girl? No ordinary thief—the local populace would have warned any such against trying me. What are you after? Who sent you?"

Laenie said nothing.

"You'll be less stubborn when you see what use I make of your—what? not lover, I think—I glimpse some resemblance around the jawline—your brother, no doubt. Your brother will make a fine meal for my pet."

Laenie couldn't suppress a gasp.

Gelvon smiled. "You see this creature?" He laid his

hand on the spherical cage. "This object is a matrix to draw the being from its world into our own. Or partly in, I should say. Hard to believe that inside this sphere is a pocket of the Shadow Realm, a tentacle extruded into our space and trapped here by my power. Imagine that a fragile construction like this network can hold such a force imprisoned. If the crystalline pattern were broken, the creature would instantly return to its own world. Amazing, isn't it?"

He met Laenie's eyes as if he actually expected her admiration. Retrieving the ritual dagger from the floor, he pricked his finger. He squeezed a few drops of blood onto the surface of the cage. They disappeared, instantly absorbed. "Tasting my blood keeps it faithful to me," he said. "But it needs much more food to thrive and grow strong. Someday it will be strong enough to act for me under its own power, instead of being constantly guided by my thoughts. Let me show you how it feeds. You'll be intrigued to see your brother devoured from inside out like a gourd infested by larvae."

Turning his back on her, he began chanting. This spell, instead of a harsh exclamation like the other two, was a crooning song. It was no more pleasant, though. To Laenie it sounded more like an insect's hum than a human voice.

The glowing creature oozed out between the sphere's interstices like a smashed worm. Once out, it appeared still less solid. It sank like heavy smoke to the floor and seeped across it like discolored oil. The thing crept toward Bronn. Laenie silently cursed her paralysis. The thing dragged itself onto the boy's body and blanketed his chest. It then sprouted swollen, pulsing fingers that groped for his face. Separate tendrils covered each of his eyes and snaked into his nostrils, ears, and mouth. Laenie's stomach churned.

She clenched her jaw. Only then did she realize that the numbness was fading. She essayed minute flexings of fingers and toes. Now that the paralysis spell no longer held her, she considered answering Gelvon's questions. She felt no hesitation about betraying Moraya to save Bronn. What held her back was the awareness that Gelvon was surely toying with the pair of them. Once satisfied with the knowledge he sought, he would kill them both regardless. Laenie tensed her arms in frustration as she saw Bronn stir with returning consciousness. He groaned deep in his chest. She heard agony in that groan and realized that he refrained from screaming only because the thing was sucking his breath.

Bronn was sometimes careless, but he didn't deserve to die for that. And when he could have escaped, he had stayed to face Gelvon with bare hands. Was there nothing she could do for him?

She mouthed a silent prayer. Suddenly, as if in answer, she recalled the one skill she had thoroughly learned during her time with Osswen. She had discovered a talent for moving small objects. Her master had considered the technique frivolous, but she'd found it useful in mitigating the endless drudgery of apprentice tasks, the tedious sorting, sweeping, and scrubbing. She began to whisper, barely a vibration in her throat. Gelvon's concentration was so deep that he wouldn't notice as long as she was careful.

The easiest objects to animate were those somehow bonded to her—such as her dagger, lying an arm's length away on the floor. She wove her net of arcane sounds, enticing the weapon to her. It slithered along the boards like a tame serpent and sliced the ropes binding her ankles. The edge would have to be resharpened later, but for now the blade slid through the fibers as through soft cheese. She continued her coaxing whisper. The knife inched up the back of the chair to her hands. Within seconds the bonds fell apart. Laenie grasped the dagger hilt in her fist and shifted it to the proper grip.

Now, another small cantrip. Nothing extravagant, summoning something out of nothing, but a slight distortion and exaggeration of what already existed. She focused on an oilnut lamp burning on a shelf not far from the center table. Her lips moved almost soundlessly. The lamp began to quiver, as if with the vibration of an incipient earth tremor. The flame inside it expanded. The vibration accelerated. Laenie tensed her knee joints for a leap. The lamp exploded into a shower of clay shards. Its flame arced like a shooting star and fastened on the skirt of Gelvon's robe.

He wheeled around with a snarl. Laenie flung one last command at the fire, which flared up to consume half the mage's robe in one breath. Gelvon threw himself on the floor and rolled to smother the flames, then jumped up. His face contorted in an attempt to articulate another spell. Before he could form the words, Laenie's dagger slashed horizontally across his midriff. He bent over, clutching the incision. Blood welled between his fingers. Laenie shifted her grip and drove the dagger straight up. It lodged in his throat, piercing the large vessel there. Laenie released the hilt and stepped back, but not quickly enough to keep the blood from fountaining over her wrist.

Breathing hard, she stared down at the sorcerer's body. She hadn't planned to kill him. Rage had swept away intellect. Her first kill, she mused, and it had to be so sloppy and thoughtless.

Wiping her weapon hand on her trousers, she turned to look at Bronn. As soon as Gelvon's attention had been distracted, the creature had been sucked back into the cage, as if by a miniature whirlwind. The surrounding air cracked aloud as it snapped back to fill the vacated space. Bronn opened his eyes. Laenie was relieved to see the light of awareness in them. She helped him stand. Though the bump on his head and the bruise on the side of his neck looked nasty, except for weakness, he seemed himself.

They tiptoed to the table where the cage sat. Absurd, thought Laenie, as if the thing could hear them. "There's your prize," said Bronn hoarsely. "Could you—could you wrap it up for the journey? I don't like looking at it."

Laenie released a pent-up sigh. Her words expressed a decision she didn't know she'd made until that instant. "I'm not taking it with us."

"What? Your assignment—"

"I was wrong," she said, "and Master Osswen is right. It *is* evil to Gate a thing like this into our world." She recalled Gelvon's words—"a fragile construction—if the crystalline pattern were broken." Surveying the cluttered table, she picked up a chunk of faceted rock about the size of a double fist. She smashed it down on the sphere.

The delicate bone network crumbled easily. Three more blows reduced it to a mound of splintered fragments and dulled crystals. There was no trace of the being from the Shadow Realm.

Bronn shook his head and brushed his hair back, as if his vision were clearing for the first time. "What about your professional reputation? Not to mention your fee?"

"Let me worry about that."

"Moraya won't like this."

"I'll tell her Gelvon destroyed the thing at the moment of his death, rather than have it captured," said Laenie.

"I suppose I wasn't much good to you, after all," Bronn sighed.

Laenie thought about his scatterbrained, hopeless stand against Gelvon. She draped Bronn's arm around her shoulders to support him. "You did fine, little brother. Let's go."

INTO THE GREEN
by Charles de Lint

Charles de Lint, of Dutch birth and currently residing in Canada, is no stranger to these collections; in the year since he last appeared here, he's won a couple of awards for fantasy—well deserved ones too. I also met him in person for the first time, and discovered his skill at the guitar—some people, as the late lamented Ted Sturgeon, no mean hand with a guitar himself, used to say, also use their guitars to paddle a canoe, and most filk singers might as well; but De Lint makes it sound rather like an Irish harp. I dislike much folk music and all so-called "filk" music, which seems to me a way of kidding music by people who have none; but his is the real thing. (Why would anyone want to write when they can sing?) I guess we're just lucky that Charles has the time and energy to do both.

S tone walls confine a tinker; cold iron binds a witch; but a musician's music can never be fettered, for it lives first in her heart and mind.

The harp was named Garrow—born out of an old sorrow to make weary hearts glad. It was a small lap harp, easy to carry, with a resonance that let its music carry to the far ends of a crowded common room. The long fingers of the red-haired woman could pull dance tunes from its strings, lilting jigs or reels that set feet tapping until the floorboards shook and the rafters rang. But some nights the memory of old sorrows returned. Lying in wait like marsh mists, they clouded her eyes with their arrival. On those nights, the music she pulled from Garrow's metal-strung strings was more bitter than sweet, slow airs that made the heart regret and brought unbidden memories to haunt the minds of those who listened.

"Enough of that," the innkeeper said.

The tune faltered and Angharad looked up into his angry face. She lay her hands across the strings, stilling the harp's plaintive singing.

"I said you could make music," the innkeeper told her, "not drive my customers away."

It took Angharad a few moments to return from that place in her memory that the music had brought her to this inn where her body sat, drawing the music from the strings of her harp. The common room was half-empty and oddly subdued, where earlier every table had been filled and men stood shoulder-to-shoulder at the bar, joking and telling each other ever more embroidered tales. The few who spoke, did so in hushed voices; fewer still would meet her gaze.

"You'll have to go," the innkeeper said, his voice not so harsh now. She saw in his eyes that he too was remembering a forgotten sorrow.

"I. . . ."

How to tell him that on nights such as these, the sorrow came, whether she willed it or not? That if she had her choice she would rather forget as well. But the harp was a gift from Jacky Lantern's kin, as was the music she pulled from its strings. She used it in her journeys through the Kingdoms of the Green Isles, to wake the Summerblood where it lay sleeping in folk who never knew they were witches. That was how the Middle Kingdom survived—by being remembered, by its small magics being served, by the interchange of wisdom and gossip between man and those with whom he shared the world.

But sometimes the memories the music woke were not so gay and charming. They hurt. Yet such memories served a purpose, too, as the music knew well. They helped to break the circles of history so that mistakes weren't repeated. But how was she to explain such things to this tall, grim-faced innkeeper who'd been looking only for an evening's entertainment for his customers? How to put into words what only music could tell?

"I . . . I'm sorry," she said.

He nodded, almost sympathetically. Then his eyes grew hard. "Just go."

She made no protest. She knew what she was—tinker, witch and harper. This far south of Kellmidden, only the latter allowed her much acceptance with those who traveled a road just to get from here to there, rather than for the sake of the traveling itself. For the sake of the road that led into the green, where poetry and harping met to sing of the Middle Kingdom.

Standing, she swung the harp up on one shoulder, a small journeypack on the other. Her red hair was drawn back in two long braids. She wore a tinker's plaited skirt and white blouse with a huntsman's leather jerkin overtop. At the door she collected her staff of white rowan wood. Witches' wood. Not until the door swung closed behind her did the usual level of conversation and laughter return to the common room.

But they would remember. Her. The music. There was one man who watched her from a corner, face dark with brooding. She meant to leave before they remembered other things. Before one or another wondered aloud if it was true that witch's skin burned at the touch of cold iron—as did that of the kowrie folk.

As she stepped away from the door, a huge shadowed shape arose from where it had been crouching by a window. The quick tattoo of her pulse only sharpened when she saw that it was a man—a misshapen man. His chest was massive, his arms and legs like small trees. But a hump rose from his back, and his head jutted almost from his chest at an awkward angle. His legs were bowed as though his weight was almost too much for them. He shuffled, rather than walked, as he closed the short space between them.

Light from the window spilled across his features. One eye was set higher in that broad face than the other. The nose had been broken—more than once. His hair was a knotted thicket, his beard a bird's nest of matted tangles.

Angharad began to bring her staff between them. The white rowan wood could call up a witchfire that was good for little more than calling up a flame in a damp camp fire, but it could startle. That might be enough for her to make her escape.

The monstrous man reached a hand toward her. "Puh-pretty," he said.

Before Angharad could react, there came a quick movement from around the side of the inn.

"Go on!" the newcomer cried. It was the barmaid from the inn, a slender blue-eyed girl whose blonde hair hung in one thick braid across her breast. The innkeeper had called her Jessa. "Get away from her, you big oaf." She made a shooing motion with her hand.

Angharad saw something flicker briefly in the man's eyes as he turned. A moment of shining light. A flash of regret. She realized then that he'd been speaking of her music, not her. He'd been reaching to touch the harp, not her. She wanted to call him back, but the barmaid was thrusting a package wrapped in unbleached cotton at her. The man had shambled away, vanishing into the darkness in the time it took Angharad to look from the package to where he'd been standing.

"Something for the road," Jessa said. "It's not much— some cheese and bread."

"Thank you," Angharad replied. "That man. . . ?"

"Oh, don't mind him. That's only Pog—the village half-wit. Fael lets him sleep in the barn in return for what work he can do around the inn." She smiled suddenly. "He's seen the kowrie folk, he has. To hear him tell it—and you'd need the patience of one of Dath's priests to let him get the tale out—they dance all round the Stones on a night such as this."

"What sort of a night is this?"

"Full moon."

Jessa pointed eastward. Rising above the trees there, Angharad saw the moon rising, swollen and round above the trees. She remembered a circle of old longstones that she'd passed on the road that took her to the inn. They stood far off from the road on a hill overlooking the Gray

Sea, a league or so west of the village. Old stones, like silent sentinels, watching the distant waves. A place where kowries would dance, she thought, if they were so inclined.

"You should go," Jessa said.

Angharad gave her a questioning look.

The barmaid nodded toward the inn. "They're talking about witches in there, and spells laid with music. They're not bad men, but any man who drinks. . . ."

Angharad nodded. A hard day's work, then drinking all night. To some it was enough to excuse any deed. They were honest folk, after all. Not tinkers. Not witches.

She touched Jessa's arm. "Thank you."

"We're both women," the barmaid said with a smile. "We have to stick together, now don't we?" Her features, half-hidden in the gloom, grew more serious as she added, "Stay off the road if you can. Depending on how things go. . . . Well, there's some as have horses."

Angharad thought of a misshapen man and a place of standing stones, of moonlight and dancing kowries.

"I will," she said.

Jessa gave her another quick smile, then slipped once more around the corner of the inn. Angharad listened to her quiet footfalls as she ran back to the kitchen. Giving the inn a considering look, she stuffed the barmaid's gift of food into her journeypack and set off down the road, staff in hand.

There were many tales told of the menhir and stones circles that dotted the Kingdoms of the Green Isles. Wizardfolk named them holy places, sacred to the Summerlord; reservoirs where the old powers of hill and moon could be gathered by the rites of the dhruides and the like. The priests of Dath named them evil and warned all to shun their influence. The commonfolk were merely wary of them—viewing them as neither good nor evil, but rather places where mysteries lay too deep for ordinary folk.

And there *was* mystery in them, Angharad thought.

From where she stood, she could see their tall fingers silhouetted against the sky. Mists lay thick about their hill—drawn up from the sea that murmured a stone's throw or two beyond. The moon was higher now; the

night as still as an inheld breath. Expectant. Angharad
left the road to approach the stone circle where Pog
claimed the kowrie danced on nights of the full moon.
Nights when her harp played older musics than she knew,
drawing the airs more from the wind, it seemed, than the
flesh and bone that held the instrument and plucked its
strings.

The gorse was damp underfoot. In no time at all, her
bare legs were wet. She circled around two stone out-
crops, her route eventually bringing her up the hill from
the side facing the sea. The murmur of its waves was very
clear now. The sharp tang of its salt was in the mist.
Angharad couldn't see below her waist for that mist, but
the hilltop was clear. And the Stones.

They rose high above her, four times her height, gray
and weathered. Before she entered their circle, she
dropped her journeypack and staff to the ground. From
its sheath on the inside of her jerkin, she took out a small
knife and left that as well. If this was a place to which the
kowrie came, she knew they would have no welcome for
one bearing cold iron. Lastly, she unbuttoned her shoes
and set them beside her pack. Only then did she enter
the circle, barefoot, with only her harp in hand.

She wasn't surprised to find the hunchback from the
village inside the circle. He was perched on the kingstone,
short legs dangling.

"Hello, Pog," she said.

She had no fear of him as she crossed the circle to
where he sat. There was more kinship between them
than either might claim outside this circle. Their Summerblood bound them.

"Huh-huh-huh. . . ." Frustration tightened every line
of his body as he struggled to shape the word. "Huh-
low. . . ."

Angharad stepped close and laid her hand against his
cheek. She wondered, what songs were held prisoner by
that stumbling tongue? For she could see a poetry in his
eyes, denied its voice. A longing, given no release.

"Will you sing for me, Pog?" she asked. "Will you
help me call the stones to dance?"

The eagerness in his nod almost made her weep. But it
was not for pity that she was here tonight. It was to

commune with a kindred spirit. He caught her hand with his and she gave it a squeeze before gently freeing her fingers. She sat at the foot of the stone and brought her harp around to her lap. Pog was awkward as he scrambled down from his perch to sit where he could watch her.

Fingers to strings. Once, softly, one after the other, to test the tuning. And then she began to play.

It was the same music that the instrument had offered at the inn, but in this place it soared so freely that there could be no true comparison. There was nothing to deaden the ringing of the strings here. No stone walls and wooden roof. No metal furnishings and trappings. No hearts that had to be tricked into listening.

The moon was directly overhead now and the music resounded between it and the sacred hill of the stone circle. It woke echoes like the skirling of pipes, like the thunder of hooves on sod. It woke lights in the old gray stones—flickering glimmers that sparked from one tall menhir to the other. It woke a song so bright in Angharad's heart that her chest hurt. It woke a dance in her companion so that he rose to his feet and shuffled between the stones.

Pog sang as he moved, a tuneless singing that made strange harmonies with Angharad's harping. Against the moonlight of her harp notes, it was the sound of earth shifting, stones grinding. When it took on the bass timbre of a stag's belling call, Angharad thought she saw antlers rising from his brow, the tines pointing skyward to the moon like the menhir. His back was straighter as he danced, the hump gone.

It's Hafarl, Angharad thought, awestruck. The Summerlord's possessed him.

Their music grew more fierce, a wild exultant sound that rang between the stones. The sparking flickers of light moved so quickly they were like streaming ribbons, bright as moonlight. The mist scurried in between the stones, swirling in its own dance, so that more often than not Angharad could only catch glimpses of the antlered dancing figure. His movements were liquid, echoing each rise and fall of the music. Angharad's heart reached out to him. He was—

Something struck her across the head. The music faltered, stumbled, then died as her harp was knocked from her grip. A hand grabbed one of her braids and hauled her to her feet.

"Do you see? Did you hear?" a harsh voice demanded.

Angharad could see them now—men from the inn. Their voices were loud in the sudden silence. Their shapes exaggerated, large and threatening in the mist.

"We see, Macal."

It was the one named Macal who had struck her. Who had watched her so intently in the common room of the inn. Who held her by her braid. Who hit her again. He stank of sweat and strong drink. And fear.

"Calling down a curse on us, she was," Macal cried. "And what better place than these damned Stones?"

Other men gripped her now. They shackled her wrists with cold iron and pulled her from the circle by a chain attached to those shackles. She fell to her knees and looked back. There was no sign of Pog, no sign of anything but her harp, lying on its side near the kingstone. The men dragged her to her feet.

"Leave me alo—" she began, finally finding her voice.

Macal hit her a third time. "You'll not speak again, witch. Not till the priest questions you. Understand?"

They tore cloth strips from her skirt then to gag her. They tore open her blouse and fondled and pinched her as they dragged her back to town. They threw her into the small storage room of the village's mill. Four stone walls. A door barred on the outside by a wooden beam, slotted in place. Two drunk men for guards outside, laughing and singing.

It took a long time for Angharad to lift her bruised body up from the stone floor and work free the gag. She closed her blouse somewhat by tying together the shirt tails. She hammered at the door with her shackled fists. There was no answer. Finally she sank to her knees and laid her head against the wall. She closed her eyes, trying to recapture the moment before this horror began, but all she could recall was the journey from the stone circle to this prison. The cruel men and the joy they took from her pain.

Then she thought of Pog. . . . Had they captured him

as well? When she tried to bring his features to mind, all that came was an image of a stag on a hilltop, bellowing at the moon. She could see. . . .

The stag. Pog. Changed into an image of Hafarl by the music. Left as a stag in the stone circle by the intrusion of the men from the inn who'd come, cursing and drunk, to find themselves a witch. The men hadn't seen him. But as Angharad's assailants dragged her from the stone circle, gray-clad shapes stepped from the stones, where time held them bound except for nights such as this when the moon was full.

They were kowrie, thin and wiry, with narrow dark-skinned faces and feral eyes. Their dark hair was braided with shells and feathers; their jerkins, trousers, boots and cloaks were the gray of the Stones. One by one, they stepped out into the circle until there were as many of them as there were Stones. Thirteen kowrie. The stag bellowed at the moon, a trumpeting sound. The kowrie touched Angharad's harp with fingers thin as rowan twigs.

"Gone now," one said, her voice a husky whisper.

Another drew a plaintive note from Angharad's harp. "Music stolen, moonlight spoiled," he said.

A third laid her narrow hands on the stag's trembling flanks. "Lead us to her, Summerborn," she said.

Other kowrie approached the beast.

"The cold iron bars us from their dwellings," one said.

Another nodded. "But not you."

"Lead us to her."

"Open their dwellings to us."

"We were but waking."

"We missed our dance."

"A hundred moons without music."

"We would hear her harp."

"We would follow our kin."

"Into the green."

The green, where poetry and harping met and opened a door to the Middle Kingdom. The stag pawed at the ground, hearing the need in their voices. It lifted its antlered head, snorting at the sky. The men. Where had they taken her? The stag remembered a place where men dwelt in houses set close to each other. There was pain in that place. . . .

*   *   *

Angharad opened her eyes. What had she seen? A dream? Pog, with that poetry in his eyes, become a stag, surrounded by feral-eyed kowrie. . . . She pushed herself away from the wall and sat on her haunches, shackled wrists held on her lap before her. The stone walls of her prison bound her. The cold chains weighed her down. Still, her heart beat, her thoughts were her own. Her voice had not been taken from her.

She began to sing.

It was the music of hill and moon, a calling-down music, keening and wild. There was a stag's lowing in it, the murmur of sea against shore. There was moonlight in it and the slow grind of earth against stone. There was harping in it, and the sound of the wind as it sped across the gorse-backed hills.

On a night such as this, she thought, there was no stilling such music. It was not bound by walls or shackles. It ran free, out from her prison, out of the village; into the night, into the hills. It was heard there, by kowrie and stag. It was heard closer as well.

From the far away place that the music took her, Angharad heard the alarm raised outside her prison. The wooden beam scraping as it was drawn from the door. The door was pushed open and the small chamber where her body sat singing grew bright from the glare of torches. But she was hardly even there anymore. She was out on the hills, running with the stag and the kowrie, leading them to her with her song, one more ghostly shape in the mist that was rolling down into the village.

"St-stop that you," one of the guards said. His unease was plain in voice and stance. Like his companion, he was suddenly sober.

Angharad heard him, but only from a great distance. Her music never faltered.

The two guards kept to the doorway, staring at her, unsure of what to do. Then Macal was there, with his hatred of witches, and they followed his lead. He struck her until she fell silent, but the music carried on, from her heart into the night, inaudible to these men, but growing louder when they dragged her out. The earth underfoot resounded like a drumskin with her silent song. The moonlit sky above trembled.

"Bring wood," Macal called as he pulled her along the ground by her chains. "We'll burn her now."

"But the priest. . . ." one of the men protested.

Macal glared at the man. "If we wait for him, she'll have us all enspelled. We'll do it now."

No one moved. Other villagers were waking now—Fael the innkeeper and the barmaid Jessa; the miller, roused first by Angharad's singing, now coming to see to what use Macal had put his mill; fishermen, grumpy, for it was still hours before dawn when they'd rise to set their nets out past the shoals; the village goodwives. They looked at the red-haired woman, lying on the ground at Macal's feet, her hands shackled, the chains in Macal's hands. His earlier supporters backed away from him.

"Have you gone mad?" the miller demanded of him.

Macal pointed at Angharad. "Dath damn you, are you blind? She's a witch. She's casting a spell on us all. Can't you smell the stink of it in the air?"

"Let her go," the innkeeper said quietly.

Macal shook his head and drew his sword. "Fire's best—it burns the magic from them—but a sword can do the job as well."

The mist was entering the village now, roiling down the streets, filled with ghostly running shapes. Lifting her head from the ground, Angharad saw the kowrie, saw the stag. She looked at her captor and suddenly understood what drove him to his hate of witches. He had the Summerblood in his veins too.

"There . . . there's no need for this," she said. "We are kin. . . ."

But Macal didn't hear her. He was staring into the mist. He saw the flickering shapes of the kowrie. And towering over them all he saw the stag, its tined antlers gleaming in the moonlight, the poetry in its eyes that burned like a fire. He dropped the chains and ran toward the beast, swinging his sword two-handedly. Villagers ran to intercept him, but they were too late. Macal's sword bit deep into the stag's throat.

The beast stumbled to its knees, spraying blood. Macal lifted his blade for a second stroke, but strong hands wrestled the sword from him. When he tried to rise, the villagers struck him with their fists.

"Murderer!" the miller cried.

"He never did you harm!"

"It was a beast!" Macal cried. "A demon beast—summoned by the witch!"

They let him rise then to see what he'd slain. Pog lay there, gasping his last breath, the poetry dying in his eyes. Only Macal and Angharad with their Summerblood had seen a stag. To the villagers, Macal had struck down their village half-wit who'd never done a hurtful thing.

"I. . . ." Macal began taking a step forward, but the villagers pushed him away.

The mists swirled thick around him. Only he and Angharad could see the flickering gray shapes that moved in it, feral eyes gleaming, slender fingers pinching and nipping at his skin. He fled, running headlong between the houses. The mist clotted around him as he reached the outskirts of the village. A great wind rushed down from the hills. Hafarl's breath, Angharad thought, watching.

The wind tore away the mists. She saw the kowrie flee with it, thirteen slender shapes running into the hills. Where Macal had fallen, only a squat stone lay that looked for all the world like a crouching man, arms and legs drawn in close to his body. It had not been there before.

The villagers shaped the Sign of Horns to ward themselves. Angharad held out her shackled arms to the innkeeper. Silently he fetched the key from one of Macal's companions. Just as silently Angharad pointed to the men who had attacked her in the stone circle. She met their shamed gazes, one by one, then pointed to where Pog lay.

She waited while they fetched a plank and rolled Pog's body onto it. When they were ready, she led the way out of the village to the stone circle, the men following. Not until they had delivered their burden to the hilltop Stones did she speak.

"Go now."

They left at a run. Angharad stood firm until they were out of sight, then slowly she sank to her knees beside the body. Laying her head on its barreled chest, she wept.

It was the kowrie who hollowed the ground under the

kingstone and laid Pog there. And it was the kowrie who pressed the small harp into Angharad's hands and bade her play. She could feel no joy in this music that her fingers pulled from the strings. The magic was gone. But she played all the same, head bent over her instrument while the kowrie moved among the stones in a slow dance to honor the dead.

Mists grew thick again. Then a hoofbeat brought Angharad's head up. Her music faltered. The stag stood there watching her, the poetry alive in its eyes.

Are you truly there? she asked the beast. Or are you but a phantom I've called up to ease my heart?

The stag stepped forward and pressed a wet nose against her cheek. She stroked its neck. The hairs were coarse. There was no doubt that this was flesh and muscle under her hand. When the stag stepped away, she began to play once more. The music grew of its own accord under her fingers, that wild exultant music that was bitter and sweet, all at once.

Between her music and the poetry in the stag's eyes, Angharad sensed the membrane that separated this world from the Middle Kingdoms of the kowrie growing thin. So thin. Like mist. One by one the dancing kowrie passed through, thirteen gray-cloaked figures with teeth gleaming white in their dark faces as they smiled and stepped from this world to the one beyond. Last to go was the stag; he gave her one final look, the poetry shining in his eyes, then stepped away. The music stilled in Angharad's fingers. The harp fell silent. They were gone now, Pog and his kowrie. Gone from this hill, from this world.

Stepped away.

Into the green.

Hugging her harp to her chest, Angharad waited for the rising sun to wash over the old stone circle and tried not to feel so alone.

EYES OF THE LAEMI
by Janet Fox

Janet Fox has not been with us since the first of these volumes; she's been too busy writing other things. I am glad that when she got around to doing a Scorpia story, she offered it to us. . . .

The landscape was bleak, ancient, eroded mountainsides and coarse grass bleached pale by summer's sun. Scorpia rode, negligent in the saddle, the tough little mountain-bred horse negotiating the terrain as if it were flatlands. He had seemed an odd beast to her when she'd studied him in the marketplace—an oversized head, a mane like a brush, standing erect, and dark feral patterns printed on his shaggy brown coat. She peered into the sun's glare, trying to find a landmark of some kind. Her throat was dry and she'd drunk the last sip of tepid water miles back.

Far off she caught the glint of reflections off brightly whitewashed walls. As she rode nearer she saw that the city was built into the side of a mountain, cubes of white clustering as close together as cells in a beehive. Ladders leaned against walls, for ingress was often from the top. Here and there was a sprawling villa enclosing a verdant garden, a luxury beyond price in this harsh land.

The streets were narrow and almost overhung in places by ambitious constructions. After negotiating one of these, she came upon an open space in which there was a public well. Old men sat gossiping in little groups around it and occasionally a housewife came to fill her water jug, shy-eyed children following or clinging to her skirts.

Scorpia slid from the saddle, leaving her beast to find the trough provided for his kind. She leaned far over the well's coping and reached far down, cupping her hands and bringing them to her mouth greedily. When she'd finished drinking, she filled her hands again and let the water run over her head, plastering down the uncut tawny hair, running deliciously down her neck and beneath the chiton-like garment of soft-worked leather she'd brought in the last bazaar.

"Long ride?"

She shook water out of her eyes. An old man was standing before her, leaning on a gnarled staff. He had long ago sustained some grave injury, a ropy scar running across his face and obscuring one eye.

She mentioned her last stop and the old man whistled through missing teeth. His cronies behind him muttered and giggled among themselves like children playing a game.

"Don't mind them. They've never been out of this village where the women huddle around their own kitchen fires or go out with faces covered, but I've seen your like before."

He mentioned a battle that to her was something out of legend. "That's where I got this," he said. "A red-haired woman, with an axe. But I bear *you* no ill will, even though I see you're of her kind."

Scorpia shrugged. "Nice of him," she reflected, ironically, thinking that she hadn't even been born then.

"But a journey through these mountains was ill-made," he continued, "Even for you, who carry a sword on your hip. There are always robbers about and some say . . . demons."

"I saw nothing but rocks, thin soil and stunted trees," said Scorpia with a low laugh.

"Oh, they'd not be seen, unless they wanted to," answered the old man, coughing and spitting a glob of phlegm into the dust of the street.

Scorpia's attention was momentarily distracted by someone who was gliding toward the well. Sun's glare made it seem an elongated, distorted shape and then Scorpia realized it was only one of the village women, swathed in heavy veils. Only a trick of the light had made her seem so strange.

She was again aware of the old man who had rambled on, oblivious of her lapse. "—blood drinkers, it's said— stronger than any man—or woman," he amended, taking in her stature.

"I've traveled far and every country seems to have its bogies with which to frighten small children—and travelers."

"No, it's truth. There have been more than one who've died hereabouts. The demon fastened upon them and night by night drained them dry. They say one should never look into the eyes of a laemi," his voice grew confused. "I forget just why."

"I'll avoid it, if at all possible," said Scorpia.

Suddenly there was a commotion in the street, dust rising as a band of mounted men rode into the square, displacing the loafers, the gossipers. "Make way, the procession!" shouted a corpulent, red-faced man who reined his wild-eyed beast straight at Scorpia to make her run, as the others had. With one hand she grasped the near rein and with the other she drew her sword. As the horse wheeled crazily around her, she gave the rider a smart slap across the back with the flat of her sword, though the weapon could as easily have been used in earnest.

The red-faced one was reaching for his own weapon just as the procession reached the square, a litter carried by four men and bearing a slight body mounded over with flowers. Quickly, Scorpia sheathed her sword and backed away, showing both palms in sign of peace. She hadn't realized that it was a funeral procession. Not that she was particularly daunted by death; she'd been waiting for something of the sort.

"The Lady Leliah," whispered the old man as the bier was carried past. The corpse was only thinly covered with a gauze drapery and its heaps of flowers. Scorpia saw that though the woman on the bier was thin and wasted, her composed face was still strikingly beautiful.

There was a further disturbance as someone crowded

past the veiled women and handsomely garbed men of
the procession. He was a gaunt man with disheveled
black hair and hectic spots on each cheek. His clothing
was half undone, wrinkled and stained. Like a madman
he made for the bier and before anyone could stop him
he was holding the corpse in his arms.

"Where are you taking her?" he shouted. "She's not
dead. She came to me just last night. She spoke to me."
The fat man Scorpia had taunted was first to reach him
and with a touch that was almost gentle and with soothing words, he began to draw the young man away from
the corpse.

"This is just what I was speaking of," said the old man.
"Leliah is said to have had a demon lover—the laemi.
That's the young Lord Peri, her betrothed. A sad day."

Peri was leaning against the well's edge when the darkly
garbed woman that Scorpia had seen before came walking by him in that effortless seeming glide beneath dark
skirts. "There she is now!" Peri shouted. "Leliah, Leliah,
come back!" His comrades restrained him and when the
disturbance had calmed, Scorpia noticed that the woman
had disappeared.

Soon all had passed by, the well somnolent at midday
as if nothing had occurred. The voices of the old men
again droned on as they chaffed each other and spoke of
events long past.

"Love sometimes brings suffering," said the old man.
His brimming eyes let fall a tear and then he roughly
wiped it away.

"I know little of it," said Scorpia, "except that what
some call love is only . . . hunger." She caught her mount
and leapt easily into the saddle, knowing that if she
waited too long the procession might get beyond her and
be lost in the hills.

"Go in peace," said the old man.

Scorpia saluted him in the way of her own people,
surprised that the gesture came so easily to her, and then
the horse broke into a gallop.

Scorpia had waited just over a ridge until the members
of the funeral procession she'd followed trickled back by
slow twos and threes. Now she reined her mount to the

top of the crest to let him pick his own cautious way down a slope of broken black rock protruding through a thin cover of soil. This land was good only for the use to which it had been put, she thought, but it was very good for that. Long before she'd reached it, she'd seen the circling of vultures, a slow vortex. Jutting angularly against the horizon were the racks on which the villagers lay the bodies of their dead. The horse had scented this place before she'd even seen the circling black wings, but the brisk, cool winds on this exposed hillside carried off most of the reek of decaying flesh and the vultures were busily at their work. Two of the birds began to squabble atop a wooden framework, and a skull, neatly denuded of all flesh, dropped and rolled toward the feet of the horse. It snorted and sidestepped in alarm. When the bones had been cleaned, she had heard, the relatives would come here to take back the skeleton which would be buried with ceremony under the floor of their house. She knew it made sense, but the sight of those dark, thrusting beaks, glittering eyes and hovering wings made her shudder. Against all reason she preferred the idea of fire—it seemed the only civilized custom.

She looked around a moment before choosing a bier. At some distance she saw what must have been the resting place of Lady Leliah, since the garlands of flowers were yet fresh, but she chose instead a taller, more elaborate framework on which hung a beautifully painted shield and other rich artifacts which told her the deceased might have been a person of substance. She smiled wryly at the thought; now a horde of vultures screamed and flapped their wings in a dark cloud atop the framework. Climbing the crude, ladderlike arrangement along one side wasn't the pleasantest thing she'd ever done, but she was too battle-hardened to delay out of squeamishness, being long inured to the sight of corpses. The lowering pale sky, the waving of long dry grass in the wind pointed up the futility of effort.

The carrion birds did not give way as she had hoped. This had been their territory for centuries, after all. She found herself facing an immense old king-bird, neck extended showing the snake beneath the feathers, a scrap of sun-dried skin depending from his beak, talons clutching a partially denuded ribcage as if it were his own personal property.

Scorpia drew her sword, feeling foolish. When she was buffeted, caught a numbing blow by a wing-bone that almost threw her to the ground, she joined wholeheartedly in the battle, sending a few feathers drifting skyward before the creature took wing with a croak of anger.

She set quickly to work, drawing gold rings off the stiff and shrunken fingers, removed a heavy gold chain with ruby pendant where it hung inside the rib cage like a glittering heart. It was not honorable work, she reflected. She was no better than the scavengers that now sat cloaked in ruffled black feathers regarding her with malevolent patience. But she had soon discovered that she had no salable talents unless she were to sell the services of her sword and it was to escape that that she had left her own land in the first place.

A shout from below brought her from her reverie. This place was so remote, considered tabu by the villagers except at certain times and with certain rituals, that she hadn't seriously considered the possibility of being discovered.

A sun-darkened face, shaggily bearded, looked up at her and she heard heavy, running footsteps and other shouts. She wasted not an instant, but leaped from the framework's height, sword in hand, straight at the intruder, who gave way, stupidly, she thought, because it meant his death.

It took a moment to dislodge her blade, a moment too long because something hit her from behind with numbing force. She went to her knees, still trying to bring her sword into play, but whoever it was hit her again and she lost consciousness.

She awoke in what seemed an instant, but some time must have elapsed because the sun was at a different angle now and when she tried to shade her eyes against it, she could not. She could move both arms only a little way. It hurt to turn her head, but she did and saw that her wrists and ankles were bound by ropes tied to stakes. She lay in an open spot, the sun broiling down. Sometime while she was unconscious she'd been stripped and before long the sunlight would possibly be lethal as well as just painful.

At first she'd thought she'd been left alone, but now she heard approaching footsteps and two shapes towered over her, silhouetted by the sun. One man was not so tall as the other and he had a greasy, thick-lipped face with pouchy little eyes that kept returning to her body.

"I still think we should have—" he said to his companion, an angular man with a seamed brown face and an over-fastidious manner. He made nervous, hand-washing movements as he spoke.

"Are you a fool, man? In this place with the minions of the gods hovering overhead? I'd as soon curse the Death Gods to their faces. No, we've done as custom decrees. 'Those who invade the sanctity of the dead shall join them.' "

The smaller man squinted upward at the spiral pattern of black wings. "The gods' will be done," he said with a shrug, "but were we not on holy ground, I'd have a better use for—"

"Cease your blasphemy," said the other, and they departed.

After a time Scorpia felt her skin begin to blister, even though the matte-gold skin of her race gave her an advantage over paler peoples. She tried to ignore the pain of it; she probably wouldn't die of exposure after all; she'd forgotten the birds. Vultures had been landing at some distance from her, kept at bay at first by her struggles to free herself. Now they only waited, strutting and preening, the sun striking bronze from their feathers. Once she was exhausted by her struggles or overcome by the sun's heat, they would likely close in. She might awaken as they plucked strips of skin and flesh. She might even live for some time under these circumstances. Thinking of this she pulled with all her strength against the ropes, feeling skin abrade and blood ooze down her wrists. There had been a very little slack to begin with and by pulling and stretching the cords she'd gained a little more, but she still couldn't reach the knots.

Though her wrists had gone numb she felt something bite deep into her flesh and she saw a glittering dark outcropping of stone under her left arm. She began to rub the cord against it, though the rope had little play. It seemed an impossible task, the sun a searing pain all along her length. She kept dragging the cord across the stone, cheered by every thread that broke and stood out raggedly. Sweat burned into her eyes and sometimes she could see nothing, only feel the dry sliding of rope across raw skin.

She woke up.

She heard raucous cries and wings blotted out the sun. Up close, she could see white parasites negotiating the bronze breast-feathers; by the vulture's size she judged it to be the old king-bird whose prey she'd taken. The skin of its neck was gray and scaly, the black beak darting toward her eye. She moved and it struck her cheekbone, the blow reverberating through her skull, nearly blacking her out again. When panic made her pull back on the ropes, she felt the one on her left wrist give way. Before the bird could strike again her left hand managed to grasp an outstretched wing. Wings buffeted madly and clawed feet scrabbled for balance. She could have been free of it merely by letting go, but her mind was no longer clear. Muscle corded along her arm as she lifted the great weight of the vulture overhead, and dashed it to earth where it lay still. Her mind spun toward unconsciousness again, for all her futile strivings against it.

She feared to open her eyes (she felt she still had eyes). There were sounds—not the raucous calls and scrambling feet of the carrion birds, but footsteps. She wondered if the villagers were coming back.

As if by a miracle the moon had risen. Between her and its chill, pale light, a narrow figure beneath an enveloping cloak of coarse weave, a cowl drawn about the face. Scorpia was unsure what to do. She wanted to speak to thank the stranger for frightening away the vultures, for surely they would have been at her before this. And yet in the moonlight there was something vaguely wrong, misshapen, about the form—too tall, too slender, the one hand exposed of chalky whiteness.

The shape knelt beside her, and suddenly she was

aware that she was free. She discovered that her own garments had been replaced though fastened awry. Nothing could stop her from striking a quick blow and running. An arm went around her, strong for all its thinness, and cold water was being dribbled into her mouth from a waterskin.

No enemy would do that. Quickly she gave over feigning, choked and pushed the water away a moment till she could drink it in safety.

"Thanks," she said after a moment.

With graceful movement the cowl was thrown back and Scorpia held her breath for fear the moonlight would expose a face alien, inhuman. His eyes were immense, almost glowing, but as she looked into them, she was reassured. Except for the slightly unearthly expression of his eyes, he was quite handsome. Unbearded, not altogether youthful, but not old, brown hair lying awry on his forehead, curling about his temples. She wondered why she had seen him as pale, since he was sun dark, even his hands.

"I decided I must release you," he said, "when I saw what happens to your enemies." He indicated the dead vulture, an inert bundle of black feathers, now as much carrion as his prey, flies gathering about him in an unlovely cloud. It gave her the uncomfortable feeling that he might have been there watching, for hours before he'd finally decided she was worthy of helping.

As she moved to rise, she cried out; the sun had burned her deeply. Her rescuer made a quick motion, surely more rapid than it should have been and lifted her easily to her feet. "We can't stay here," he said almost apologetically. "If those who tied you come back to see how matters are progressing, they'd be particularly pleased to surprise me as well."

"Are you some sort of grave robber," she began, stopping herself from adding the word, "too." They strode quickly along, mostly from his volition. He was quick to catch and set her upright when she stumbled.

"*Some* sort of robber," he said with the smile that had seemed strange to her at first, a quirk of the lips suggesting secrets.

They ended their journey at the mouth of a cave at the

top of a rock-strewn slope. "But this looks like the den of some animal," protested Scorpia as he ushered her inside.

"My den, I suppose," he said with a laugh. Lamps burned with a steady glow from niches in the walls and the floor was strewn with boughs of pungent evergreens.

"Well, it's not exactly—" she began.

"Not what?"

"Not what I thought it'd be. It's almost . . . homelike."

"My den, your den," he said, bending to create a sort of couch from a mound of the branches and the luxuriant pelt of some animal. The sharp scent of evergreen rose around her as she sat. They shared a sparse meal of dried meat, bread and wine—plain fare, but there was a piquancy about the flavors that she couldn't explain, just as she couldn't explain to herself why the robber's face seemed somehow familiar. At one angle she would almost be able to speak a name, then the lamplight would flicker and he was a stranger. When she asked his name, he paused a moment before saying Zaer, so she was certain this was an alias, but when confiding her own name she found herself poised to pronounce the syllables of her true name, the one given her by her mother and that she would pass on to her own daughter (should she have one). By an effort of will she recovered.

"Scorpia," he said, mouthing the word as if to taste it. "That has a nice ring of hostility."

"It's my battle-name," she found herself saying, somewhat stiffly. She couldn't explain why, but she had the feeling he had *known* what she was about to give away— that in fact, he might at this moment know her birth name.

"But you must excuse me; weariness is giving me strange thoughts," she said in hopes of clearing her mind of what surely must be delusion.

"You never did tell me what you were doing in the Fields of the Dead," said Zaer.

"I suppose I was doing the same thing you were," she said, too tired to lie about it.

"A thief could do worse than steal from the dead," he said, rising to go to the back of the cave a moment, and continuing his ruminations as he did so. "After all, they don't need their trinkets and make no outcry when they're relieved of them." He returned with a magnificent onyx and gold neckpiece. "Truly, I have no use for this myself, so you may as well have it." Before she could answer he was fastening it around her neck and touching her more than was necessary to arrange it against her breast. "They say onyx is a charm against the laemi, or other demons of the dark. But I don't think that you will really need the protection," he went on, bending forward to kiss her. "Only the one night—I promise it."

As his arms came around her, she thought momentarily that the promise was all wrong, somehow. Forever, wasn't that the vow? His hands were colder than they should have been as she put them against herself to warm them.

As her garment was gently undone and pressed back, she winced and cried out (it almost seemed she had to see the angry redness of her skin to remember she'd been badly burned). Stubbornly, she embraced him again. Things had progressed too far to stop them now, but she knew that burned as she was—everywhere—only an acrobat would have been able to make this anything less than a painful experience.

When she awoke, with no memory of having gone to sleep in the first place, she lay, torpid and half-exhausted on the fragrant bedding, remembering. The memories seemed jumbled, thoughts slipping back crazily to other men and other times, but somehow he had managed to cause no pain; just the opposite. She smiled and turned over, fully expecting to look into Zaer's face, but all she saw was that she was alone in the cave, all the lamps burned out and a pale morning light seeping in from the entrance. Maybe he'd only gone out for water or to answer a call of nature, she decided. Languidly, she lay back. It would be worth the wait.

As she lay there, she began to notice how the debris from which the impromptu couch was formed dug into back and shoulders. There was the scent of some animal heavy on the air, the moldering pelt on which she lay, or— She wondered why she hadn't noticed these discomforts last night. She had only begun to consider this when she heard footsteps. When she realized that it was the footsteps of more than one man and sat up to look around for something to use as a weapon, it was already too late. The next moment the cave was overcrowded with armed men. One of them tucked a sword-tip familiarly under her chin before she could do anything further.

Surprised, she recognized the slate-blue steel of her own blade a moment before she recognized the rotund man who held it. He had been in the funeral procession.

"Gone," said a voice and she recognized the young nobleman named Peri.

"This sword is mine," said Scorpia. "Where did you get it?"

"That may well be," said the fat man. "I thought the sewer rat who sold it to me could not have come by it honestly. You were at the funeral." His eyes twinkled in a doughy, porcine face. "It probably is your weapon, since you don't look dressed without it."

Peri bent to retrieve Scorpia's garment and with a low curse threw it at her. "Leave her be, Jul, let her cover herself, even though his mark is on her for all to see, just as it was on Leliah. Gods, if I had only known in time!"

Another man approached carrying a handful of pendants, rings, bracelets. "See, he hesitates not to rob even the dead."

"And dress his harlot in the spoils," said Jul as Scorpia struggled into the disheveled garment. She remembered she was still wearing the neckpiece and when she reached up to touch it her fingertips found a rough spot on her throat, like a rash.

"That stuff is trash compared to what he took from me," said Peri. "But I swear we'll find him and cut out his heart." He looked in that moment almost as insane as he had at the funeral, and Scorpia felt a pang that Zaer must lead the life of a hunted animal. "I don't think you'll find him," she said. "He left sometime in the night. He could be far from here by now."

"Give her to me and I'll find out where he's gone," said Jul, licking fat lips.

"I have a better idea," answered Peri. "She goes with us, as bait."

Scorpia stood on a narrow balcony, scents of heavy foliage and exotic flowers rising from the garden below.

Peri's house was one of those she'd noticed upon approaching the city, with luxuriant gardens encircled by walls of whitewashed stone. She saw the silhouette of a sentry on the wall's top. As it always did, her gaze wandered to a branch of a tree that grew near the balcony, not near enough to reach, even though she had climbed to stand on the very edge, but one leap would be enough to allow her to catch hold of it, from there to be borne to the ground by her own weight, or so she hoped. It seemed just possible, if she didn't fall short and hit the ground at some distance below.

A lassitude overtook her, a recurring weakness she couldn't explain, and as she had a dozen times before, she drew her gaze away from the tempting branch.

Night was falling, but she could still see well enough to track a figure moving through the trees. She had earlier recognized it as Peri, whom she'd often seen walking in the garden after sunset. Tonight he didn't seem to walk alone; a heavily cloaked shape kept pace. When he reached a clearing, a ring of trees around an ornamental pool that flickered in moonlight, it almost looked as if Peri and the strange figure embraced, but light was failing fast and it may only have been a trick of light and shadow. She strained to see more, then started as a heavy hand was laid on her shoulder. She turned to look into Jul's shrewd little eyes.

"What are you doing here?"

"I've taken this watch. I wondered if . . . you might be lonely."

"Not that lonely," she said shrugging off the hand. She studied him, her eyes lingering at the hilt of her own sword riding his fat hip. He outweighed her twice over, probably, but— As he grasped her strongly and tried to bring her face close to his, she struggled, realizing there was muscle under all that bulk. "Your master is in earshot should I wish to call out," she said, indicating the clearing in the garden.

"I doubt he'd hear you; he's much preoccupied of late," said Jul, but he let her go.

"I've noticed him walking there late in the evenings, as if waiting for someone. Probably some slut from the city. So much for his faithfulness to Leliah."

"You know nothing of his torment. He's confided in me that he's seen Leliah's shade, heard her calling to him. No doubt he thinks he walks with her there."

"Fine. I'm captive of a madman."

"And mine as well," said Jul, a sigh rippling his bulk. "For all the good it does me." He stalked off, she supposed, to take a post outside her doorway. Scorpia rearranged her nightdress, which was like all the garb she'd been given, flimsy or useless or both. She supposed she might as well retire; after all, one could only pace the chamber so long without getting weary of looking at the wall frescoes.

Sometime later, she awoke to some sound she couldn't at once identify, and lay quietly waiting. Someone was crossing the chamber. She thought first of Jul, but this figure moved lightly, unerringly. She wished for a weapon, but only clenched her fists and forced herself to pretend to be asleep.

When whoever it was leaned over the bed, she threw a punch, but didn't feel the expected jolt since somehow her wrist had been caught and held in an unyielding grip.

"Your greeting is enthusiastic, as always," said Zaer. His eyes gave back the moonlight like some animal's. She was inexplicably afraid a moment, then calmed. Though she knew he had spoken, it was as if nothing disturbed the silence. She told herself he must be speaking in a low whisper.

"You shouldn't have come."

"I tried not to." She felt him shrug as he lay next to her in the darkness. "A creature of impulse."

She tried to tell him that this was a trap, but once he touched her it was impossible not to respond.

The next clear memory she had was of being thrown out of bed, to hit the tiled floor with a grunt.

It looked as if an army had invaded her bedchamber and Zaer was backed against the wall weaponless as the guards closed in. Scorpia caught the man nearest her with a double-handed blow to the back of the neck and he crumpled, and as if this were a signal Zaer leapt among the guardsmen. She saw him swing his hand. One man went down, the other grabbed his face, blood, black in the moonlight, trickling through his fingers. Zaer must have carried a concealed dagger, she rationalized, as he went through his enemies like a reaper through a field. His shape, made grotesque by the shadows of wind-tossed trees, poised on the balcony's edge and was gone. She wondered if he had made the leap she had so often considered, and ran with the two guardsmen still standing to the balcony to look down.

She was in time to see him cross an open patch of moonlight and then disappear into the trees. The branch was where it had been, swayed only a little by the wind.

Scorpia was surprised to see Peri come into her chambers next morning. She hadn't seen him except at a distance since she'd been imprisoned here. "Let me go," she said. "Bring an end to this. You've already lost one man."

"Two. But this only proved that I was right. I'll drain the blood from that snake's body and Leliah will be avenged."

"Yes, I've seen how you revere her memory from my balcony there every evening."

"A part of me will always remain faithful to her."

"I know which part will *not.*"

For a moment Peri drew closer, hectic spots on each cheek. Something nagged at Scorpia's attention, a path of angry-looking pinprick marks on Peri's throat, disappearing into his collar.

"Don't try me too far. I need you only to draw that . . . animal."

"He's twice the man you are for all your armies. When you speak of him, call him by his name."

"Very well," said Peri with a slow smile. "I'll call him by his name. Laemi!"

That evening Scorpia eyed the nearby branch and began to tear at the hem of her nightdress; the excess cloth would wind around her legs and get in her way. She tried not to think of Zaer, for when she did, she knew she would want to wait, even though logically staying here as bait in Peri's trap wasn't what she'd call an act of love. She poised on the edge, muscles trembling, crouched and jumped. Darkness blurred by, the jagged shapes of leaves and then her hands were talons gripping the rough bough and her weight was swinging the branch downward. The action felt good; it didn't call for endless speculating about a situation that just didn't *feel* right. She jarred to the ground, still more or less on her feet.

As she did, she heard a shout from behind her and whirled around. Jul was pounding toward her. There had probably always been a sentry posted in the garden, she realized. He would have been in the balcony's shadow beyond her view. She began to run, since she didn't think Jul could keep up with her for more than a few yards.

A shimmering white shape appeared before her, making her veer off, realizing too late that it was nothing but a statue. Her detour sent her into the clearing where she interrupted Peri with whatever harlot he'd hired for the evening. Only the tableau was subtly wrong; Peri was as still as death, head thrown back, eyes empty. The one that held him was chalk-white of skin, the hands elongated and ending in dark clawlike nails, the head a bulging white hairless dome. The lower part of the face, below the beautiful dark eyes, bore no mouth but a bristling tangle of fine translucent tentacles, dark now and tumid as they clung to Peri's throat.

Scorpia stood a moment in shock. Peri had been right— the demon, the laemi. A thrashing in the underbrush heralded Jul and she heard his indrawn breath as he took the picture in. He held the sword—her sword—out in front of him and in his moment of shock, she took the weapon from his unresisting hand.

The monster had sensed or seen them; it was turning, and the old man's warning, "Never let the laemi look you in the eyes," came back to her. Squeezing her eyes closed, she swung the sword blindly, hoping not to hit Peri, but so repulsed by the creature that she took that chance. The familiar shock of the blade biting deep told her she had hit something and droplets of moisture pelted her face.

When she opened her eyes she saw blood of a rich purple color jetting from a deep gash in the neck of the monster. As she leaned over to make sure of it, poising her weapon over its body, she was caught by the gleam of those eyes. "Zaer," she said in anguish. "I didn't know it was you." The face moved, blurred and she could see that it was a composite of all the men she'd known and cared about, but she still couldn't keep herself from telling the monster how sorry she was.

From somewhere, as if in distance, she could hear the rasping gurgles of the beast's last breaths, but it raised a long hand toward her and she felt her birth-name dropped back into her consciousness, as if it were something he knew was precious and wanted to return.

"I pitied you and all the time the thing had me in thrall," said Peri. "Give me the sword—give it to me. It meant to kill us both."

For a moment she held him off at arm's length until Jul came to draw him away. Scorpia withdrew as well. When those dark eyes glazed over, she knew she'd be looking into the face of a horror.

"It needed us," she said, assuming a practical tone. She wished she could put the image of Zaer from her, but she knew she would in some way continue to cherish it. If love was an illusion, it was a powerful one.

"A monster," railed Peri.

"It was only . . . hungry."

JEWELS
by Linda Gordon

Another story about a mercenary—but it couldn't be more different from the first story in this volume.

"Your son for the jewel." The gray-haired man's lavender gaze slid over Blackwood's figure, bouncing from her well shaped legs, to curved form, to broad shoulders, to endowed chest, to strong arms, to sword at her side. He met her dark gaze, desire flaring.

Blackwood's eyes narrowed. A breeze danced across the balcony and tossed a strand of her coal black hair. "I need money," and my son, she thought. "How bad do you want your jewel?"

"Money?" The man laughed, his wrinkled hands grasping his walking stick. "I have long ago learned there are more important possessions than such." His humor faded and he coughed. "Your son for the jewel," he said deliberately.

Blackwood gritted teeth together. "There will be expenses, wizard."

The mage's gaze grew distant as he thought, then finally he nodded. "Very well, bounty hunter, you will have your expenses." He brought a pouch out from under his dark cloak and tossed it to her.

The woman caught it, judged the weight of the pouch, then nodded.

"There is a matter of time." The mage coughed again. "I need the jewel or soon—" He stopped talking and shrugged.

"Yes," Blackwood said icily, "you indebted yourself to it." Her lips tightened into a mock grin. "Your soul for the powers."

His smile was almost apologetic.

Her dark eyes grew cold. "And you misused your powers, making them vile."

With back slightly bent, he leaned on the walking stick and left the balcony, then worked his way into the large stone commons. A fire crackled in the fireplace that took up one wall, and the man stood by it. Flames flickered, danced, and reflected in his gaze as he stared down.

Blackwood followed the mage, stopping to stand by the fire. "Or," she continued, "your powers have made you evil." She watched his face for a reaction.

"I am spoken of, I see."

"Yes, Zuriel." Her gaze shifted to the fire. "The villagers are terrified of you. They can pay no one to come near save for your precious offerings!" She almost spat the last words.

"They found you!" Zuriel whirled around to face her, using the walking stick for balance. "They are not *my* offerings! I demand no such thing." His jaw worked in anger, giving a life of its own to his aged face.

Blackwood stepped closer to the mage, hand on swordhilt. "I should see to you right now."

He smiled thinly. "Then you would never find your son."

Blackwood forced her hand away from weapon. "Do not lie to me."

"Lie?" He shrugged. "I am beyond lying, woman."

"Why do you have the fire outside if you desire no offerings?" Her eyes narrowed. "Is it not a signal to those below that you want such?"

"*I,*" he jabbed a finger at his chest, "*I* never desired an offering. It was that wretched jewel."

"Surely." She paused, brows furrowed. "That is the reason you want the jewel returned." She clenched, then released fists. "The reason you hold my son for the return of the stone."

Zuriel stood quietly, hand on the mantle for support. "I regret the youngling had to be involved."

Blackwood grunted disbelief. "And you regretted the other younglings as well. All the offspring of those people below who were sacrificed to you for the well-being of the village."

"It was their decision, not mine."

"Where is my son?" Blackwood crossed arms over chest, dark gaze boring into the wizard.

"My—"

"Minions?" she interrupted angrily.

"My minions," he allowed, "have him safely locked away."

"Safely?" Her skin crawled. "Where, in one of your dark, damp dungeons? Chained to a wall?" Her hand slipped to swordhilt.

Zuriel laughed, amused. "And you think he is tortured at each sun's passing?" The humor faded. "I no longer possess the jewel. Think on it, woman."

Blackwood snorted. "It matters not. Once you have doings with the Evil Ones, you become forever a part of them. My son—"

"Has he his father's eyes?"

"What!" She frowned. "You have not seen him?"

The wizard turned back to the fire. "I have no time to peer upon such things."

"Surely. To peer upon such innocence would doubtless bring out the human in you. If there is any left. Where *is* my son?"

"Does he?"

"What? Have his father's eyes?" She nodded. "Yes."

Zuriel smiled, the dancing flames reflected in his gaze. "Ah."

"He has his father's same thick blond hair, his father's broad shoulders."

"He must be three, maybe four seasons. Can he resemble his father so?"

"Yes. He even has the intelligence his father once had." The mage looked at Blackwood and her gaze locked with his. "The man I knew then is now gone. There will be only one such as my son."

"Yes."

"Wizard, where is he?"

Zuriel laughed. "I tell you, then you go after him, and I do not get my jewel returned." He grinned. "You think me daft?"

"How long do you have left for the return of the stone?" Blackwood's eyes scanned the mage's form. Is he wasting away before my very gaze? The darkness around his eyes is deeper now, he seems to be older, more bent than when I first looked upon him.

The wizard coughed, a rattling sound now in his voice. "I slowly die before your eyes. The jewel, woman, find it and bring it here. Quickly."

"How do I know my son will be returned unharmed if I bring you the stone?"

"You have my word."

Blackwood turned toward the fire. "Your word?" She grunted. "That and some coin will buy me a manwhore."

"*My* word!" He turned around and slowly walked to the doorway, back obviously bent, weight supported by the walking stick. "Let us speak of the bounty hunter's word."

Blackwood paused, watching, then followed in strides. "My word is good, wizard."

The mage continued silently, leading her down the torch-lit hall to the huge thick wooden doors. He stopped. "You are a bounty hunter, one who hunts human prey." He pointed at himself. "*I* have never done such." He motioned toward the large metal door ring and Blackwood grudgingly grasped it and pulled the door open.

"I hunt only those who have done wrong. No others." She followed him outside, letting the door slowly close on its own. "Why should you hunt when the prey is brought to your feet? At least I take no offerings."

"And you have never killed?" The mage followed a stone path toward the large outer yard, feet shuffling, the walking stick now a true support. He reached a shaking hand out and gently touched a flower here, a vine there, as he carefully moved past.

"Of course I have killed. Some deserve such."

"One will accept one's own doings more easily than will another."

"Then why did you send for me, a lowly bounty hunter?" Blackwood stopped walking as she watched Zuriel halt, and at a molasses pace, turn to face her.

"A bounty hunter has few fears. The others—" He shrugged. "They fear the rumors and would not come, even if I called to them."

"Rumors!" Her gaze slipped to the huge fire burning a distance away. "Sacrifice is no rumor, wizard. The villagers are at this moment gathering, to offer you another youngling."

"Superstitious drivel." Zuriel turned and looked toward the village. "Someone down there has the stone. I went, for reasons you need not know, to the village and while there, someone, a pickpocket, snatched it."

"How? Where did you carry it? In a pouch at your side?" She grinned as if the thought was so unbelievable as to be humorous.

"Yes." The wizard turned and continued toward the fire, moving gingerly as if each step caused him pain. "The warmth feels good to my bones."

Blackwood fleetingly thought of running her sword through him, but it was not her way. He would have to face her, and she would first know where her son is.

They stood near the huge fire, their forms small next to the tall, leaping flames. Blackwood stepped back, the heat more than she could stand. "You wore that precious stone of yours in a pouch! I cannot believe it." She shook her head. "One such as you would be cautious, I would think."

"The villagers fear me, true enough, but the one who stole the jewel is new here. He was unaware of my— status with the others."

"So he, or she, took advantage of the vulnerable, and visible, pouch strings."

"Yes."

Her eyes narrowed in suspicion. "He? You know it was a man who stole your stone?"

Zuriel turned away from her, glancing at the sky, the trees, the fire. "Just a guess, woman."

She crossed her arms, dark eyes intent on him. "Tell me who I look for."

"I know not. Just go to the village and ask. Someone will tell you."

"They will tell me, yet they would not tell you?" She laughed. "A thing is amiss here, wizard."

"Find the jewel and return to me." He faced her. "Your son for the jewel."

"My son is more precious than any fool stone of yours!" She moved toward him. "Where is he!"

"Here. He is here, woman. Locked away where not even the sun can find him. Away where there is naught save darkness and loneliness. Away where the dark spirits await."

"You bastard!" Blackwood drew sword and held the tip at the mage's throat, forcing him to straighten slightly. "If harm comes to him, in any way, you will pray to your God for the sweetness of death."

"Try to kill me," he challenged.

The urge to push the blade struck, but she pulled back. "No. With each passing moment you spend without your precious stone, you suffer. You have aged since my arrival."

"Yes," he said, "but I will not age beyond a certain point, a point unknown to me." He smiled wryly. "Difficult to believe I was birthed the same season as you, is it not?"

"Yes." She lowered the sword to her side.

"Time is wasting. Your son pales from the darkness that surrounds him." Zuriel's voice took on a taunting tone. "There are many creatures of the dark, woman, many who at this very moment seek out the warmth of your son's body. He—"

"Stop it!" Blackwood jabbed the sword point into the wizard's chest above his heart. "Begin your prayers." Her lips pulled back, baring teeth. "Do it quickly, wizard—"

"Yes, and he is chained to the cold, damp wall, he whimpers day and night, and refuses the food I offer. He complains of the things that crawl in the mush. Does he have no knowledge of the value of food, no matter its source?"

Blackwood stepped closer to the mage, pushing a little harder on the sword, eyes glaring.

"And he whines that his arms hurt because his feet do not touch the floor." Zuriel sneered. "I cannot help it if the chains are at a man's height."

"No!" Blackwood fought the urge to put all her might behind shoving the blade.

"The water I offer is fresh from the drainage trough yet he complains of its smell and refuses to drink."

"Enough!" Blackwood forced herself to step back from the wizard and sheath her sword. She drew a small pouch from inside her jerkin. "Here, here is your damnable stone!" She jerked the pouch, breaking the leather strand. "Your jewel, wizard, here in my hand." She ignored the string of pain that burned around her neck from breaking the leather tie.

Zuriel stepped closer to the fire, drawing Blackwood toward him. He held out his hand. "Give it to me."

"As you said, my son for the jewel." She clenched the pouch, knuckles white.

"How did you come to have my jewel—" He stopped talking for a moment. "Ah, the villagers."

"Yes," she hissed, "the villagers. They knew you would be sending to hire someone to find and return your stone. They needed only to wait."

"What if I had sent vengeance down on them?"

"They had the stone and knew your strength was within it."

"I see, so they just waited for the time when I was looking elsewhere, to steal my pouch."

Blackwood frowned in puzzlement. That did sound convenient. "Yes, maybe." She stepped closer to the wizard who had moved nearer the fire. Sweat beaded on her skin. "You were careless to carry a thing of such importance in a string pouch." Her frown deepened. "Very careless." She studied his face. Deep wrinkles etched his skin and a pale white-blue color emerged in blotches.

"They know the only way I can be killed is if the jewel is thrown into a fire."

Blackwood tossed the pouch into the air and caught it.

"I *will* throw it if you do not show me my son, Zuriel."
She moved as if to throw.

"No!" The mage held his hands up. "Wait." He
coughed. "If you throw it, I will perish."

"Yes." She feigned a throw.

"Wait!" He smiled leeringly. "Your son has little time
left. Already he has sores from bites, and the black skin
has formed on his hands. Give me the jewel."

She suddenly threw the pouch with all her might, into
the fire, rage deep in her gaze. She watched as the
leather bag disappeared somewhere deep in the fire's
flames. Her face felt flushed from the heat and sweat
trickled down between her breasts, darkening the front
of her jerkin.

Zuriel jerked as if his whole body spasmed and he
doubled over. He stayed bent over for a moment, then
slowly straightened. His face held an expression that
puzzled Blackwood. It looked as if he were relieved.
"Your son is free."

"What?" Blackwood saw more changes in the mage's
body; the darkening of the blue color in the skin, the
appearance of more wrinkles, the hair getting snow white.

His gaze met hers, but instead of showing anger there
was only compassion. "Even I could never find the strength
to do what you just did."

Blackwood stood with mouth agape. "The fire—the
offering. You!"

"Go to your son." Zuriel smiled warmly.

A painful guilt mixed with a lonely ache and stabbed at
Blackwood's heart. "You want to die."

"The jewel gave me powers, but it also made me
something I was not. Evil." He coughed. "It was a bad
thing, but I was not aware of such until too late." His
violet gaze met hers. "My release is welcome." He turned
toward the fire and stood in silence for a moment. "Did
you love your son's father?" he asked quietly.

Blackwood reached into her pocket and brought out
the real jewel. Her dark moist gaze fell on the stone for a
moment. "I still do." She tossed it into the fire.

Suddenly something touched her leg and Blackwood
whirled around, then looked down. Genuine joy brought
a wide smile to her face.

The little blond boy held his hands out to her.

Blackwood noticed the small hands were still the same color as always, not black as Zuriel had said, and she scooped him up in her arms. She squeezed him close to her chest for several moments. "Wood-son," she whispered, "I feared I would not see you become of the age when you take a name of your own."

"I liked it here, but I missed you, mother." Wood-son wrapped his arms around Blackwood's neck and hugged.

"You liked it here?" Blackwood frowned.

"Yes, Zuriel taught me songs, told me stories."

"He caused you no harm?"

Wood-son shook his head, then pulled on a thin leather string around his neck. "Look!" He brought the string up and out of his jerkin. "He made this."

Blackwood looked at the small carved wooden piece on the end of the leather strand. There were lines and circles etched into the surface. "Is it magic?"

Wood-son's violet gaze looked at the object then at Blackwood. "Yes! He said it would 'tect me always."

Somehow, Blackwood believed that. "He really made it for you?"

"Yes, and he said it was for me so I could 'member him."

Blackwood hugged her son again. "Remember him well."

"When I get old enough for my name, can I choose it?"

"You are supposed to choose your name."

"Then I want Zuriel."

"Yes," Blackwood said giving Wood-son a quick squeeze, "that will do well."

"Where is Zuriel?"

Blackwood's dark gaze swept to the fire. For a moment, she thought she saw the dark uneven form of a man standing deep inside the flames, but the moment was too brief.

She could not, would never be sure.

DANCE OF THE HEALER
by M. R. Hildebrand

Every year I try to present at least one "first story" by a new writer. And this one gave me a great deal of pleasure; not only because the story is a good one, but because the writer is an old friend.

Hildy, as she is known widely to fans in the Phoenix area, is the wife of fan and writer B. D. (Bruce) Arthurs. He, like Hildy a member of a local writer's group started by Jennifer Roberson (who appears elsewhere in this volume), made his debut in these pages with "Death and the Ugly Woman." Hildy also runs (and from a wheelchair) a series of conventions and the like that would make a strong man blanch.

Now she has managed to send me a story too.

S herlin walked quietly through the dark streets, the stars blinking above in silent company. The only sound was the steady, soft clicking of meditation beads slipping through her fingers. It had been a long and difficult delivery, but successful, ending with a healthy mother and child. Her feeling of satisfaction was matched by a purely physical tiredness.

When she had first come to live in Heracilis, she had twice been attacked by footpads. Sherlin had explained, as she checked their bruises and set their broken bones, what a Dancer was and what that meant. Since then, she had formed the habit of clicking softly in the night to announce her presence.

Coming to her home, Sherlin realized that something was wrong. Cermis, her apprentice, should have had a light burning for her. *Not again* ... She pushed the intruding, frightening thought away. She slid through the door and into the room with a smooth fluid motion, slamming the door back against the wall. Nothing moved. She listened. Nothing breathed. Carefully, she skirted the table and other objects scattered over the floor.

Reaching the fireplace, she took down a candle and lit it. The light showed her to be a woman of above average height, solidly built, dressed in a long, narrowly cut, calf-length over-tunic split to the hip. As she turned, the over-tunic flared slightly, showing the underskirt to actually be loosely cut trousers.

There was no sign of Cermis, except perhaps the traces of blood discernible on the floor. Cermis' attackers might easily have left the blood; Sherlin had been teaching her apprentice the Dances of Life and Death, as well as healcraft and meditation, for five years.

Food and dishes were scattered over the floor from the overturned table. Sherlin bent and felt a piece of bread. Whatever had happened had taken place early last night. The healer walked over to her workbench. Her dark eyes checked over her supplies. Nothing had been disturbed. Crossing to the opposite wall, Sherlin opened a large chest and felt quickly through it. Frowning, she straightened. Her hands began to worry the beads at her waist as she stood lost in thought.

Then Sherlin went to the door and gave an undulating but piercing whistle. Leaving the door slightly ajar, she turned back to the fireplace and rekindled the fire. Before she was finished, a small figure, shapeless in layers of dirty rags, slipped into the room.

"What's wrong, Dancer?" it piped, taking in the state of the disorderly room.

"Cermis is missing," Sherlin said, her low voice retaining its usual calm, hiding the fear she felt, "probably taken last night, about an hour after dark. Do you know anything about this?"

"Nah. I was on the Street of Fish, in Merlik's doorway by then. I din't see her yesterday, but I figured she was with you."

"Thank you, Rabbit." Sherlin looked up from the pan of water she was placing over the now crackling fire. "Go find Snake for me. Tell him I need him."

Snake arrived as the first sunbeams struck the door. His dark curls were disordered, his clothing slightly awry on his slender, newly-adolescent body. His voice shook slightly in spite of his effort to sound unconcerned. "Rabbit said Cermis was gone—taken!"

Sherlin looked up from her teacup. In the early morning light, her calm golden face was gilded to an exotic mask. "She was taken from here by force at about the second hour after dark." She gazed at the youth with slanted dark eyes, noting his concern.

"What do we do now?"

"I am going to sleep." The healer rose and took a small pouch from the chest, handing it to the youth. "You will use all of your talents and sources to find who took Cermis, and where." A surprised look crossed his face as Snake instinctively hefted the pouch.

"You may need all of it," Sherlin said as she unfolded her sleeping mat. "Check the brothels and slave caravans, of course, but I'm afraid it won't be that simple." She settled on the spread mat, then continued. "That pouch was left intact and my supplies as well. Some of those are even more valuable." The healer's voice continued calm, but her hands fretted at her beads. "Look for anything out of the ordinary . . . Tonight is the dark of the moon and the longest night of the year."

Snake's face was pale with fear as he nodded wordlessly and left. In the echoes of the slamming door a keen ear might have heard, "And the gods go with you. *Child, oh child* . . ."

The smell of dead fish added to the town's usual smell of woodsmoke and sewage told Sherlin that her small guide was leading her toward the riverfront. It was not a district she knew well; if anything, it was less law-abiding than her own neighborhood. A sudden turn and they were passing warehouses, great weathered sheds that bordered this portion of the river.

"Rabbit, are you sure this is where Snake said to meet him?" Sherlin asked as she hurried after the scurrying figure, cloak flapping about her legs. She had expected a magician's lair, not a merchant's. Cermis being stolen just prior to the potent conjunction of moon and solstice was a coincidence too significant to ignore.

"Yep, said to hurry. Said there wasn't time to spare." The small legs pumped even faster. The bag on the small back squirmed as it was bounced.

A bend in the road suddenly revealed an old, weather-beaten house. Its walls stood clear of its neighbors, a rarity in this crowded district. The lengthening shadows made the old house look even more sinister. Across the street, Snake stood watching the sky.

"What have you found, Snake?" Sherlin asked.

"I hope it's where Cermis is," the youth answered quietly, a slight edge in his voice. "I couldn't find anything definite, but this house has a bad reputation. A dark magician is said to live here. Old Nimian said that whores disappear regularly." He shrugged slightly. "Rumor has it they're used somehow to extend the magician's life. According to the old man, the magician is over a hundred years old.

"The gates are always shut and no one can get in." Snake looked at Sherlin defiantly. "Jopa the Thief tried to get over the wall, but something stopped him. He can't remember what it was—but he hasn't been sober since then."

The youth looked back at the sky, away from the healer's eyes. "Maybe I'm crazy, but when I get close to the wall or gate my skin prickles. Another thing, I've been watching for almost an hour and I've never seen a bird go near the house. They fly up and down the river. They light on the other roofs. But they don't go near the house or the trees in the garden. I want to try something, but I wanted you here to see.

Turning to Rabbit, he asked, "Did you bring the rats?" Rabbit grinned and held out the writhing bag.

Sherlin watched carefully as Snake threw a squirming

rat toward the top of the wall. As the animal reached the top it stopped in midair, then fell, squealing in agony. Hitting the street hard, the animal lay still, unconscious.

"Try it again." Sherlin asked thoughtfully. "No, no," she added, forestalling Rabbit's reach into the bag. "Use that one again." The healer nodded toward the unconscious rat. This time, the rat sailed unhindered over the wall.

After several more rats had failed to go over the wall unless they were unconscious or dead, Sherlin turned to Snake. "I will need a blanket and several strong people."

"What good will it do Cermis if you're on the other side of the wall but unconscious?" the youth asked. He shook his head. "We don't even know for sure she's in there."

"This house is surrounded by a strong magic spell that is indetectable from ten steps away. To cast a spell of that strength and subtlety requires a great power." Sherlin looked straight at the youth. "Sacrificing a virgin, especially one being taught The Dances of the Universe, tonight would gain a sorcerer incredible amounts of power."

Snake stared back, his jaw set. "I know you can heal better than anybody I ever heard about, but what can you do against a sorcerer that good? It won't help Cermis if you just go and get killed."

"I can't say I won't be killed, Snake, but I won't be totally helpless either. Not all of the Dances of the Universe are as simple as the Dances of Life and Death." Sherlin glanced at the creeping shadows, her face tight with anxiety. "The sun will be down soon and I'd rather not go over the wall in the dark."

It was obvious that Sherlin was determined to get into the house, and soon. Snake turned to Rabbit. "Climb on the roof over there and check out the best place for her to go over the wall. I don't want to toss her onto something that will break her back."

Snake turned back to Sherlin. "I may not know much about magic, but that long tunic isn't suitable for housebreaking. Go change into that black outfit you wear when you teach Cermis to Dance."

*   *   *

The sun had just touched the horizon as Sherlin's entranced body flew over the wall. Only a slight muscle spasm marked crossing the barrier.

"She's down. Doesn't look broken," came the call from Rabbit on the warehouse roof. The group of street dwellers that had tossed her over looked relieved.

At that assurance Snake began to call softly from the street, pleading with Sherlin to wake up and help Cermis. Rabbit's silence informed him that Sherlin was not responding. Dusk fell, and Snake paused for a moment. Then, carefully remembering Sherlin's instructions he called, *"Sherlin, linbao mun Chieu-li."*

"She's twitching!" Rabbit squeaked.

That yell was the first conscious impression Sherlin received. The second was a stab of memory; Chieu-li couldn't need her. Chieu-li was dead . . . but Cermis wasn't. Memory came flooding back; Sherlin opened her eyes and got to her feet. Rabbit announced it with a triumphant squeal.

"I am awake, Snake." The healer spent a few minutes moving through several difficult routines, loosening her stiff muscles. Then she called, "Throw over my equipment. I am ready to go in."

She caught the awkward bundle carefully. Sherlin removed the torch and laid it down. Moving swiftly, she tucked several small packets into pockets concealed about her close-fitting tunic. Finally, she took the silver knife Snake had insisted she carry and slipped it into her sash.

Sherlin picked up the unlit torch and made her way through the garden. Her black leather slippers glided soundlessly through the dry grass and leaves. The woman was aware of her own fear, aware that she was doing this because she had to do *something*. She could not lose another young friend. Not if there was any possibility of saving her.

When the healer got to the door, she simply reached out and gently opened it. Why lock the door when a spell so powerful guarded the wall around the property? Entering, Sherlin probed her surroundings carefully. Dust and staleness lay on the air, which was as heavy and still as if she were in a tomb. A faint blue glow from the walls and ceiling showed that she was in a broad hallway. It ran across the front of the house and seemed to continue around the corners. Dark places on the interior wall indicated doorways. There was no physical sound, but magically the house resounded with echoes of spells which existed now or in the past. No single spell could be discerned among the psychic din.

Silently, carefully, Sherlin moved, all senses alert. The first doorway showed only black, musty stillness. She lit the torch, revealing a room empty save for some heavy, dark furniture and a tightly shuttered window opposite the door. The healer was turning to continue down the corridor when a faint movement of air alerted her. She spun, seeing two large, black manlike shapes lunging toward her.

When the first creature was slightly more than an arm's-length away, Sherlin moved. She thrust the pitch-laden torch into its face as she Danced, turning and sliding swiftly, smoothly past it. That same turning continued into an upthrusting kick into the torso of the second monster. She turned immediately back to the first creature. It mewled in agony, beating at the burning pitch. A swift double-kick behind the knees brought the creature down to the floor. A fast two-fisted blow broke the thick neck with an audible snap. Whirling back to the second creature, she found it facedown on the floor, dark ichor oozing from its lifeless mouth.

She scooped up the guttering torch and nursed it back to full flame, watching the dark for another attack. Moving cautiously, Sherlin checked the other rooms on that portion of the hall. All empty.

She turned the corner and found herself in darkness. She could still feel the heat from the torch on her skin, but not see its light. Moving back, Sherlin found the darkness still surrounded her. Tendrils of sorcery edged around the Dancer's mind, trying to enter. She blocked them with an orderly pattern of thought. Abruptly, the tendrils withdrew, taking visible form and coalescing into a bright faceted mirror into which Sherlin found herself suddenly drawn.

She turned to flee, only to find herself enclosed by

mirrors. She was naked, and her nude image was reflected from every possible angle, even underfoot. Sherlin struck the mirrors, first physically, then psychically, with no results. She realized she was trapped out of body. The mirrors did not exist on a physical level. But if she couldn't escape, her body would either be killed or die eventually for lack of food and water.

Sherlin took up a meditation pose, legs folded beneath her. Her mind became calmer, and she began to recall one of her talks with Master Hu, so many years and miles away. He had said that the most advanced adepts could move not only their minds but their bodies by conceiving the new surroundings so completely that they "fooled the universe" and were there. Sherlin had not advanced far enough to do this on the physical plane but perhaps. . . .

She stood and placed her hand against one of the mirrors. Shutting her eyes, the Dancer envisioned herself on the outside of the globe of mirrors. But when she opened her eyes, she still saw herself reflected over and over into infinity.

Sherlin slumped against the glass. She couldn't fail. It was not only her own life at stake, but Cermis' as well. She closed her eyes again, steadied her breathing, and began the mental exercise called the Dance of Forgetting. She guided the details of her prison out of her mind, every angle and curve to both the mirrors and her reflection in them. Then she rebuilt the corridor, its mustiness and murky depths.

Suddenly the universe shifted. Her eyes flew open as her spirit poured back into her body, receiving a quick glimpse of the mirrored sphere popping like a soap bubble.

The Dancer quickly checked her surroundings; nothing had changed in the dark corridor except the brightness of her torch. Sherlin rose, the guttering torch in her hand, and quickly checked herself. Her body's slack fall had added another layer of soreness to the bruises from her toss over the wall, but basically she was still in good shape. She continued carefully down the corridor, continuing to check each room. More empty rooms.

It was too easy. Neither trap had been insurmountable. Sherlin knew she was not unusually strong in magic; she had left the temple with her training unfinished. Nor was she physically unbeatable, despite her training in the Dances. Why weren't there more attacks? Her mind worried at the problem.

Turning the next bend in the hall brought Sherlin to an abrupt halt. Before her was a black wall reaching from side to side and top to bottom of the corridor. Probing at the barrier with the torch, she found that she could not quite touch its surface. Nor did the torch's light reflect from its surface, but vanished into the blackness. Sherlin contemplated the barrier. Slowly she brought her hand forward, stopping when she felt the terrible cold of the blackness. Cold this intense could burn as badly as fire. *This* was the true wall around the sorcerer, untouchable either by physical tools or flesh. It reeked of terrible sorceries.

Sherlin went back to one of the empty rooms. She threw the bolt before placing her torch in the wall bracket. A quick check of the wardrobe and the musty bed and its hangings provided nothing more sinister than dust and a dead moth or two.

Satisfied, she pulled one of the pouches from a pocket, and took out a small handful of carved flat stones. She raised them to her forehead for a moment, then placed a stone in each corner, their carved faces looking outward. From the center of the room, Sherlin pointed toward each of the stones, speaking a short syllable. Speaking the syllable more slowly, the Dancer drew an arc diagonally overhead, turning and repeating until the room was covered and floored with protection.

Sherlin lay down and began a breathing mantra. The Dance was complex and she had not performed it since leaving the temple. When she reached the needed level of calm, Sherlin began to direct her spirit in the proper patterns. Her third eye—that which observed the nonphysical—opened.

Sherlin stood on a hazy gray plain. Her black clothing was now white silk, and each ankle was circled by a light, black band. A black tower stood nearby, reaching up out of sight. Her astral self moved smoothly and swiftly as thought, circling the windowless, featureless tower. Approaching closer, she felt again the coldness. Sherlin closed her eyes and resumed the patterns of the Dance.

When she opened her eyes again the plain was slightly brighter and the ankle-bands slightly heavier, but the tower still stood, strong, black, and cold. Again and again the adept danced to a higher level, each being brighter and more defined, the grays shifting toward colors.

Still the tower walls stood unbroken. Each level higher also increased the weight of the bands. The weight was reflected in the patterns of the Dance until it became a slow, strained effort.

Sherlin knew she could dance no higher. She opened her eyes; there again was the tower. She had lost. The Dancer hit the wall in angry despair. Suddenly she straightened in realization. She had touched the wall! The barrier was weakening! The tower was still solid, but it *was* weakening.

She had to go higher. Master Hu had said that the black bands were of her own making. That they were formed of self-deceit, and the closer she came to the essence of the universe the heavier the falsehood weighed, simply because a part of her knew that it to be false. Could she rid herself of them? Master Hu had told her she could, but repeated attempts had failed.

To rid herself of the bands she would have to remember the most painful times of her life. Not just remember them, but relive them and the emotions she had felt. Only then could she overcome her feelings of guilt.

Rather than that, she had left the temple, abandoning further studies in magic, and become simply a healer. She had roamed the world until she found a home in Heracilis, far from any reminder of the past. Now the past was Cermis' only hope. She folded into a lotus position and began.

She was an excited eight year old, watching Mother preparing a tea tray for Father and his important guest. The mandarin Ling-Po was the richest and most important man in town. Father was to lead a caravan escorting Ling-Po and his gifts to the emperor. Sherlin could hardly wait to tell her best friends about this!

She walked slowly, balancing the tray with great care

and pride, as she came quietly into the room. Sherlin watched in horror as the mandarin's gesturing hand struck the tray. Hot tea spilled onto her and on the mandarin's robes.

"Clumsy girl!" her father snapped. His hand lashed out, slapping her face. "Pick up this mess and remove your miserable self."

Full of confusion and anger, Sherlin bent to pick up the broken teapot. "Go, child." Unnoticed, her mother had entered, bringing a cloth. Sherlin hurried to the kitchen. Only then did she allow tears to silently form.

After her mother had taken a fresh tray to the men and returned, Sherlin asked, "Why was it my fault the tea was spilled and the pot broken? Lord Ling-Po hit the tray."

Her mother shook her head sadly. "Child, you must learn proper humility. We live among barbarians, but civilized people, in our homeland to the east, make it the woman's place to bear blame. We must save face for fathers and husbands wherever possible."

"I don't care," Sherlin muttered to herself. "It isn't right or fair. I hate them both! I hope I never see them again." The thought went through her mind many times that day. Her father left with Ling-Po to see to the last minute preparations, and Sherlin was asleep before his return. When she woke next morning, the caravan had already left.

Three weeks later, a man came to see Sherlin's mother. A while after he left, Mother called her in from play. Her mother's face was as serene as always, but Sherlin could tell something was very wrong.

"Sherlin, your father is dead. Bandits killed him." Her mother paused to allow her to understand what had been said.

Sherlin's first numb thought was, "I will never see him again." Never to run to her father again and get a hug. Never to hear his funny stories of other places and strange things. Grief blossomed in her. Then came the thought, "Maybe it was my fault."

After a moment her mother reached out and smoothed Sherlin's hair. "Your father didn't own enough yaks and mules for such a large caravan as Ling-Po's, so he rented some from Taj Singh. Your father had to give Singh a paper that said if your father didn't return the animals Singh would own our house and furniture. The bandits left nothing; Taj Singh now owns everything. We must leave tomorrow."

Sherlin felt real fear. *"Where will we go?"* she asked.

"I don't know," was her mother's quietly desperate answer.

The next morning Sherlin and her mother ate what little food was in the house, took their clothing, and left. *"Where are we going Mother?"* asked the frightened girl, trying to appear calm.

"We are going to the temple." The smoothness of her mother's face was belied by red-rimmed eyes.

"Will we live there now?"

"No." Sherlin's mother stopped walking and looked straight at her daughter. *"I have no way to earn money except by cooking, cleaning, or pleasing a man. It is all I know. I have no friends or relatives here to help find a servant's position, so I must go to a house of . . . joy."* A fleeting look of bitterness broke the customary calmness of her face at the final word.

She continued, *"I can't take you with me. Even young as you are, they would see you as another body to be sold. I am taking you to the temple to be trained as a magician or healer, so that you never have to make this choice."*

Sherlin didn't understand what her mother was saying, other than she would be taken to the temple and left there. She was numb, unable to understand how or why her world had collapsed so suddenly. All she could think of was other children saying that bad children were taken to the temple and left. She must have been bad. She had caused her father to die, and now her mother was leaving her.

Sherlin drew a shuddering gasp, tears streaming down her face. The pain of her father's loss was balanced by the new understanding of a mother's love. How well her mother had understood her; Sherlin would never have adapted to a brothel. She glanced down; only one ankle-band remained. Taking control of her breathing, Sherlin once more plunged into the past.

*   *   *

"Hi, Sherlin. What are you studying so hard?" Chieu-li came into the cell. The only other easterner in the temple, she had adopted Sherlin as an older sister. Her bright cheerfulness had made her very dear to the more serious, studious girl.

"The positions of the Dance of Fire Calling," Sherlin said proudly, setting the scroll to one side. "Master Hu says now that I have called Air and Water Elementals, I can start to study Fire. It is one of the most dangerous dances, and a major step toward becoming a master."

"Then it's settled? You're going to learn to be a master?" There was a teasing note in Chieu-li's voice.

"I think so. Master Hu says I have much self-examination ahead before being fully qualified, but he thinks I have the talent."

Just then a dark head poked in the doorway, "Sherlin, come quickly. There is a breech presentation in the infirmary, and with Yirna sick there isn't anyone able to turn the baby."

"All right, Namling. Don't panic. I'll be there in a minute." Sherlin rerolled the scroll and placed it on a shelf. "Leave the scroll alone," she said, ruffling Chieu-li's silky, black hair as she left the room. "And stay out of trouble, Little Monkey."

It was not only a breech baby, but a big one. Sherlin and Namling worked the night through, struggling to turn the baby and ease the mother's task. Finally the baby arrived safely. Sherlin felt a glow of happiness as the dawn's light lit the way to her cell.

Entering she stopped short. A smell of burning was in the air, and a small black lump lay in the middle of the floor. Her puzzled glance rose to the table, where a loosely rolled scroll lay. She began to scream, and everything went very far away . . .

Sherlin found herself back in her own body, tears again flowing freely. Great gasps racked her body. This time she allowed herself to cry for a few moments before calming herself. It was only right that she shed tears for those she loved. She had never allowed herself that before.

Sherlin now remembered what Master Hu had told her, "Of the twenty-seven poses and nine patterns of the Dance of Fire calling, only two poses in proper order are necessary to summon the elemental. The remainder are meant to control and dismiss." Yes, she was, in part, responsible for Chieu-li's death. It had been careless to leave the scroll in her room. But it had taken both Chieu-li's disobedience and pure bad luck to complete the tragedy.

Standing, she stretched and began to Dance. Higher and higher on the planes she rose until her own essence merged with that of the universe. From this viewpoint, the black tower was no longer an unbreachable monolith, but a tunnel leading inside itself. Sherlin began to dance down, concentrating herself on the inner side of the wards. As she neared the physical plane, her movements became slow and fluid so as not to disturb other wards the wizard might have set.

As Sherlin's astral shelf reached the physical plane, she realized her caution had been unnecessary. The wizard had already summoned the demon. All his attention centered on the creature contained within a large chalked pentagram. The demon noted Sherlin's arrival with a quick appraising glance, but gave no other sign. Cermis' unconscious body lay within a second pentagram to the side, and Sherlin went to her.

"I want a full fifty years," the wizard haggled. "After all, she's not only a young virgin, but a magic apprentice."

"I don't care," the demon responded. "I've held time back from you for almost a thousand years. No matter what the stories say, it gets harder each time. Ten years is all I can manage."

Now that she had gotten here, what could she do? The bargaining went on as Sherlin looked around the room. Outside the pentagrams, piles of notes and scrolls were neatly stacked on every available surface. It reminded her of the temple library, and of her last completed lessons with Master Hu. It would be dangerous to call elementals into the room, but better that than to allow the wizard to bargain away Cermis' soul. She began the Dance of Water Calling.

When the Water Elemental began to materialize, the wizard stopped short and looked around. "All right, twenty years," he said hurriedly, "Someone's attacking and I haven't time to argue further. I need power quickly." He began the ritual to bind the demon to his agreement. As soon as the water spirit was fully materialized, Sherlin ceased the Dance, loosing it to do as it would. Then she started the Dance of Air Calling. As the water spirit moved through the room, the papers and parchments began to develop puddles of dark, ink-stained water around them. The wizard's chanting became more harried, developing odd pauses as he peered intently at the increasingly soggy manuscript in his hand.

The air spirit began to materialize, first as a mild breeze and then as a strong wind. The soggy piles began to topple across the floor. A brazier began to give off thick smoke as the water spirit wandered past; the air whipped the smoke around the beleaguered wizard. One of the wet piles toppled across a corner of the demon's pentagram, smearing the carefully chalked line.

With a quick pounce the demon crossed the pentagram and grabbed the wizard. The sorcerer's scream was cut off as teeth sank into his throat. His dark hair whitened and his flesh withered as the demon fed upon his blood. It crooned in a crazed tone, "In the end it all comes to me, oh yes. The girls and the blood, the blood, oh yes, the blood." The wind and water continued to churn around the room, making a weird accompaniment to the demonic crooning.

Sherlin shuddered, trying not to watch or listen. The demon, finished, dropped the shrunken body. It powdered upon impact with the floor, dissolving into the black pools of inky water. Giving the intact pentagram and its contents a regretful look, the demon vanished.

Relief washed over Sherlin in a wave of tiredness. Slowly, she danced the dismissal for both elementals, then returned to her physical body. Several hours of physical inactivity had stiffened her bruised body. She made her slow, painful way back to Cermis' side. There was no black, cold wall to stop her now, the wizard's wards having vanished with his death.

Waving hartshorn under Cermis' nose brought her to spluttering wakefulness. "Come on, I want to go home." Sherlin's voice was sharp with exhaustion.

"What. . . ?"

"I'll tell you tomorrow. For right now let's just go home." The healer staggered, and Cermis put an arm around her as they left the house. Tomorrow, Sherlin decided, she would tell everyone what had happened. Everyone. It would be a long letter to Master Hu, but a necessary one. She would also have to talk with Cermis and decide whether she would try to return to the temple.

But for now she was going to bed. The night sky blinked in agreement.

ONE NIGHT AT THE INN
by Millea Kenin

About half the stories I get deal with the common conflict—at least in volumes like this—between the woman who wants to be either a swordswoman or a sorceress—and has talent only for the other. Stories like that come in so often that they must be saying something very important about women, I suppose. Otherwise I might get one every couple of years instead of—as I do—getting fifteen or twenty every year.

Millea Kenin, married to an entertainer, is an old friend; she has two kids, Rohana and Leon, who are about the age of my own younger two. (It always surprises me to find out that her kids are grown up—like mine—but I suppose that never ceases to surprise any mother.)

I've heard it said that every innkeeper in the Reaches of Aldery is a retired swordswoman. My mother was certainly no exception. Since she got the wound that lamed her, she'd been the keeper of the Golden Cock. (Don't smirk. I see you know that story. So did everyone in the neighborhood.) The picture on the signboard was a rooster and had been for years before she took over the place. She'd have liked to change the name, but people would have laughed worse than ever if she'd done so without an adequate excuse. This she never had until the night I'm telling you about.

My mother wanted me to follow her trade, and never let me forget it. "There's always a place for my daughter in the apprentice corps of Lord Rakelly's guard, and my old comrades would do right by you." She frowned at the open account book in front of her at the kitchen table, then looked up at me, pushing back her hair. "But you've got to start soon if you're ever going to, Velle; you've turned fourteen."

"Why you think anyone who bleeds every time she scrapes a carrot would survive even one battle—" I wound a rag around my finger. "No, Mother, I won't do it. Moranne would take me on; she told me so."

"If I could pay her fee! No, Velle, there haven't been any sorcerers, or sorceresses in this family yet, and I'll be happier if there never are. Oh, the sweet Brothers damn and blast this account book!" She slammed the ledger shut, put it on a back shelf and began to stir the soup of the day.

She was not in the mood to bear taunting, but I said recklessly, "How about on my father's side?"

"Your father was a wandering musician, as I've told you before, and the Brothers bless the day he chose to wander on! But if you'd shown any signs of musical talent, I'd have scrimped and saved to get training for you."

"I can whistle—"

"And don't you dare! Who knows what you might whistle up?"

"Moranne. And she could teach me."

My mother snorted. "An hour she talks to you about herbs and you think you know it all." She tasted the soup and wrinkled her nose. "You haven't been cooking up potions in the kitchen again, have you?"

"No, Mother. Not since I promised."

"A good thing too. What would become of the roof over our heads if word got out that our guests tend to fall asleep at the table or start seeing visions—or drop dead?"

As the sun went down, the common room started to fill up. Mostly the guests were locals, in for a few beers and a gossip, but there were a few travelers who needed a hearty meal and a room for the night. Kep, the elderly handyman, was stabling their horses and I was bringing their bowls and platters, while Mother drew beer and ale from the kegs or poured wine.

Suddenly the door was flung open hard enough to crack the frame. One by one, three hulking figures shoved their way in, cracking it worse. The last one didn't duck low enough, cracked his head as well as the lintel, and swore.

"Bring us something to drink, wench!" boomed the first of the brutes, in a voice that rattled all the crockery. He banged his fist down on the bar hard enough to knock chips out of the hardwood.

My mother put three large, full tankards in front of them. Each drained his in one gulp and handed it back for more. Now the top was off his thirst, the leader took a mouthful, spat it onto the floor and threw the tankard after it. "Haven't you got anything better than this goat piss?" he roared.

One of his companions tasted his, frowned thoughtfully, then spat and threw his tankard likewise. "Dog piss, not goat piss," he said after deep consideration.

The third had drained his second tankard, but now he too threw his on the floor, bellowing disgustedly, "Chicken piss!"

"*Chicken* piss, you ass?" one of the others snorted.

"Ass piss!"

The one who had snorted clouted the third fellow on his already sore head. That one took a wild swing at his erstwhile comrade and swept all our precious glassware to the floor.

By their size, shape and smell, and by their total lack of manners, these three could be nothing but giant hill trolls. What they were doing in this region they hadn't said, and I couldn't guess. Trolls—at least large ones—don't usually travel much, since they've got to find a place big enough to hole up in between sunrise and sunset every day.

Though my mother's too lame for active guard duty, she's well up to breaking up the usual public room brawl. She couldn't have taken on three trolls single-handedly when she was at the top of her form, but I think for a moment she almost forgot. She looked up at her sword hanging decoratively on the wall—then looked away quickly. She must have been hoping, as I was, that none of the trolls would notice the sword. One of them could have killed somebody with it before he broke it.

As for the other guests, they'd be no help. None of them were armed or looked tough, and by now they were all cowering in the corner farthest from the bar. Kep peeked in the doorway and retreated quietly toward the stable.

"What are we going to do?" my mother muttered, running her fingers through her hair. "I can send Kep to fetch the guards from Rakelly's Keep, but by the quickest they could get here the place'll be in smithereens. My old comrades would do me a favor if they could, but Lord Rakelly will charge me an arm and a leg for their time, the old skinflint. And don't say Moranne! She lives farther from here than Rakelly's Keep, and she charges more!"

I didn't mention Moranne's name, but I started thinking about what she might do in this situation. Probably any one of a thousand things—but there was one thing she might do that I could do. "Don't worry, Mother," I said. "I'll handle it."

The trolls had stopped fighting long enough to start yelling again for something fit to drink and pounding the bar apart.

"Tell them I've gone to get the best stuff in the house, *on* the house," I grinned. My mother gave a worried sigh and tried to grin back. I don't know why she thought a tiny drop of one of my potions on the wrong spoon would have untoward effects, but a whole potful wouldn't be enough to quell three trolls; but I hastened into the kitchen. A few minutes later I came back, trying to look as seductive as I could while staggering under the weight of our biggest cauldron, now doing double duty as a punch bowl. I put it on a table and invited them to sit around it.

The first one took a chair, which smashed beneath his weight. For a second I was afraid he'd take offense and overturn the punch bowl, which would wreck everything. (I'd used up all I had of the special ingredients, aside from virgin's blood—a drop from my cut finger—but more of that I'd rather not spare either.) The troll noticed that the table was at the right height when he was sitting on the floor, so he magnanimously swept the other two chairs out of the way and said, "Wench, fetch us some cushions." This I did, and served their first helpings of my special punch. "Not bad," admitted the leader, ladling himself a refill.

"Not half bad." The second elbowed him out of the way and messily refilled his own tankard. I hoped they wouldn't spill so much they wouldn't get an effective dose.

"Elephant piss," said the third, but he took a refill too.

One of the others raised a hand to clout him. The punchbowl rocked, and the other two grabbed it to steady it. The troll with the upraised hand stopped with it in midair, unclenched the fist and started wiggling the fingers. He looked at them cross-eyed and began to giggle.

"What's so funny about those knuckle sausages?" growled the leader.

The cross-eyed troll laughed harder than ever. "You're funny too," he said.

"In a pig's eye," rumbled the first, but then he broke out laughing too.

"Pig piss," said the third troll, draining his tankard yet again.

"In *your* eye," said the first troll, and by now all of them were laughing uproariously. "Say, wench," the leader went on, "give some to our friends—" waving his hand to include the whole cowering company. "On us." He hefted out a bag of gold coins and started throwing them around.

"Not the house special," I said. "This is all I've got of it, hardly enough for you three big men."

"Men? We're trolls—highest form of life, wench, 'n' don't you forget it. But give our good buddies a round of dog piss, or whatever they've been drinking."

Mother and I scrambled to obey. Then I made sure the shutters on all the eastern windows were drawn back. "Why— Oh," Mother said. The trolls had stopped paying attention to the other guests and were telling each other stupid jokes. The local people began quietly slipping out the wrecked doorway, and my mother took the overnight travelers up to their rooms. I stayed to keep an eye on the three, but there was no need.

"Knock knock," said one.

"Who . . . uh, who's there?" the second asked slowly.

"Man piss," mumbled the third.

"Piss off," said the first, "you're uh, making me forget. Oh yeah . . . it's . . . uh, Ida. Knock knock who's there Ida."

"Ida . . . who?"

"Ida . . . uh, Ida know who."

"Neither do I."

"That's . . . that's the *answer*, meathead . . . Ida . . . know . . . who."

"Oh." He thought hard, and added, "Any . . . any more to drink?"

The leader slowly picked up the whole cauldron, held it up and tipped the dregs into his own mouth, then let it fall with a crash. "There *was*," he said.

"I oughta . . . oughta hit you . . . for that."

"Ne'mind. Why . . . uh, why does the chicken?"

"Why does the, uh, chicken . . . do what?"

"I ain't gonna give you no . . . uh, clues!" Gradually their laughter became slower and slower.

My mother came down and we sat in a corner with our arms around each other. Neither of us felt like trying to sleep, or like talking. There was no sound for hours but occasional bursts of slow, rumbling laughter; the candles were out and the fire had burned to embers, but the three creatures of darkness took no notice. Less typically, they also did not notice as the darkness gradually lessened.

Then the first beam of sunlight shone in the window. There was one horrible cry, three giant voices in unison, in agony—then total silence. The growing light showed them motionless and gray, three ugly stone statues.

"Don't tell me what you put in that punch, Velle," said my mother—as if I would have. "Brothers bless you for thinking of it. Not too much damage done, and what the quarrymen will charge to break these up and haul them away won't be a quarter of the fee for calling in the corps."

"Besides, we've got the trolls' gold," I said.

"Oh, yes? You know, of course, how to take the curse off it?"

"No, but Mor—" I bit my lip.

My mother grinned. "Moranne does? Then she can have it as her fee for taking you off my hands."

So she sent Kep off to ask Moranne to come to the inn as quickly as possible (what with all that gold lying around, still cursed). I'm not sure his explanation of the need for her presence made much sense; come to think of it, he'd hidden from most of the exciting part, and Mother and I hadn't taken time to explain to *him*. At any rate, when Moranne walked in, her pale face went even paler, and she gasped, "What's been happening here?"

So I told her the whole story, and sat back waiting for a pat on the head. What I got felt more like a swift kick in the butt.

"Oh, no! No, Jolynne, I can't take this—any of it but the standard ten percent de-cursing fee, that is. I owe it to the Brothers and my conscience to teach Velle at my own expense, before it's too late, if it isn't already."

My mother looked just as daunted and confused as I felt. "What do you mean, too late?"

"Well, in the sweet Brothers' names, Jolynne, do you have your human guests killed for being obnoxious and disorderly?"

"But these were *trolls!*" I burst out.

Moranne just gave me a look that made me want to sink into the floor. Before I could figure out how to do so, however, who should come bustling in through the broken doorway but old Lord Rakelly himself, white mustaches bristling; he'd overheard the last few words.

"Quite right!" he said. "Only good troll is a stone one, *I* always say. Heard about your little adventure here, Jolynne, and wondered what you were planning to do with these fellows." He gestured toward the three seated, hulking stones.

"Break them up for rubble, I suppose," my mother sighed, pushing her hair back from her brow again.

"No, don't do that—I'll buy a couple of them to stand at either side of my gate."

She brightened up at once and began to haggle, but I didn't listen to the details, because Moranne took me aside and began, in an undervoice, to give me a lecture which has since become far too familiar, about how trolls and gnomes and merrows and so on were here in Aldery before we humans came, and how little incidents like this increased the threat of war between our kinds, and— But you don't want to hear that.

You do want to hear about the name of the inn? Oh yes, I was going to tell you. Mother still has the biggest and ugliest looking of the trolls in the innyard; it's quite a local attraction. Moranne keeps me too busy for me to go back and visit very often, but last time I did, I found that Mother'd had the sign repainted with a picture of all three, and the words on it now are: The Stoned Trolls.

KEYS
by Mercedes Lackey

Misty Lackey, when she sent this story to me, accompanied it with a letter that began (in red ink), "I said I wasn't going to do another Tarma and Kethry story for S&SV. So I lied."

How can you reject a story after that? Especially when Tarma and Kethry have been special favorites with the S&S readership ever since their first appearance here.

She is also the author of a very good trilogy: ARROWS OF THE QUEEN, ARROW'S FLIGHT, and ARROW'S FALL, also published by DAW, about a special elite corps of messengers. At least I liked it, and it's not that easy for me to find anything I like to read anymore. Maybe it was in spite of the sentient horses; I tend to dislike horse stories (defying the tradition) because I was a farm girl and had no sentimental feeling about horses. For me horses were just big animals which ate too much hay (which I had to shovel) and demanded altogether too much shoveling in other ways.

She stood all alone on the high scaffold made of raw, yellow wood, as motionless as any statue. She was cold despite the heat of the summer sunlight that had scorched her without pity all this day; cold with the ice-rime of fear. She had begun her vigil as the sun rose at her back; now the last light of it flushed her white

83

gown and her equally white face, lending her pale cheeks false color. The air was heavy, hot and scented only with the odor of scorched grass and sweating bodies, but she breathed deeply, desperately of it. Soon now, soon—

Soon the last light of the sun would die, and she would die with it. Already she could hear the men beneath her grunting as they heaved piles of oily brush and faggots of wood into place below her platform. Already the motley-clad herald was signaling to the bored and weary trumpeter in her husband's green livery that he should sound the final call. *Her* last chance for aid.

For the last time the three rising notes of a summoning rang forth over the crowd beneath her. For the last time the herald cried out his speech to a sea of pitying or avid faces. *They* knew that this was the last time, the last farcical call, and they waited for the climax of this day's fruitless vigil.

"Know ye all that the Lady Myria has been accused of the foul and unjust murder of her husband, Lord Corbie of Felwether. Know that she has called for trial by combat as is her right. Know that she names no champion, trusting in the gods to send forth one to fight in her name as token of her innocence. Therefore, if such there be, I do call, command, and summon him here, to defend her honor!"

No one looked to the gate except Myria. She, perforce, must look there, since she was bound to her platform with hempen rope as thick as her thumb. This morning she had strained her eyes toward that empty arch every time the trumpet sounded, but no savior had come—and now even she had lost hope.

The swordswoman called Tarma goaded her gray Shin'a'in warsteed into another burst of speed, urging her on with hand and voice (though not spur—*never* spur) as if she were pursued by the Jackels of Darkness. Her long, ebony braids streamed behind her; close enough to catch one of them rode her amber-haired partner, the sorceress Kethry; Kethry's mare a scant half a length after her herd-sister.

Kethry's geas-blade, Need by name, had woken her this morning almost before the sun rose, and had been driving the sorceress (and so her blood-oath sister as well) in this direction all day. At first it had been a simple pull, as she had often felt before. Both Kethry and Tarma knew from experience that once Need called, Kethry had very little choice in whether or not she would answer that call, so they had packed up their camp and headed for the source. But the call had grown more urgent as the hours passed, not less so—increasing to the point where by midafternoon it was actually causing Kethry severe mental pain. They had gotten Tarma's companion-beast Warrl up onto his carry-pad and urged their horses first into a fast walk, then a trot, then as sunset neared, into a full gallop. Kethry was near-blind by the mental anguish it caused. Need *would* not be denied in this; Kethry was soul-bonded to it—it conferred upon her a preternatural fighting skill, it had healed both of them of wounds it was unlikely they would have survived otherwise—but there was a price to pay for the gifts it conferred. Kethry (and thus Tarma) was bound to aid any woman in distress within the blade's sensing range—and it seemed there was one such woman in grave peril now. Peril of her life, by the way the blade was driving Kethry.

Ahead of them on the road they were following loomed a walled village; part and parcel of a manor-keep, a common arrangement in these parts. The gates were open; the fields around empty of workers. That was odd—very odd. It was high summer, and there should have been folk out in the fields, weeding and tending the irrigation ditches. There was no immediate sign of trouble—but as they neared the gates, it was plain just who the woman they sought was—

Bound to a scaffold high enough to be visible through the open gates, they could see a young, dark-haired woman dressed in white, almost like a sacrificial victim. The last rays of the setting sun touched her with color—touched also the heaped wood beneath the platform on which she stood, making it seem as if her pyre already blazed up. Lining the mud-plastered walls of the keep and crowding the square inside the gate were scores of folk of every class and station, all silent, all waiting.

Tarma really didn't give a fat damn about what they were waiting for, though it was a good bet that they were there for the show of the burning, and not out of sympathy for the woman. She coaxed a final burst of speed out of her tired mount, sending her shooting ahead of Kethry's as they passed the gates, and bringing her close in to the platform. Once there, she swung her mare Hellsbane around in a tight circle and drew her sword, placing herself between the woman on the scaffold and the men with the torches to set it alight.

She knew she was an imposing sight, even covered with sweat and the dust of the road; hawk-faced, intimidating, ice-blue eyes blazing defiance. Her clothing was patently that of a fighting mercenary; plain brown leathers and brigandine armor. Her sword reflected the dying sunlight so that she might have been holding a living flame in her hand. She said nothing; her pose said it all for her.

Nevertheless, one of the men started forward, torch in hand.

"I wouldn't," Kethry said from behind him. She was framed in the arch of the gate, silhouetted against the fiery sky; her mount rock-still, her hands glowing with sorcerous energy. "If Tarma doesn't get you, *I* will."

"Peace," a tired, gray-haired man in plain, dusty-black robes stepped forward from the crowd, holding his arms out placatingly, and motioned the torch-bearer to give way. "Ilvan, go back to your place. Strangers, what brings you here at this time of all times?"

Kethry pointed—a thin strand of glow shot from her finger and touched the ropes binding the captive on the platform. The bindings loosed and fell from her, sliding down her body to lie in a heap at her feet. The woman swayed and nearly fell, catching herself at the last moment with one hand on the stake she had been bound to. A small segment of the crowd—mostly women—stepped forward as if to help, but fell back again as Tarma swiveled to face them.

"I know not what crime you accuse this woman of, but she is innocent of it," Kethry said to him, ignoring the presence of anyone else. "*That* is what brings us here."

A collective sigh rose from the crowd at her words. Tarma watched warily to either side, but it appeared to be a sigh of relief rather than a gasp of arousal. She relaxed the white-knuckled grip she had on her sword-hilt by the merest trifle.

"The Lady Myria is accused of the slaying of her lord," the robed man said quietly. "She called upon her ancient right to summon a champion to her defense when the evidence against her became overwhelming. I, who am priest of Felwether, do ask you—strangers, will you champion the Lady and defend her in trial-by-combat?"

Kethry began to answer in the affirmative, but the priest shook his head negatively. "No, lady-mage, by ancient law *you* are bound from the field; neither sorcery nor sorcerous weapons such as I see you bear may be permitted in trial-by-combat."

"Then—"

"He wants to know if I'll do it, *she'enedra*," Tarma croaked, taking a fiendish pleasure in the start the priest gave at the sound of her harsh voice. "I know your laws, priest, I've passed this way before. I ask you in my turn—if my partner, by her skills, can prove to you the lady's innocence, will you set her free and call off the combat, no matter how far it has gotten?"

"I so pledge, by the Names and the Powers," the priest nodded—almost eagerly.

"Then I will champion this lady."

About half the spectators cheered and rushed forward. Three older women edged past Tarma to bear the fainting woman back into the keep. The rest, except for the priest, moved off slowly and reluctantly, casting thoughtful and measuring looks back at Tarma. Some of them seemed friendly—most did not.

"What—"

"Was that all about?" That was as far as Tarma got before the priest interposed himself between the partners.

"Your pardon, mage-lady, but you may not speak with the champion from this moment forward—any message you may have must pass through me—"

"Oh no, not yet, priest." Tarma urged Hellsbane forward and passed his outstretched hand. "I told you I know your laws—and the ban starts at sundown—Greeneyes, pay attention, I have to talk fast. You're going to have to figure out just who the real culprit is—the best I can possibly do is buy you time. This business is combat to the death for the champion—I can choose just to defeat my challengers, but they *have* to kill me. And the longer you take, the more likely that is."

"Tarma, you're better than anybody here!"

"But not better than any twenty—or thirty." Tarma smiled crookedly. "The rules of the game, *she'enedra*, are that I keep fighting until nobody is willing to challenge me. Sooner or later they'll wear me out and I'll go down."

"*What?*"

"Shush, I knew what I was getting into. You're as good at your craft as I am at mine—I've just given you a bit of incentive. Take Warrl." The tall, lupine creature jumped to the ground from behind Tarma where he'd been clinging to the special pad with his retractile claws. "He might well be of some use. Do your best, *veshta'cha*; there're two lives depending on you—"

The priest interposed himself again. "Sunset, champion," he said firmly, putting his hand on her reins.

Tarma bowed her head, and allowed him to lead her and her horse away, Kethry staring dumbfounded after them.

"All right, let's take this from the very beginning."

Kethry was in the Lady Myria's bower, a soft and colorful little corner of an otherwise drab fortress. There were no windows—no drafts stirred the bright tapestries on the walls, or caused the flames of the beeswax candles to flicker. The walls were thick stone covered with plaster—warm by winter, cool by summer. The furnishings were of light yellow wood, padded with plump feather cushions. In one corner stood a cradle, watched over broodingly by the lady herself. The air was pleasantly scented with herbs and flowers. Kethry wondered how so pampered a creature could have gotten herself into such a pass.

"It was two days ago. I came here to lie down in the afternoon. I—was tired; I tire easily since Syrtin was born. I fell asleep."

Close-up, the Lady proved to be several years Kethry's junior; scarcely past her mid-teens. Her dark hair was lank and without luster, her skin pale. Kethry frowned at that, and wove a tiny spell with a gesture and two whispered words while Myria was speaking. The creature of the Ethereal Plane who'd agreed to serve as their scout was still with her—it would have taken a far wilder ride than they had made to lose it. The answer to her question came quickly as a thin voice breathed whispered words into her ear.

Kethry grimaced angrily. "Lady's eyes, child, I shouldn't wonder that you tire—you're still torn up from the birthing! What kind of a miserable excuse for a Healer have you got here, anyway?"

"We have *no* Healer, lady." One of the three older women who had borne Myria back into the keep rose from her seat behind Kethry and stood between them, challenge written in her stance. She had a kind, but careworn face; her gray and buff gown was of good stuff, but old-fashioned in cut. Kethry guessed that she must be Myria's companion, an older relative, perhaps. "The Healer died before my dove came to childbed and her lord did not see fit to replace him. We had no use for a Healer, or so he claimed, since he kept no great number of men-at-arms, and birthing was a perfectly normal procedure and surely didn't require the expensive services of a Healer."

"Now Katran—"

"It is no more than the truth! He cared more for his horses than for you! He replaced the farrier quickly enough when *he* left!"

"His horses were of more use to him," the girl said bitterly, then bit her lip. "There, you see, *that* is what brought me to this pass—one too many careless remarks let fall among the wrong ears."

Kethry nodded, liking the girl; the child was *not* the pampered pretty she had first thought. No windows to this chamber, only the one entrance; a good bit more like a cell than a bower, it occurred to her. A comfortable cell, but a cell still. She stood, smoothed her buff-colored robe with an unconscious gesture, and unsheathed the sword that seldom left her side.

"Lady, what—" Katran stood, startled by the gesture.

"Peace; I mean no ill. Here," Kethry said, bending over Myria and placing the blade in the startled girl's hands. "Hold this for a bit."

Myria took the blade, eyes wide, a puzzled expression bringing a bit more life to her face. "But—"

"Women's magic, child. For all that blades are a man's weapon, Need here is strong in the magic of women. She serves women only—it was her power that called me here to aid you—and given an hour of your holding her, she'll Heal you. Now, go on. You fell asleep."

Myria accepted the blade gingerly, then settled the sword across her knees and took a deep breath. "Something woke me—a sound of something falling, I think. You can see that this room connects with my Lord's chamber—that in fact the only way in or out is through his chamber. I saw a candle burning, so I rose to see if he needed anything. He—he was slumped over his desk. I thought perhaps he had fallen asleep."

"You thought he was drunk, you mean," the older woman said wryly.

"Does it *matter* what I thought? I didn't *see* anything out of the ordinary, because he wore dark colors always. I reached out my hand to shake him—and it came away bloody!"

"And she screamed fit to rouse the household," Katran finished.

"And when we came, she had to unlock the door for us," said the second woman, silent till now. "Both doors into that chamber were locked—hallside with the lord's key, seneschal's side barred from within this room. And the bloody dagger that had killed him was under her bed."

"Whose was it?"

"Mine, of course," Myria answered. "And before you ask, there was only one key to the hallside door; it could only be opened with the key, and the key was under his hand. It's an ensorcelled lock; even if you made a copy of the key, the copy would never unlock the door."

"Warrl?" The huge beast rose from the shadows where he'd been lying and padded to Kethry's side. Myria and her women shrank away a little at the sight of him.

"I may need to conserve my energies. You can detect what I'd need a spell for. See if there's magical residue on the bar on the other door, would you? Then see if the spell on the lock's been tampered with."

The dark-gray, nearly black beast trotted out of the room on silent paws, and Myria shivered.

"I can see where the evidence against you is over-whelming, even without misheard remarks."

"I had no choice in this wedding," Myria replied, her chin rising defiantly, "but I have been a true and loyal wife to my lord."

"Loyal past his deserts, if you ask me," Katran grumbled. "Well, that's the problem, lady-mage. My Lady came to this marriage reluctant, and it's well known. It's well known that he didn't much value her. And there's been more than a few heard to say they thought Myria reckoned to set herself up as Keep-ruler with the Lord gone."

Warrl padded back into the room, and flopped down at Kethry's feet.

"Well, fur-brother?"

He shook his head negatively, and the women stared at this evidence of like-human intelligence.

"Not the bar nor the lock, him? And how do you get into a locked room without a key? Still—Lady, is all as it was in the other room?"

"Yes—the priest was one of the first in the door, and would not let anyone change so much as a dust-mote. He only let them take the body away."

"Thank the Goddess!" Kethry looked curiously at the girl. "Lady, *why* did you choose to prove yourself as you did?"

"Lady-mage—" Kethry was surprised at the true expression of guilt and sorrow the child wore. "If I had guessed strangers would be caught in this web I never would have. I—I thought that my kind would come to my defense. I came to this marriage of their will, I thought at least one of them might—at least try. I don't think anyone here would dare the family's anger by taking the chance of killing one of the sons—even if the daughter is thought worthless by most of them." A slow tear slid down one cheek, and she whispered her last words. "My youngest brother, I thought at least was fond of me."

The spell Kethry had set in motion was still active; she whispered another question to the tiny air-entity she had summoned. This time the answer made her smile, albeit sadly.

"Your youngest brother, child, is making his way here

afoot, having ridden his horse into foundering trying to reach you in time, and blistering the air with his oaths."

Myria gave a tiny cry and buried her face in her hands; Katran moved to comfort her as her shoulders shook with silent sobs. Kethry stood, and made her way into the other room. Need's magic was such that the girl would hold the blade until she no longer required its power; it would do nothing to augment Kethry's magical abilities, so it was fine where it was. Right now there was a mystery to solve—and two lives hung in the balance until Kethry could puzzle it out.

As she surveyed the outer room, she wondered how Tarma was faring.

Tarma sat quietly beneath the window of a tiny, bare, rock-walled cell. In a few moments the light of the rising moon would penetrate it—first through the eastern window, then the skylight overhead. For now, the only light in the room was that of the oil-flame burning on the low table before her. There was something else on that table— the long, coarse braids of Tarma's hair.

She had shorn those braids off herself at shoulder-length, then tied a silky black headband around her forehead to confine what remained. That had been the final touch to the costume she'd donned with an air of robing herself for some ceremony—clothing that had long stayed untouched, carefully folded in the bottom of her pack. Black clothing; from low, soft boots to chainmail shirt, from headband to hose—the stark, unrelieved black of a Shin'a'in Sword Sworn about to engage in ritual combat or on the trail of blood-feud.

Now she waited, patiently, seated cross-legged before the makeshift altar, to see if her preparations received an answer.

The moon rose behind her, the square of dim white light creeping slowly down the blank stone wall opposite her, until, at last, it touched the flame on the altar.

And without warning, without fanfare, *She* was there, standing between Tarma and the altar-place. Shin'a'in by her golden skin and sharp features, clad identically to Tarma—only Her eyes revealed Her as something not human. Those eyes—the spangled darkness of the sky at midnight, without white, iris or pupil—could belong to only one being; the Shin'a'in Goddess of the South Wind, known only as the Star-Eyed, or the Warrior.

"Child." Her voice was as melodious as Tarma's was harsh.

"Lady," Tarma bowed her head in homage.

"You have questions, child? No requests?"

"No requests, Star-Eyed. My fate—does not interest me. I will live or die by my own skills. But Kethry's—"

"The future is not easy to map, child, not even for a goddess. Tomorrow might bring your life *or* your death; both are equally likely."

Tarma sighed. "Then what of my *she'enedra* should it be the second path?"

The Warrior smiled, Tarma felt the smile like a caress. "You are worthy of your blade, child; hear, then. If you fall tomorrow, your *she'enedra*—who has fewer compunctions than you and would have done this already had you not bound yourself to the trial—will work a spell that lifts both herself and the Lady Myria to a place leagues distant from here. And as she does this, Warrl will release Hellsbane and Ironheart and drive them out the gates. When Kethry recovers from that spell, they shall go to our people, to the Liha'irden; Lady Myria will find a mate to her liking there. Then, with some orphans of other clans, they shall go forth and Tale'sedrin will ride the plains again, as Kethry promised you. The blade will release her, and pass to another's hands."

Tarma sighed, and nodded. "Then, Lady, I am content, whatever my fate tomorrow. I thank you."

The Warrior smiled again; then between one heartbeat and the next, was gone.

Tarma left the flame to burn itself out, lay down upon the pallet that was the room's only other furnishing, and slept.

Sleep was the last thing on Kethry's mind.

She surveyed the room that had been Lord Corbie's; plain stone walls, three entrances, no windows. One of the entrances still had the bar across the door, the other two led to Myria's bower and to the hall outside. Plain wooden floor, no hidden entrances there. She knew the blank wall held nothing either; the other side was the courtyard of the manor. Furnishings; one table, one chair, one ornate bedstead against the blank wall, one bookcase, half filled, four lamps. A few bright rugs. Her mind felt as blank as the walls.

"Start at the beginning—" she told herself. "Follow what happened. The girl came in here alone—the man followed after she was asleep—then what?"

He was found at his desk, said a voice in her mind, startling her, *He probably walked straight in and sat down. What's on the desk that he might have been doing?*

Every time Warrl spoke to her mind-to-mind it surprised her. She still couldn't imagine how he managed to make himself heard when she hadn't a scrap of that particular Gift. Tarma seemed to accept it unquestioningly; how she'd ever gotten used to it, the sorceress couldn't imagine.

Tarma—time was wasting.

On the desk stood a wineglass with a sticky residue in the bottom, an inkwell and quill, and several stacked ledgers. The top two looked disturbed.

Kethry picked them up, and began leafing through the last few pages, whispering a command to the invisible presence at her shoulder. The answer was prompt; the ink on the last three pages of both ledgers was fresh enough to still be giving off fumes detectable only by a creature of the air. The figures were written no more than two days ago.

She leafed back several pages worth, noting that the handwriting changed from time to time.

"Who else kept the accounts besides your lord?" she called into the next room.

"The seneschal; that was why his room has an entrance on this one," the woman Katran replied, entering the lord's room herself. "I can't imagine why the door was barred. Lord Corbie almost never left it that way."

"That's a lot of trust to place in a hireling—"

"Oh, the seneschal isn't a hireling, he's Lord Corbie's bastard brother. He's been the lord's right hand since he inherited the lordship of Felwether."

The sun rose; Tarma was awake long before.

If the priest was surprised to see her change of outfit, he didn't show it. He had brought a simple meal of bread and cheese, and watered wine; he waited patiently while she ate and drank, then indicated she should follow him.

Tarma checked all her weapons; made sure of all the fastenings of her clothing, and stepped into place behind him, as silent as his shadow.

He conducted her to a small tent that had been erected in one corner of the keep's practice ground, against the keep walls. The walls of the keep formed two sides, the outer wall the third; the fourth side was open. The practice ground was of hard-packed clay, and relatively free of dust. A groundskeeper was sprinkling water over the dirt to settle it.

Once they were in front of the little pavilion, the priest finally spoke.

"The first challenger will be here within a few minutes; between fights you may retire here to rest for as long as it takes for the next to ready himself, or one candlemark, whichever is longer. You will be brought food at noon and again at sunset—" his expression plainly said that he did not think she would be needing the latter "—and there will be fresh water within the tent at all times. I will be staying with you."

Now his expression was apologetic.

"To keep my partner from slipping me any magical aid?" Tarma asked wryly. "Hellfire, priest, *you* know what I am, even if these dirt-grubbers here don't!"

"I know, Sword Sworn. This is for your protection as well. There are those here who would not hesitate to tip the hand of the gods somewhat."

Tarma's eyes hardened. "Priest, I'll spare who I can, but it's only fair to tell you that if I catch anyone trying an underhanded trick, I won't hesitate to kill him."

"I would not ask you to do otherwise."

She looked at him askance. "There's more going on here than meets the eye, isn't there?"

He shook his head, and indicated that she should take her seat in the champion's chair beside the tent-flap. There was a bustling on the opposite side of the practice ground, and a dark, heavily bearded man followed by several boys carrying arms and armor appeared only to vanish within another identical tent on that side. Spectators began gathering along the open side and the tops of the walls.

"I fear I can tell you nothing, Sword Sworn. I have only speculations, nothing more. But I pray your little partner is wiser than I—"

"Or I'm going to be cold meat by nightfall," Tarma finished for him, watching as her first opponent emerged from the challenger's pavilion.

Kethry had not been idle.

The sticky residue in the wineglass had been more than just the dregs of drink; there had been a powerful narcotic in it. Unfortunately, this just pointed back to Myria; she'd been using just such a potion to help her sleep since the birth of her son. Still—it wouldn't have been all that difficult to obtain, and Kethry had a trick up her sleeve— one the average mage wouldn't have known; one she would use *if* they could find the other bottle of potion.

More encouraging was what she had found perusing the ledgers. The seneschal had been siphoning off revenues; never much at a time, but steadily. By now it must amount to a tidy sum. What if he suspected Lord Corbie was likely to catch him at it?

Or even more—what if Lady Myria *was* found guilty and executed? The estate would go to her infant son, and who would be the child's most likely guardian but his half-uncle, the seneschal?

And children die so very easily.

Now that she had a likely suspect, Kethry decided it was time to begin investigating him.

The first place she checked was the barred door. And on the bar itself she found an odd little scratch, obvious in the paint. It looked new; her air-spirit confirmed that it was. She lifted the bar after examining it even more carefully, finding no other marks on it but those worn places where it rubbed against the brackets that held it.

She opened the door, and began examining every inch of the door and frame. And found, near the top, a tiny piece of hemp that looked as if it might have come from a piece of twine, caught in the wood of the door itself.

Further examination of the door yielded nothing, so she turned her attention to the room beyond.

It looked a great deal like the lord's room, with more books and a less ostentatious bedstead. She called Warrl in and sent him sniffing about for any trace of magic. That potion required a tiny bit of magicking to have full potency, and if there was another bottle of it anywhere about, Warrl would find it.

She turned her own attention to the desk.

Tarma's first opponent had been good, and an honest fighter. It was with a great deal of relief—especially after she'd seen an anxious-faced woman with three small children clinging to her skirt watching every move he made— that she was able to disarm him and knock him flat on his rump without seriously injuring him.

The second had been a mere boy; he had no business being out here at all. Tarma had the shrewd notion he'd been talked into it just so she'd have one more live body to wear her out. Instead of exerting herself in any way, she lazed about, letting him wear *himself* into exhaustion, before giving him a little tap on the skull with the pommel of her knife that stretched him flat on his back, seeing stars.

The third opponent was another creature altogether.

He was slim and sleek, and Tarma smelled "assassin" on him as plainly as if she'd had Warrl's clever nose. When he closed with her, his first few moves confirmed her guess. His fighting style was all feint and rush, never getting in too close. This was a real problem. If she stood her ground, she'd open herself to the poisoned dart or whatever other tricks he had secreted on his person. If she let him drive her all over the bloody practice ground he'd wear her down. Either way, she lost.

Of course, she might be able to outfox him—

So far she'd played an entirely defensive game, both with him and her first two opponents. If she took the offense when he least expected it, she might be able to catch him off his guard.

She let him begin to drive her; and saw at once that he was trying to work her around so that the sun was in her eyes. She snarled inwardly, let him think he was having his way, then turned the tables on him.

She came at him in a two-handed pattern-dance, one

that took her back to her days on the plains and her first instructor; an old man she'd never *dreamed* could have moved as fast as he did. She hadn't learned that pattern then; hadn't learned it until the old man and her clan were four years dead and she'd been Kethry's partner for almost three. She'd learned it from one of Her Sword Sworn, who'd died a hundred years before Tarma had ever been born.

It took her opponent off-balance; he back-pedaled furiously to get out of the way of the shining circles of steel, great and lesser, that were her sword and dagger. And when he stopped running, he found himself facing into the sun.

Tarma saw him make a slight movement with his left hand; when he came in with his sword in an over-and-under cut, she paid his sword-hand only scant attention. It was the other she was watching for.

Under the cover of his overt attack he made a strike for her upper arm with his gloved left. She avoided it barely in time; a circumstance that made her sweat when she thought about it later, and executed a spin-and-cut that took his hand off at the wrist at the end of the move. While he stared in shock at the spurting stump, she carried her blade back along the arc to take his head as well.

The onlookers were motionless, silent with shock. What they'd seen from her up until now had not prepared them for this swift slaughter. While they remained still, she stalked to where the gloved hand lay and picked it up with great care. Embedded in the fingertips of the gloves, retracted or released by a bit of pressure to the center of the palm, were four deadly little needles. Poisoned, no doubt.

She decided to make a grandstand move out of this. She stalked to the challenger's pavilion, where more of her would-be opponents had gathered, and cast the hand down at their feet.

"Assassin's tricks, 'noble lords'?" she spat, oozing contempt. "Is this the honor of Felwether? I'd rather fight jackals—at least they're honest in their treachery! Have you no trust in the judgment of the gods—and their champion?"

That should put a little doubt in the minds of the honest ones—and a little fear in the hearts of the ones that weren't.

Tarma stalked stiff-legged back to her own pavilion, where she threw herself down on the little cot inside it, and hoped she'd get her wind back before they got their courage up.

In the very back of one of the drawers Kethry found a very curious contrivance. It was a coil of hempen twine, two cords, really, at the end of which was tied a barbless, heavy fishhook, the kind sea-fishers used to take shark and the great sea-salmon. But the coast was weeks from here. What on earth could the seneschal have possibly wanted with such a curious souvenir?

Just then Warrl barked sharply: Kethry turned to see his tail sticking out from under the bedstead.

There's a hidden compartment under the boards here, he said eagerly in her mind. *I smell gold, and magic—and fresh blood.*

She tried to move the bed aside, but it was far too heavy, something the seneschal probably counted on. So she squeezed in beside Warrl, who pawed at the place on the board floor where he smelled strangeness.

Sneezing several times from the dust beneath the bed, she felt along the boards—carefully, carefully; it could be booby-trapped. She found the catch, and a whole section of the board floor lifted away. And inside—

Gold, yes; packed carefully into the bottom of it—but on top, a bloodstained, wadded-up tunic, and an empty bottle.

Now if she just had some notion how he could have gotten into a locked room without the proper key. There was no hint or residue of any kind of magic. And no key to the door with the bar across it.

How *could* you get into a locked room?

Go before the door is locked, Warrl said in her mind.

And suddenly she realized what the fishhook was for.

Kethry wriggled out from under the bed, leaving the hidden compartment untouched.

"Katran!" she called. A moment later Myria's companion appeared; quite nonplussed to see the sorceress covered with dust beside the seneschal's bed.

"Get the priest," Kethry told her, before she had a chance to ask any question. "I know who the murderer is—and I know how and why!"

Tarma was facing her first real opponent of the day; a lean, saturnine fellow who used twin swords like extensions of himself. He was just as fast on his feet as she was—and he was fresher. The priest had vanished just before the beginning of this bout, and Tarma was fervently hoping this meant Kethry had found something. Otherwise, this fight bid fair to be her last.

Thank the Goddess this one was an honest warrior; if she went down, it would be to an honorable opponent. Not too bad, really, if it came to it. Not even many Sword Sworn could boast to having defeated twelve opponents in a single morning.

She had a stitch in her side that she was doing her best to ignore, and her breath was coming in harsh pants. The sun was punishing-hard on someone wearing head-to-toe black; sweat was trickling down her back and sides. She danced aside, avoiding a blur of sword, only to find she was moving right into the path of his second blade. Damn!

At the last second she managed to drop and roll, and came up to find him practically on top of her again. She managed to get to one knee and trap his first blade between dagger and sword—but the second was coming in—

"Hold!"

And miracle of miracles, the blade stopped mere inches from her unprotected neck.

The priest strode onto the field, robes flapping. "The sorceress has found the true murderer of our lord and proved it to my satisfaction," he announced to the waiting crowd. "She wishes to prove it to yours."

Then he began naming off interested parties as Tarma sagged to the dirt, limp with relief, and just about ready to pass out with exhaustion.

"Sword Sworn, shall I find someone to take you to your pavilion?" the priest was bending over her in concern. Tarma managed to find one tiny bit of unexpended energy.

"Not on your life, priest. I want to see this myself!"

There were perhaps a dozen nobles in the group that the priest escorted to the lord's chamber. Foremost among them was the seneschal; the priest most attentive on him. Tarma was too tired to wonder about that; she saved what little energy she had to get her to the room and safely leaning up against the wall within.

"I trust you all will forgive me if I am a bit dramatic, but I wanted you all to see exactly how this deed was done," Kethry was standing behind the chair that was placed next to the desk; in that chair was an older woman in buff and gray. "Katran has kindly agreed to play the part of Lord Corbie; I am the murderer. The lord has just come into this chamber; in the next is his lady. She has taken a potion to relieve pain, and the accustomed sound of his footstep is not likely to awaken her."

She held up a wineglass. "Some of that same potion was mixed in with the wine that was in this glass, but it did *not* come from the batch Lady Myria was using. Here is Myria's bottle—" she placed the wineglass on the desk, and Myria brought a bottle to stand beside it. "Here—" she produced a second bottle "—is the bottle I found. The priest knows where, and can vouch for the fact that until he came, no hand but the owner's touched it."

The priest nodded. Tarma noticed that the seneschal was beginning to sweat.

"The spell I am going to cast now—as your priest can vouch, since he is no mean student of magic himself—will cause the wineglass and the bottle that contained the potion that was poured into it glow."

Kethry dusted something over the glass and the two bottles. As they watched, the residue in the glass and the fraction of potion in Kethry's bottle began to glow with an odd, greenish light.

"Is this a true casting, priest?" Tarma heard one of the nobles ask in an undertone.

He nodded. "As true as ever I've seen."

"Huh," the man replied, bemused.

"Now—Lord Corbie has just come in; he is working on the ledgers. I give him a glass of wine—" Kethry handed the glass to Katran. "—he is grateful; he thinks nothing of the courtesy, I am an old and trusted friend. He drinks it—I leave the room—presently he is asleep."

Katran allowed her head to sag down on her arms.

"I take the key from beneath his hand, and quietly lock the door to the hall. I replace the key. I know he will not stir, nor even cry out, because of the strength of the potion. I take Lady Myria's dagger, which I obtained earlier—I stab him." Kethry mimed the murder; Katran did not move, though Tarma could see she was smiling sardonically. "I take the dagger and plant it beneath Lady Myria's bed—and I know that because of the potion, she will not wake either."

Kethry went into Myria's chamber, and returned empty-handed.

"I've been careless—got some blood on my tunic; no matter, I will hide it where I plan to hide the bottle. By the way, the priest has that bloody tunic, and he knows that his hands alone removed it from its hiding place—just like the bottle. Now comes the important part—"

She took an enormous fishhook on a double length of twine out of her beltpouch.

"The priest knows where I found this—rest assured that it was *not* in Myria's possession. Now, on the top of this door, caught on a rough place in the wood, is another scrap of hemp. I am going to get it now. Then I shall cast another spell—and if that bit of hemp came from this twine, it shall return to the place it came from."

She went to the door and jerked loose a bit of fiber, taking it back to the desk. Once again she dusted something over the twine on the hook and the scrap—this time she also chanted as well. A golden glow drifted down from her hands to touch first the twine, then the scrap—

And the bit of fiber shot across to the twine like an arrow loosed from a bow.

"Now you will see the key to entering a locked room—now that I have proved that this was the mechanism by which the trick was accomplished."

She went over to the door to the seneschal's chamber. She wedged the hood under the bar on the door, and lowered the bar so that it was only held in place by the hook; the hook was kept where it was by the length of twine going over the door itself. The other length of twine Kethry threaded *under* the door. Then she closed the door.

The second piece of twine jerked; the hook came free, and the bar thudded into place. And the whole contrivance was pulled up over the door and through the upper crack by the first piece.

All eyes turned toward the seneschal—whose white face was confession enough.

"Lady Myria was certainly grateful enough."

"If we'd let her, she'd have given us all the seneschal stole," Kethry replied, waving at the distant figures on the keep wall. "I'm glad you talked her out of it."

"Greeneyes, what she gave us was plenty. As it is we'll have to send a good chunk of it back to Liha'irden to bank with the rest of the clan possessions. I'm not really comfortable walking around with this much coin in my saddlebags."

"Will she be all right, do you think?"

"Now that her brother's here I don't think she has a thing to worry about. She's gotten back all the loyalty of her lord's people and more besides. All she needed was a strong right arm to beat off unwelcome suitors, and she's got that now! Warrior's Oath—I'm glad *that* young monster wasn't one of the challengers. I'd never have lasted past the first round!"

"Tarma—"

The swordswoman raised an eyebrow at Kethry's unwontedly serious tone.

"If you—did all that because you think you owe me—"

"I 'did all that' because we're *she'enedran*," she replied, a slight smile warming her otherwise forbidding expression. "No other reason is needed."

"But—"

"No 'buts,' Greeneyes. Besides, I happen to know you'd have more than repaid anything I did. Puzzle *that* one out, oh discoverer of keys!"

DRUM DUEL
by Gerald Perkins

Gerald Perkins resubmitted this, at my request, early in my reading for V. He had submitted it the previous year for IV, and I had liked it then, but the anthology was full. No one regrets more than I the inelasticity of typeface. But since this anthology has become an annual event, I can request that something I particularly like be resubmitted the next year. And if I can remember the story a year later before I reread it, I know I've got a good one.

"I'm afraid we're in trouble, Renaya." Yin spoke softly over the mutter of drums as he let the door curtain to their guest hut drop. "Otu thinks I know about the weapon that kills at a distance with no mark."

Renaya finished tying the length of silver-white silk that served as her breastband. She tugged at it to make the knot fit better between her breasts. She arched an eyebrow and touched her ear: Listeners?

Yin shrugged and nodded: Possibly.

"Where have you been?" she demanded. "We'll be late to the feast."

"Out walking on Drum Mountain." He shed his gray-green Dragon Priest's robe. In breechclout and sandals he stepped to his side of the hut.

The mirror, a treasure from the mainland, reflected them both for an instant. The contrast between them startled and intrigued Renaya. Yin was small, lean and hard. Violent attacks of seasickness had stripped him of all excess flesh, but in no way prevented him from doing his share of work on their voyage. His shaven head gave him an ageless quality.

Where Yin was short, she was tall. His faintly yellow tan skin looked sallow when compared to her rich red mahogany. She touched the silver combs that held the mass of her silver-white hair off her neck. The hut was stifling in the tropic evening.

Her sword belt and heelless thigh boots hung on the wall. She felt naked without them. Yin turned his head to follow the direction of her look. He knew of the throwing needles in the lining of her band, under her breasts, the hard circles of disks pressing her cheeks under her breech-clout, and probably suspected the poison in the combs.

"So that's why you're late," she said. "Did you enjoy the view?"

"Peace, Renaya. I need something to do while you and N'dea's troupe try to kill one another. The view was excellent, as you would expect from the central peak of a volcanic island like this. I was surprised to find that the top is flat with nothing to block the view but a small circular wall of loose stone and a pile of bamboo under a shelter. Otu's man said that certain rituals are held there."

Renaya grinned in admiration. In a few disinterested, didactic sentences Yin had told her he had been shown the one area of the island so far forbidden to them, that he had not found the thing they had been sent to find, and that the chief priest of the island had sent his number one thug along. He even managed to sound bored.

"Let's go." Renaya held back the door curtain. "They're drumming in the guests." The "guests" were chiefs of recently conquered islands in the archipelago. Yin passed close. She murmured, "Still no luck converting Chief Hansa to peaceful ways?"

"None. He is completely under the spell of Otu. Has N'dea told you anything?"

"Not yet." They started walking toward the fires and the men waiting for them. "I don't understand Otu."

"In all your travels on the Dragon and the seas around it, have you never before met a man with a message from 'higher spirits'?" Yin asked. " 'Ware, Renaya. I'm being led while you're being held back. Something will happen tonight." Then their escort met them.

Renaya drank from the gourd of palm wine she shared with Yin. She kept her thumb over the hole so that it looked as though she drank more than she did. Yin let the colorless fluid run down his arm into a sponge under his robe. A breath of humid air made Renaya glad of her undress. The islanders wore only clouts and shell and feather jewelry, their dark, oiled skins gleaming in the torchlight. Yin was dressed for summer on the high plains at Dragon's Heart, far too warm on this hot night. Sweat beaded his head and darkened his robe, concealing the wine stain.

Conversation on the platform was subdued. Hansa tried to jolly the other chiefs, with no effect. Otu kept silent. He was young for a man who held the position of spiritual leader of the most powerful island in the confederation. She could feel his stare on the back of her neck. No one spoke to Yin and her, although they occupied seats of honor.

Yin leaned past her to scoop mashed root from the platter they shared. "I'm blessed if I know what it is that fascinates me about Drum Mountain," he said. "Whenever I think about it, it seems there's something so obvious, something I already know, that I'm a fool for not recognizing it."

Renaya shrugged.

A burst of laughter came from the place where many of the Drum Dancers sat. There were so few women on the Dragon who followed the way of the sword that to find these privileged warrior women was a refreshing experience. Renaya smiled, recalling tales told and boasts exchanged. More than boasts, actually, but a good swim and a long soak in the sun banished cramps and bruises. N'dea, the premier dancer, had taken to calling Renaya "Sun Friend" for her habit of basking long after even the dark Islanders had taken refuge from the tropical glare.

N'dea got to her feet in a space made by her friends. She beat a short, complicated rhythm in the dirt, then sat down again to the accompaniment of more laughter.

As though that were a signal, drums began on the side

of the village center opposite the cooking pits. The first dancers were men carrying clubs, spears, and shields. "At least they have the courtesy not to tell how they conquered a local island," commented Yin. They were replaced by women dancing everyday tasks. The men returned with an acrobatic dance that left plenty of opportunity for solo efforts directed at the watching women. The women's second dance was slow and sensuous, done to muffled drumbeats. One of the junior Drum Dancers asked for N'dea's permission to join the wild, frankly erotic mixed dancing. N'dea smiled and nodded.

When the young couples had vanished into the night, conversation rose to a more normal level. One of the visiting chiefs had joined the group dance. Now the others talked more freely. One of the Drum Dancers started a tale that had the others laughing above the crowd noise. She jumped to her feet to mime the climax, then collapsed in ribald laughter.

Renaya grinned as she slipped off the guest platform. Perhaps a joke would bring action where a week of diplomacy and spying had not.

N'dea greeted her with a raised hand and a flashing smile as the other dancers made room for her. "Did you hear the one about the trader's daughter?" Renaya asked. At the climax she danced the trader's double-hulled canoe, rocking at its anchor, pots and tools a-rattle. Yin, bless his sharp ears, banged an empty bowl, sending it clattering along the platform. That broke the dancers up.

Loorsh, second dancer, told an improbable tale about a mermaid and a war party.

Renaya followed with the tale of a couple caught at the critical moment on the slope of an erupting volcano. To suggest the slow swaying, rolling motion of the ground she danced as though she were on a huge elastic surface. When she completed the joke, there was dead silence.

"It is told much better on the drum," said Otu.

N'dea's face went blank, then sad. "Oh, Sun Sister, I wish you hadn't done that."

Renaya turned toward the Islander priest. Otu stood on the guest platform, arms crossed, looking out at the assemblage. "In three days let the Dragon's bodyguard meet the Drum's servant."

*   *   *

"Renaya, it is to be to the death," whispered Yin, pouring oil on his hands.

"Of course." Renaya rubbed the scented palm oil over her shoulders and down across her breasts. Her three days of confinement in the guest hut had been spent in exercise and meditation.

N'dea, Sword Friend, I didn't mean it to come to this.

At Yin's confirmation of her expectations, her surroundings took on a sudden, almost painful, clarity. This was more than honor or seeking lost knowledge for the Dragon Priests. This was her life! She snorted softly. Wasn't it always?

Yin finished her legs and began to work on her back. "These people don't realize how much of the local dialect I understand. Renaya, N'dea has over a dozen kills in personal drum combat."

"I'm unarmed."

"Not even those small throwing discs you hide so intimately?" Yin managed a shaky smile.

"They'd bounce out of my clout. I do have this." Renaya pulled out a long pin with a dull silver head that held her hair rolled at the base of her neck. She rolled it more tightly and reinserted the pin.

"Poisoned?"

"Yes, but it leaves obvious signs. You have an escape route planned?"

"Of course. I saw to our supplies and moved the boat under the pretense of fishing. I'm being very confident and very dense."

The evening was cooler on the drum mountain than it had been at the feasting. Men grunted under flaring torches as they laid the last of the horizontal bamboo barriers in place between the contestants and the watchers. Lengths of hollowed bamboo bound together into bundles somewhat taller than a man, they defined a space between the drum and the grassy center of the mountain top.

Renaya studied N'dea where she stood in a pool of light near the entrance. She turned in place as her attendants oiled and massaged her, too. Loorsh gave her a cup to drink.

Behind Renaya was the drum. Huge; its diameter was easily the length of six tall men, its surface half a man-height from the ground. Covered with the seamless skin of some ocean leviathan, it was supported above a pit by posts and removable stone sides.

The breeze shifted for a moment. Renaya smelled the pungent stink of the crowd, the tropic night, her own sweat, the sweet, oily, reek of the torches that illuminated the scene. Interesting that none of the conquered chiefs were there.

Loorsh brought Renaya the same bowl N'dea had drunk from. Yin's touch was reassuring, but she was certain nothing had been added. The contents smelled of earth and tasted like old spit. She took three mouthfuls. She felt keenly the breeze on her body, nipples hardening for a moment before a tingling numbness spread outward from her stomach. She tested her limbs. They worked with their accustomed smoothness. She pinched herself. Ah! Pain was deadened. Why, when dancers fought weaponless?

"Yin, how do you kill in a drum duel?"

"With the drum, but blessed if I know how. All you can do is follow N'dea's lead and try to better her at it. Can you?"

"Yes." It was time to go. Yin made a cup of his hands. Renaya stepped up onto the rough surface of the drum skin.

Rrum, brum! The drum made a sound like distant thunder as she walked slide-footed toward the center. There were smooth spots worn on the skin. N'dea favored them. Why? The footing was better in the rough places.

The audience surrounded the barriers on the grass except at the entrance, watching through the lengths of hollow bamboo. It was mostly armed men. Hansa and Otu occupied the center of the side toward the main village. Beyond them a rainstorm illuminated the next island with its ghostly lightning.

Yin followed N'dea's attendants through the zig-zag entrance. That head shake meant he was trying to remember something; probably what the drum reminded him of.

N'dea turned in the center of the drum, her face looming and vanishing in the torchlight. "I am sorry my spirit sister," she called, "but this is how it must be. Once you know our secret, you cannot leave."

"Know what?" Renaya wanted to shout.

N'dea began to dance, a simple two beat rhythm, moving slowly away. The drumhead tension changed with her motion. The sound was almost too low pitched to hear. Renaya felt it in her bones. Renaya followed N'dea's rhythms, then began elaborating on them.

Room toom. Room toom. Room rum, toom rum. Rumrum roomrum, rumrum toomrum. Toom rum, room rum.

N'dea wasn't expecting her to take the beat away so soon. The game was: match the other's rhythm, then take it away. N'dea took back the lead. This could be fun, tiring, but fun if N'dea weren't trying to kill. How was she going to do it? How?

N'dea was magnificent as they circled in their dance. She showed to Renaya as shadow and gleams reflected from her streaming ebony skin. She wore only a clout as black as her short hair. Her large, flat breasts rested against heavy muscle and hardly moved as she danced.

Soft weight tumbled down Renaya's neck to between her shoulders. Where was the pin? She stamped and saw it bounce halfway to the rim. Two beats later it vanished over the side. N'dea took advantage of Renaya's distraction to increase the beat.

Rum room. Rum TOOM! The watchers sometimes sank half out of sight when the dancers hit a beat together at the drum center or floated below when they lifted off the skin as the drum responded.

Odd how silent the drum was. They were wearing each other out just moving on the drum. They should be shaking the island with their noise. Where was all that effort going? And why did N'dea always retreat to certain positions on the drum?

Renaya stumbled over a complex rhythm of N'dea's and the audience flinched.

Renaya felt hot, dizzy, tired. She couldn't match N'dea's rhythm patterns any more. She tossed her head to get the hair out of her eyes. The pin was long gone and now there was nothing but bare hands and the dance. Every step of N'dea's tireless legs sent a jolt of agony through Renaya. She slipped. N'dea continued to seek the half-worn spots on the drum in the increasingly complex pattern of her dance. Could they be important? Every beat seemed to gather inside and add to the building pressure. She would fly apart if she had to take much more!

Soul of the World Egg! That was how a drum dancer killed! Find the rhythm that poured the sound too deep to hear into your opponent's body until she burst! Break the beat! Break the beat! Make another.

The Dragon take faulty memory! She knew a way, if she could think of it. But the time, oh, the aching time! Yes! When? What? That silly, twirling dance learned to entertain the Ironton miners? Down until her butt touched the skin. Up, fly, tuck and roll, and land in the center.

THOOM!

She nearly bounced N'dea right off the drum with that. Would that count as a win?

Room, room, toom. Room, toom, toom. Room, toomtoom. Room, toom TOOM. Roomroom TOOM. Roomroom TOOM. ROOM toomtoom.

That did it! She had a breathing spell at least. N'dea obviously had never danced a rhythm not based on a heartbeat before. Could she find N'dea's bursting point in three beat; find it before N'dea caught on?

N'dea stopped dead. The break in the dance shocked her, tore her out of her trance. She stood panting, sucking air in huge gasps, trying to understand this new rhythm. She couldn't.

N'dea screamed and leaped. Renaya dodged, but not before N'dea laid gouges across her face, just missing her eye. So that was legal, was it? Now they were on her ground. Renaya smiled a fighting grimace. She would, by The Dragon, do it to a beat!

One, drop, bounce. On the side, tuck, kick. Damn, N'dea saw that coming. Awkward landing, up, three. Stiff hand, elbow, heel. N'dea was good at hand-to-hand, too. One, up. Ah! Her leg! Around, two. Fall away from N'dea's kick at her knee. Around. Strike. Miss. Bounce away. They were falling into the two beat again. Where was N'dea? On the far side of the drum, dancing again. It had to end. It had to end.

Renaya leaped from her side of the drum. Her hands were busy at her waist even as she straightened from her somersault. N'dea moved a split second late. Renaya landed just short of halfway and was already on her way up when N'dea added her force to the bounce. Instead of being tossed off the drum, Renaya shot straight up, twisting in midair, coming down at N'dea's back. She whipped the silken strangler's cord that had held her clout in place around N'dea's neck. She gave a quick tug. There was a dull snap not audible a pace away.

She caught N'dea's body as it fell, concealing the broken neck from the watchers. She dropped the cord near her breechclout. As she rose to her feet, Yin passed the zig-zag barrier to the arena. The Drum Dancers were close behind.

"Can you do one more stunt to hold their attention while we get out of here?" he signaled.

Renaya's legs threatened to give way as she dragged N'dea's body to the edge, laying it down gently. She looked back to where Yin should be, took a deep breath and jumped a third of the way down the drum. She flipped forward in midair, rolled, and hit the center full force.

TH-WOOM!

She felt the air stream by her sweaty skin, tug at her hair. She kept her hands out, legs slightly parted. Ah, to make love to the night!

Yin was standing at the edge with his back turned. Renaya's feet hit just short of the drum supports. She did a forward roll over the edge.

Yin grunted as Renaya landed on his shoulders. Her long legs snaked around and locked behind his back. He stood for a moment in the stunned silence of the crowd before slowly walking toward the exit.

"You tickle, Renaya," he muttered.

Renaya almost laughed. "Shave-pate, this is hardly the time for that." Nonetheless, she gave a small wiggle of her hips, glad to be alive.

"If you make me fall, we're dead," Yin grunted. "Wave

to the crowd, be the victor." She did as he told her. The Drum Dancers met them at the exit.

"You fought well." said Loorsh, her voice catching. "Y-you knew nothing a-and yet you triumphed over the best of us. We will take you to your boat." The milling crowd made no move toward them as Yin carried Renaya off in the midst of the Drum Dancers. Otu had the wisdom to remain silent.

A hundred paces down the mountain, Yin began to pant. A loose stone in the path nearly spilled them both, but he staggered on. She gasped as he dug his fingers into hard knots of muscle. "I can't carry you any farther," he said.

"Aieee!" The cry hung on the cool night air. "She is dead! Her neck has been broken."

Loorsh signaled. The other dancers stepped away. "N'dea broke her honor when she broke the dance. We will not stop them," she nodded sideways toward the shouting crowd, "but neither will we help." The dancers vanished into the undergrowth.

Yin grabbed Renaya. "You'll have to make another three hundred or so paces. Then we'll come to a stream that feeds the river that empties into the bay where I moored the boat. The only high fall is the one where all the show-offs go to impress their lovers. Know which one I mean?"

"Yes."

"All right. Remember to dive to the left. From there it's an easy swim to the boat. Watch out for rapids on the way."

At the stream Yin stripped off his robe and sandals. The sandals went into the flow. The robe followed after he tore a strip of the dull material to wrap her white hair. They plunged into the fast, shallow water barely ahead of the mob.

The rest of the journey was nightmare. They were dragged over stones, smashed against rocks, tumbled over small falls, and half drowned in the pools beneath them. Renaya's cramped legs would hardly support her through the shallows. More than once she thought she'd broken bones when they were whirled through the rapids. Several times they hugged the banks or cowered behind stones as search parties passed by. The dive off the high falls was almost a relief.

Renaya luxuriated in the brilliant morning sun as she sat at the tiller. The small boat was a dot on an infinite surface of wrinkled blues and greens. The Islanders gave up pursuit shortly after dawn, when a freshening wind proved that even their best war canoes couldn't travel upwind as well as a properly rigged ship. Renaya stretched lazily, enjoying the sun on her skin and the salty wind that whipped her hair about. Retching sounds from the cabin made her smile sympathetically.

"How do you feel, Yin?" she called.

"Like The Dragon had its claws in my guts and was twisting. How else would I feel?" came the reply. "If I live to get back on The Dragon, I'll never leave solid land again. I swear it; body, mind, and spirit; I do swear it."

"Well, come up on deck. If the fresh air doesn't make you feel better, at least you won't stink up the cabin any more. Bring me some food while you're at it. I'm famished."

Yin's pale face appeared in the hatchway. "How you can eat, I don't know. Oh, for The Dragon's sake, you're still naked."

"The sun . . ." Renaya began.

"I know, the sun is your friend. Even the Islanders know enough to protect themselves from 'your friend' in these waters. Here." Yin tossed up a light, hooded, cotton shift. He followed it with a package of hard rations. "I'm afraid this is all we have until we reach shore," he said, taking the tiller.

"What, I ask you, am I doing here?" he exclaimed with a theatrical gesture at the rolling horizon. "I'm a priest and a scholar. I should be safely ensconced in the library at Dragon's Heart.

Changing the subject, Renaya asked, "Did you find what Abbot Lorn wanted?"

"I wish I knew exactly what it is he wants," he replied. "If I did, I'm not sure I'd tell him. I did get what we were sent after. Did you hear me while you were dancing?

That change from two beat to three was a stroke of genius."

"Yin, I didn't hear you. I just felt that rhythm pounding in me until I was ready to burst. Can that kill at a distance? If it can, why didn't it kill the watchers? Or N'dea?"

Yin's eyebrows rose in surprise. The look he gave Renaya was one of great respect. Then he bent over the side, trying to spew up food his stomach didn't have. When he had recovered he said, "I think the tubes cause the sound to cancel itself somehow. The researchers at Dragon's Head will have to look into it. I can see how the Drum Islanders get their reputation, though. If an invader comes, the tubes pointing toward that bay are removed and the dancers begin.

"Did you know that military men break step when they march over a bridge? Otherwise it might collapse. I think the effect is the same. The sound that reaches the beaches doesn't have to be very loud, but it builds in the body. An opposing force could be half dead before they met the Drum Islanders and not even know it. Of course they have warriors to do the actual fighting.

"Otu realized the drum materials could be easily transported. The Drum Islanders would show up with the women and the drum. No one would pay them any attention because warriors on both sides would be dancing their threats. Then ritual battle becomes conquest.

"I don't think they live long, the Drum Dancers. The drug helps and they know where to stand to minimize the sound they receive, but . . .

"That's why the dance had to be to the death," said Renaya. "Once we'd seen the drum in action, we were bound to figure out how it worked. We'll have to watch out for ambushes before we get to Dragon's Heart. She pulled in the sail as the wind shifted. "What will happen to the Drum Islanders, I wonder?"

"Probably nothing. Otu called the contest and lost to The Dragon. I expect the drum will be returned to a defensive weapon."

Renaya gave him a sharp look. "She had me beaten you know. If N'dea could have returned to the dance soon enough, she would have killed me. I had to go outside the dance to live."

"It hurts, doesn't it, to kill one so like yourself, a 'Sword Sister'?" Yin asked gently. "As Loorsh said, N'dea broke honor first. Besides, your honor extends far beyond one island."

After a while Renaya said, "I wish we could have saved my boots and sword."

"Oh, didn't I tell you? They're in your chest below."

Renaya reached to embrace Yin, but before she could, he succumbed to another attack of seasickness.

THE EYE OF TOYUR
by Diana L. Paxson

It's nice every year to get a manuscript which I know before reading it will be just about what I want. Diana Paxson has been writing about Shanna since the beginning of these anthologies, and I always know her stories will be excellent.

I really don't need to say anything more to introduce the story, but those of you who like Diana's work might like to know that she has produced three more novels: two in her Westria series; SILVERHAIR THE WANDERER and THE EARTHSTONE, and a sort of sequel (it has some of the same characters) to BRISINGAMEN, called THE PARADISE TREE. She has also written a major novel about Tristram, which I haven't read yet. Knowing Diana, I am sure it will be as good as all her other books.

T he falcon hung in mid-heaven, a black cross against the blaze of the setting sun. Shanna took a deep breath of clean air, releasing the strain of another day of travel as she let it out again. From the hollow where the caravan was settling down for the night she heard shouting, but she did not look down.

The flicker of a wingtip set Chai in a sideways slide across the sky; she rocked a little, holding her new position, waiting once more for some small life on the moor below to misjudge the peacefulness of the evening and betray its position. The noise from the caravan grew louder.

"A witch! There's a witch in the caravan! The spirits have told me—" A shrill voice pierced the babble.

The falcon's wings folded, and like a bolt from heaven she fell. Shanna heard a single, stifled squeal as she struck, and a puff of fur floated on the still air. Then she turned to look down at the caravan. Men were running toward the center of the circle of parked wagons. In its midst a scrawny shape swayed and mumbled, overshadowed by the rotund splendor of the archpriest of Toyur.

"Witch" was a title with many meanings in the Empire of Bindir, but in the mouths of war-priests it meant magic of the blackest kind—or whatever they chose to define as sorcery.

Chai's sharp beak tore at flesh and fur. Leaving the falcon to her meal, Shanna lengthened her stride down the hill.

"I knew those two would be trouble—from the very first mile I knew it—didn't I tell you so?"

Shanna grinned as the caravan mistress came out of her tent, broad, graying, with a high-colored face lined and weathered by years on the road. Bercy had been foretelling disaster from the moment they moved out of Otey. It was no wonder if one of her predictions had finally been fulfilled. Especially this one—Shanna had been keeping a wary eye on the archpriest and his pet witchfinder too.

"The gods have spoken—" the archpriest's fruity tones rolled over the murmur of the crowd. "We must seek out the guilty one!"

Bercy set her fists on her hips, glaring. They were big fists, quite capable of laying out a drunken drover with one blow, but not much use against the powers of darkness. Shanna realized that her own hand had dropped to the hawk's-head pommel of her sword and made herself let go. A blade was no more use than fists here.

"I thought you promised me an easy duty!" she grinned, and after a moment Bercy managed a wry answering smile.

Everyone who survived the plague at Otey had been

eager to get out of the city once the gates were opened again. Bercy would probably have promised anything to replace the guards she had lost, and Shanna was tired of traveling alone. Besides, she had taken an immediate liking to this big woman who with the help of her three sons continued to run the hauling business she and her husband had begun.

But the witchfinder was right about one thing—the trip had been haunted by misfortune. One of the new drovers was a trouble-maker, and there was a Bindiran merchant who seemed to feel that his wealth gave him the right to constant complaint.

"It's true that we've had no trouble from outside the caravan, but the journey itself—"

The caravan mistress was not listening. The ring of people wavered as a tousled head of wheat-colored hair thrust through. It belonged to Awrdin, Bercy's youngest son.

"That boy! He'll ruin us—all muscle and no brain—by Hiera's headpiece! Why do these things always happen to me?" Bercy shifted into motion again as Awrdin reached the center of the crowd, and Shanna followed her.

"Now see here!" the boy's voice cracked, and someone snickered. "This talk of witches is . . . is ridiculous! If you believe this creature, you're as crazy as she is! You can't go upsetting the caravan this way—"

"Silence, stripling, if you do not wish the Spear of Toyur to point at you!"

Awrdin gaped as the archpriest turned on him, saw his mother approaching, and blushed.

"Awrdin, be off with you, don't you have work to do?" Bercy stepped between the boy and the priest, and he scurried off gratefully. "What's all this, now?" She surveyed the ring of avid faces.

Shanna stayed a half step behind her, poised and ready, though most of those in the forefront were beginning to look as if they wondered what they were doing there too. The archpriest stood in majestic silence, fingering the amulet cases sewn to the baldric he wore. His medium twitched at his feet, her possession having apparently progressed past speech.

"She said there's a sorcerer, mistress—and it might be

true!" offered one of the drovers finally. " 'Tis natural for one ox-yoke to break during a journey, but three of them, before we are two weeks on our way?"

"If someone is tampering with the gear we will deal with him," answered Bercy, frowning. "What is all this talk of witches?"

"Ox-yokes are nothing—" the archpriest gestured contemptuously. "But if Evil walks among us it must be rooted out before it grows!"

What, exactly, are you asking to do?" Bercy sounded uneasy.

"Asking?" the archpriest shook his head as if he pitied her. His gaze slid past, for a moment fixed distastefully on Shanna, then moved on. "Woman, I am invoking the Law of Toyur; I rule here now. We will not leave this place until the spell-casters have been found!"

"But why should the archpriest want to stop for a witch hunt? I thought he was in a hurry to get to some convocation in Bindir—" Shanna set down her mug of beer.

"Well he's going to be late anyway because of the plague," said Bercy. "He must have been desperate, to join a caravan with a woman in charge. I've seen it rankling him!"

Shanna remembered how the archpriest had looked at *her*. A woman warrior was an anomaly even in the north. Shanna suspected that the prejudice against her would get worse the closer she got to Bindir. She already had the curse of the Dark Mother to bear—was she going to run afoul of the god as well? She found her thoughts echoing Bercy's. *Why do these things always happen to me?*

"Maybe he figures to make points if he has a few trophies to show for the delay!" Bercy's florid face grew redder.

"Trophies?"

"Magic bones—you'll see— And there isn't a damn thing I can do!" Bercy stomped across the tent, stopped as her nose brushed the faded canvas, and whirled.

"Because of the war?" asked Shanna.

"These days the spear-temple near *owns* Bindir. The

Dorian Alliance can have Dard and welcome. Hiera's holy elbow, that's not what hurts trade! It's the Brotherhoods, pushing the Hundred to slap on more restrictions in the name of the emergency. They'll stop soon as it begins to hurt *them*, but by then us little folk'll be run under—you'll see!" She stopped for breath at last.

"The Emperor's not controlling them?" Shanna stretched out her arm and Chai sidled down it to a perch on a packsaddle. "Shame to him, then, eh Chai? He breaks his bond!" The bird stretched her neck and gave a scornful "ker—"

"Shanna, sometimes I could swear that bird talks back to you!" said Bercy, momentarily distracted. "It's a wonder how you let her run about unhooded and all!"

"She's very tame—" Shanna said quickly.

That had been a slip. It would be bad enough if anyone realized Shanna was the one who had been overshadowed by the battle goddess in Otey. She could imagine what the witch hunters would say if they knew that Chai was not really a bird. . . .

Toyur was a god of Justice as well as of War. She wished she could say the same of all His servitors.

It was time to change the subject. She looked up at Bercy.

"About tonight, where do you want our guards to be?"

The torches flickered and failed and flared again; light chasing shadow crazily across the ring. Drums set the heart racing; the earth shuddered to the thud of booted feet as the people stamped out a circle. Chai fidgeted on Shanna's shoulder and she reached up to stroke the smooth feathers.

"I don't like it either," she said softly, glad of the duty that kept her armed and on guard outside the ring, but there's nothing we can do."

Bercy had been right about the power of the Temple. Once the laws against sorcery had been invoked, religious law took precedence. None of the merchants in the caravan would protest; she could not even count on Bercy's own men. They could be depended on to fight off bandits or break up fights in the encampment. But no one dared oppose the God of War.

Chai chikked angrily, and Shanna turned and saw the falcon's golden eye burning in the torchlight.

How much, she wondered, did Chai understand? In their own valley, Chai's people could take avian or human shape at will, but when she had agreed to take the falcon with her to Bindir, Shanna had not thought to ask what kind of mental processes were possible in feathered form.

> *"Behold, the ring of fire flames high.*
> *The justice of the God draws nigh!*
> *Within this circle all be bound*
> *Until the guilty one is found!"*

Half a hundred voices joined in the chanting, and if some of them were less than full-throated, their weakness was hidden by the compulsive beat of the drums. The archpriest moved majestically into the center of the circle, encased in a blood red cope emblazoned with the chain and spear of Toyur. The ornaments on his baldric tinkled as he lifted his baton. The drumming pattered to silence. A little raggedly, the chant ended as well.

"The gods have spoken!" The archpriest boomed. "Evil walks among us. It must be cauterized before we reach Bindir!"

He gestured, and his servant led out the witchfinder, dressed in a fantastical garment of animal skins sewn with clattering bits of iron and staggering as if half tranced already. She hung back, as if frightened by the people and the fire, and the priest bent over her, whispering. For a moment his bulky form hid her entirely from view.

Shanna's lips thinned. She had thought the medium might have made her accusations simply to get attention, but now she wondered. Clearly the archpriest was in control of what was happening here.

> *"Beat the drum and sing the spell—*
> *Seek the sorcerers, seek well!"*

The people took up the new chant. The drums pulsed insistently, and the witchfinder's disjointed movements eased as the rhythm mastered her. Louder the people sang; ever more quickly the medium danced, widdershins whirling, spinning around the ring.

> *"By the body and the bone*
> *Thus the Evil one is known!"*

Shanna felt the earth vibrate as men stamped out the rhythm. Torchlight pulsed and she blinked, fighting its fascination. Even outside the circle it compelled her—dark wings fluttered in her awareness and she fought the pull of the Marigan's power.

"Not again!" she whispered. "Don't let Her take me—" Fists clenched until Shanna's nails bit into her palms; then a sharper pain brought her to her senses again. She blinked, felt the wet warmth of blood on her arm, and realized that Chai had pecked her.

She drew a deep, shuddering breath. Had she frightened the bird, or had Chai understood and used the pain to distract her?

Then the witchfinder screamed. Drums thudded suddenly. Ignoring the ache in her arm, Shanna pushed in beside the caravan mistress to see.

"Here—here! The demon smiles behind his eyes!" The witchfinder clutched suddenly at one of the drovers. In an instant the archpriest's guards had him pinioned. His fellows had melted away to either side as if they feared contamination. The man was a shirker, and quarrelsome; it was not surprising he had no defenders. A low, ugly, murmur rumbled around the ring.

Shanna had heard that sound before, when men wanted to burn the plague hospice in Otey. And the battle goddess had come to defend it—but innocent as well as guilty would die if Shanna let the Marigan possess her again.

"Ai—the magic bone—see!" The medium fell back into the archpriest's arms, brandishing something that gleamed pale in the torchlight.

Shanna shook her head, denying the red pulse of violence without and within. The drumming and chanting resumed. The witchfinder jangled and flapped in wavering circles. Almost immediately she struck again, a merchant this time—but having given her first accusation its blessing the crowd was caught up in the madness. And yet again she whirled around the circle, and this time she plucked the magic bone from the breast of Bercy's boy Awrdin.

Shanna felt her friend begin to move and clapped a hand over her mouth as her oldest son grabbed her from the other side.

"Bercy, be still!" she hissed, "or they'll seize you too! We'll save him, I promise you—"

Shanna felt the fight go out of the older woman. In the same moment the witchfinder swayed and fell. The archpriest's men carried her away, after the prisoners. Shanna released her grip on Bercy, for there could be no more accusations now.

"Toyur has pointed out the guilty ones—" intoned the archpriest. "Tomorrow, His Justice will be done . . ."

It was midnight, and the caravan mistress had fallen into a drugged sleep at last. Shanna paced the perimeters of the encampment, seeking solace in the cool night air. The tents of the merchants and the drovers rolled in their blankets beside dying fires were dim shapes in the darkness, and the rolling heathland beyond an indistinct mass of shadow that sloped upward toward the distant hills.

"Not the Justice of God, but the greed of men!" Bercy had mumbled as oblivion took her. And that was certainly true. The arrest of the drover had prepared the way for that of the merchant, which had probably been the archpriest's real goal. The temple inherited the goods of those claimed by the god. And Awrdin? That accusation, she supposed, had been pure malice.

"The poor lad! And I've promised his mother he won't die—ah Chai, was I wrong to stay silent?" The falcon shifted uneasily on her shoulder and Shanna sighed.

She had seen no way to stop what was happening, but her own inner judge accused her of cowardice. Even if Chai understood, in bird-form there was nothing she could do to help. But had there been others who doubted? Would they have followed Shanna's lead if she had dared to declare that this was wrong?

In any case, the moment for protest had passed.

Her wanderings had brought her around by the privy trench. As she turned, she saw someone coming back up the path. Shadowed by a cloak, the features were unreadable, but there was something in that stumbling gait—

Shanna waited, and as the figure passed her, reached out suddenly.

"Don't hurt me!" It was only a thread of sound. Shanna tightened her grip, and drew the witchfinder away with her, off the path.

"Be still. I want to talk to you."

There was a fallen log in the thicket behind them. Shanna pushed the woman down.

"Yes, mistress—" Her hood had fallen back, and Shanna saw pinched features white in the waning moonlight.

"How long have you been in the service of Toyur?" Shanna asked harshly.

The woman shrugged. "Long. My parents cast me out when the spirits began to visit me. I would have died in the streets of Straith if the priests had not taken me in."

"And the god speaks through you?"

"The priest says so, and he should know!" the witchfinder's laughter was just a little mad. "I know only the weight when the god approaches, and how my body aches after. Please do not hurt me—" Her mood shifted suddenly, and she gazed up at Shanna with frightened eyes.

"Does *he* hurt you?" Shanna asked softly. The woman rocked back and forth on the log, turning her face away. Impossible to tell how old the creature was—her body was twisted with age or illness, but her eyes were still a child's.

"When I grew older, the spirits stopped coming; now the priest makes me breathe sacred smoke, and the god comes, but he is heavy, too heavy for me to bear. . . ." She bent until her forehead rested on her knees, and stayed there, shuddering. Shanna repressed a stab of pity. She too, had known what it was to be ridden by a god.

"What is the magic bone?"

The woman straightened, giggling suddenly. "If I had one I would show you! The spirits still talk to me sometimes, you know. They are telling me about you now, warrior woman—they say you smell of magic!"

"If I had any magic, do you think I would let you burn those innocents you accused?" Shanna exclaimed.

The witchfinder's eyes filled with tears. "It is the priests who burn them. When the sacred smoke takes me, I do not know what I say. You are like me—there is a shadow between you and the power that pulses in your soul."

Shanna sat back, staring. It was a lie—a lie! She had no magic but her skill with a sword. If she believed that there was something in her that invited the attention of the goddesses who had haunted her, her world would be unmade.

"If you do not believe it," a still voice spoke within, *"Bercy's son may die."*

The first time Shanna had put herself into jeopardy for someone's child she had earned the curse of Saibel. What price would she pay to save this one? *I cannot do it, and even if I were willing, I do not know the way!*

"Let me go," whimpered the witchfinder.

There was no strength left in Shanna's hands or in her will; her fingers released their grasp and the woman scurried away. But the warrior remained where she was. Chai spread her wings and slid across the air to perch on a dead branch; Shanna could feel the question in her golden eyes.

"Search-sister," whispered Shanna. "What am I to do?"

It seemed to her then that words formed in her awareness. But from where did they come?

"Hawk eyes see all . . ."

The drumming was different in the morning—not the compulsive pattering that had whipped men to frenzy the night before, but an ominous slow heartbeat that paralyzed the will. High clouds covered the sky, filtering a pale, pitiless illumination that showed only too clearly the marks of fatigue and fear.

Shanna saw shadows like bruises around Bercy's eyes and knew her own face was just as haggard. *We all look as if we were on our way to execution . . .* she thought bitterly. Chai's talons dug into her shoulder, and she welcomed the pain. *And if the innocent perish, something in each one of us who just stood by and watched it happen will die as well.*

She realized that she had made a decision at some moment during the darkness. The executions must be stopped, even if she had to give up her will to the mindless fury of the Marigan again.

The stakes were prepared already. The dismal procession wound towards them, guards and victims, weighted with chains. The witchfinder, white and shivering, crouched at the archpriest's feet. The low chant vibrated in Shanna's bones.

"Toyur, Toyur is just and sure . . ."

Bercy's grizzled head moved back and forth like a wounded animal's. Seeing the older woman's pain, Shanna thought then that perhaps her own barrenness was a blessing. Children made you too vulnerable. In one night the caravan mistress had become old.

They were chaining the prisoners to the stakes now, piling wood around them. Shanna took a deep breath and let her awareness sink inward, seeking the red tide of power. But this cold-blooded killing was the antithesis of the bloodlust that had called up the Lady of Ravens. Panicking at the emptiness, Shanna reached deeper than she had ever dared to do before.

"Toyur, Toyur, the god is near . . ."

Her spirit trembled in the balance, and slowly she became aware of an eternal watchful patience whose Presence became ever stronger as she became the focus of its passionless attention.

It seemed to her then that she stood in a lofty hall before a throne. Others waited along the wall, but they were silent. It was the One on the throne who compelled attention. Shanna peered through the shadows, seeking to see, but the shape shifted. For a moment she thought it was a wolf that sat there, but the wolf was bound. Then she realized that the form was that of a warrior with only one hand. She came closer. Was he wearing a helm? No, the head of a hawk rose above those human shoulders, that swiveled to fix her with one amber eye.

"Lord, see how Thy priest profanes Thy Justice!" Shanna's spirit cried.

The vision had flashed into being in a moment. With doubled sight she saw the radiance of the hawk-headed god and the pallid flicker of the torch as the archpriest, in full finery, started toward the first of his victims.

"Toyur, Toyur, the god is here!" chanted the guards.

"Let the will of Toyur be done!" cried the archpriest, lifting his brand. And at the same moment, a voice spoke in Shanna's soul—*"The Eye of Toyur sees all!"*

The Eye! The hawk's bright eye! Shanna took a step forward, thrusting out her arm so that Chai could run down it, swinging, flinging the falcon into the air. Up, and up like a thrown spear she flew, and even the archpriest looked up to see her climb the sky. Her cry seared hearing, and then, too swift for human vision, she struck.

A scream of rage; a thunder of flapping wings. The torch flew from the archpriest's hand as he fell backward, flailing. Then the falcon released him, something clutched in talons that wrenched it open as she lifted and scattered its contents across the grass.

Shanna sprang, clutched, held her prize high.

"What is it?" "What happened?" came the babble. Somebody laughed as the archpriest groaned and tried to sit up again. His men started forward with drawn swords, but now the other guards from the caravan moved out to face them. The medium had collapsed into a tattered heap of garments, weeping softly.

"Behold the Justice of Toyur!" cried Shanna, showing them what she held—a piece of bone carved with sigils.

"A magic bone!" said one of the men. "I don't understand—"

"They were in one of the cases on the archpriest's baldric," answered Shanna. "He set his witchfinder on the accused, and gave the bones to her to produce by sleight of hand!"

"She's the witch!" gasped the archpriest, pointing at Shanna. "She spelled the bird to attack me—"

"Toyur Himself inspired the bird, this is the proof of it! Charlatan, the god disowns you!" Shanna replied.

"Burn him!" cried someone. "Burn the witchfinder and her master!" Dull acceptance had turned to anger, as furious against the archpriest as it had been against those he accused. Men surged toward him, but his guards surrounded him; they turned back on the witchfinder but Shanna was standing there.

"Leave her alone—he drugged her—she was only a tool!" She gestured with drawn sword. "It's the man you want—look, he's getting away!"

The archpriest had made good use of their distraction. He was already mounted, and two of his men were swinging into the saddle. Baying, the crowd streamed after them.

And then it was quiet. The light grew ever brighter as sunlight burned the clouds away. Someone had released the archpriest's victims, and Bercy was shaking and hugging her youngest son while his brothers looked on and grinned. The witchfinder was still huddled in the grass. She looked ancient now, but Shanna found her reserves of pity dangerously low.

"Get up, woman" said Shanna, "and be gone. If the archpriest escapes the drovers, I doubt I can save you again. There is enough silver in this pouch to keep you for a time. Let us call it a fee for your reading of me—" She tossed her the bag.

Shanna felt the breath of displaced air and turned to offer her arm as Chai swept down.

"So, my friend, you did understand me," she said softly as the falcon sidled up to her usual perch on Shanna's shoulder. "And I begin to think that I may learn to understand you." For a moment she stood very still, opening her inner ear, letting her mind float free.

"*Finally* . . ." The sleek head swiveled to fix her with a luminous amber gaze.

Shanna grinned. The witchfinder had disappeared, and Bercy was on her way to her tent with her family. The rest of the men were dark dots on the moor. Still smiling, Shanna walked across the field and stamped out the torch that was still smoldering in the dew-damp grass.

PEET'S BRIDE
by Dana Kramer-Rolls

Dana Kramer-Rolls is another writer whose stories I can
depend on to be quite professional. The first one she
sent in this year was too long for me. (In general, although this anthology is theoretically open to stories of
up to 10,000 words, in practice I seldom buy much over
4,500 words, and everyone seems to think I should make
an exception for *their* story.) It's good to be able to say to
a pro that the story's fine but too long for me and know I
won't get any flack, just a shorter story.

That's the difference between a pro and an amateur,
or, as someone once said, "The amateurs were in one
corner talking about ART and the pros were somewhere
else talking about contracts."

Dana is one of the professionals from the start; she
began her career writing games and "participatory
adventures"—which I don't read or participate in. But
she also takes the time now and then to write an artful
little story like this one, which shows (if it needed showing) that the work of a professional need not be a
disqualifier for the artistic.

"Can't we take a break, yet?" Gorak moaned,
the cart tethered to his huge shaggy body groan-
ing along on the rough road.

"Stop complaining, Gorak," Meera snapped wearily,

wiping the gritty sweat from her face on the back of her hand. She gave another hopeless tug at the leather shirt, but it still stuck to her back, and it still chafed her neck.

"At least you could get off and walk," the beast whined.

The pitiful, if endless, carping from so hearty a beast struck her as comical, and she grinned, shrugged and hopped off the still moving cart. Besides, she was really quite fond of her companion, although he was sometimes so bright for a draft animal it was uncanny.

She casually reached out to snap off a branch of the fragrant flowing shrub at the road's edge.

"Ouch!" She pulled her hand from the plant, as if it were suddenly made of fire.

Then she spun around and shouted at Gorak, "Damn it all, stop that. Your sense of humor will send you to the glue works . . ."

"Stop what?" the animal protested, turning its shaggy head at her and digging in his heels, the cart suddenly tipping dangerously.

"You mean you didn't say anything?"

"No, I didn't," Gorak pouted, indignantly.

"Ouch! Help, help, somebody," The voice called out from somewhere behind the bush.

Meera cocked her head, cautiously. "You wait here with the cart. I'll go look." She pulled her staff from the cart, gave it a self-reassuring shake, and plunged into the brush.

"Whooooaaaaaa!" Her feet almost immediately flew out from under her, and she bounced and slid down the steep, sandy slope. She stabbed at the ground and grabbed for whatever passed for vegetation, but that only made her tumble painfully to the bottom. Finally she stopped and, blinking the silt out of her eyes, she looked up in time to see Gorak and the cart at the edge of the slide.

"No, Gorak, don't . . ."

She scrambled out of the way of the avalanche of beast and cart as it made the inevitable trip to the bottom.

"Great!" she harumphed, hauling her bruised body upright, and giving Gorak a very unsympathetic medical inspection. "Look at that. Just look at that," she shouted, waving her arm over the smashed, overturned cart. "That is everything we own." She picked up and dropped one smashed bottle of potion after another. "How are we going to make a living? Crone's Hell, how are we going to get out of here?"

"Oh, please help me." She turned in the direction of the voice. She had forgotten about him, but now she turned her wrath toward the skinny young man who was securely tied to a tree not ten feet from where she stood.

"Help you? You . . . you . . . What are you doing tied to a tree?" she asked, her curiosity outweighing her anger.

"Well, you see, in the days of King Condol, of old," he began.

"Keep it short," she said, in no uncertain terms.

"All right. But, well, it's embarrassing. I'm a sacrifice to a dragon."

"You're a WHAT?" Meera and Gorak chimed in unison.

"Well," the young man said, blushing, "they needed a virgin, and girl virgins were hard to find."

"Watch it," Meera snapped hotly.

"Well, it's a small village, and well, oh, never mind," he cried miserably. "Just leave me here. Go on. But," he added, looking up hopefully, "could you at least get this dratted branch out of my back before you go? Being dragon lunch is bad enough, but . . ."

"Oh, shut up," she growled. "You're as bad as Gorak."

"I'm not a virgin," the oxenlike animal protested.

She ignored him and went on, "Besides, boy, how do you expect us to get out of here? Fly? In case you don't know, flying spells don't grow on trees." She sat down hard on the ground, turning her back on both the boy and Gorak.

"Don't mind her," the animal said, cheerfully. "She gets like this. Meera's really a pussy-cat, you know. Name's Gorak. What's yours?"

"Peet. Glad to meet you," the tied boy said politely. "Oh, here we go again. . . ."

His words still hung in the air as the huge scaly beast swooped over the party, huge wings beating hot smoke smelling of sulfur.

Meera looked up, her eyes bulging and her mean funk forgotten. "Is that HIM?"

"Her," Gorak corrected casually.

"All right, her, then. How can you tell?" Meera muttered.

"It's easy. Now if you read all those books you make me drag around . . ."

"Don't start that again, Gorak. Please. How do we get OUT of here?" she said desperately.

"Oh, we have a little while. I think he, er, she, is just sizing me up. She's been doing that all morning. We've got about half an hour. Of course, if she's not fussy about virgins—by the way, are you a virgin. . . ?"

Meera swooped up her staff and lunged at the boy.

"Sorry, sorry, just asking," he spluttered.

"Well, don't" she snarled.

"She's not," Gorak whispered, ignoring the frosty look from Meera.

"At least *she* wants me," the boy said wistfully, staring after the rapidly disappearing speck in the blue sky. "You don't know how awful it is being the runt of the litter in a small village."

"Wanna bet?" Meera hissed, more to herself than her party.

"Why don't you get out the spell book and see if we can do something to get out of here before *she* comes back?" Gorak said with broad, if somewhat sarcastic, patience.

"If you untie me, I'll help," the boy said hopefully.

"If I untie you, you'll bolt for the hills, leaving me and Gorak as the first and second course. You'll stay put," she added, diving into the wreckage of her traveling spell shop.

"If you untie *me*," Gorak said, coldly, "I could help move some of that trash around so you *could* find something useful."

She cut the animal's harness, and the two now rummaged in the rubble. "Here, here, push, Gorak," she gestured excitedly.

She soon extracted a tattered volume whose title, *Ancient Spells for All Occasions,* glowed in a sort of tarnished gold.

"Pater Omnes must have something useful," she muttered, rapidly turning pages.

"Father Everything indeed!" Gorak muttered. "You humans are so gullible. I would suggest you dig out Gregorious the Hermit's . . ."

"Oh, hush. What is this? Look, Gorak. This part here." She held the book up for the animal to see. "What do you make of it?"

"What? WHAT?" Peet shouted, with desperate impatience.

"Quiet!" the other two shouted in unison.

"Well, Meera, it looks to me like a changing spell. But it takes a lot of stuff . . . I don't know if we even had half of this stuff before we crashed."

"WE crashed? WE crashed?" she spluttered.

"We don't have all day," Peet implored.

Meera and Gorak looked back at the book, and then at each other, and both broke out into gales and peals of laughter. "Are we thinking the same thing?" she asked, the tears squeezing from her eyes as she fought to control the mirth.

"I think so," the great oxen said, shaking back and forth like a huge brown fur haystack.

"All right, Peet, this is it. This spell is a changing spell, which means it turns things into other things, like princes into frogs. But it usually needs a virgin. Or at least that's easier to work, for reasons which don't concern you."

"That's obvious," Peet offered. "Virgins are more, well, more impressionable.

Meera raised an eyebrow in admiration. "Good. It's a pity we didn't meet under other circumstances. You might have made a sorcerer. Have you ever seen or heard of baby dragons in these parts?"

"Can't say as I have," the boy answered.

"Neither have I, not for ages. I'll bet old Fire Mouth up there hasn't picked you off because she's in love, or lust, or something like that. It must be lonely for her," the sorceress added, with some feeling.

"You want to change *me* into a DRAGON?" Peet shrieked.

"Well it's either that or . . ." Gorak said, finishing by grinding his teeth suggestively.

"What's so wrong with being a dragon?" Meera asked. "What do you have back there?" she said, shaking her head in what she supposed was the direction of the village. "Think of it. You could be the father of a whole race of new dragons."

"I could?" Peet breathed, his jaw dropping as the enormity of the offer hit him.

"We'd better get started," Gorak said, using a voice usually reserved for small, stupid children.

Meera shook out her long, raven black hair and propped the book up on a stack of broken cart parts.

"If you untie me, I could help. Please?" Peet pleaded, and this time she cut him loose.

"All right, Gorak, see if you can bring me some wartbush leaves. I'm sure I can smell some over there," she ordered and the beast lumbered off. "Try not to eat them all," she shouted after him.

"Peet, somewhere in that trash heap there is a vial with pink stuff. If it's still intact! It should be in a small pouch of white threep fur." She kept her two impressed assistants busy collecting enough ingredients to bake a royal wedding cake, which in some sense was what she had in mind. She set up her tripod and cauldron, which sported a new dent, poured in the last of her water from a leather bag, and chanted up a small, but adequate fire. Finally she was satisfied, more or less (some of the plants were substitutions, and that made her nervous, but there was no helping it).

"Here she comes again," the prospective bridegroom cried out, excitedly standing on tiptoe and pointing to the approaching spiral of smoke headed their way.

Meera pulled on a short ceremonial cloak of purple wool lined in threep fur, a little warm for the season, but it was what came to hand. She raised her staff and started to chant, but stopped short, muttering, "Damn," as she burrowed once more into the heap of cart debris, throwing objects dangerously all around her.

"Careful!" shouted Gorak.

"Hurry!" shouted Peet.

"There!" shouted Meera, emerging triumphantly with a silver filigree helmet, holding a huge golden sun's eye in place over the forehead. It was her favorite possession. She settled it on her brow, straightened up and began again.

"Powers of earth, of face and form," she intoned, dropping a handful of leaves in the water.

"Powers of fire, of spirit and love," she went on, pouring out three drops of the precious pink stuff.

She went on with the spell, Gorak rocking back and forth with impatience as the shadow of the giant creature preceded it into the clearing. Peet was standing in the center, shaking with fear and anticipation.

"Powers of air," Meera went on, rushing the spell as fast as she dared. "Breath of life," she went on, hoping she had gotten it right, and crumbling some petals of the same fragrant flowering shrub that had gotten them into all this.

"Power of water," she finished, mumbling the real words of power, reading them carefully from the spell book. Then she breathed into the mixture three times, and unceremoniously dumped it on the unsuspecting Peet.

Nothing happened.

The dragon's head had already appeared over the edge of the forested pit. They could hear the flap of her wings as they tore the air and the hoarse caw of her call.

"*Mentu kaxon greebe nunt*, damn it," Meera shouted again, pounding the end of her staff on the ground.

"She's beautiful," Peet said, his face glowing with adoration. Slowly a shimmer began to form around the boy. Meera held her breath. Gorak held his breath. The scrawny boy was definitely growing, his clothes shredding effortlessly around him. And he was sprouting little wings. The great female circled above, more than curious.

Now Peet was covered with shining gold and green scales in beautiful contrast to his mate's golden red, shot with hints of purple. He turned his now elongated head to Meera, and said, "Thank you so much, Meera. Good-bye, Gorak. I can never thank you both enough . . . caw, caw . . ." Then it was over, the newly formed dragon rising shakily on his new wings, guided tenderly by his lady as they soared off for their mating dance in the far mountains.

Gorak snorted sentimentally. Meera wiped away a tear.

"I don't suppose you would care to make me human?" Gorak asked, almost knocking her to the ground with an affectionate nudge.

"I'll think about it," she answered, not too gruffly, as she fondly scratched the beast's furry head. "But in the meanwhile, let's see if we can clean up this mess, and find a road out of here," she snapped in her old familiar fashion. "After all, flying spells don't grow on trees! And neither do mugs of ale," she added, throwing back her shoulders. Yes, she was very pleased with the day's work.

WARRIOR'S WAY
by A. D. Overstreet

I have been asked again and again why I buy the occasional warrior story, but invariably reject the very similar Samurai story. That's easy; fantasy is escape literature, and I reject any story which is too tightly pinned down to any particular space or time.

I am not myself a devotee of the martial arts; I suppose, if I had to be anything, I would be sorceress rather than swordswoman. Fortunately, I don't have to choose. And the various adventure tales of swordswomen keep coming in year after year and people keep buying the books, so I suppose a lot of people are interested in the art of the warrior. But women writers, especially, seem to feel that a warrior's story is incomplete unless it triumphs over sorcery as well. Don't ask me why; I haven't the least idea. I only know that these stories seem to work better than the others.

Maybe it's because in a daydream—which is what all stories are, when you come right down to it: shared daydreams—there is no extra charge for anything; so the writer can have the best of both worlds. I have been writing for about forty years, and I never found that

"He who lives more lives than one
More deaths than one must die . . ."

And the writer is the only person I know of who can live more lives than one.

S ure the blind man would recognize the sound,
Kwannon let five gold coins fall one by one on the
small, wood table. She let her pleasant look carry
in her voice. "Sir, tell me what you know of the Eye of
Dhyana."

The grizzled sage reached for the coins. The outer
corners of his hollow eye sockets crinkled; and a faint
grin flickered over his lips. "In the land of the Githrodi,
high in the Mountains of the Sun, in the Valley of the
River of Wind, in an ancient temple rests the sacred Eye
of Dhyana."

"That's where it *was*, Master Keane." The ragged teeth
of impatience gnawed at her, but the Githrodi warrior
did not bother to tell the Sage of Redstone that what he
called temple was more sanctuary than place of worship.
"It was taken, and I've tracked it this far."

Gravely the old-timer nodded. "No doubt by the trail
of dead men. I've heard of the curse."

The warrior laughed, a sound as lean and hard as her
own well-trained muscles. "A trail obvious to one who
looks for meaning in any death." Outside the tiny, neat
cottage, Kwannon's mare stamped. Her attention split
briefly, the woman kept her gaze on the old sage. "The
curse, however, is only that of humankind's own greed
for a two-inch, perfect emerald."

Keane laughed also, a delicate tone befitting his frail
form. "But you are no thief."

"If it takes thievery to recover the Eye, then, yes, I
am." Five more coins rang on the wood planks.

The sage tilted his head back, as if listening to some far
voice. "The Eye sees cold hands about it, yet the hands
are now where none can see."

"You speak in riddles. You mean those who took it
are dead. This I know."

"As well as those who brought it here. I speak also of
where it is now." Rising stiffly, Keane walked deliberately to a cupboard across the room. Opening one door,
he eased his hand onto a leaded crystal decanter filled
with a dark liquid. He turned to hold it out to the
warrior. "Though it be early in the day, a small libation?"

Warriors drink no such poisons, but she guessed refusing the sage's offer of hospitality might forestall his frustratingly slow way of giving information. "I'll accept water, thanks." With the ingrained grace of the gentlewoman, Kwannon accepted the offered chair and sat facing the Sage of Redstone. She could smell the sour tang of the blood red wine.

Finally, Keane set down his mug, his wine only half finished. "All who bore the Eye were doomed from the start. He who sent for it made sure of that. Their blood makes the Red River even redder."

Though his pause seemed endless to Kwannon, she stayed calm and in combat stance even while seated. Sages had their own timing; she would not rush him. When he took another sip of the wine he seemed to relish, Kwannon winced, internally. Even in front of the blind she would not vary her stolid expression. She knew how well the blind sensed their world. Because unseeing, they were often unseen and so heard things unspoken before the sighted. Her patience grew thin.

As if he had eyes to see, Keane turned his head toward her. "The Eye of Dhyana is between heaven and earth, between wind and water."

"More riddles."

His voice was brittle as cheap glass. "A warrior of the Githrodi should understand both riddles."

Slowly, Kwannon set down her mug and darted her gaze about the small space. How did he know that? A guess from the tone of her voice or the sound of her walk? Or had the Sage of Redstone some informant's knowledge of her arrival? Smoothly she rose. "My thanks, Master Keane."

Rising, the sage held out his hand. "I wish you could stay longer. Your voice is so pleasant; strong, yet calm and determined. I hear so few like that."

Kwannon nodded once; it was indeed her voice that betrayed her. Or was it? "Another time, perhaps. Tell me one thing more, please. How'd you know I'm a Githrodi warrior?"

"Your voice is sure, your tread strong and confident, and your smell too fresh for a townsperson. You're a warrior, and only the fearless Githrodi wear no armor."

Kwannon stepped around the table to grasp the old

one's hand. Truly, the blind do see more. Not all in the Downlands recognized her for a warrior—some to their sorrow. Scanning the dim room again, she confirmed her first impressions; Keane was no danger to her in himself or in any possible connections to whoever now held the Eye. Kwannon offered the gentle sage more than gold. "Did you know the River of Wind is not a river?"

His quick grin told her he welcomed her gift of knowledge. "It is not?"

"It's wind moving across the valley floor so steadily it's like a flowing of water. The Sanctuary of Dhyana lies at the upper end of the valley where the wind starts. Some say it's Dhyana who causes the wind, but it's just air falling down the high peaks and blowing into the valley. The valley's shape channels the wind."

As always, outside the cottage the Githrodi warrior breathed deeply. She gagged. While the air inside was stuffy, the outside was much less fresh. Downlander towns always stank; Downers must not know cleanliness and health were related. On her journey from the Mountains of the Sun, Kwannon had seen much sickness. She snorted. Downlanders! *And they call* us *savages*.

Her mare snorted but not this time to answer Kwannon. All at once, the warrior stepped up into the saddle. The mare cranked her head toward the disturbance on the other side of the rutted dirt street. Close-lipped, Kwannon took in a leather-garbed tough assaulting a young woman. Near the warrior, a small clutch of Downers turned to her. One—from his smug attitude and fine, untorn clothes a merchant—lifted both hands to her. "You've got weapons. Help her!"

Already Kwannon had noted the expression on the face of the woman struggling helplessly. "No," she said firmly. "I do not interfere. She chose the victim's way. And so've you if you don't confront a bully in your own town." Not looking back, the warrior rode past both groups. Only her keen hearing stayed tuned to danger from her back. Kwannon ignored the futile taunts from the Downlanders: "Craven mountain vermin!" "Highland scum!" Let them protect their own if necessary. Women were not vulnerable unless they chose to be. All Githrodi believed only one class was truly at risk and that class was children. If an adult chose the way of the victim, he—or she—could as well choose another way.

The warrior rode with her head easily erect, her brow smooth and not squinched into wrinkle lines. Her eyes were slightly narrowed, her features composed. Strength flowed in the lines of her body, even in her hairline. At her left side, thrust through her belt, rode her lightly curved long sword and its shorter companion sword, both housed cutting-edge up in the fine elkskin sheaths she had herself made. Her ready position even astride was almost unconscious; so long had she practiced maintaining combat stance that such was her everyday posture.

She considered Master Keane's riddles. His hint that a Githrodi warrior should understand guided her. Heaven was fire, the creative force; and earth, strategy or the yielding substance through which creation manifested itself. Water was the spirit of constance of flow; and wind, other ways. As for the other riddle, that could be the Void. No one could see there. Void was one of the five aspects of life, the last that she did not yet understand. Void was nothingness, what-is-not. Fah!

Urging the mare, she wanted to be rid of the stench of the town of Redstone. The pervading noise made such pandemonium that she found it difficult to distinguish individual sounds. Redstone was not a healthy place for a mountain warrior. Soon the houses sat fewer and farther apart and she entered the farming countryside. On a rise some distance ahead she saw a tower. On its top burned a huge bonfire, the flame strands whipped around by a wind not felt on the road. Surrounding the base of the tower, great oaks moved in a rhythm to match that of the windtossed flames. On the right flowed the Red River. Such a simple riddle after all! The Eye of Dhyana was in that tower.

Kwannon leaned back, just slightly shifting her weight. The mare stopped, her rump brushing the dirt of the road. The warrior called to workers in the field to her left. "What tower is that?"

The wizened woman closest to the road straightened, rubbing her back. "Black Tower."

Did these impoverished Downlanders have a dearth of imagination as well? Every town Kwannon passed through had its dark tower of some sort, usually inhabited by some equally dark practitioner of the black arts. She looked again to the lofty tower. It appeared built from some dark, perhaps black, stone. "Thank you, grandmother. Who lives there?"

"Nane ye want to see." The crone spat loudly. "Nor he ye. But if'n ye want a name, he's known as Edan Eblis." Quickly she made some sort of definitive motion with her right hand over her breast. Kwannon noted others in hearing range doing the same.

"Magus?"

The squinty confusion told Kwannon they did not know the term, but the old woman whispered, "Death wizard. Leave him be, young-un. I heard tell he's a-looking fer fresh blood. Young blood."

Then Kwannon was certain the Eye of Dhyana was in the dark tower. Old legends told of blood sacrifices to pervert Dhyana's gentle compassion. As the magi at the sanctuary suspected, a necromancer had purloined the holy stone of meditation, for its deeper powers were greater than its intrinsic worth. Kwannon knew she must be careful now. All the same, she could crush ten opponents with her spirit alone; could she not overcome one lone necromancer with spirit and sword?

"Thanks, grandmother. Blessing of the day to you." The warrior shifted her weight a bit forward to urge Jahael. The buckskin moved three steps and stopped as a small child darted in front. The battle-trained mare would not trample a child since she, too, was Githrodi born and bred.

"Come back here, you worthless mullock!" The man in a fine cloth coat and leather boots brandished a braided whip. Fieldhands jumped away from his clumsy rush. Calmly astride the stopped mare, Kwannon turned her head to look at him. He stopped hard at the edge of the road and swallowed noisily. "That's my chattel." His fearladen stutter was barely concealed. *He* recognized her profession.

Only Kwannon's eyes looked down to the child. "Is that your father?"

One tiny, scratched hand reached out to the mare. The child shook his (her?) head. "Ain't got no paw or maw.

Him's my master." New scarlet bruises covered the pinched face beneath jumbled and matted dung-colored hair. The clothing was equally jumbled and dung-colored; through tattered gaps showed older bruises and welts. The metal collar was tight enough to wrinkle the pale skin. Clinging now to Jahael, the small, androgynous creature stared up at Kwannon. "Please help me."

Her voice warrior steady, Kwannon—for the moment—ignored the brute with the whip. "Don't you know what I am, child? I am a Githrodi warrior. Don't you fear me? *He* does."

"Ain't as skeered of you as of him." The child grabbed at Kwannon's boot. "Please. Don't let him beat on me no more." He (she?) tugged at the warrior's leg. "Please, mountain lady, take me with you."

As warriors see all, even the most trifling detail, Kwannon duly noted the minute traces of rust on the collar. She bent down to feel around the metal till she found the catch. In one hand, she snapped the weakened iron, then tossed the collar to the man. "Do you object?" In his eyes and miniscule shift of weight, Kwannon saw the origin of his intent to use the metal-tipped whip on her. Before he could make the obvious decision that such would be unwise, Kwannon moved, almost imperceptibly. Jahael reared; her forehooves slashed at the air. When the buckskin came down, she faced him. The warrior drew neither sword since she had no intent to cut the fool. He was no warrior, not even a fighter, but a simple farmer. "Do you object?" she repeated.

He squeaked something that sounded vaguely negative. After that, the warrior put the Downlander to the back of her attention. At full carrying volume, she called out, "Does anyone else object? The child is free to go with me or to stay." She got no verbal answer, but the workers' physical attitudes assured her no one wished to protest the warrior's rescue of the serf. "Child, walk beside my horse. I'll not have you up here to get your fleas and lice all over me or Jahael." *Or let these Downers accuse me of kidnapping.*

So she would not exhaust the gaunt urchin, Kwannon restrained her mare's pace. The mettlesome Jahael pranced sideways, almost jogging in place. She bobbed her head vigorously up and down; often she whickered, so eager was she to move out at a more comfortable ground-covering gait.

In spite of an openly hurtful limp, the child suddenly smiled hugely. "He's nice."

"Who?"

"Your horse. He's jus' . . . real fine."

"She. Jahael is a mare."

"Oh. Yes'm. She."

While that might have been the ideal time to determine the child's gender, Kwannon decided such a question would be offensive. Surely the youngster had been hurt enough. "I am Kwannon. You?"

"Name's Druce, mam."

They trained them young! these Downlanders, to obliterate personal identity. The Githrodi, as all Uplanders, know well the link between who you are and what you are named. As Uplanders matured, names attached themselves according to personalities. Names mean something, as Kwannon's meant mercy. "How many years have you?"

Gawking at the warrior, Druce frowned. "What, mam?"

Blast the Downers' dialects! "How old are you?"

The child stopped, patently thinking hard, brow furrowed, mouth working around the question. "Ten, mam. I think."

So old! Yet so tiny. Why, a Githrodi cub of six would be that tall yet have more flesh on solider bones. The righteous fever of anger crackled through Kwannon. Feeling her tension, Jahael prepared to charge. The warrior murmured, "Soft, my friend." Obviously Druce saw no change in either woman or mare. Waiting to let the little one rest flopped at the side of the road, Kwannon let her anger sort itself out. Perhaps the ubiquitous poverty in the Downlands bred neglect, but even in lean times the Githrodi fed their cubs first. Indeed, no Uplander would allow a child to be so ill-fed as well as so ill-treated.

During the next hour, Kwannon paused three more times to rest Druce. Nearing the river at last, the warrior noted a side path down to the riverbank. Though the sun was nearly at zenith, Kwannon insisted the child bathe before eating. A small pocket of water eddied downstream of a bend in the river. There the current looked safe. "Take this." Kwannon handed Druce a stone vial. "Wash with it. Hair. Everything. Be sure you get your whole self under water."

Removing her boots, the warrior stood on the bank, her toes touching the water, in case the child had trouble in the river. Beyond the sheltered pool, the swift red current carried debris. The child waded into the water fully clothed. "Stop. Take your clothes off first." Quickly Druce obeyed and dropped the rancid clothing next to Kwannon. Knowing now the ex-serf was female, Kwannon watched as the child ducked under the water.

After a time, Druce popped back up, spitting water. "I can't stay under too long."

"No need. Just get wet all over." Kwannon nearly laughed when she saw the child rub the vial itself over her dingy flesh. "I will help." Kwannon waded in and opened the vial to pour liquid soap into the small palm. At last, she had to tell Druce exactly how to bathe; the child admitted she did not know how to wash because she never had. No wonder Downlanders smelled so bad! Kwannon gathered up the tattered clothing and dunked the mess as well. Scrubbing them herself, she said, "This soap will get rid of parasites on you and your clothes." Seeing Druce did not understand, she added, "Your fleas and lice."

Spreading the shabby homespun trousers and tunic on the grassy bank to dry in the sunshine, the warrior offered Druce her gray wool cloak to keep warm. While it was hot even in autumn for the Uplander, the air temperature was far too cool for the Downlander girl. "Eat." Kwannon passed Druce a hunk of bread with a sliver of cheese on it, along with a twig of pemmican. When Druce had trouble chewing the dried ration, the warrior offered more bread and cheese. Soon the youngster slept in the sunlight while Kwannon watched from the shade of an old oak.

After a while, the warrior laughed. "Now what've I done!" To rescue the battered child, the Githrodi warrior had acted as spontaneously as she had refrained from aiding the town woman. What was she to do with Druce? The warrior had a mission that the girl could only hinder; yet Kwannon had taken up the ingrained Githrodi responsibility for a child. All at once, the warrior sighed. Her eyes widened. Such confusion was unseemly for warriors. Thoughts only slow action.

Hunkering down beside the girl, Kwannon brushed the dull but now golden hair back from the bruised forehead. *Everything has its own timing, and this child's interferes with mine.* Softly Druce whimpered in her sleep; she turned toward Kwannon to snuggle against the woman's legs. The bruises on her neck were turning dark, but the pasty look was gone. Kwannon felt the harsh prickling on the insides of her eyelids and the sudden aching rush of compassion down through her throat and into her belly.

Brusquely she stood and stalked toward the river. What was happening? Had something gone wrong with her warrior's timing? Surely she was not in the falling time of her warrior's way. She was not old, not yet thirty. Through her clothing, Kwannon touched the minute scar on her belly, the touch of the healer-mage sought by female warriors. "I have renounced children," she said to the rose-red waters. "I have renounced family. No foes can hold aught over me."

After tugging on her boots, Kwannon deliberately resumed her combat stance, too stiffly. The Githrodi warrior glared at the child till she woke. "Time to move, Druce. Dress yourself."

"Yes'm. Where's we a-going?"

"I'll find a place for you. I've neither time nor inclination to protect you."

"Please, mam, not too close. He come on after me."

"To the Mountains of the Sun, then. He'll not follow you there." Now why in the name of Dhyana did she promise that? Of course any Githrodi family would take Druce in and rear her well; but the warrior had no time—the Eye was too close. Oh, all right, afterward she could take both Eye and child to the Valley. "You must watch after yourself. Do exactly as I say."

"Yes'm!" Handing the thick cloak back to Kwannon, Druce smiled.

The rigid warrior felt her heart beat faster and then stop for the space of three beats. After mounting Jahael, Kwannon held down her hand. "Ride behind me now."

The sky clouded. A chill breeze soughed off the blood-red river. Feeling the shivering behind her, Kwannon untied her cloak from the saddle and fastened it around both of them. Though the girl could not see out, she seemed happy enough to snug herself close to the warrior. The warmth against Kwannon's back gave comfort, and she eased her too rigid posture. She nodded. The tension would slow her movements. The girl's presence both caused it and relieved it. Children! How frustrating they are!

Close up, Kwannon saw the tower was indeed black stone, dull and smooth, of a kind unfamiliar to her. No chisel marks showed, and the stones fit tightly together without mortar. A narrow path led from the road to the base of the hill, where a stair cut from the living rock rose to the tower itself. Kwannon swung her right leg over Jahael's neck and slid to the ground. "You, Druce. Slide into the saddle. Do as I say. Wait for me here. Stay on Jahael. Should anyone try to get you, ride away or let her fight. I'll find you later."

"How long will you be?"

"I don't know."

"Can't I come with you? I could help."

"You could not. Obey me."

The small girl gulped. "Yes'm!"

The Githrodi warrior strode to the foot of the long staircase. From the tower's vantage, they must already know of her arrival. She went up the stairs, slowly, deliberately; her gaze was direct, yet she perceived all around her. Quiet surrounded her. Even the river's rush seemed muted. No bird sang; no small squirrel rustled in the drying oak leaves. The wind's song was faint. Only the raging fury of the fire on top of the black tower sounded normal. The acrid scent of smoke permeated all. At the top of the worn stone stairway, she came to a six-foot-square landing. The door was the same black material as the tower; it had no latch. On the left side, the door was an inch from being entirely closed.

Kwannon let the smile flow on the inside of her features. *So, he waits for me.* With that, her conscious thinking ceased. All the thoughts she needed for the next few moments were already thought through; all her years of training and practice welled up to the ready. In one smooth, deliberately calm motion, her right hand grasped the hilt of the sword to draw it; her left followed in a preordained rhythm to the companion sword. Both hands gripped the weapons easily, thumbs and forefingers floating, other fingers gradually tighter to the little fingers. Her right leg jerked up and her foot snapped out, striking the door to hurl it open. Yelling, Kwannon leaped into the opening.

Before her left foot met stone flooring, Kwannon studied the room. As big around as the tower itself, it boasted a fireplace directly opposite the doorway. To her right a stone staircase hugged the outer wall. A table with four chairs occupied the center and cupboards lined the left curve.

Five fighters waited in the round room. Directly to her left, one poised to strike. An axman with shield hovered on the bottom stair and two swordsmen crouched near him. One other, patently the leader in thigh length chain armor, stood with his back to the fire, heavy sword dangling in his right hand. The swordsman to her left swung. Her left foot contacted pavement. Turning on the heel, she presented her back to him. She bent her right arm up and over her head with the sword braced on her left arm to parry.

The youth was a head taller and much heavier. The force of his blow staggered Kwannon into the doorjamb, but the flat of her blade deflected his dual-edged sword harmlessly up and over her head. Knowing how he must move to deliver the beheading strike, she thrust her left hand back. The slim companion sword cut through his heavy leather armor and plunged into his abdomen. She angled the blade upward with a downward twist of her wrist; two sideways twists sliced the blade through major arteries. Though her blow was delicate, shock of surprise lifted the man up on his toes. He was dead, open-eyed, before she pulled out the blade.

The second swordsman was already moving in with a downward body-cleaving blow. Her sword still in parry position, she stepped forward. His power swept his long sword on down as she flicked her blade around to cut below his jawbone and through the throat. The third aborted his own cleaving blow from the other side and

stepped into a spreadlegged ready stance, point of blade
on guard. Kwannon knocked his blade to her left and
spun left to swing her long sword around and cut his
throat. Already at full charge, the bellowing axman drove
his massive weapon down. Over his shield, she could see
only his fervent eyes. Kwannon flowed forward and flicked
her sword up to his wrist. The force of his blow helped
her keen blade cut cleanly through muscle and bone. His
shield lifted to protect him from the expected overhead
blow; but the smaller Githrodi warrior continued her low
movement, rotating clockwise. As she came down on her
left foot, her companion sword cut through his lower
belly and its leather armor; then the long sword cut up
under his ribs nearly to his backbone.

During the five-step blitz, Kwannon saw the headman
moving around the table, obviously to join axman and
swordsmen in surrounding her. Now she slowed as he
had, her own sword on guard. The falling axman was not
yet dead but definitely out of the fight. The leader paused,
a tankard in his left hand, not thrown as was his original
intent. She waited to see if he would vault over the table
at her. Seeing he would not venture near the bodies and
their slick blood carpeting the floor, she did not give him
further time to fully analyze her movements to his
advantage.

Kwannon leapt onto the table and over it to face him
directly. He hoisted his tankard in a mock salute. She
wiped her companion blade on her trouser leg and slid it
back into its sheath. The other sword she put on guard,
aiming the point at his chest. Casually, he lowered his
own very long sword.

All at once, he dashed her bladetip to her right. Instead of moving in to him, Kwannon turned the opposite
way and jumped over his low-slashing blade. Landing on
the raised hearth, she brought her blade down and cut at
his neck. The metal gorget above his chain mail blunted
her blow but not his surprise at her lightning move. She
dodged his continued sweep and placed her back to the
bodies.

Roaring his full-mouthed battle cry, the massive swordsman rushed in with a full-bore overhead strike. Kwannon
blocked it, her right arm overhead and sword braced

down her left arm. The enormous power of his two-handed blow rocked her. He smiled as he swung the sword in a continuous arc to ram in another overhead attack from the opposite side. Bracing her blade in both hands, she took the strike overhead. His great strength almost crushed her to her knees; even through the heat of the fight she felt the jar in her wrists. By catching the blow near the hilt, she saved her sword from breaking in two. His arc continued down and up and around. The third blow repeated the first. She sidestepped, darted forward. Kwannon thrust the point of her sword through his open mouth and into his brain. She stepped back fast to retrieve her blade before the corpse crashed into the table. The thick wood fractured and tankards flew into the air to spill the remains of their bitter-smelling ale.

Kwannon knelt beside the dying axman. He had long moments to live; the agony of his violent death leaked from his eyes. The Githrodi warrior drew her short companion sword and cut swiftly though delicately across his throat to bring cease to his pain.

Conscious thought returned as Kwannon carefully wiped both blades. Her breathing slowed. She was sore but uncut from blocking the brutal blows. They had been good fighters, even the youngest by the door. These swordsmen relied on the greater lengths of their blades, and all depended on their colossal strength. Their chief error was not knowing her tradition of fighting as well as she knew theirs.

Her back to the outer wall, the warrior edged slowly up the stairs away from the raw smell of death. As she tested each stone riser before firmly settling her weight, her long sword probed ahead for trip wires. Inside the tower the quiet was palpable and intense. Straining, the warrior heard nothing beyond the lightest touch of her own tread and the delicate flow of her breathing. On each dim-lit landing, she faced a door. She listened before trying each latch; but each door proved locked. Up and up she groped in the silent gloom into ever greater warmth. Her sweat oozed, collected, and trickled down her sides, her back, and between her breasts. The rolled band on her forehead dampened but kept the salty flow from her eyes. Nearing the sixth landing, she saw light flickering out onto the stairs. The rancid odor of decay came ahead of the light. Swords in hands, Kwannon entered the room at the top of the tower.

He was waiting for her. The sallow necromancer was clean-shaven, his noble features as handsome as any Uplander's; but his expression was close and tight. He wore black tunic and trousers, and brown knee-high boots; a sable cloak rippled from his shoulders to brush the floor. His teeth showed white and straight, unusual for a Downlander. "Welcome to my workshop, great warrior of the Githrodi." A thin snigger oozed through his lean nose. "No other could best all five of my guards. Though you do spill a great lot of blood, you are much too fast. You take no pleasure in severing limbs nor in letting blood." His lackluster voice was flat.

Even as Kwannon watched him, she scanned the circular room. A dismembered cat lay in its pathetic parts on a stained wood table. Nearby, a dying gutted bird fluttered truncated wings. Bottles and vials stood in exact order on shelves. A circle of small rectangular gaps in the roof revealed the leaping fire overhead. Through the slits dribbled molten silvery metal; heat flames tongued the fall lines. So black was the space enclosed that light seemed to flow in but not out. Looking directly at the blankness, the warrior saw nothing, not even darkness. When she turned her gaze back to the necromancer, the very edge of her vision caught a wink of luminous green in the center of the void.

While the necromancer wore no weapons, Kwannon knew no worker in supernatural thing was ever defenseless. Already he had told her he had ways to see where he was not. "You are Edan Eblis." His curt nod confirmed what she knew. "I am Kwannon. I take no pleasure in killing. You know I am a Githrodi warrior. You also know I came for the Eye of Dhyana which was stolen from our sanctuary in the Valley of the River of Wind."

The graying wizard rounded his eyes. "Such a thing stolen? If you can find it here, you may take it."

Kwannon did not move. "It is in the Void."

For a long moment, he stared at her intently, his cold gray eyes steady; then he lifted long-nailed hands to chest height. The backs were toward Kwannon; she noted the long brown hairs curling past the second knuckles. His head lowered to jut forward on top of the spine. "Take it if you dare, harlot."

"You will not allow this." She stood still.

"You are correct." The twisting of his mouth was meant to be a smile; but without the eyes' cooperation, the effect was a grisly smirk. "You will die trying. How sad for you, warrior. To die having failed makes your death useless to you. Indeed, how useless your life, then."

Still inwardly relaxed, Kwannon maintained her combat stance. Her sword angled downward, its companion braced along the back of her left arm. "You're a fool or mad to think that."

"Am I?" Still, he did not move from his position. "Nevertheless, I do understand what you call the way of the warrior. You act out of concern for others."

Slowly the tip of her sword rose. His weapons were words as well as magic. Yet his knowledge of warriors was incomplete. Warriors act beyond love and grief; they do not think of success or failure.

"Death is the way of the warrior. Since you are as one already dead, you've come to the right place to embrace your destiny."

Kwannon let the hint of a smile show itself. His understanding was immature. Long ago, she resolved to accept death; and that was not the same. "You, however, are afraid to join those you love." Neither death nor dying attracted the death wizard; the dead lured him.

He seemed to grow slightly taller, his head pulled back. "You'll find me impossible to kill." Both hands flipped forward. Blue sparks jumped from fingertip to fingertip and then arced from his hands.

Dropping to one knee, Kwannon crossed both swords over her head. Where they touched, the blue lightning bolt struck. The shock punched into her shoulders. Before he could gather energies to attack again, the warrior vaulted into a full lunge, both swords prepared to cut.

From beneath his voluminous fur cloak, Edan Eblis yanked out a small child, hands bound with rough rope. As Kwannon dropped flatfooted from midstride, Druce gawked at her. "I'm sorry, Kwannon! I did like you said, honest. I stayed on Jahael, but he done something to her and she jus' stopped and he grabbed me."

"Stop your everlasting drivel, cowpat!" The necromancer clamped his bony, long-fingered right hand around the little girl's neck. "You see, warrior, I know you better than you can imagine. You do have something to lose. Observe." He aimed his left forefinger at a large black marble basin. The red water in it swirled, whirlpooling left and darkening. "Show what I witnessed earlier today."

While Kwannon watched, her attention split on image and wizard, the water cleared to picture the riverbank where she stood by the child. She saw herself tenderly touching the freed serf.

"Back off, warrior trollop. You care for this miserable pile of excrement. Her life depends on you."

Kwannon's unwanted affection for Druce burdened her with a life to lose other than her own. Thoughts crowded in. His word weapons were effective; she could not find her no-thought status. Indecision weighed down her shoulders. The necromancer meant to torture and kill Druce no matter what his lies indicated. What was more important now, the life of one small child or the Eye of Dhyana with its countless powers? Should she try to rescue her small charge or abandon her and snatch the Eye from the evil intent of the death wizard?

The swords hung loose in her grip, useless in the pangs of her indecision. Yet one consideration never emerged. She never thought of saving her own life. All her thoughts soared far above mere concern for her own welfare. No! Kwannon had not lost her way for such was the Way of the Warrior. Almost instinctively her body moved back into combat stance; swords moved into position as if with a will of their own. She would rescue both Eye and Druce. As her confusions smoothed and vanished into the region of no-thought, one hint of failure touched her. He already drew on the power of the Eye. Kwannon's war cry filled the chamber.

Hurling the child against the wall and knocking her senseless, Eblis sidestepped and arched his hands. A red dagger spewed from his right palm to strike Kwannon as she dodged to her right. The eldritch weapon pierced her left lung and vanished. Pain seared her chest. Each breath renewed the agony. She yelled again, a guttural sound, to get into rhythm. When she was sure of cutting the man, he was instantly not there but a foot to her left.

Another red dagger vanished into her abdomen. Sword high, she dashed quickly in and drove downward. Evading the cut, he appeared to her right. She scooped the sword up from below and missed again. A third red dagger darted from his hand to the hollow of her right shoulder. Her right sword arm weakened. Tightening her left fist, she struck at his face. Again, he was not there but to her left, his hands spread. She darted in to strike his chest with her left shoulder just as she breathed out yelling. This time she caught him. He bounced back about ten feet. His face darkened to a purple; the veins on his neck and temple bulged. She surged between him and the fallen child. Trying to dodge another red blade forced her on one knee, the dagger scorching through her right thigh. Her strength drained through the invisible holes left by his ethereal weapons.

Once more he gave her his ghastly smirk. "Tired, girl? How long can you keep this up? Mere physical stamina is no match for the power on which I draw." He stepped toward her, his nostrils flaring. "Die now, warrior, by the very power which you come to steal from me." Holding out his hands to the blackness, he spoke words strange to Kwannon. A thread of shadow surfaced to move toward the necromancer's cupped hands.

Slowly Kwannon rose. She could not defeat him with swords. His magic was keyed to her blades. She tossed both her swords onto the stone paving.

For a moment, the clatter distracted the death wizard. As he looked at her, the somber thread retreated. "Surrender or not, hill woman, you die. Then I will tear the child apart slowly as sacrifice."

Her strength gone, Kwannon stumbled. "Neither, evil one." Taking a sluggish, harrowing step, she tottered toward the Void. The shadow thread emerged again and drifted toward his hands. After another of her slow steps, he closed his hands over the tenuous strand. Taking another step, Kwannon grew yet weaker as the necromancer flourished. Strength scintillated through his waxen eyes and skin. With another step, the molten flow from the roof touched her right shoulder. In another, the liquid silver burned through to her bone, then into the bone.

His hollow cry bounced off the walls. "By the power of Dhyana, slut, you kill yourself."

Kwannon reached the dull horizon of the Void. She neither paused nor questioned her action. She crossed from what-is into what-is-not.

She was as blind as the old sage of Redstone; but like him, she knew where she was going. She reached out her hands. She was cold, shivering from an iciness deeper than the worst winter in the Mountains of the Sun. Weariness tugged at her bones as her hands closed on a faceted gemstone two inches across. The lethal chill emanating from it permeated her flesh and her bones. She lifted the Eye in both hands over her head. The Void thinned to translucent smoke as she turned to face Edan Eblis. He seemed larger; he had drawn much power before she cut off his source.

"Die, foolish warrior. You don't know how to channel the mana of the eye." Hands clasped, the necromancer pointed his left index finger at her.

Resolution filled Kwannon. Strength returned. She felt no pain now from either physical or mystical wounds, nothing except the rightness and fullness of her way, the Warrior's Way, the spirit of winning whatever the weapon.

A shadow grew from Edan Eblis' fingertip. It reached toward her.

"Your way is mine, Dhyana," said the warrior. "Through me, stop the evil that would use you to destroy life."

The nebulous power line entered the Void and touched her. Not scorching, it burned her flesh worse than the touch of the molten silver. Invisible fire crawled along her hands. Dark force and pain sheathed Kwannon. The black line of agony left the wizard's finger and insinuated itself into the fiery field of her tortured spirit. He seemed elated now, his eyes wide with passion. "As slowly and painfully as you die, even more so shall the child die as innocent blood sacrifice to the infinity of Dhyana's power."

Torment washed over her. Every joint throbbed from the sensation of being torn apart. The insubstantial fire baked her nerves, scalded her muscles, and ravaged her organs. Her vision blurred and her head ached from the fierce, surreal heat. Because the Eye had its own timing, she would no more rush it than she had rushed Master Keane.

"Let it go," the death wizard mouthed at her. "Your pain will end."

Yes. Yes, he was right. The Eye of Dhyana was the source of her anguish. Exquisite pain dragged at her sinews and lowered her hands. Now at eye level, the glittering Eye shook in her weakening grasp. Kwannon knew pain from her many battles, but no human should bear such racking dolor without losing consciousness. Her fingers opened. The Eye balanced, rolled. No! she raged at herself. Don't think! Do! Focusing her concentration on the emerald, Kwannon yelled her battle cry.

Edan Eblis screamed. His flesh withered and his bones burned. The burning and wrenching on him outside the what-is-not of the Void was real. On Kwannon in the Void, the energies had no existence. His limbs sundered from his torso and his burning body riven, he shrieked endlessly. His eyes were the last to blaze. The warrior witnessed the necromancer's death orgasm till the whites blackened and the dismembered parts fluttered to the stone floor as gritty ashes. As she sounded her final victory cry, her knees buckled. Together, pain and consciousness fled.

The fire on the roof was out when Kwannon woke. A small candle lit the dark room. Eyes crammed shut, Druce knelt beside her; both tiny hands clutched the emerald. The child sobbed, moaning, "Don't die," over and over. As Kwannon watched, the gaping wound on her right shoulder closed, bone and flesh. When she turned her head to see more clearly, the motion startled Druce. "Oh, Kwannon, you're alive! I was so scared you'd die."

"I do not die." Rising, the Githrodi warrior closed her hands over the girl's small fists with the emerald Eye within. If Druce without training could heal such a pernicious bone wound now, how much more could she accomplish through the Eye with proper education in meditation? "You are meant to bear this." From beneath her shirt she tugged out a silk pouch. "Put the Eye of

Dhyana in here." Then she tied the long thongs around Druce's waist.

Checking the gutted bird, she found he had already given up his life. She picked up her swords and cleaned them carefully before she returned them to their sheaths. Her thoughts moved as carefully. The Eye of Dhyana had its own way even to the theft of itself to bring together a Githrodi warrior and this precious child. Looking at the girl watching her so intently, Kwannon decided she was in the falling of her Warrior's Way and in the rising of another, rarer and more difficult. "I'll watch over you, Druce. I choose to be your personal Lifeway Guardian. Come. We'll see what he's done to Jahael. Then we go to the Mountains of the Sun." Gently, and with great respect, Kwannon, the Githrodi Guardian, led the embryonic healer-mage down the stairs and out of the black tower of the dead.

SPOILS OF WAR
by Jennifer Roberson

There are a few writers I buy from every year, whose work I know beforehand that I can accept because they have their own following. In this category, the first is Jennifer Roberson. I look forward to reading these new stories, I guess, as much as the fans do.

But isn't that what writing is all about anyhow?

All around her the arrows sang. It was a sibilant song of death, she thought: whining, humming, buzzing . . . the percussion of iron on wood . . . the crescendo of human screams. But the melody did not please her.

The wood was alive in her hands. Its touch was security, nameless progenitor of satisfaction. It was not *pleasant* to kill a man, but if she missed he might kill her.

Carefully she wound fingers around the leather grip. Four years before the fingers had been callused, the hands of a competent archer; now they were soft and white, the hands of the mountain lord's lady.

Right-handed, she cocked the red-fletched arrow. The shaft was banded black-on-red-on-white, the colors of her husband; the colors of the lord. The arrows singing by her were fletched in white, with triple bands of black. The colors of the enemy who sought to take the castle.

Four years. But she had not forgotten how.

Stone merlons warded either side, cutting off the angles. But to sight she needed room; to kill she needed sight. And so she stepped away from the merlons and stood before the crenel that reached her hips but no higher; she was an easy target now, in her lord's tricolor tunic. Black-on-red-on-white.

All around her, the arrows sang.

Unsmiling, she chose her target: a man in black and white. Unsmiling, she loosed the arrow . . . and it sang, how it *sang*, slicing through the sky . . . she heard the distant crescendo; she heard the archer's scream.

She took an arrow from the quiver; nocked, sighted, loosed; heard the song and heard the scream, enjoying neither of them. Knowing that even the death of one enemy might save the life of a friend. Might save the life of her lord.

A step. She knew it. She knew the hand that touched her own as she reached for another arrow; the fingers that closed on her wrist and drew her behind a merlon. And knew the voice as well; in bed, it whispered love words.

"Enough," he said. "Enough. This is no place for you."

Red-on-black-on-white. But the silk of his tunic was torn, baring silver ringmail. She looked into his face and saw blood and grime and enduring strength; in dark eyes, determination. He had slipped the ringmail coif and she saw sweat-damp hair pressed flat against skull except where the weave of the links had formed a pattern.

Fingers lingered against her hand. "Enough," he said again. "I see what it does to you."

Her hand tightened on her bow. "Do you send me down from the wall?"

He was grim, but also gentle. "I must. I must. For my sake as well as your own; I fear that I might lose you."

An arrow sang beside them and shattered against the stone. Neither of them flinched. "Will you strip me of my honor?"

Now he did flinch; her tone was truer than the arrow. "This is not a question of honor . . . it is a question of life."

"*You* risk yourself."

He said nothing, knowing better; he had said it before, and was made to suffer for it. And yet he knew, as she did, there was no need to speak; between them lay the words: *War is made for men.*

"Go down," he said. "Remember that I am your lord."

She did not move, though she thought the bow might break. "Will you strip me of my honor?"

The tension sang between them.

His dark eyes were fathomless. "I do not wish to lose you."

"If you send me down, you will."

He could be harsh, but now he was not. In his face she saw regret commingled with admiration. "You are a willful woman."

"You knew that four years ago."

Surprising her, he laughed. "Oh, aye, I did . . . it was why I wanted you."

"And now you fight a war."

Grimly, he said, "I keep what is mine. Cattle, castle, wife." Seeing her face, he smiled. "In no particular order."

She took an arrow from her quiver. "I will not go down from the wall."

Over the crenel, he looked at the enemy. And then he looked at his wife. "I will let you keep your honor if you promise to keep your life."

Unsmiling, she nocked the arrow. As he watched, she loosed it, and listened to its song.

They came to her at sundown and said the war was done. They told her the lord was dead. The enemy had won.

"Yes," she said; her quiver was empty. For her the war *was* done.

They took her to his body. Around it stood other men—black-on-red-on-white—warding their lord against arrows. But one had been enough. Through an eye, it touched the brain.

She knelt. She laid down her bow for the first time since dawn. She touched his face and knew him gone, his spirit had flown free. In silence she closed his other eye, and then she rose to face his men.

"The lord is dead. The war is done. The enemy has

won." She looked into their faces. "Put down your weapons and open the gates; the victor is now the lord."

One man stirred. "Lady, what of you?"

She did not smile. "I am part of the spoils; it is the way of war and women."

As one, they looked at their lord. And went to open the gates.

The victor came before her in the hall of the castle keep. *His* hall, now; no more was it her husband's. All around her the candles blazed as she waited on the dais.

He was not old, but neither was he young. Years of warfare and its trappings had ruined the hair on the top of his head so that he wore a graying, grizzled cap where the coif had rubbed him bare. Ringmail glittered; his tunic was black and white.

In silence, she waited. She was not a meek woman and gave him no meekness now; proudly, she waited. Watching the man who had killed her husband; who had taken cattle, castle, wife. In precise and particular order.

He halted before the dais. He was armed, as a victor should be, with knife and sword and pride. "He fought well."

His voice was a hoarse rumble: bellowing orders ruined a throat. "Yes," she said, "he did. He did not care to lose me."

Something moved in his eyes. "I saw you on the wall."

Unsmiling, she lifted her chin. "How many did I kill?"

"How many arrows loosed?"

"Thirty," she told him clearly, "banded black and red and white."

He nodded once, unsmiling. "Thirty of my men."

It did not please her to take the life of a single man, but she knew, if she had to, she would be willing to do it again. In war, it was simply practical; the *im*practical did not survive.

"The lord is dead," she told him formally. "This castle and all its holdings, including inhabitants, are yours to do with as you will."

He did not move, but faced her. "Was he kind, or was he cruel?"

"Both and neither," she told him, "as all men are, dependent upon their needs."

"Have you children?"

"None, my lord," she said steadily. "It was his greatest regret."

"And did he beat you for it?"

"No, my lord. He did not."

His voice was very quiet. "Did you love your husband?"

She swallowed tightly. "Once, I hated him, when he stole me from my father, who taught me what honor was. But my father *also* taught me there is no honor in hatred, and so I let it go. No more did I hate my lord, but neither did I love him."

"Four years," he said hoarsely, and she saw the tears in her father's eyes.

She went to him. She took his battle-scarred hands into her own and kissed them tenderly. "I swear, it does not matter. I knew you would come one day."

CHOLIN OF CARNEL
by B. A. Rolls

I thought, when I read this story, that the colorful language and the way in which it was crafted would show readers what I meant when I spoke of fantasy writing. I suppose I mean that it arouses in my mind images which for some reason remind me of the earliest fantasies that I read—in a long life spent in reading a lot of fantasy. That's why I want to share it with my readers. I have read many stories on this same theme and they didn't move me at all; but here is a story which, for me, tells what fantasy is all about—it's the art of sharing our daydreams. B. A. Rolls is British, and, as far as I know, no relation to Dana Kramer-Rolls.

A t the confluence of the Oisen and Vital, below the Connatain Mountains, stands the Aldorite. The name applies to the whole complex and to the temple itself: tier upon tier of colonnades and curving balustrades in white marble ornamented with pale green jade and chalcedony, rising abruptly from the flat alluvial plain.

Cholin stood beside the white road, wrapped in his cloak against the evening chill; the low red sun stretched his shadow across the piazza. He ignored the suspicious glances from the lines of suppliants waiting to enter the public booths. The tall, spare young man was dressed like a noble, or at least a scholar, but carried no sword or tablet. He was an enigma, a source of irritation.

Cholin summoned his determination. Impatiently, careless of the murmurs, he strode along the lines, past the booths, into the Aldorite itself.

"Yes?" Cholin started despite his studied self-control. He blinked, his eyes still unaccustomed to the gloom. A priest in heirarch's vestments was standing a few paces away.

"I seek advice and succor."

"The public booths are without. They are well patronized, but even the longest wait ends."

"My problem is not one that can be resolved by sound advice or simple physic," said Cholin. "Nor do I wish to consult acolytes whose powers are limited to the evocation of elementals and principals. I seek revenge."

"You can pay for your perseverance?" Cholin thrust his hand into his pouch and dropped the emerald into the priest's hand. One of the finest jewels of the House of Carnel that by some chance the reavers had missed. The priest gave the stone the most casual of glances before saying:

"Wait." With a swish of robes he was gone. Perforce, Cholin waited. Around him, the cavernous temple was never silent: from altars and fanes along the immense nave orange and red shafts of light glowed on tapestries of green, russet and silver, accompanied by muttered incantations and more disturbing sounds. The portal, illuminated by the last dying rays of the sun, seemed suddenly attractive.

"Come." Cholin followed the priest across the echoing vault of the nave into a maze of corridors as narrow and black as a crypt. Then, before he could feel confined, they had emerged into a room well lit by cressets set high on the wall. Light from a brazier flickered on the swarthy face of a priest who regarded Cholin expressionlessly.

"Be seated." He waved Cholin to a bench. "Relate the nature of your request." Unlike the acolytes in the public booths, Cholin noted, these priests adopted no portentous speech or air of remoteness, as if their powers were such that pretension was beneath them.

"I am Cholin—late of Carnel. My father was Galmer, chief merchant and seyyid of that House."

"Ah." The priest leaned forward. "The House of Carnel." He gestured to an acolyte who placed an open book before him. "The Aldorite maintains an efficient intelligence system. Ah, yes. Galmer, dealer in gems, craftsmaster. Widower, two children: Cholin, educated by tutors and at the Elstern Academy; Petra, educated at the Convention of Chieves." He raised hooded eyes to Cholin. "I recall that Galmer cherished social ambitions that aroused the displeasure of the nobility. When the House was sacked and the members of the Household were slain, suspicion naturally fell on the Heavenborn.

"So—you seek revenge." Cholin nodded silently.

"I see." The priest closed the book. "Allow me to clarify points that may have eluded me. You are clearly not without funds, and gold will buy men. Why have recourse to the supernatural? Unless, of course, you suspect your enemy retains powerful sorcerers or owns secretions of outstanding virtue."

"I concede your point," said Cholin. "I might discover the identities of the men who struck the blows, and naturally I wish to bring them to account. But such men do not act alone: a noble or nobles ordered the murders. I want to inflict a terrible vengeance on my real enemy, the Heavenborn. Or that part of it that refuses to see the unarmed as human."

The priest nodded. "You are alone? No retainers, mercenaries?"

"An army is beyond my means, and a dozen men are no better than one."

"You have explored other ways of obtaining justice?"

"The College of the Sacred Will? I endured several homilies on the virtue of accepting the Will as manifested by the placing of the Heavenborn above us. The archons of the God-Emperor's courts? What magistrate would investigate a case in which a noble may be involved?"

"So, rejected by the representatives of heaven, you turn to those of hell. Well, we of the Aldorite have no love for the nobility. We shall aid you.

"But first, a warning. We issue no guarantees." His raised hand stilled Cholin's protest. "Oh, we shall do our part, but the forces beyond the Web are at best unpredictable, at worst dangerous. Should the demoniac manifestation refuse aid, there is no sanction we can apply.

"Now, please remove all iron and secretions* from your person. My colleague will take care of them." Cholin removed knife, buckles, a selection of secretions set in rings and armlets.

As he did so two more priests entered, leading a shambling, blank-featured man clearly dulled by some drug. Before Cholin could speak the priest murmured:

"The man is a condemned murderer from the cells of Duval. He will die in any event and his death here will be less harrowing than at the hands of the public strangler. The Web cannot normally be pierced by will alone; life force is required."

Grimly, Cholin forced himself to watch as the priest took up a knife of volcanic glass—no iron, of course—and raised it.

"Split, substance of the Web," he cried. "Hear us, powers beyond the Web. Accept our offering and manifest yourselves." As he spoke the cressets dimmed and glowed red. Abruptly he brought the knife down into the spine of the slouched miscreant and there was a sullen growl, like underground thunder.

The stroke had been swift and merciful; the man collapsed without a sound. Cholin, his whole body tense, stared past the brazier where resins smoked and flared to where the room grew misty, then red, and finally cleared.

Cholin and the priests faced, not a stone wall, but a scene in hell itself. The pathway had been opened, the Web breached and the demoniac forces invoked.

On a skin-strewn dais sat the demon, blacker than a starless night with eyes like twin yellow lamps of evil. Around him sprawled lesser inhabitants of the foul re-

---

*When the energies beyond the Web impinged upon the world, deposits were often formed at vortices from matter derived from limbo, or perhaps from the essence of the Web itself. Secretions were possessed of various specific or general virtues, detecting or warding off sorcerous activity; some even imparted paranormal powers. Counterfeit secretions also enjoyed a wide circulation.

gions, some of human appearance, others of repellent aspect.

Defying all natural law a stream of blood spiraled from the hole in the dead man's back into a blackened bowl held by the demon, leaving the body white and flaccid.

The demon touched his lips to the bowl, then held it out to his minions. Like a tide of horror they crawled forward, reaching for the smoking container. Beautiful young men and women struggled with scabrous beings, but Cholin noticed that they were careful not to spill a single drop. The demon raised his eyes to the priests.

"The Web is rent," he said. "Raakuk attends. He and his loyal companions have fed. What is your petition?" Succinctly the priest recited Cholin's grievance and his desire for revenge. When he had finished, the demon laughed, the inside of his mouth glowing like a furnace, and beckoned to Cholin.

As Cholin approached, the heat of the lands beyond the Web beat on his face and arms. He was aware of the intense regard of the demon's court, but he looked steadily back into the yellow eyes.

"You do not show fear," rumbled Raakuk. "I like that. Your motives appeal to me, Cholin of Carnel. I tire of listening to petty squabbles; it is refreshing to meet true hatred in your soft breed. Were you less tractable your nobles would have vanished long since. The sheep must accept the wolves or learn to be wolves themselves.

"The offering was good: rich blood heavy with sins. I am disposed to be generous, and will assist you. Not too much, for to remove every obstacle would reduce my amusement in that farcical struggle you mortals call life." He turned to an attendant.

"Throw the mortal Starfire." A scaly horror fumbled in a chest and produced a bundle wrapped in rags, which he tossed toward Cholin. The object glowed momentarily as it passed the junction between the two worlds.

Cholin unraveled the swathings to reveal a heavy, cross-hilted sword of springy, well-tempered metal. It balanced easily, despite its weight.

"Starfire is demon-forged," Raakuk told him. "It will not hew stone blocks or any such banality, but it will prove more reliable than mortal blades. Naturally, it is free from iron and is hence indetectable by thaumaturgy, nor will it respond to sorcerous incantations."

Cholin murmured thanks, hoping that the alleged dangers of accepting demon gifts were pure propaganda on the part of the College of the Sacred Will.

"You serve my purpose as well as your own," continued the demon. "The pressure of the College on the Aldorite increases daily. I tell you this that you may understand my uncharacteristic generosity, which never stems from disinterested charity.

"In addition, I am moved to grant you a familiar." Cholin started. A demoniac familiar would place him on a par with the greatest sorcerers. And yet, to spend his life with some foul creature, nurturing it with his blood . . . But he had no choice: if any course were more hazardous than accepting a demon gift, it was to reject it.

Raakuk looked around his retinue, from time to time glancing at Cholin with sardonic amusement. At last he spoke.

"Ailuah." Amid silence one of his company approached the dais; Cholin's first reaction was relief that it was at least human.

"Ailuah," purred Raakuk, "do you agree to serve this mortal, to take his blood and in return channel the forces of the Web to his aid?"

The creature raised her head, and Cholin realized that the demon woman was beautiful. A somber, tainted beauty, but undeniable. Thick black hair framed a face arresting even with the hatred burning in her dark eyes as she regarded Raakuk.

"Taming you has been a challenge, Ailuah," said the demon, "but entertaining. Well?" The woman glanced toward Cholin.

"I accept, Lord." Raakuk smiled. Then, with a dark blur of motion, he grasped the woman's arm and flung her toward Cholin. Her body glowed briefly as it passed through the Web and her shriek of pain still echoed as she fell before him.

Raakuk nodded to the priest who had performed the sacrifice and his knife flashed out to leave a red line on Cholin's forearm.

"Mortal," said the demon, "your familiar is now part

of you until death divides you. Ailuah, take your new master." The woman looked up at Cholin, her face unreadable, then she bent and her lips fastened on the scratch. Her tongue stroked his flesh and for a moment his resolution wavered. Did even his slaughtered family justify this association with evil?

"She will serve you well," said Raakuk. "She has her own reasons to hate the Heavenborn. Bring me more blood soon, priests. Let the Web return." His voice faded and when Cholin looked up he faced the stone wall. But it had been no illusion. On the floor were Starfire and the drained body of the criminal; at his side knelt the demon girl.

In an antechamber Cholin studied the woman, who watched him warily. She wore only a coarse shift, her feet were bare. He turned to a priest.

"She cannot leave like that."

"I shall fetch clothing," replied the man, "together with water, unguents and other materials that females need." He paused. "Raakuk granted aid beyond my expectations, but I am uncertain whether you are to be congratulated." Cholin nodded curtly. The priest had expressed his own feelings.

An acolyte entered with clothing and toiletries which he laid before Ailuah. Another handed Cholin a forged license to carry Starfire; a third set down the packet of iron and secretions. The priests filed out, leaving Cholin and the woman alone. He felt awkward, unsure how to treat her.

"Would you prefer that I withdraw?" She shrugged.

"There is no humiliation I have not experienced." Her voice was low and pleasant, her tone revealed no emotion. Cholin compromised by turning his back as he resumed his accoutrements. When she walked round to stand before his he was surprised. Washed, dressed in dark green, her hair free of tangles, she could have graced any gathering of nobles, merchants or scholars. She came closer as he opened the secretions and prodded them with a forefinger.

"This—and this—are of moderate if unspecific utility. The rest are fakes, although this ring has a certain aesthetic appeal."

"They are all guaranteed by the College, and very costly," protested Cholin querulously.

"Nevertheless, it is so," said Ailuah, losing interest.

"How can you handle secretions and bear the proximity of my steel knife?"

"Naturally I am more sensitive to such things, but familiars have normal fleshly attributes, though we are very strong physically. The situation is otherwise if we call on the forces beyond the Web."

"Come," said Cholin, "let us leave." Momentarily forgetful of her origin, he put his hand on her shoulder. She smiled up at him, and he saw her canines were long and sharp. Instinctively he jerked his hand back and she turned away, her smile gone.

"An adaptive process," she said. Neither spoke as they followed the waiting priest through the corridors to leave the Aldorite by a side door. Out in the dusk Cholin voiced his fears.

"About the nature of our compact. Is it true that you rely on my blood for sustenance?"

"Well, only partly," said Ailuah. "I need food like any mortal—largely I am an ordinary mortal—but all who have been beyond the Web lack something we can obtain only from human blood. The amounts are small; clearly I could not derive sufficient nutriment from your blood alone without killing you. Perhaps the science of biochemistry could have identified the deficiency, but such skills were lost eons ago."

"Science?" Cholin was amused. "I take it you reject modern scholarship that holds such things myths."

"Indeed," said Ailuah, "they once existed, when Earth was young and sorcery itself a myth. Science was the systematic study of knowledge, neutral, not relying on effort of will or supernatural force. Had we science today we should control the Web."

"How do you know?" Banter was gone from Cholin's voice. "Who are you?"

She shrugged. "An unremarkable daughter of the nobility, who expected nothing more than to be traded off in marriage for dynastic advantage. But my father had many daughters, so I was allowed to study at the Secular College in Albdrovah. There I studied the fragments of knowledge that have survived from the far past. The study of physics, of the forces that operate whether or not man observes them, the strange interrelationships of physiology, the arcane lore of mathematics, that enable us to build models of the world in marks on a piece of paper.

"I was ignored by my House, and I was happy. But my father was angered by what he saw as pointless erudition, and reasoned that my price from the Aldorite was worth more than my dubious marriage prospects."

Cholin was silent for a moment. "Ancient lore was not encouraged at the Elstern Academy, yet I have often wished I knew more—"

"And now, master?" said Ailuah. "What is your present wish?"

"We travel south, to learn what we can around my home. I shall procure mounts—unless you have alternative means of transport."

"In this world I am bound by its laws," said Ailuah. "Demoniac forces are not to be unleashed for trivial convenience."

Their first task was to identify those who had sacked the House of Carnel. Close by the ashes of his home, Cholin made discreet inquiries, learned of a cottager who saw the reavers pass. They waylaid this unfortunate, but he recognized Cholin and refused to speak. Perhaps, like most peasants, he believed the actions of the Heaven-born might not be questioned; perhaps he feared reprisal.

Cholin offered him gold, then, exasperated, reached for his blade, but a hand touched his wrist. Ailuah came forward, held the man's eyes with her own, ran her tongue suggestively over her long canines.

"Perhaps you do not fear death. Do you fear hell? Shall I drink your blood and commit your soul to possession of the forces beyond the Web?"

The peasant whimpered, spoke in a rush. "It was Taifel's Guard, I recognized their emblem. Sacred Will, forgive my weakness—" He was still sobbing when they left.

When they had ridden in silence for a time Cholin asked, "Can you do that?"

Ailuah shook her head. "It was simply a device, to frighten him."

At a nearby hostelry they reserved a room and cleared it of all traces of iron. Ailuah knelt on the floor, her eyes closed. Sweat started out on her face as she made the effort of will necessary to wrench the fabric of reality and force it to reveal the information she sought. Then abruptly her shoulders slumped and she would have fallen had Cholin not caught her and carried her to a pallet.

"Master," she whispered, "Taifel's Guard are at the provincial capital, Albdrovah." She held Cholin's arm when he would have straightened.

"I'm sorry, but I need—" Tears of weakness leaked from her eyes.

"My blood?" She nodded. "Very well, what must I do?"

"Just lie down." Cholin watched apprehensively, then he caught at her wrist and a ceramic knife tinkled on the floor.

"I'm not trying to hurt you," protested Ailuah. "My teeth would bruise your flesh. A knife cut is less painful and heals quickly."

"Raakuk only bound us until we were parted by death."

"No familiar can harm its master. Besides—" Cholin waited, but she said no more. Ashamed of his suspicions he picked up the knife and placed it in her hand. In fact, it was less unpleasant than he imagined: her warmth beside him was almost comforting.

"Ailuah," he said gently, "what's it like, to you?" She turned her head, her dark hair hiding her expression.

"Think of eating food so rich it sickens you, but you cannot stop. But familiars derive comfort from their masters' proximity, even if they disgust them."

"You don't disgust me," said Cholin. "My poor Ailuah. As if I could pretend to virtue, after seeking the aid of the Aldorite."

She murmured, "At least you try to hide your feelings."

That night, Cholin was visited by dreams of the panic-filled screams of his sister as she was violated and flung into the flames. All imagination, since he had returned from Elstern when the ashes of the House were cold. He cried out, flailed at immaterial assailants.

He felt Ailuah's touch and woke, clinging to her hand

until, ashamed of his weakness, he released it. As if divining his mood, she returned quietly to her pallet.

When they reached Albdrovah, its streets were crowded, for Festival time approached, when young men of the Heavenborn were initiated into adulthood. Ceremonies at the Sacred College alternated with contests of daring in which more than one embryo noble would perish. Large numbers of the unarmed were also likely to be killed, but no one tallied these casualties. Nonetheless, each merchant and entertainer hoped that the displeasure or high spirits of the Heavenborn would strike elsewhere.

Ailuah's expression softened as she pointed out the places she had known when she was a scholar, ignored by her noble House. The town was of some antiquity, with narrow, cobbled streets lined with stone houses topped by high-pitched roofs faced with a characteristic, dark red glazed tile.

They soon found that Taifel's Guard was lodged at a large inn near the outskirts of town. Here the innkeeper, assessing them as neither wealthy nor influential, scowled.

"I trust your requirements are not grandiose. Taifel's Guard occupies the domaine rooms and the garden suite is reserved for His Nobility the Heavenborn Surthal. We have only attic rooms available and for these I require a week's tariff, payable in advance."

"Your terms are quite satisfactory," said Cholin, unlacing his pouch. The proprietor grunted and called his daughter to attend them: Mylena, a plump, bovine girl, pretty in a vacant way.

Cholin had not missed Ailuah's start at the noble's name. "You know of this Surthal," he asked as Mylena opened the ledger.

"He's hardly the most humane of the Heavenborn," she said obliquely, "yet he considers the unarmed beneath his notice. Such a massacre seems out of character."

Mylena seemed distraught; her hand trembled as she entered their names and Cholin had to remind her to inspect the license that permitted him, a commoner, to bear arms. Perhaps she cared less for the income Surthal brought.

When they were in their room Cholin said, "If you stay

here, I'll see what I can find out about Taifel. That Mylena may prove knowledgeable."

"I thought we were here to look for Taifel's Guard, not chase women," said Ailuah tartly. For a fact, Cholin found the ruminant Mylena unappealing, yet he felt mis-judged, and answered sharply:

"We need to learn their numbers and movements. Perhaps you can't kill me directly; persuading me to abandon all caution is scarcely different."

"Get yourself killed without my help, then," snapped Ailuah. "At least I—" She broke off, sniffed and strode from the room, slamming the door.

A short while later Cholin was staring moodily into his ale. Mylena's information had been willingly imparted, but uniformly depressing. Taifel's Guard consisted of a score or so experienced men who, once the noble and his son arrived, would all remain at hand. So much, at least for the time, for his idea of waylaying them in groups of one or two.

He tried to convince himself that Ailuah had behaved unreasonably, but he was uncomfortably aware he had treated her badly, with scarcely more sensitivity than the noble who thought the unarmed less susceptible to pain.

He set down the ale. Trained by the austere Elstern dominies to control his appetites, he was too abstemious to lose himself in drink. He looked up as voices sounded in the entrance lobby.

Respects, Captain Taifel," fawned the proprietor. "Your Nobility, an honor to have my poor hostelry graced by you and your noble son." Unnoticed in the shadows, Cholin tensed. As well Starfire was in his room, or he might have been tempted to attack them forthwith. He smiled wryly; such an action would confirm Ailuah's poor opinion of his judgment.

Ignoring the innkeeper, Surthal beckoned to Mylena, who approached reluctantly. He twisted her face to the light.

"You should begin to exercise your prerogatives," he told his son, a pale, waspish youth. "You can use her when we return from the College."

"But I'm to be married after the Festival," said Mylena tearfully.

"Sacred Will, slut," barked Surthal. "You don't mention your lowborn ruttings in connection with the wish of a Heavenborn." Cholin felt a rush of sympathy for her as she fled but, after all, he was not even able to pursue his own interests.

He pushed aside his untouched ale. No point in prevarication. The good opinion of the demon girl was more important than he had been willing to admit. He must find her and apologize. As for the Guard, perhaps a better opportunity would arise after the Festival.

Before he could rise, Mylena slipped back into the tap room, looking nervously over her shoulder.

"Captain Taifel's learned you've been asking about him," she told him. "I heard him say he'd teach you to be less curious." She reached beneath her skirts and brought out Starfire. "I thought this might help."

"Where's Ailuah?"

"In the garden. She's crying, but she won't say why."

Cholin closed his eyes briefly. "Tell her I say she's to flee, to save herself. Tell her also—no matter. Go quickly; I can hear voices."

Taifel led about a score of men into the room, probably the whole band. Not a man spared Mylena a glance as she scuttled out.

"Mercenary," said Taifel, "you have been asking impertinent questions."

"I'm unattached," said Cholin politely. "I'd hoped for a vacancy. Here, let me buy you a drink." Taifel ignored this, gestured to one of his men.

"Gessner, teach this oaf a lesson." Cholin sat motionless, his mind in a turmoil. If he did not resist, they might do no more than beat him—no, he would be a sheep no longer.

Cholin gripped his hilt, hidden by the table. He had been instructed by the finest fencing masters; now his application would be tested.

He sprang to his feet; Starfire gleamed in the dull light as it sliced into Gessner's neck. Before the body could fall he ran forward, slashed at another man's face, and on the backswing brought the blade across a third Guard's shoulder.

By now the Guards had their own swords out, but the

clutter of tables hampered their movements. One man became entangled in a bench; Starfire leapt out and punched a hole clear through his mail. For all Raakuk's disclaimers, this was no common blade.

Bludgeoned by Taifel's curses, Guards retreated, formed a well-spaced line, clearing the tables as they advanced. Cholin knew that once he was forced against a wall he was lost.

How many had he eliminated? Four? Five? No matter, there were still too many. Only in legends did one man overcome many trained warriors. So much for his mission of revenge, which would end ingloriously on this blood-soaked floor. He hoped that Ailuah would be well away before the Guard thought to avenge their losses on his companion.

The door crashed open and Ailuah stood framed in the doorway.

A Guard laughed. "Here's our entertainment, for after—" He reached for her, but with a lithe motion she eluded him, leapt on his back. Her demoniacally enhanced muscles held him for a moment, then her teeth darted to his throat.

The ashen-faced Guard staggered forward, blood seeping through the fingers clawing at his neck. Taking advantage of the diversion, Cholin flung a stool at one man, thrust at another, who went down in a crash of mail and splintered benches. A flurry of strokes and he was through. He backed to where Ailuah stood unmoving, her hands hanging loosely at her sides.

"Run," Cholin whispered. "I'll try to hold them."

"No," said Ailuah, seeming to rouse herself from her trance. She raised her hands in claws over her head, her breasts strained at her blouse as she filled her lungs.

"Forces of the Web," she screamed, "attend!"

There was a sullen rumble and the room behind Cholin and Ailuah darkened to a somber red. Silver traceries ran along Ailuah's hands and sparked at her fingertips. Her face distorted with the effort of sorcerous activity in the presence of so much iron.

And yet iron was uniquely vulnerable to demoniac power. The coruscating energies leapt from her fingers to ground on the mailed shirts of the Guards. Blackened shapes were hurled across the room to twitch on the floor.

The rest was slaughter. The powers of the Web and Starfire tore at the Guards until finally only Taifel remained. The drained, exhausted Ailuah slumped to her knees, the crackle of energy gone. Taifel's white face stared into Cholin's.

"Why?" he croaked.

"I am Cholin of Carnel," said Cholin. Comprehension and despair flickered across Taifel's face and he leapt forward with a howl to meet the demon blade.

Cholin knelt beside Ailuah, pressed her lips to a slash on his forearm. Then the door opened and both looked round. In the doorway stood the smiling Surthal, holding aloft an armlet set with a milky, translucent sphere.

"Insolent upstart," he said. Extending the armlet, he advanced. Ailuah whimpered and agonizing pain struck deep into Cholin's side. As Surthal came closer, it spread into hip and spine.

"Iron," gasped Ailuah. Dimly, Cholin understood. The noble was holding a secretion that acted through the agency of iron. He fought the pain, slashed down and his knife fell from his belt and slid across the floor. The agony receded. Thank the fates, thought Cholin, that he had discarded all other iron in deference to Ailuah's sensibilities.

He raised Starfire and the disbelieving noble thrust the secretion forward.

"Starfire contains no iron," Cholin told him. He chopped down and the secretion shattered, the matrix that imparted its powers gone forever.

Before he could strike again, Ailuah slipped before him, pushing the hair from her face.

"Hello," she said, "dear father."

The fear on Surthal's face turned to terror. He ran, his features slack with panic. At the far side of the lobby he tripped and fell down the stairs. Cholin sprang after him. A few moments later he returned slowly.

"Dead," he told her. "Broke his neck. So, he was your—the one who sold you to Raakuk." She nodded, drew a harsh breath.

"When I was beyond the Web, I used to swear I'd

endure anything if one day I could repay Surthal. And you—you have avenged your family."

"I suppose so." Cholin made an unconscious motion as if to cast away his blade, but controlled his impulse and began to clean it. "I can feel only disgust that I have slain these men. Doubtless they were guilty of great crimes, and not only against the House of Carnel, but they lie dead and others, whose crimes are as great, stalk abroad unscathed. And should I have cared had the victims not been my family, my friends, my retainers?"

Ailuah came closer. "It's to your credit that you have no love of killing. But don't exaggerate. True, the administration of justice should be the domain of impartial public functionaries, but where are they? If you can't punish all crime, should you not bring retribution when it lies within your power?

"I too closed my mind and accepted the benefits of wealth and power. But I don't allow myself to become enervated by guilt; I act willingly with you, not simply because you can command me."

Cholin turned abruptly to face her. "Ailuah, why did you come back? I didn't deserve your help. You'd have been free to return to Raakuk and ask him to release you." She turned her head in the way that had become familiar so that her hair hid her face.

"Why? Perhaps because I'm attuned to your blood, and it's better here than beyond the Web. Perhaps because you tried to be kind to me, as if I were not a creature of evil. But mostly—you recall I said that familiars were in many ways normal people? Well, I was a woman before I was a familiar. I imagine Raakuk foresaw that as a result of our intimate contact I should become attached to you, even though I nauseated you. It would appeal to his sense of humor."

"For once," said Cholin, "I think Raakuk may have been oversubtle." He reached out, drew her closer. She stiffened for a moment, then relaxed.

Suddenly Cholin tensed. "Sacred Will, I'd forgotten the son."

"Pienet, here? We must find him before he summons help."

Before they could reach the door it burst open, and in

came the epicene youth himself dragging Mylena, disheveled and with her lip swollen and bleeding.

"Unarmed slut," he shrilled, "you need instruction—" He stopped before the scene of carnage, his jaw almost comically agape.

Cholin slammed the door; Ailuah moved to block the other exit. Mylena pulled free, shrank back.

"What is the meaning of this outrage?" Pienet demanded nasally. Even now, he seemed unable to conceive that he was in danger.

Cholin spoke in a low tone, taut with menace:

"I am Cholin of Carnel; my esche* is Ailuah. Now listen: if you wish to live, tell us why Surthal ordered the destruction of my House."

Pienet's eyes turned to Ailuah, widened as he recognized her and appreciated her altered appearance.

"I have not forgotten," said Ailuah, "the enthusiasm with which you urged the sale of 'that girl with her head stuffed with worthless learning.' You would be foolish to expect sympathy from me."

The youth trembled, his certainties, his superiority, all destroyed.

"I know only that an emissary from the College at Tsenelan came to see Surthal, a Votice of the Pontifex himself. They were closeted for perhaps an hour; I was not privy to their discussion. Then His Nobility called Taifel and gave the order." His voice cracked. "I know no more, I swear. You gave your word."

Cholin hesitated. To release the stripling would be dangerous. Yet it was true that, at least by implication, he had promised. He glanced at Ailuah, who shrugged. Lowering Starfire, he stepped aside.

There was a high-pitched animal sound. Mylena ran across the room, holding aloft the knife Cholin had hacked from his belt. Pienet stared at her in shock, too stunned

---

*Partner, also term of endearment; roughly, dearest. Actually, a contraction of the Derelian phrase *essiente tarache*, beloved companion. The terminology reflects the view of the ancient Derelians that emotional and intellectual compatibility was of the highest importance. Sexual adjustment they regarded as fortuitous, and of no great moment.

to defend himself as Mylena drove the dagger once, twice, three times into his body until he collapsed face down over a bench.

In the silence that followed Ailuah walked over to the girl and took the blade from her unresisting hand.

"Where's your father?" she said gently.

"Dead. At the last he tried to protect me. Useless. Useless to defy the Heavenborn. Now we shall all die."

"Nonsense," declared Ailuah. "The Heavenborn have been defied. We still live. Wash the blood from your hands, gather all the money from the inn, flee with your lover. Change your names and seek a remote location; no one will connect you with events here."

The young woman straightened, responding automatically to the aristocratic command in Ailuah's voice.

As she left Ailuah looked at Cholin. "What now, master?"

"Ailuah," said Cholin, "let us be done with talk of master and slave. We fight the Heavenborn as comrades, warrior and sorceress."

Ailuah shook the hair back from her face and smiled. "To Tsenelan, esche?"

Cholin smiled in return. "Where else?"

RITE OF VENGEANCE
by Deborah Wheeler

Every year I receive many stories on this same general theme. Why do I usually take them when they are written by Deborah Wheeler and turn them down when they are written by anyone else? It's the writing; she certainly can turn out a good story.

In addition to being an excellent writer, Deborah is also a very good chiropractor.

Tyr Swordsister cursed aloud and reined her startled warhorse under control. The black stallion arched his neck and reared, scattering the loose shale under his hooves.

She leveled the tip of her best sword at the witch who had appeared suddenly around a bend of the trail. "One trick, witch, and you're dead."

"No tricks," the other woman agreed in a soft voice. She pushed back the hood of her long silvery robe, revealing a pale, rather homely face framed by iron-gray hair. Her brow was bound with a fillet of copper and a bloodstone shone on the ring on her left hand.

"Ha!" Tyr spat, indulging her temper. "Who the hell are you, traveling alone in these lands?"

"If I asked you for your true name, would you tell me? Give such power into the hands of a stranger, and on the very threshold of the Djenne Wastes? You can call me Elarra."

The witch stepped forward and laid a hand on the stallion, who quivered under her touch. "I'm heading north."

"Into the heart of the Wastes?"

"Elarra glanced at the sword which Tyr still held, pointed at her heart. "I'd travel with you if we follow the same path, Tyr Swordsister."

"How did you know who I am?" Sudden sweat gleamed on the muscles of Tyr's forearms.

"How many sword-bearing women does our world know? And how many of those ride a black stallion—Hellsteed he is called, is he not?"

Tyr found herself smiling. "There's not many who can understand why I named him that."

"A mount who can carry you to the very depths . . . and then back again," Elarra said, stroking the stallion's nose. "Which way do you ride now?"

The warwoman sheathed her sword. "North, like you. You looking for company?"

"Do you think we met by chance?"

"I think that *chance* can be arranged," Tyr said. She nudged the stallion with her knees as the witch began walking with painful slowness along the narrow trail. "I know nothing of your goals, or you of mine."

"There's a small village within reach by nightfall. Scrub gatherers, living in the shadow of the Djenne. Makes sense you'd night-over there."

"You sound like you know these parts. You been here before?"

"Yes," Elarra replied, and quickened her pace.

The village was heart-tearingly poor, little more than a twist of a street bordered by single-room huts, half of them empty. Children peered out with haunted, hungry eyes before their mothers hushed them back. Tyr accepted water and shelter, but would not take any food. Horse and rider quartered together in an abandoned hut.

"Curse them," she muttered, spreading grain from her meager store on Hellsteed's blanket. "They left these people nothing!"

Elarra stirred from where she sat at the glassless window. "There is such hatred in your voice when you speak of the Djenne."

Tyr's body came instantly tense. "I never said *Djenne*—"

"You didn't come by your training by happenstance, Tyr. You would have been ten or twelve when the Djenne Raiders swept through Arcady, slaughtering the Swordsister clans. Maybe you escaped by luck, or were sold as a slave and later freed yourself. What I feel in your heart is the loneliness where your clan should be—and the depth of your bitterness."

In the shadows, Tyr's dry eyes glittered. She sat down beside her saddle and took out her two swords and her whetstone. "I asked before, what the hell are you doing here, nosing around their back door?"

"Like you, I seek the righting of wrongs."

"Djenne blood."

"No."

Tyr awoke to a room flooded by moonlight. The black stallion shook his head restlessly and pawed the remnants of his straw. Elarra was gone. Soundlessly, she crept to the window.

The village lay still, but there was a quiver in the air, just barely perceptible to Tyr's preternaturally sensitive ears. Such a trembling as might be made by horses galloping across the barren hills to the north. Such a sound as haunted her nightmares.

Moving stiffly, Elarra crept into the hovel, her gray robes almost invisible in the moonlight. "Tyr—" she whispered, but the warwoman was already saddling her horse.

"Witch, can you fight?"

"Tyr, there's nothing here for them. They'll only be a few—"

The stallion pranced, sweating in anticipation as the warwoman led him outside. She swung up and felt him responsive and eager between her thighs. The villagers streamed from their huts, gathering in little knots of terror. They saw Tyr's sword, saw the fire in the eyes of her warhorse. A baby started crying.

They came bounding over the last gentle stretch of

hills, five or six mounted on small fast horses, barely the size of ponies. Tyr's teeth flashed in the moonlight as she waited until the Raiders had bunched together in the narrow funnel at the base of the hills. Their torches gleamed like a reflection of the Hell she would shortly send them to.

She touched the stallion with her heels. Like a quarrel from a crossbow, he hurled himself forward to meet the foremost rider. The pony, a roach-maned dun, staggered as the black shouldered him aside. The Raider's lance wavered, but before he could recover, Tyr stood erect in her stirrups and slashed downward with a double-handed blow. She saw his weirdly painted face upraised to her for a helpless moment before her blade snagged on bone and she jerked it free.

The coppery taste of blood filled the air, with a scream that died suddenly. The other riders streamed past the warwoman and wheeled their mounts. Hellsteed leapt for the nearest, ears flattened to his skull and his teeth bared.

"Arcady! Arcady!" The battlecry tore from Tyr's lungs as another Raider went down beneath her bloody sword. She and the stallion were now a single fighting unit, slashing at the faceless enemy. Madness pounded through her veins.

Sudden stillness pooled around Tyr's final triumphant cry. She reached down to quiet the stallion, feeling his hide slick and hot beneath her touch. Two of the Djenne ponies, still on their feet, wandered aimlessly until they were caught. The villagers stood murmuring, clustered around the fallen bodies.

Tyr's ears caught the groan which could only have come from a wounded man. She jumped from the stallion's back and elbowed her way in, her sword hungry to finish its work. The Raider, his face distorted under its faintly luminescent paint, writhed on the ground, chest and shoulder covered with blood.

"Stand back," Tyr commanded the villagers.

"No!" Elarra appeared from the crowd and knelt awkwardly at the man's side. "I think I can save him."

"Are you crazy, witch? That's a Djenne devil you're talking about. The world will be better off without him.

Besides, do you want him running back with news of both of us? What will happen to the village once the Djenne learn they've stood up to them?"

"This wasn't a serious raid, only a scurry. Any fool could see that. None of these boys has earned his manhood token—"

"So I should let this one live to earn his—in the blood of these people?" Tyr demanded.

Elarra stood, her face unreadable in the flickering torchlight. "If he lives, he will limp home with a tale of a demon warrior who rides a supernatural horse and wields an invincible blade. His pride won't let him say anything less. By the time the Raiders hear the story, they'll believe that it was only with the intervention of the land-spirit herself that he escaped at all."

Tyr paused for a moment before sense took over. She shrugged. "It's on your head if you're wrong and these people suffer."

"That's what I'm trying to prevent," Elarra said and turned back to the wounded Djenne.

Tyr sat against the dried-mud wall of the hovel later that night. She had tended the minor cuts and muscle strains that she and the stallion had sustained, but she was still too keyed up to sleep. She waited for the adrenalin to drain from her system, rehearsing her plan of attack. She would approach the Djenne encampment by stealth, staying hidden until she was near enough to make a suicide raid. She did not care what happened to her then as long as she took Chandros to the grave with her. But how could she expect Elarra to understand that dedication?

Chandros . . . Chandros the Warlord who had single-handedly transformed the Djenne from a loosely organized bunch of nomadic raiders, making life uncomfortable for their neighbors but not doing much more damage than that into . . . into the blood lusting horde that had slaughtered her clan, and too many others.

Chandros . . . would be older now, and slower. Fat perhaps, or at least complacent. Since his rise to power no one had challenged the Djenne Raiders. They rode where they would, took what they wanted—goods, slaves, lives. Until now. Until Tyr.

The light of the moon soaked the tiny room, as cold and sterile as her heart.

Elarra looked up as Tyr strode into the tiny hut she had set up as an infirmary. The warwoman's cheek shone an angry red where a Djenne lance had grazed her. It would leave a scar.

"Is he fit to ride?" Tyr demanded.

"He'll live, but I'd hoped . . . not for a few days."

"We haven't got a few days." Tyr hauled the youth to his feet with one hand, her fingers clamped around his throat so that he was forced to meet her eyes.

"Listen, Djenne pig! I'm going to walk into your home camp at your back. Whether you are still alive to see it is up to you." She twisted his head around and shoved him toward the door.

Outside, Tyr shouted for the villagers to bring one of the captured ponies. She was about to haul the Djenne youth to its back when Elarra caught her.

"Leave him. Let me come with you instead," cried the witch.

"You? What good could you do me, after last night?"

"You seek the Warlord Chandros, and an end to Djenne tyranny. So do I."

"By sparing this cub to kill again?"

"You can get me past the Djenne guards—"

Tyr released her hold on the youth's collar and stared at the witch, who had surely taken leave of her senses.

"You will never be able to fight Chandros on your own terms, with this boy or without him. You are a mighty warrior, Tyr, but you are not invincible. Not against his black arts."

"Chandros . . . I want Chandros." Tyr could feel the fire of her hatred even as she whispered his name.

"Then listen to me! Join forces with me! Leave this child here. Let's go together to the heart of the Djenne. We'd make a good team, wouldn't we?"

It went against all her years of bitterness to show mercy to a single Djenne, even helpless and wounded as this one was. With more roughness than necessary, Tyr shoved him at Elarra.

"Keep him," she growled. "Feed him, dose him. I don't care as long as he stays out of my way. And that goes for you, too, witch. I've had enough of your interference. The next trick you pull will be your last."

The Djenne were not expecting any trouble. The guards were lax, looking more to each other than the heights.

Traces Of their nomadic heritage were everywhere, but the arrangement of the tents spoke of layers of addition, not careful spacing for easy takedown. Toward the western border stood something which should have been anathema to the Raiders . . . a stone building.

A temple, Tyr thought, noticing its roughly pyramidal shape, but given the Djenne mentality she could not be sure. She had never seen any evidence that they reverenced anything, certainly not human life.

The wind that blew through her cropped hair turned chill as Tyr sank into the rhythm of the life below. Hours passed, and she took some dried meat from her pouch, chewed it slowly to edibility, and sipped stale water from her skin pouch. Night came, and torches were lit. The pattern of the guards changed, but there was no sign of uproar about the missing youths. Perhaps the young hot-bloods often disappeared, their fate considered to be their own business.

Midway through the night, Tyr crept back to where she had left the stallion. She led him higher into the badlands to a well-hidden drycove that she had mapped out earlier. The Djenne Raiders might have grown careless with time and unbroken success, but she did not want to take any chances until the time came to strike.

There was an ironic justice about her plan, for it had been at night that they had descended upon her clansite. All her years of struggle, of steeping herself in bloodshed to prepare for vengeance still paled beside Tyr's memories of that night. Even mounted on their ponies, the Raiders had seemed larger than life, their painted faces like the masks of demons against which no human warrior could stand. And Chandros . . .

She remembered Chandros, astride a huge animal reek-ing of blood and armored with unnatural tokens. A necklace of curved, bifurcated teeth swung from the beast's thick shoulders. Behind the Warlord hung an image of crimson dust, something with a long, articulated neck that waved like a slaver's whip, something whose leering fangs dripped poison to the soul . . . something before which even the most seasoned warrior paled, and froze . . . and died.

Except for a few terrified half-grown youngsters, Tyr among them.

I must not remember it now, except as a reminder of my cause, I must remember the fury and not the fear. It was all a child's imagining anyway, the natural heritage of a night of horror, she told herself, checking the sharpness of her best sword for the third time.

Tonight it will be different.

They were well within the outermost circle of the camp before they were spotted. The guard gave a sharp whistle and lunged at them with his spear. Tyr sent Hellsteed into a neat turn on his forequarters and signaled him into a *capriole.* Snorting in excitement, the black stallion lashed out with his hind legs just as the Djenne came within range. The explosive power of his kick caught the man squarely on the chest at the point of maximum power. Tyr heard the snap of shattered ribs before she wheeled the stallion and urged him into a tight canter.

The alarm was up and Djenne burst from their tents. Years of easy victories might have softened their alertness, but could not undo generations of constant struggle on the very borders of survival. The boys who had ridden on the village were children compared to the grim warriors who bore down on them now. It took the Djenne only a few moments to shed their layers of sleep-induced ease and show their true ferocity.

Tyr dropped the reins on the black's neck and used her favored two-handed sword technique, aptly named *grasshopper of death*. Battle-madness rose like a mist behind her eyes. She caught her breath as her blade sliced through a man's cervical spine, and then she stopped thinking.

Slash!—and curving around with deceptive slowness—

now her sword whirred past her ears, crooning devastation like a lullaby—

Slash! Another Djenne down, this one only wounded before Hellsteed's iron-shod forefeet caught him. Tyr, caught in the orgy of battle, did not pause to see if he was really dead, he or any of the others. Some she saw, others she only felt before her sword sliced through their living flesh.

The attacks redoubled as she came within sight of the pyramid. The encampment must be pouring out its manpower at her, desperate to protect its heart. Torchlight streamed from massed lights held by Djenne slaves. Hellsteed, now bleeding from a criss-cross of superficial cuts, screamed and struck out at the men who crept behind to hamstring him.

The pyramid door opened.

Djenne warcries died suddenly, even the shouting of the slaves. The crowd melted back to a half-circle, well out of reach. Incensed at the disappearance of his enemy, Hellsteed rose in a *levade* and bellowed his challenge.

Tyr, breathing hard, changed to a one-handed *iron fist* grasp and laid her other palm on the stallion's hot neck. She kept her eyes upon the empty threshold which streamed light that was cold and blue.

A crowned figure stood silhouetted upon the stone threshold. It raised its arms in a commanding gesture, and Tyr could see that it bore a wickedly curved saber in one hand and a scepter in the other.

"Begone, foul desecrator of the Sacred Ground of the Djenne!" The voice boomed out, eerily unhuman in its distortion.

Tyr felt her gut spasm in recognition. The light behind the figure soared suddenly and then died in a cascade of greenish sparks that spilled out onto the ground. The stench clawed at her throat.

Suddenly he was in front of her, almost underneath the black stallion's nose. In the uncertain torchlight, his mask flowed from human parody to demonic. The horns and other things which formed his crown glowed and shifted. Tyr could not see his eyes within the darkness of his sculpted orbits. Before her own throat could dry to disaster, she shouted, "Slayer of Arcady, prepare to meet your doom!"

Tyr pressed her knees into the bulk of Hellsteed's strength and placed her free hand upon the sword hilt, changing to the subtle, deadly *black comet* grip. It had taken her years of stubborn desperation to master it, the mounted attack which had no defense known to any of her teachers. The stallion sensed Tyr's impending strike and leapt forward, angling his body into the proper position.

But Chandros was no longer there. Instead, a pace beyond the spot where the Warlord had stood, a hell-black dragon known as the inferno-drake bared its sulfurous fangs. Exhaling noxious vapors, it stood fully a horse's height above Tyr's head.

The Djenne crowd murmured and drew back. Tyr felt the black shudder in fear. Then her own fury took hold again and she applied her heels to his flanks.

One swipe of the drake's enormous paw shook Hellsteed from his gallop. He staggered, fighting for balance before the next thunderous blow slammed him to the ground. Tyr kicked her feet loose from the stirrups and was already rolling free when the stallion's body met the packed earth with a bone-shattering impact. She darted in, the razored tip of her sword sweeping toward its unguarded belly. The monster loomed above the war-woman, its effluvium filling her lungs. Screaming her battle-cry, she slashed upward.

But her sword never whispered through the unclean flesh of the demon drake. Before she could touch it, it vanished into mist and a dozen emerald eyes surrounded her in the torchlight.

Tyr found herself in the center of a nest of giant serpents, filling the air with their furious hissing. Her wrists were seized in manacles of cold, mottled flesh. Other snakes whipped round her feet, threatening her balance.

The largest of the serpents drew itself up before her, as tall as a man. Its twin green eyes seethed with malevolence, echoed by a third eye, as crimson as spilt blood, in the center of its slanting forehead. It wavered, regarding her as if it found her helplessness appetizing.

Then it struck.

Tyr saw the slight tensing of the serpent's muscles which preceded its attack, and hurled against her living chains. The fangs of the giant snake bit only air, but it recovered with demonic speed and coiled round her waist.

The warwoman did not wait for the relentless compression which would squeeze first the strength then the very breath from her body. She threw all her power into a sinuous twist. The smaller snakes, caught by surprise by the lightning speed of her effort, gave way. Her arm was free! Without pausing or changing her grip, she slashed at the king snake with a basic *chopping wood* blow.

Tyr's blade touched the scaled hide, but before it could penetrate the bone to sever the reptile's brain, the snake screamed, an eerie, blood-chilling wail, and launched itself at her. Even her trained reflexes were too slow for the supernatural speed of its attack.

Fire lanced through Tyr's chest as the serpent sank its fangs into her breast. Pain and searing heat shocked her and she fell to her knees. The smaller snakes redoubled their hissing, loosening her bonds in preparation for joining their leader in the death-strike.

Desperation sent Tyr staggering back to her feet. She knew that if she delayed even a moment, she would be lost, and all her hopes of vengeance with her. She gasped, her lungs straining for air which gave no strength. Her vision sank toward gray and her sword slipped from her numbing fingers.

At that moment, Hellsteed plunged into the nest of writhing serpents, trumpeting in rage and fear. His iron-shod hooves trampled the lesser snakes as he reached bared teeth toward the hideous beast.

Tyr raised one hand, but she could not speak to command the stallion to safety. Through the spreading paralysis in her chest, she felt a tug as Hellsteed caught the giant snake behind the head and yanked with all the might in his powerful neck. The snake released its hold, twisting to meet this new attack.

Hellsteed reared, lashing out with his forefeet. For an instant the snake dangled helpless and inert from his jaws. Then its tail whipped around toward the stallion's shoulders.

It was no longer the gently tapered tail of a serpent, but the venomous barb of a giant scorpion. Hellsteed's teeth slipped from the hard shell of the lion-sized insect. Its pincer claws grabbed and tore at his sleek hide, leaving streaks of blood. Pushed past the limits of his courage, the horse threw himself backward in panic. The scorpion struck once more with its stinger, missing as Hellsteed's battle-trained reflexes sent him scrambling beyond its reach.

Then it turned its glittering multiple eyes on its helpless human victim.

Tyr sobbed in impotent rage. The lesser snakes lay limp at her feet, her blade within reach, the enemy clear before her. But the chill of the serpent's poison clawed at her heart, rapidly draining the last of her strength.

Tyr knew she could never reach the scorpion at sword's length. She allowed herself to sink into a crouch, forcing air into her lungs for a final effort. She picked up her sword and held it at a low, oblique angle, ready for an opening to the insect's vulnerable belly. In a lightning move it seized the blade in its pincers, wresting it away from Tyr's weakening grasp.

Snap! The reverberation of the shattered blade filled Tyr's skull. If the thing could break a piece of tempered steel that had already weathered countless battles, what chance had any other blade? What chance had she?

Hopeless or not, Tyr still had a weapon besides her bare hands and feet. She slipped her dagger from the top of one boot, holding it carefully shadowed. She waited, heart drumming, for the final strike. . . .

Even though she was prepared, the suddenness of the scorpion's attack astonished her. Without thinking, her years of training seized her, holding her hand steady until the final moment when she leapt between the awful reaching pincers, under the very shadow of the deadly stinger.

Tyr drove the tip of her dagger between the chitinous plates of the scorpion's neck. The point easily pierced the flexible armor and she had only to push it home to sever its vital nerves.

Pincers clacked in outrage as the scorpion flung itself upward. The curved talon at the end of its tail lashed the air, scattering drops of poison that burned whatever they touched.

Tyr scarcely felt the pain as the dagger was wrenched from her fingers. She felt only the growing pool of quiet as the insect retreated into the night and the Djenne muttered, drawing in for the kill.

" 'Steed . . ." Tyr forced the sound from her ragged throat.

The black stallion turned, his tail still held at a defiant angle even though his ears were pinned tightly against his neck. White ringed his eyes, and mingled blood and sweat drenched his hide. He shuddered and dipped his head. Summoning the tatters of her strength, Tyr caught the near stirrup with both hands. Hellsteed, trained to assist a rider vaulting to his back, steadied his gait, but there was little more he could do to help her. In a few more seconds the Djenne would close in. Grunting with the effort, Tyr reached up to the saddle—it was too high, and the serpent's poison sang in her ears.

The nearest Raiders were almost upon her. She drew in her breath for one last try just as Hellsteed leapt into a gallop. The impetus swept her feet out from under her. Tyr's grip tightened convulsively as she flexed her thighs, drawing her legs forward. She touched the ground and put her last energy into a final spring which would make the difference between a bloody death and a chance for escape.

The earth itself seemed to rise up beneath her. Tyr felt her feet soar upward, grazing the stallion's flank. At the top of the arc, she hooked her right knee over the saddle.

Hellsteed galloped like a demon horse for the safety of the hills. Tyr hauled herself into the saddle, her fingers twining in his mane. The stallion lunged up the rocky slope.

On and on he stumbled through the night, the heat from his exertion blanketing the warwoman. She lurched in the saddle, barely conscious.

She never knew if they were followed. There were no sounds of pursuit, but her sight and hearing wavered, blending into a nightmare kaleidoscope. Finally the black stallion came exhausted to a halt and her fingers loosened their grip on his mane.

Tyr slipped from the saddle, already unconscious.

Through waves of pain and heat came blessed, soothing cool—at first only a tendril, then an insistent caress, over and over again, stroking her cheek, her thighs, her chest that was a strongbox of darkness. Finally Tyr opened her eyes and there sat the witch.

What the hell are you doing here? Tyr thought, but her mouth made only helpless, empty sounds.

Elarra put down the herb-soaked cloth she had been using to wipe her wounds. "Almost lost you," she said. "What a fool thing to do, riding alone into Chandros' campment."

Tyr smiled crookedly and her voice found itself in a croak, "Damned near got him, too. If it weren't for his magic, he'd be a dead man."

"You didn't listen, did you?" Elarra demanded, looking as if she would like to take Tyr by the shoulders and shake some sense into her. "I told you back at the village what would happen."

"You tried to sneak a free ride with me." Tyr cleared her throat, feeling surprisingly fit. The witch knew her remedies, whatever else she might say about her.

"I *told* you— Oh, what's the use arguing with you? Eat something." Elarra thrust a metal trail dish into Tyr's hands.

Tyr heaved herself up and regarded the contents of the plate. "Spiced beans and greens? *This* is food for a sick woman?"

"You're in no position to argue. Or shall I describe the condition I found you in? If your horse hadn't the sense to follow the path back toward the village. I'd have been too late."

"You were following me. Why?"

"Did you hear anything I said to you? Chandros has got to be removed before he does more evil."

Tyr looked up from her meal, her expression curious and evaluating. Tell me why *you* want his hide."

"You grew up in Arcady, you don't remember the Wastes before Chandros. The Djenne were raiders, true, but not a scourge. They're not a true clan, you know.

Men aren't born into the Djenne. They come from villages and herder clans all through this land—wild kids who'd tear up everything their parents fought for. So they run away to the Djenne and do crazy stupid things.

"You sound as if you approve of them!"

"They cost the villages, true, but less than if they had to deal with the youngsters actually living there. Some Djenne grew up after a few years, went back home to a life of hard work and no future. They painted their faces so that they wouldn't be recognized, so they need not be ashamed of what they did in their youth. Others stayed until the Waste caught up with them. That was before Chandros."

"Chandros," Tyr said thoughtfully. "He changed them, didn't he? So they became more than a safety valve for hellraisers."

Elarra nodded, her gray eyes bleak. "They struck farther and farther from the Wastes, pillaging and destroying instead of merely harassing. They leveled your clansite."

"And yours?"

"You haven't guessed why I know so much about the Djenne? I was one."

"A woman? But I saw none—"

"The Djenne, unlike your people of Arcady, do not admit that women can ride and fight with the best. I was careful they didn't find out. It was easy until Chandros' magic . . ." Memory clouded her face.

"He scared the shit out of you?"

"Do you think a little thing like his illusions could frighten someone who could ride with the Djenne Raiders and keep such a secret? Even if I hadn't witchblood, I'd have felt his evil. He doesn't work with symbolic or natural magic the way true witches do. He uses elemental forces—instinctive fears that give body to his attacks."

The inferno-drake, the snakes, the scorpion . . . An atavistic shiver clawed at Tyr's spine as she realized how deeply Chandros had tapped her primal fears.

"Yes, those, but also something worse. He invokes the very spirits of land and heaven, using their power to extend his control, slowly poisoning their essence."

"The Wastes . . . a spirit?"

"Dry, wild—like a wiry old mother with dust on her bare feet and weeds braided in her hair. Clean, uncompromising—she kills you or she tames you. She makes you find out who you are and what you want—fast. Not a bad place to be. But now . . . Can't you feel how she's changed, grown bloated with the lifeblood of Chandros' victims?"

Tyr shook her head.

"I felt her," Elarra whispered. "I felt her even as far away as Ryley Witch-heart, where I put my life back together again after I escaped what the Djenne had become. We've got to stop him before it's too late."

"Too late?" Tyr cried bitterly. "It was too late the day he marched on Arcady!"

"Each time he feeds her with blood she grows further and further from her true form. Soon she will rise, not the clean spirit that made the Waste a haven for wildness, but a ravening figure of death."

Tyr sat silently, imagining the force behind Chandros' power given a form—a shape vaguely, obscenely female, lusting for blood. Each drop that fell upon the land would feed her hunger. "I tried to kill Chandros. I think, at the last, that I touched him, but nothing more. And if you and Hellsteed hadn't rescued me . . ."

"I can stop him," Elarra said with quiet intensity. "But I could never get to him through his guards."

"You, who rode with the Djenne as one of their own? Did your witchlore turn you into a female-eunuch?" Tyr demanded spitefully.

Elarra drew up her long gray skirts. One leg was normal, muscular and straight under its curl of fine hair. The other ended above her knee in a shiny-skinned knob, raw and oozing through its bandages on top of the crutch that supported it. Tyr swallowed, realizing what it had cost the witch to race to her aid.

"Not even magic could give back what Chandros had taken from me," Elarra said.

"Daylight, moondark, it doesn't make much difference," Elarra commented. The two women crouched together in Tyr's lookout above the Djenne encampment, their bodies touching. The wind blew the witch's gray hair to an unruly froth.

"They'd be waiting for me at night," said Tyr.

"Hardly. Does that look like a camp on guard? If anything, they're complacent with one more victory they didn't have to fight for."

"And us? How hard are we going to have to fight?"

"Was getting as far as the pyramid a fluke? Can you do it again?" Elarra turned and began a careful descent.

The witch's words had lost their power to sting Tyr. "Even with my second-best sword."

"That's all you have to do, then. Get me there. We'll make a good team, I promise you."

"What are you going to *do?*" Tyr followed, genuinely curious. "Fight a magical duel with him?"

When Elarra did not answer, Tyr supposed she was concentrating too hard on her precarious footing to speak. Only later did she realize there might be another, less bearable reason.

Even burdened double, Hellsteed cut through the outer Djenne defenses like butter. Tyr, guiding him with her knees, slashed down the defenders who were no more effective than they had been on that fateful night. She fought soundlessly, all joy in battle drowned in the fear of what she might have to face at the pyramid.

The Djenne resistance thickened until their progress was like sloshing through a noxious quagmire. This time the Raiders had a chance to mount and counterattack from horseback. It made no difference to Tyr's sword. The Djenne ponies staggered before the black stallion, squealing in panic as he sank his huge yellow teeth into their flesh. They were trained to be transportation for lightning raids, not targets themselves.

Chandros stood outside the pyramid, his crown glittering like an offence to the sunlight. Tyr reined Hellsteed to a halt in the little clearing at his feet. The Djenne drew back from them as before, content to let the Warlord do their fighting for them.

"Begone, foul invader!" he shouted. "You cannot touch the sacred leader of the Djenne."

"You bastard, did you think I was that easy to kill?"

"Arcady is dust beneath the might of the Djenne. It was a mistake to let any of that spawn survive, but it is a mistake easily rectified."

Chandros raised his arms above his head, this time bearing only the scepter. Tyr kept her eyes from examining its ornaments too closely in the bright day. What she could see of his crown was enough to turn even the most stalwart stomach. He began a slow chant in an alien, guttural language. His flowing robes swirled around him as if they had living energy of their own.

"Witch, do your part!" Tyr hissed over her shoulder.

"It's too soon. We'll have to force him—can you take the scepter?"

"And have him turn into something I can't handle when I'm that close? I've done my job getting you this far; it's up to you now. Or do you let others do *all* your fighting?"

"No!" Elarra loosened her grip around Tyr's waist and slid to the ground. She stumbled as her false leg gave way, but then recovered and stepped forward.

"By the wind which is our spirit, by the salt which is our strength—" Elarra cried out in a clear, ringing voice. The massed Djenne recoiled as if she had bodily struck them. Chandros paused in his chant, his robes falling still.

"I call challenge upon you, Chandros Out-lander!"

"A woman—but she knows the code!" A voice rose from the crowd.

"I do not acknowledge your right!" Chandros shouted, his sonorous voice suddenly raw. "You are not Djenne!"

"I do not acknowledge your right to be here, either," Elarra retorted. "Did you spend ten days alone on the Waste with no one but the vultures to guide you? Did you win your manhood token? Who among the Djenne bears the brother-knife with your own blood upon it?"

She turned to the Djenne Raiders, now restless, muttering their agreement. "Listen, O Djenne, listen and decide if I have the challenge right! I have seen the moon rise over the Barren Peaks ten times! I have carved the sign of ritual passage upon my own breast! And where is Pauce, who bears the knife of Ylar?"

A tall Djenne stepped forward. "Chandros is our War-lord, leading us to victories we never dreamt of before. Ylar is a cripple, if he still lives. Why should I listen to the words of a woman?"

Moving slowly, her stiffness apparent only to Tyr, Elarra approached the Raider. He bent his head to catch the words too hushed for others to hear. Then she drew out someting from a hidden pocket and placed it in his hand. Tyr saw him blanch and nod his head in agreement. He raised his voice as Elanna returned to her place in front of Chandros.

"She has the right!"

"But, Pauce, a woman," came the protest. "Since when have the Djenne accorded *women* the right?"

Pauce turned toward the questioner, his brow red and furrowed. "Since when have the Djenne been too cow-ardly to accept a challenge? Chandros is either Djenne or he is dead!"

As the Djenne cheered their agreement, Chandros shook his scepter and called aloud, "Come forth, then, and see what doom you have laid upon yourself!"

Instantly a billow of putrescent yellow smoke began to swirl around the Warlord. Vague shapes moved in its currents and the outlines of Chandros' form began to blur. Bile rose in Tyr's throat, caustic and unbidden, as she remembered the horror she had so narrowly escaped.

But Elarra was shouting, too, her hands thrust aloft and the bloodstone ring flashing to life. The yellow smoke dissipated into tatters. Chandros shouted an obscenity at her and she laughed.

"You cannot use my fears against me, imposter! I am no tribal brat to be cowed by a bit of trivial magic! Surely you can do better than that for the honor of the Djenne!"

Exultation steadied Tyr's heart as she realized what Elarra was doing. She needed to force him deeper into his defenses, where she could strike at his very source.

The air between the embattled pair grew thick, rip-pling with waves of supernatural power. Chandros shook his scepter, the bones and horrendous carved objects rattling like the chains of doom. Elarra's ring cast a deep crimson light, staining their faces like freshly spilt blood.

Her voice soared above the rumblings of the Warlord's spells.

Stalemate, thought Tyr.

With a horrendous cry, Chandros wrenched himself from the deadlock. He drew a wickedly curved knife from the folds of his robes and pointed the tip at his own chest.

"No! Stop him, Tyr!" Elarra screamed in real panic. Tyr dug her heels into the stallion's sides and he hurled himself forward, but they were too late. No human agency could have stayed Chandros' hand. Blood ran down the front of his robes and spattered the dust at his feet.

Thunder rocked the cloudless sky and several of the Raiders fell to their knees, keening in terror. Tyr reined Hellsteed to a halt. The ground quivered beneath him and she jumped from his back, steadying him with her warrior's touch.

Chandros stepped back, his face unreadable behind his ritual mask. The ground where he had stood, where his blood lay like scattered coins of death, began to bulge upward. More wails of terror came from Djenne throats, and then all sound was torn from them.

The bulge grew to the size of a barrow-grave, and then a small hill. Tyr did not need to pull the stallion from its spreading arch. He shivered and danced backward, his ears pinned back in fear. Chandros had retreated to the stone threshold of the pyramid, and the Djenne were well out of the way. Only Elarra had not moved, and the wave of earth lifted her up and up. Her face was impassive, her voice still, her hands clasped together before her breasts.

Tyr realized it was not only the light of the bloodstone ring that made the earth seem red. It was actually turning crimson, as if it were being soaked with human blood.

Crack! The bulge split open at Elarra's feet with a deafening whipsnap. The earth beneath Tyr shuddered, but she kept her eyes upon the crest of the unnatural hill. A huge, misshapen hand emerged from the crevice in a volley of loose soil and pebbles.

"Aiee! The Earth-mother herself to eat us!" screamed a Raider among the gibbering of his fellows.

Tyr dug her fingers into the heavy leather of the stallion's braided reins, praying that she would not faint.

Another hand emerged, as big as the warwoman's torso, and then two arms leading to narrow shoulders and a squat neck. The head raised blind eyes to scan the terrified crowd. The Djenne were on their knees, cowering with their faces hidden in their hands. Only Tyr, who was too frightened to move, Elarra on the mound, and Chandros Warlord were still on their feet.

The hillock began to crumble as the monstrous blood-drenched figure clambered out. Tyr could see that its form was vaguely, almost indecently female, a perverted reversal of the nurturing land-spirit Elarra had described.

Chandros began to laugh. At first slowly, a barely recognizable grumble, then louder it came, shrieking up the scale to hysteria.

"Eat you! She'll eat *you*, witch!" he screamed.

The Earth figure stooped toward Elarra, who stood small and frail at her feet. The mouth which was no more than a tooth-edged gash opened wide, wider, stretching to encompass her. Elarra seemed mesmerized, unable to move, impotent against the battering, elemental blood-lust which emanated from the giant.

Tyr closed her eyes, fighting for the courage to move. Elarra had risked *this* in joining forces with her—she could not leave her to die alone, not like this. . . . She dropped the reins and forced her hands toward the hilt of her second-best sword.

Before she could draw the blade, however, Elarra stumbled clear of the rubble, for a moment beyond the reach of those massive hands. She reached the level ground and turned to face her adversary. She lifted her hands high above her head, the light from her ring shifting in rainbow glory from red to orange, down through the spectrum to deep violet. Sparks flew from the ring. They landed with a hiss at the feet of the lumbering Earth giant, who came to a halt, bellowing threats.

Tyr could no longer see Elarra clearly, the witch was so enveloped with shimmering purple light. She seemed to grow taller and thinner as the purple faded to mauve and then to silver-gray. A chill wind, carrying the tang of alkali from the Wastes, whipped through the encampment. There was no question now that Elarra had grown, almost to the height of the monstrous figure she faced.

The wind sang wildly, scouring tears from Tyr's eyes. It pulled Elarra's hair into a halo of untamed glory. It distorted her flesh, whittling her curves into hard, bony angles.

The shrieking voice of the wind filled Tyr's head, freezing her hand on her sword, freezing her very thoughts. Then it was no longer the wind's voice, it was Elarra's, or rather what Elarra had become.

Not Elarra . . . the land-spirit of the Djenne. The Djenne herself, a mirror of what she had been, of what she was meant to be. She stood, clean and wild, before the bloated atrocity Chandros had created from her. She sang, forcing memory, evoking truth . . .

The blood-soaked figure wavered, her hunger melting in Elarra's clean song. Chandros shouted incoherently and rushed at her.

Tyr, understanding, dropped her sword and sprinted for all she was worth. Before he could reach the Earth figure, she caught him around the waist, throwing him heavily to the ground. He fought her with insane strength, and it took all her wrestler's tricks to keep him pinned and immobile.

"Get off me, you interfering bitch!"

"And let you feed that *thing* with more death?" Tyr shrieked back. She tightened her lock on him. One flicker of her attention toward the two elemental figures, and he might squirm free. She shut her ears to the Djenne's untamed song, to the blood-lust in the Earth figure's rumble. At last Chandros collapsed, limp in the leverage of her hold. His muscles went slack, then papery beneath the iron of her grasp. She dared to look up—

To see *two* Djenne land-spirits like mirrors of the same self, both singing, both swaying in the whirlwind of their own wild natures. But which was Elarra, which the real land-spirit?

The nearer of the two figures turned, her robes swirling in a medley of silver and violet and dusty brown. Her hair flowed around her body like spun steel, like silk.

Her eyes were blind, white as clouds or the salt crusts on the alkali lakes. Without a backward glance, she strode toward the heart of the Wastes. Her feet passed through the tents of the Djenne without a trace of damage, but when they touched the squat stone temple, it crumbled to dust.

The remaining figure wavered in the silence of the other's passing, shrinking slightly. "Elarra," Tyr called. "Elarra, you've won. Come back to us!"

The Djenne spirit who had been Elarra sank to her knees, and Tyr could see the tears gleaming on her face. But she looked out through Elarra's eyes.

"Elarra?"

"Human flesh . . ." came the voice, soft and reedy as a desert breeze. "Cannot return . . ."

"You gave yourself to that thing—to stop Chandros?" Tyr gasped, fighting against her own tears.

Slowly the Djenne spirit nodded. The color was fast draining from her, brown and purple fading first, leaving tone upon tone of gray.

I thought no one else could hate him as I did . . . Elarra, trapped in the form of a land-spirit and forever barred from her own kind, was willing her own dissolution.

"No! There must be some other way!" Tyr scrambled to her feet. Somewhere among the Djenne Raiders, Hellsteed whickered, an echo to her own anguish.

"Where . . . is there a place for me . . . now?"

"At my side."

Tyr thought she saw the ghost of a smile pass over the figure's face before she slipped sideways, collapsing into ash. Tyr felt something inside her snap, something which even the Djenne devastation of her clan could not break. Over the years, she had wedded her soul to vengeance, and now it had been not her own swordskill but the heroism of the crippled witch which had ended Chandros. She buried her face in her hands and sank to the earth— the earth Elarra had sacrificed herself to cleanse.

Hellsteed's neigh reached her through blankets of pain. He reared, lashing out, as a Raider tried to seize his reins. Tyr spurred herself into action, picking up her sword where it lay in the dust. The Djenne parted before her, standing back as she swung on to the stallion's back. She wheeled him in a circle, searching the crowd for any sign of impending attack.

Pauce raised his voice. "The Warlord is dead."

"And the Djenne free to be as they were," Tyr replied.

He lifted one hand to show the brother-knife Elarra had returned to him. Another Raider, examining the ash where the witch's land-spirit had disintegrated, handed a small object to him. He held it out and approached Tyr.

"Go in peace," he murmured, and dropped Elarra's bloodstone ring into her hand.

Tyr felt a slight shock as the metal touched her skin, but she hid her reaction, guiding the black warhorse from the encampment with her grimmest warrior's face. It was not until they were well up into the hills that she allowed herself to respond to the thought which had formed in her mind as the concentrated energy of the bloodstone flooded through her. The words bore the unmistakable tang of Elarra.

"We make a good team, don't we?"

BLOODSTONE
by Mary Frances Zambreno

Under ordinary conditions the mention of a vampire would be enough to get a story an instant rejection slip. Vampire tales are pretty hackneyed by now, no?

No; at least not when they're like this one.

A good thief should be more careful of what she stole, Aeres thought as she rested on the dank straw of her cell. One blue eye and one brown-hazel considered the opposing wall philosophically. A good thief should be particularly careful not to get caught after accidentally stealing a vampire's bloodstone. Bad enough to wait here wondering if the judge would chop off her right hand or her left for stealing; worse contemplating how long it would take the vampire to track her and what he might do when he found her. Was it better to have one's throat ripped out before or after judicial dismemberment?

The room was suddenly very cold. She tensed, then deliberately half-lidded her eyes. Darkness gathered around her.

The vampire was standing just outside her cell door. Quiet as—as the moon, he'd come. More quietly than a thief.

He smiled ferally, revealing pointed teeth. She gulped and sat up quickly.

"I haven't got it," she said. One chance, now. Talk fast. "But I can get it back for you. For a price."

His hand touched the cell door. There were rings on three of the long fingers: sapphire, emerald, opal. Why couldn't she have stolen one of *those?*

"Where is it?" he said softly. His voice was cold and even. Remote.

"In the tabernacle of the city cathedral," she told him baldly. "If you go within a hundred paces of it, you'll melt like tallow."

The fingers clenched. He snarled soundlessly, and she drew back against the wall.

"You—gave the Eye of Rom—to the *church?*"

(The great red gem had its own name? Interesting.)

"Well, it wasn't *my* idea," she said, talking faster. "I got caught with it, and of course they recognized what it was. I could steal it back, though—if I could get out of this cell."

Flat, empty eyes measured her through the bars of the cell. "And once you had stolen it again, you would bring it to me?"

"Why not?" she said, drying sweaty palms on her tunic. "It's *yours,* isn't it? You could follow me wherever I took it, unless I managed to kill you. Which isn't likely, is it? If I'd known it was a bloodstone, I'd never have taken it in the first place—no matter how big and pretty it was! Now all I want is my freedom, and you can give me that."

She was talking too much, but it worked: he was listening. She held her breath.

"All very true," the cold voice said at last, contemptuously. "And very well. You may steal it—tonight."

Of course; they would be searching for the owner of the bloodstone now, and he would have to flee the city. Her theft had betrayed him.

"I can," she said, though he hadn't really asked a question. "They won't be expecting me tonight."

He pushed the door; it swung freely. "Bring it to me at the cloth-man's house, by the river. Ask for Lord Porphyro."

Aeres scrambled to her feet. "Um—my lord? There's still the little matter of the prison guards."

"They won't bother you," he said. He smiled again, and she shivered. Poor guards. "Bring me the Eye of Rom before dawn tomorrow, little thief, or you will find yourself wishing you were back in your cell awaiting punishment."

The darkness swirled. Almost before she could think, he was gone, leaving behind only a chill in the air and in her stomach. She wasted two whole minutes making sure he was gone before she risked slipping out into the prison corridor. By dawn tomorrow and it was full night now—not much time. Delicately she stepped over the one guard who sprawled in her way: he was snoring, so at least they weren't all dead. And at least she had the chance she'd been praying for.

The cathedral was almost empty and no more heavily guarded than usual. She waited in the shadows of the apse for her eyes to adjust to the candles. Singers practiced in the choir for dawn services and two priests waited to hear late confessions at the back, but no one was near the altar. Good. The tabernacle of the receptacle reflected mellow golden gleams down the right aisle. Now, to get close to it.

There were acolyte's robes in the vesting chamber at the rear of the church. Aeres appropriated a loose, hooded robe and a small broom, and began to sweep her way up the nave. A good thief worked with the materials at hand, and she wasn't likely to be questioned if she kept her head down and her hood up. She swept carefully, stopping now and again to push debris into dark corners and under floor coverings as a lazy servant would. At the altar rail, she sighed audibly—not that anyone was near enough to hear, but a good thief also stayed in character—before making her reluctant obeisance and beginning to sweep the steps.

She was into the side altar in a few moments. Her heart pounded as she leaned on her broom, apparently to consider the amount of work ahead of her. The main floor was rugged, so she had an excuse for starting at the back. Head bent, she made for the shadows. With one hand she felt inside the stolen robe for her kerchief: she wasn't a priest, to touch any bloodstone casually. Best be careful.

One arm slid inside the golden tabernacle doors, felt around among jeweled plate and other articles. Pity she didn't dare take more than the bloodstone. Ah! There it was. Pity too that she had to take *it* back to the vampire. She'd never stolen anything half so grand before. It was worth the risk, even if it had gotten her caught like that—

"Brother, what are you doing?"

She froze, fingers tight on the cloth-wrapped stone still inside the tabernacle. A rusty-black priest stood just at the corner of her vision, regarding her suspiciously.

"Dusting, father," she said, trying to keep her voice rough and low.

"*Inside* the tabernacle?"

"All surfaces gather dust, father," she replied, moving her arm within the golden door as if flicking away grime. Her fingertips skidded on a slick, faceted surface, and she flinched at the small shock that ran up to her shoulder.

"What are you holding, brother?" The priest grabbed her arm and pulled it out. Of course she should have opened her fist and let the stone fall still hidden, but somehow she didn't, couldn't. Her whole arm was tingling.

He forced her fingers open. The stone lay glowing dully on her palm, cradled against her bare fingers and putting the candles to shame. The priest gasped.

"The vampire's stone! Why—" Keeping his grip on her arm, he reached up to pull off her hood with his free hand. "The thief with the odd-colored eyes! But the watch had you safely jailed!"

Her eyes had always made her too easy to identify, but Aeres was past regretting that now. Her attention was fixed on the stone, which sat between her body and the priest's like a fat, setting sun. She didn't think she could let go of it if she tried.

"Take it, father," she said uncertainly. "It burns . . ."

"Of course it burns you," he snapped. "You are sinful, and a woman besides. Here, give it to me."

Not like that, she tried to say. It isn't burning like that. There's no pain, no pain at all. But it pulls at my soul. Cold fire—

The priest's thick hand covered the stone. Almost she cried out as he cut off her sight of it: for a moment she thought she had. But it was the *priest* who screamed aloud.

"Aiee!" he wailed, waving a smoking hand like a great fish as he capered about. Aeres watched, dazed. "Fire! Fire! It burns!"

Well, of course it burns you, one part of her mind said to him coldly. *You're a coward and a hypocrite and stupid to boot.*

The stone glowed lambent blue, like the heart of flame. Fascinated, she stared at the priest in the light it cast, Seeing right down to the core of his scruffy little soul. Her blue eye glowed with the gem; her brown eye darkened, blackened, burned. She watched in awe as he ran up the nave to a holy water font and thrust in his burning hand. Clouds of steam issued forth. A voice whispered: *He was weak.* The jewel honored strength and courage and intelligence, the understanding within her said, of which the priest evidently had little. And she had enough? It didn't hurt her.

Aeres lifted the gem; something sang in her blood. Yes, this stone could be used to drain a man of life and will as the vampire used it, but it was more, so much more. It called again, it called her, and now she could See clearly . . .

The priest was yammering hysterically. "Guards! The woman! The witch! *Guards!*"

She thrust the stone into the front of her tunic and vaulted over the altar rail all in one motion. The acolyte's robe hammpered her, so she stripped it off as she ran. Left was the chancel, and there she went, skittering around the benches like a waterbug on a calm lake. If she could get out into the streets—

The chancel door was locked. She swung around, but the way was already closed by the priest. His burned hand was black and dripping, and his eyes were wild. Behind him, the church filled up with guards.

"Witch," he hissed at her. "Undead, unclean—"

He thought *she* was the vampire? Well, of course— she'd touched the stone. She crouched before the priest, breathing heavily; the jewel was a great burning weight between her breasts. Through the stone she could See all the little veins running through the priest's body, See his heart pulse and beat, See the thoughts running in his feeble little brain. She studied him, then reached out with her mind and gave an odd little push. He crumpled. Dead? No—moaning and clutching his head. She gave him a Vision she found in the recesses of his own soul, and he writhed, gibbering. Then she was past him and away, out into the streets to find the hidden corners that every good thief knows as well as she knows her own name.

The jewel still burned, showing her things. She nearly stumbled: her pursuers were little flames in the night behind her, scared and anxious little flames. The city around her glowed with life; all she had to do was head for the cold and empty places, and hide. It was almost too easy.

She rested in one of the empty places briefly, pulling the stone out of her tunic to stare at it. What *was* this Eye of Rom? No ordinary bloodstone, surely. And no wonder the vampire valued it! Killing would be so easy with this gem for a weapon. It had been well-wrapped when she'd first taken it—did the vampire realize that she could touch the thing? No, or he would never have risked letting her steal it back for him. Or would he? He couldn't get into the cathedral himself, and the stone was still tied to him in its way. Would he, could he even consider letting her go now that she knew so many of its secrets? Now that was the question.

Slipping the rest of the way through the city streets was no harder than hiding had been, though she took care to avoid late travelers. She ignored the door she had been told to ask at, instead climbing to the one open and lighted window of the cloth-man's house. Now she hid in the curtains by the window alcove, and peered through the cracks in the cloth. The Eye of Rom she left where it was, uncovered. Yes, she could See the vampire: all dark-red blood, he was, pulsing sluggishly. His mind was impatient, busy with schemes: so. He didn't think she could do it, did he? Well, he would learn. Bracing herself, she pushed one velvet curtain aside.

"Good evening, my lord," she said formally. "Or should I say good morning?"

He whirled; she'd surprised him. Good.

"I told you to ask at the door, little thief," he said, straightening slowly. There was wine and a full cup on the table in front of him. How convenient. "You're early."

"Not very," she said, ignoring the first sentence. No sense telling him she'd wanted a private look. Let him wonder for a little. "It's nearly dawn."

"Ah, yes. Dawn." He smiled lazily, charmingly, terrifyingly. "Have you the stone?"

"Right here," she said. "It wasn't easy—"

"Give it to me." His voice cracked.

"Certainly, lord. It's why I came." Moving closer to the table, she reached inside her shirt. The stone winked on her palm. "Now what?"

He leapt as soon as he saw her touch the gem, but Aeres was ready. She flipped the contents of the wine cup into his face. He pulled his head back, closing his eyes instinctively and exposing his throat. With the jewel in her open hand, palm out, she caught him against the throat with it. His hands ravened against her arm, but she held firm, pushed forward, down. His breath came in gasps.

"Ah, vampire!" she said, laughing. "Did you really believe I would trust you tamely? I said I'd bring it to you, and I have, but the Eye of Rom is *mine!*"

His eyes started out of his head. "You—witch—"

"Who, me? Not hardly. The stone has all the power, lord, and a mind of its own. All I have is the strength to use it, and for my strength it chose me. You didn't count on that, did you?"

The jewel was blazing now, warming her arm to the shoulder. Her blood burned in her veins, and Porphyro sank uncomprehendingly to his knees. "You—can't—you haven't—"

She laughed again, exultantly. "Why not? The strongest will holds *this* bloodstone!"

She pressed harder; he withered. The world began to blur around her, echoing the startling blue flame of the stone. She could hear other voices in the gem now, crying out for vengeance. The powerful mind of the vampire beat against hers, struggling for release, but she was stronger. He'd underestimated her, had he? Most people did, but the stone knew better. Poor little sneak thief that she was, with just enough wit and will to survive—

It was enough.

When the flames cleared from her mind, Aeres was alone in the room with the stone still glowing faintly in her hand. Automatically she tucked it under her shirt—tried to calm her racing heart. This was done. And next? She was hungry and tired, but there were plans to make. She had to go somewhere to find out about the stone, what it was and what it could do. That later. Porphyro's mind was in the gem, trapped along with those he'd killed. Did that make her a vampire? She didn't think so—she'd tasted no blood flowing through the stone—but she'd have to find out. *Most* important for now was the strictly practical matter of getting safely out of the city with her prize.

First things first: food, and supplies for a journey.

"Well, Porphyro?" she said aloud, considering the room around her. "What shall we eat tonight? Or aren't you hungry?"

A spirit's unheard-scream of rage answered her. She smiled. No doubt it would take him a while to settle in. Exploring his mind was going to be fun, once he did. So was exploring this house and its possible riches, before she left the city. In fact, the whole world seemed to be turning into a thoroughly interesting place.

Now that she had an Eye to See it with.

SWORD SINGER
by Laura J. Underwood

In reading for this anthology I always get plenty of evidence that you shouldn't write much of a cover letter, because almost everything necessary should be on page one of your manuscript anyhow. Credits outside the field you are trying to sell in, like this beginner who cited credits from "Horse and Horseman" and assorted credits from newspapers and poetry, don't belong in your cover letter. I don't really need to know anything except your previous sales in the fantasy field. Everything else is irrelevant.

Mist crawled across the road that ran a winding track through the bog-infested ground. It crept about the legs of the iron-gray stallion who took nervous steps at the urging of his rider. Cloaked more against recognition than the weather, the man still managed to exude an air of lordliness as he sat proud in the saddle and forced the beast to follow the old road.

At length, he came to a ramshackle hut flanked by outbuildings. Dismounting from the jittery stallion, he drew a sword and scabbard off his saddle pack. He stared at them with awe and respect. He was interrupted when a swamp bird squawked sharply in the nearby trees, spooking some small vermin out of the brush. The horse started as it bolted between his legs, causing the beast to rear and stamp with fear. The man swore as the horse nearly trampled his leather-shod feet. He wrenched the reins to bring the stallion back under control, angrily cuffing the beast for good measure. Still cursing, the man tied the stallion to a standing pump. He grumbled to himself as he started for the door of the hut.

Light slithered out of the cracks around the wood. He could smell the acrid smoke of a log fire and the aroma of stew simmering over the flame. Clutching the sword and scabbard close, he threw a furtive glance at the fog and the darkness before knocking on the door.

Presently, the structure shook as someone slid the bolt. It opened, and a very young woman peered through the gap. She had soft brown eyes and a handsome face. Her hair was dark, braided down the back to her waist, but he could see the single streak of silver that broke its rich chestnut—the mark of her kind. She was dressed in a tunic and leather breeches.

"Can I help you?" she asked in a musical voice that almost sang its words.

"Are you the sword singer called Marta?" he asked.

"Yes," she replied.

"I have a task for you," he said.

"The smith is not here," Marta offered. "He has gone to the village for supplies, and I do not expect him to retun before tomorrow."

"I have no need of a smith," he assured her. "It's your services I require."

Marta frowned. "May I know of the task?"

"May I come in?" he responded in kind.

"I'm not supposed to entertain guests in the absence of my father."

The man sighed. "I have not come all these leagues to be entertained by a girl who reeks of sulfur and steel," he said, sounding fierce. "Do you not know me, girl?"

Marta shook her head. That only served to increase his ire.

"I am Brak Wolfson, Warlord of the North Hall!" he growled. "I need a sword singer, not a bedwarmer!"

Flinching, Marta refrained from making a retort. She had heard tales of this Brak Wolfson and his barbarous

North Hall. None of it was good, and his presence here was unnerving.

"You've come an awfully long way to seek a mere sword singer," she said, meekly avoiding his cruel gaze. "Are there none in the smithies of the North Hall?"

"Are you so well off, girl, that your father would approve of your refusal to give me the service I desire?" Brak retorted, gesturing to the rundown area around them.

"My task is that of all my kind." Marta replied, trying to keep the quaver out of her voice. "I sing to the sword as it is being forged, and since my father will not return before tomorrow . . ."

"And I told you that I had no need of the smith!" Brak said vehemently. "Only the sword singer!"

"Then, you have only to tell me your task, and I will let you know if I can perform it," she insisted.

His face hardened into a perturbed mask. "Very well," Brak said. "Some sword singers can heal the flaws of a blade badly forged. I have none in my hall who can do the task as well as the tales I hear of you, Marta. They say you have the power to heal a blade that is broken."

"Only if I was the singer whose voice forged it," she said, shaking her head. "If the sword was properly sung to by another at its forging, I cannot."

"It was not," he assured her. "It was badly forged, and without the song of a sword singer to aid it. It carries a flaw in its steel."

"How can you be sure it was not sung to at the forging?"

"I was there," Brak replied.

Marta sighed. This warlord, like many of his kind, was stubborn and rude. If her father were here, she might feel better about telling Brak to go back to his North Hall, but in the smith's absence, she felt uncertain. Her instincts told her to quickly bolt the door and refuse him entry. He was a powerful, large man, and she was a mere sixteen winters.

Not that she wasn't capable of fending for herself. After all, she was a sword singer. She'd had the best teacher—her own mother. She had once been sword singer to a smith in the North Hall, just as Marta's father had been his apprentice. They fell in love, but the smith was a jealous sort who refused to allow them to wed.

They had no choice but to elope, leaving the boundaries of the North Hall far behind in their desire to escape the old smith's wrath. Her father set out to start his own smithy, and it had not been an easy task. The old smith sent searchers for a time, forcing the young couple to set up a forge far from normal trade.

Out here in the swamp, they did business with travelers, until the new trade route was established. It was a longer route, but it was not so ugly as the swamp. In time, their business fell to almost nothing. Still, they had persevered through the hard times. Then, just a few years ago, Marta's mother had fallen ill and died, leaving a grieving husband and son, and a daughter born with "the kiss of the sword," the silver streak that marked her as a sword singer.

Marta was about to follow her instinct and close the door when Brak quickly drew a pouch from his belt. He jingled it within her sight. Marta almost gasped. She knew the clink of gold, and the pouch appeared hefty with the weight of it.

"This," said Brak, looking at her with a chilling gaze, "will all be yours—if you will sing to my sword and heal its flaw. There should be enough here to buy you a whole new smithy."

"So much," Marta said. "Why?"

"That, girl, is my affair. All I ask is for you to sing the flaw out of my sword."

Brak smiled, and Marta caught the malign mask behind it. She wanted to withdraw—but all that gold. Her father's anvil had cracked—the main reason he had gone to the village. He was hoping to scrape together enough commissions from the farmer folk to pay for a new one. Brak's gold would be a blessing.

"Well?" Brak asked, half teasing as he shook the bag.

Marta nodded in spite of the ill boding she felt. Brak practically pushed her aside as he swept into the hut. She quietly shut the door as he glanced around the room.

"So, your father leaves you alone, and you so young," he said in a coy fashion.

"I'm used to it since mother died," she replied. "But I'm not entirely alone. My brother should return soon."

A lie, she scolded herself. She had no idea as to when her older brother Hanson would return. Since he knew their father would not return until the morrow, Hanson had gone to visit the lady he was courting in secret. Father did not approve. The lady was wed to an old, fat merchant who traveled often.

Brak nodded. "We shall need to work quickly so I can be on my way. Here is the sword."

He held forth the scabbard. Marta took it, noting the finely wrought workmanship of the leather. She took hold of the ornate grip. The feel of it brought back the dreaded chill. Slowly, she drew the sword from its scabbard.

Marta almost held her breath when she beheld the most perfect blade she had ever seen. Her father was a great smith, but nothing he had ever made could match this. She could not bring herself to believe any smith could forge a blade as fine and keen without a sword singer to shape its power. She turned it over in her hands, trying to ignore the deathly cold it exuded.

"Where is the flaw?" Marta asked.

"Inside," Brak said.

Marta frowned. "How do you know that?"

"I had it examined after forging because something was not right with the weight of it. The sword singer in my own smithy found the flaw, but she was not able to heal it."

"And you expect me to be able to do so?" Marta said.

"One who can heal a broken blade should have no trouble," Brak insisted. "My own sword singer said so."

Marta was not sure. She sighed and carried the sword through the door that led to the smithy. Close to the forge was her magic circle. Brak followed her into the room. He stood back in the shadows to watch as Marta prepared the ritual taught to her by her mother. She placed the sword on the etchings in the middle of the circle and took her place at the northern end. Sitting with her legs crossed, she took several deep breaths and closed her eyes. When she felt calm within herself, she began to sing a song of warding that would close the circle around her and keep out bad influences. She felt the flux of power moving in and the air around her, gently closing the circle. Marta changed her melody, directing it toward the sword.

The sword began to glow as her magic forced it to rise. Its point aimed itself at the earth that birthed its ores, using her song, she called to the spirit of the sword, and it responded. Waves of cold were emitted by it. Marta scowled, but she kept on singing. The steel seemed reluctant to reveal its flaw. She intensified her song into one of true seeing, and as she did, the sword gave up its secret. With her mental eye, she could see the location of its flaw.

Marta felt the cold increase. The flaw was not an ordinary one. It ranged deep in the metal, a hairline crack from tang to tip, as if the forger had purposely done something to the metal. Marta shivered. Why would anyone place such a flaw in the steel on purpose?

She let her mind's eye rove the length of the blade as she continued to sing her song of true seeing. Designs were visible now, glowing where none had been. Marta saw runes of an unknown nature. The cold seemed to emanate from them.

Carefully, she changed her song to the special one of healing. Starting with the tip of the sword, she moved her mind up the crack a few inches at a time as she used her song to remeld the metal. Almost all of her concentration went into the work. A very small part of herself remained detached and curious. Why those runes? Why such a crack? Why the cold? Why was Brak inching closer? Why . . .

"Too many questions," a voice chided. *"Heal me and be done! I've work of my own to do!"*

Marta had kept her eyes closed, but now she opened them and looked right at the sword. An essence was writhing about the blade. Malicious eyes now gazed at her from stones in the hilt.

The sword was alive!

"Yes, little one," it whispered. *"I do, indeed, live. Now, stop wasting precious time! I've work to accomplish!"*

"What work?" Marta's mind asked as her song carried on with the healing. She was halfway done with it.

"What work is there for a sword?" it replied. *"I was wizard-forged to kill a man who cannot die by natural means."*

"What man?" Marta demanded.

"What does it matter to you, girl!" the sword rudely retorted.

"I must know if I am to be able to heal you completely."

"Then join me in treason, girl, for by healing me, you make yourself a party in the death of the High King!"

Marta's song faltered. The High King was the magical ruler of the realm. There were rumors that he had roused the wrath of several Warlords by insisting they pay more taxes while the poorest peasants should pay none. But he was well warded and guarded by many magics. Yet, she could feel the power in this sword and knew now the meaning of the runes. They were death glyphs, charged with the power to destroy its intended. Yes, such a sword as this could kill the High King and throw the realm into the hands of tyranny, were it not for the flaw in its making. That could cause its wicked magic to go awry.

Marta ceased her song, allowing the sword to fall. Its point pierced the floor of the forge deeply enough to make it stand upright. The eyes glared.

"Traitor!" Marta called aloud, scrambling to her feet.

Brak was already charging into the circle, scattering the magical protection with his anger. He wrenched the sword out of the floor. Marta tried to run for the door, but the Warlord blocked her route of escape. She backed away in fear as he pointed the sword at her.

"So," he said. "You have learned the truth—just like the last sword singer."

"You had it wizard-forged to kill the High King!" she blurted.

"Yes—and it will succeed now that you have healed its only flaw. The fool who forged it was loyal to the High King. He secretly gave it the flaw as the wizard was giving it life and purpose. Only I didn't find out until the forging was complete and the wizard was testing it. The damned sword killed the wizard of its own accord, and I knew then that something had gone wrong.

"The flaws pervert the purpose of the sword," Marta said as she backed into the cracked anvil.

"Clever," Brak said. "The last sword singer found out much sooner and threatened to give away the plot. I took her life with this sword—just as I must take yours now!"

"No!" Marta cried.

He raised the sword high to deal a death stroke. Marta reacted out of fear. She threw herself over the anvil as the sword descended. Landing on the floor, she filled her lungs and threw back her head to sing one long, powerful note.

The sword gave a shriek as the sound touched the remaining inch of its flaw near the tang. Its screech caught Brak in mid-swing. The sword literally tore itself from his hands and struck the surface of the anvil. Its blade shattered, sending large and small shards in different directions.

Marta ducked, covering her head with her arms. Some needles of metal pricked her and she cried out, but her own pain was overshadowed by a guttural howl of agony. Marta raised her head in time to see Brak keel over. A large shard of the blade was lodged in his chest.

Tears ran down her face as she struggled to regain her footing. The shards of the sword were everywhere. She could feel a few small ones jabbing into her arm and shoulder. Sobbing, she began to remove them. Her hands shook from the painful task.

All around her, the cold permeated the air. It swirled close to her, then it fled as though the essence that gave life to the evil sword had been freed.

Foolish Brak. He should have realized. A sword singer good enough to heal a broken blade would also have the power to break it.

STORMBRINGER
by Steve Tymon

Usually I reject a story out of hand if a writer can't spell "sorcerer," figuring that if he can't spell a word so intimately connected with sorcery, he doesn't know enough about it for his writing to be worth much.

However I can, and occasionally do, break all my own rules if the story really grabs me.

Then why have rules at all? Well, you should see some of the stuff I get. So if somebody couldn't be bothered to learn the basic rules for submitting manuscripts, why should I be bothered with their stories? It isn't as if the rules were so hard to learn; every high school worth its salt now requires students to submit term papers typed and double-spaced. When I'm editing an anthology, I read more than most teachers, and I value what's left of my eyesight.

This story grabbed me from the first page.

Her name was Winter, and she came in on the storm, a woman wearing armor of darkest black, riding a winged horse like shadow across the lightning-cloaked clouds, thunder echoing all around. She brought with her weapons of magic—a sword of purest light, and a jewel of great power that was warm against her, concealed against her chest. And, too, she kept a dagger of sharpened glass, lacking any magic at all, but thin and transparent and very sharp, hidden beneath the armor of one arm. And last, she brought light into the darkness—a simple magic, the slight glow surrounding her—for this was a place of perpetual night where the stormswept winds called out her name: dead souls, some she had known as friends, calling to her in warning, telling her to run, to hide, to turn away from the greater darkness ahead, but she would not. It was far too late. Already *he* would know of her coming, of that she was certain, and so she rode through the darkness and the rain, on toward the great fortress of Akmar and the sorcerer-king who waited there. After ten long years, she was coming home.

The usurper saw her, of course. He had always seen her. The first time he had touched his stepdaughter, the vision had come—something about a dark battle between them, nothing more, yet he did not fear. He was one of the greatest of sorcerers in an age of great and powerful sorcerers, was Merikor, and he knew full well that no mere child could ever defeat him. And, so knowing, unfearful of the vision, he had committed the atrocity that would bring it all to pass. And now it had come back to him at last, borne on wings of shadow, a spot of brilliance on the edge of a storm, bringing things of power. Confident, he made ready to battle, to claim his prize, preparing his trap.

And above, circling, the stormbringer forced back the rain and the clouds that she might see the fortress below. What she saw bore little resemblance to what she had once known: the walls were cracked and shattered and had grown thick with vines, the crumbling stones were much darker than she remembered, and there, in the courtyard, was a small tomb, a recent and inappropriate addition to the ruins around it. Even without reading the inscribed runes, she knew who it was, yet she shed no tears—her mother had been lost to her long before her departure, long before that ugly night, and the act had only confirmed it. Rather than sympathy or support, her mother had blamed her for what had happened, and even now, after all the years, she still felt the anger and the horror of the moment, all the pain of betrayal. But her anger had given her the strength to live and the will to seek and learn the ways of sorcery, and in that she had been successful. Yet even as she grew in power and skill, she knew she would never equal *him*, not if she were to live a thousand lifetimes. But, of course, in time, she realized that was the key.

She urged Abraxas downward. The stallion's hooves struck sparks against the cold stone of the courtyard, and then he cantered to a stop, folded his wings, shook his head and mane, and waited for her command. Dismounting, she whispered a word in his ear—he would stay until she returned, or until her death, whichever came first—and then she turned to the keep, to the heavy, locked doors. Crossing the courtyard, the rain falling around her but *never* ever touching her, she paused before them and gestured slightly with one hand. The thick wooden planks burst into flame and vanished. She stepped inside.

It was not at all as she had expected.

Within was a vast hall, cheerfully lit with many torches, a roaring fireplace. Rich tapestries decorated the walls, and by the light from the windows, one might have assumed it was a bright and sunny day outside instead of the storming darkness that served for reality. Beneath her boots, there was a thick carpet, and before her, a long and ornately carved table, piled high with fine meats and fruits on silver platters. There was wine in crystal carafes and goblets of purest gold from which to drink it, and even the tablecloth was woven of the finest silks, interspersed with gold thread and the occasional jewel. In all, it was a setting for the most special of occasions, a setting for a festival or celebration.

"Either one will do," came a man's voice. At the far end of the table, a mist coalesced out of the air, took form, and became a bearded, seemingly-young man who settled himself comfortably into the tall, thronelike chair that was there. Her stepfather smiled sweetly at her.

"You could call it a celebration, I suppose," he continued, "for you have returned, and I intend to have you again as I once did. Surely a festive occasion."

"As diseased as ever," she answered, drawing nearer the table. She shielded her mind more thoroughly—no more of that—then gestured with one hand. There was a sparkle of light, and in her grasp, her sword appeared, its light strangely subdued by the magics in the air. "But here, I'll cut out the cancer."

He laughed, the sound echoing in the vast hall.

"Winter," he said, speaking her name, "after all these years, still as foolish as ever. Do you honestly think you could best me in any form of combat, either by steel or spell?"

He did not wait for her answer, but instead stood and smoothed his red silk robes.

"No," he continued, answering for her, "you will not win. I can't think of what ever possessed you with the idea that you might."

She shook her head. "You still stink of arrogance," she said. "I'm hardly as weak as you seem to think."

He nodded slightly at that. "Perhaps not."

He looked past her and made a slight throwing gesture with one hand. From somewhere behind her came a brief flash of light. Without turning, she knew that the doorway was gone, that a wall of solid stone had now replaced it, sealing her in. There would be no escape.

"It's the storm, I suppose you mean," he continued. He looked at her. "So tell me, what thing have you brought with you that has such power, such magics that it can disturb the very elements with its passage?"

"My secret," she answered, smiling slightly.

"Indeed?" He shrugged. "No matter. You can afford me few surprises, child, and as for secrets, you have none from me, not even your body."

Her grasp tightened on her sword, her lips grew thin.

"Yes," he went on, "I see you remember. You were always better looking than your mother, and certainly the more entertaining in bed. Shall we try it again?"

She slammed the sword hilt down hard against the table. Cloth, wood, silver and food all vanished with a flash of light. There was nothing between them but a length of floor and carpet.

"We shall try something, yes," she agreed, "but it won't be quite what you expect."

He stifled a bored yawn.

"As you will," he said, and then he moved one hand in front of himself. As he did, his robes became metal, blood red in color, and in one hand, a sword of darkest shadow appeared—a death-blade, whose merest touch would kill.

"You still have a chance to surrender," he warned. "After all, I would not prefer to kill you. But once the battle is begun—"

"Once the battle is begun," she finished for him, "I will send you to join my mother."

He laughed again. "Fool, little fool," he said, though his words now seemed strangely loud, almost thunder. "Like her, you choose to die. So be it."

There came a final flash of light from the torches, and then they were gone, as were the tapestries and the fireplace, even the fortress walls. They stood on a vast and empty plain, beneath a starfilled sky. And then, in the starlit darkness, he came toward her.

She retreated, making the quick gestures that would bring additional light, more than was afforded to her by her sword. Around them both, a slight green glow sparkled into existence. But what it revealed was no longer human.

There, within the armor, staring at her with hellish red eyes, was a skull, an image of death. And of the armor itself, it now seemed ancient and corroded, with bone showing through the gaps. It raised its sword to strike.

And she brought hers forward, blindingly fast.

The two blades met with the sound of thunder. Fire leaped at the contact, and lightning suddenly blazed around them, surrounding them in blinding light, yet neither gave ground. They stood, motionless, blades locked in the midst of flame. For the moment, it appeared they were evenly matched. And then, slowly, inexorably, he forced her down.

"No!" she shouted, then let slide her blade. The other crashed to the ground. Winter turned and slashed down, but it was too late. With a clap of thunder, her blade struck the earth, the ground shaking with the impact, but he was already gone.

"You're stronger than I remember," he said, watching from nearby. "Quicker too. Evidently you draw power from another source."

She said nothing, but only turned to face him, her sword raised and ready. He shrugged.

"Be silent, then," he continued. The skull grinned at her. "But here, let's be fair. I'll add more strength of my own."

And then he rushed at her, a sudden blur in the darkness.

The swords clashed, shadow against light, and the thunder once more echoed about them. Though Winter blocked the attack, the force was such that she was hurled through the air, crashing to the ground some distance away.

He did not give her a moment to recover. He charged after her, his sword raised for a killing stroke, but this time it was she who dodged and brought up her blade. The edge slashed across her stepfather's blood red armor, cutting deep.

He gave an inhuman shriek, and a deep darkness seemed to flow from the wound. But to Winter's horror, he turned to continue the attack, his strength and speed undiminished.

The blades met again, and the flames erupted about them. Winter fell back, both from surprise and the force of the blow, and the usurper seized upon the moment to press his attack.

He struck, and again, and each time, she retreated before the fury of the assault. Her counterblows had no effect, and for the first time since she had arrived, she began to fear, to doubt her plan.

Desperate, she called forth a death spell, that which could shatter worlds, one of her strongest weapons, and hurled it full force at her enemy.

Unharmed, her stepfather began to laugh.

"So at last we go to spells," he said, tossing aside the black blade. It spun upward, sparkled and vanished. "As you will, then."

Reaching up with skeletal hands, he called down the darkness from the sky, from the empty places between the stars.

And the shadows came down, like claws, black and long, covering the entire sky above, the talons spreading as if to pluck her from the ground. Retreating, she threw her full strength into a spell of brilliance, far beyond the dim green radiance that surrounded them. There came a burst of light, blindingly bright, and this she sent upward—a counter-force, a beam of purest energy.

It struck the descending shadows—now glistening with scales like the claws of a great dragon—and they exploded bursting into a cascade of sparks and flame.

But, amid the falling flames, her stepfather only laughed.

"Excellent, daughter, for a first move." He raised his arms over his head, as if pulling something from the very ground itself. "But how will you do against this?"

And the ground itself reached up from below, tendrils made of iron and stone. They closed tight over Winter before she could move, and a moment later, where there had stood a woman remained only a pile of stone.

He resumed his proper form, then sighed. His temper, his damnable temper. He remembered the sweetness of her body, as it had once been. The regret was that he would not be able to touch her again.

"A shame," he whispered, "tragic loss."

But, as he began the gesture that would bring him back to his fortress, back to his world, flames suddenly lanced down from the sky, drawn from the myriad stars and suns, and fire exploded over him. From somewhere came Winter's laughter.

"Did you think it could end so easily?" she said, a mocking voice from the flames. "How weak you must think I am."

He did not answer. Instead, he made quick, desperate gestures, yet the fire continued to burn. Already it glowed white hot.

"It won't go out so easily," said Winter, "or have you discovered that?"

"Enough!" he shouted.

And the world was gone. So too the flames, and even the stars.

They were in a darkened place, where light played like wind, where no substance was underfoot. They were in a place yet virgin of life, unformed, a place without time and boundary—a universe before its beginning, in another time. Winter was but a shadow among shadows, and she could sense him too. And then there came his laughter, this time echoing, as if in a large and empty room.

"We duel, then, in darkness primordial," he said, unseen. "And from this place, daughter, there will be no leaving, for either of us, until it is decided, for this is all there is—for you, for me, for this moment. This is all."

Winter hesitated, then made the decision. She pulled forth the jewel from around her neck, a thing of brilliant light. It had cost her much to find it, the lives of many to obtain it, but for its price, there was no greater weapon. She reached into it with her mind, felt its power of life, of light and creation, and it was upon this that she drew, that she conjured, that she performed her greatest spell.

The darkness coalesced quickly, the years whispering by in seconds, eons gone in the merest of moments. The first fire was begun.

"No!" Winter heard her stepfather shriek. "No!"

And yet it went on. There was a blinding explosion and the darkness was filled with millions of lights, expanding outward, growing. The first stars were born, and then others. The galaxies began to form, and all the worlds within. She felt the first beginnings of life—indeed, it was she who caused them—and all the cosmos blossomed like a flower on the first touch of Spring's rain. The darkness was cast aside, and where nothing had been before, now there was substance.

And still it went on.

Other worlds exploded into being, the fires sparkling across the vast darkness and forming into spirals and spheres and irregular shapes, and time rushed forward, ever faster. And, through all of it, she was the creator, the duelist, the Goddess who brought light and life and called down the winds of time themselves. It was her greatest spell, the very antithesis of darkness, of death, of *him,* and she was not pleased, for it seemed he could not stop her.

And then realized that he would not want to.

Winter heard the mocking, victorious laughter of her stepfather. Silent, she watched the trap close around her, the stars growing red. All that she had done, all that she had created, was plagued by the subtle poisoning of entropy. All would collapse and fall away in time, and to win, he needed only to wait. And so he did as the stars exploded, vanished, or simply faded to black and chill. Time whispered on, millennia upon millennia rushed past, and when it was done, the spell was ruined, gone, and all was as it was before, empty and lifeless and dark.

And through it all, the laughter continued, echoing, echoing, until the last stars winked out. The duel was finished, the weapon exhausted. There was no more.

There came a flash of light. They were again within the great hall, the table returned, as were the tapestries and all the rest. It was as it had been before, save that Winter was weak from the effort, while her stepfather seemed not disturbed at all.

He stepped forward and yanked the jewel from her neck. Holding it up before himself, he smiled.

"A Jewel of Creation," he said. "Precious rare. I am surprised that you found it, and that you knew how to use it."

She said nothing. Defeated, she kept her head bowed, staring at the ground.

"Ah," he whispered, touching her chin. His hands were ice cold. "Such sorrow, such loss in your look."

He forced her to look up at him.

"But if it's any consolation," he went on, "I knew you had the jewel from the first. I recognized its power, even though you tried to conceal it from me, and so I set the trap. You've only yourself to blame for stepping into it."

And then he paused. His smile was not a pleasant thing. "And now it seems I rape you again, my daughter," he finished.

He grabbed her armor. In his hands, it tore like tissue, exposing one breast. He reached for her.

And it was then she moved: her slender dagger, clear like ice, sharper than the sharpest razor, slid into her hand from its concealment, and before he could react, she sank it deep into his heart.

Stunned, he tried to speak, staring at her, but he could not. His mouth moved, but blood only bubbled out, and then he fell to his knees. She followed him down.

"I never intended to win," she said, coldly watching his death, "not with sorcery. I knew I could not, not against you, though I knew you expected me to fight on those terms."

He was shaking now, trembling. He managed to shake his head. The question remained in his eyes.

"I was your weakness," she answered. "That, and your own arrogance. I knew you would want to repeat your crime."

She suddenly yanked free the dagger. Blood spattered. "And I knew you would never expect something so simple as a knife," she continued, "something so obvious as a weapon without magic. That was *my* trap."

And then paused, and added, smiling coldly, "But then, you've only yourself to blame for stepping into it."

And slashed open his throat.

It was a special blade, made of a special glass. It parted flesh like air, bone like water. Her cut nearly took off his head. Certainly, it ended his life.

He fell forward, into her arms, and a moment later, there was only dust and his empty robes. She had always suspected he had lived far longer than any mortal man should—one of the benefits of sorcery—and now it was confirmed, now that the ages had returned to him at last.

Slowly, she picked up the jewel, then stood and tossed aside the knife. It shattered against the floor, a delicate crystal sound. Turning, she waved one hand and the door returned. Beyond, outside, Abraxas still waited, his head tucked under one black wing as if to hide from the falling rain. He looked up as she stepped through the door.

She started toward him, but paused when she saw the small tomb, there in the courtyard. She reached out to gently touch the rainswept stone—it was horribly cold—and for a moment, just a moment, she allowed the tears to come at last. All the distant memories that went with them swept over her: something about a child, something about a happier time, something about someone she only vaguely recognized, a stranger. She wondered, could it be her?

And then, still crying, she turned quickly and pulled herself up onto the winged stallion, urging him forward and up into the night until they were merely a small point of light that circled once, twice—

And then vanished into the raging storm, never to return.

SORCERESS OF THE GULLS
by Dave Smeds

"Sorceress of the Gulls" was one of those stories which came in too long for this anthology, but I knew the author was sufficiently professional to cut it. He had, after all, sent me the excellent "Gullrider" for SWORD AND SORCERESS IV.

I seem to be harping a lot on professionalism in this set of introductions; I deal with so many amateurs and their amateur effusions that it's a relief to get something which is thoroughly professional.

What is the big difference between the professional and the amateur? I have heard many criteria; but mine is that the professional knows what he or she is doing, and if the amateur does things right, it's a lucky accident.

G an found the baby lying in the snow where her mother had left her.

Swaddled in a single thin cloth, the infant wailed and shivered, startling the jackdaws in the heavily weighted pines above. Snow from the birds' departure settled down on her tiny face, white traces that melted instantly, running off her cheeks like tears.

Gan scooped the child up and nestled her awkwardly against his body, unsure just how to hold her. Newborn. Two or three days old. A little blue in the lips and the tip of the nose, but not so cold that she had been harmed.

Placing his back to the wind, he hurriedly unwrapped her, examined her, and covered her again. No deformations. A fine, healthy child. Cast off, then, simply because she had the witchglow.

The baby's cries stilled as Gan held her close. A nimbus of energy hovered in the air around her small body, a pale lavender radiance almost invisible in the daylight. She exuded magic as conspicuously as the geysers of the nearby hills exuded clouds of steam into the crisp winter air. The wizard could not help but rouse from his den, even on such an inclement day as this, and seek out the source of that power.

No death so young for this one, Gan vowed. Such talent was not to be squandered. He would raise her, even if it meant the end of his bachelorhood.

But first things first. She needed a wet nurse. And even before that, a name; wood spirits were known to steal babies without one.

"Kari," he murmured, testing the sound of it. Pleased, he smiled and started back the way he had come.

Kari virtually skipped down the path to her home. Crossing the small brook that trickled past the cottage, where her father grew riverwort and moly herbs for his potions, she danced across the stepping stones and flicked her bare toe impishly into the water. She sailed into her father's workroom. Gan looked up from the yellowed parchment on the table and raised a craggy, graying eyebrow.

"You've the look of a lobsterman who's just caught a rare blue for his dinner pot," he said.

"It's nothing," she said smugly. "It's just been a good day."

He marked his place with a conch shell paperweight. "Did you go up to the oaks and gather splayed mushrooms as I asked?"

At his tone, Kari's exuberance dwindled like a cooking fire doused with sand. "Of course I did. Here." She held out her basket.

He peered inside. "These are hardly enough for the elixir. You could have gathered them in half an hour. What kept you so long?"

Kari sighed. She was almost eighteen. Why did he insist on treating her like a child? "I stopped in the village."

"Ah. To see that boy of Ortor's again?"

"His name is Ren. And yes, I saw him."

Gan's expression blackened. "Sit down."

Ignoring the stool, Kari plopped straight down on the floor amid the detritus of the past month's potion-making, incense-burning, and spellweaving. "I'm sitting."

"This has got to stop. You've made a mockery of your studies all summer."

"I didn't know being a magician meant being celibate," Kari replied. "It wasn't that way when you were my age, from what I'm told."

He glared at her. "I didn't sacrifice all these years so that you could run off with the first young buck who tumbles you."

Not again. How many times had she heard the word "sacrifice?" "Pa! I *love* Ren."

"You can't expect a common fisherman's son to understand your calling. He'll just want you to have his babies and keep his house."

"Well, that would be my choice, wouldn't it?"

"I'll not have it," Gan declared. "You were meant for more than that." He gestured at the basket. "Now go get me more mushrooms."

Kari opened her mouth, but stopped before speaking. She shuffled out, head down.

Kari meandered along the beach, heedless of the incoming surf, even when it rolled up above her ankles and soaked the hem of her singlet. The coast was deserted. Most of the able-bodied adults of the nearby hamlets were out at the Deeps for two weeks, harvesting the annual run of swiftfish. Including Ren. He had left the day after her argument with her father. She had a fortnight in which disobedience was not an issue, and an uneasy sort of peace reigned.

Gan had always expected much of her. But why should she slave away memorizing incantations when magic came so easily to her? She'd taken only a month to learn to weird iron from its ore. She'd learned to charm fleas out of her bedding on only the second try, and got them to jump into the hearth flame on the tenth. In a few years she would outstrip Gan entirely. He had said as much. Why drill so intensely that she had no life outside of wizardry?

"You have the potential to do things no sorcerer in living memory has done," her father would say. But he never specified what those things were. As she had grown older she had realized he himself didn't know the answer, except to assure her that she had not done them yet.

In one sense he was right. She had neglected her studies. She had ruined the charm on a fishhook simply because she'd forgotten to rinse it in salt water before she renewed the spell. She'd learned the procedure at age ten; there was no excuse for such a mistake other than lack of attention. And she'd made a hundred bumbles like it in the past year. Gan was right about Ren's character, too. Had it not been so, the scolding would never have stung her.

At the headland she climbed the bluff, stood amid the succulents and spiny heather, and gazed out at the sea. The surf lapped calmly at the shore. Mild weather. The swiftfish would be running thick. The wind pressed her singlet tightly against her calves, drying the damp hem, whipping it with lighthearted vigor.

At least the sand crabs and kelp pods kept her company without judging her. But it was not enough. She wished the wind would take her up. She wanted to fly away.

A shadow crossed over her. She ducked. A great gull passed over, suspended on the thermals of the bluff, a vast, milk-white bird. Two more followed, distinguishable by the fringe of gray feathers at the edges of their wings. They landed a few hundred paces up the cove.

Kari watched in fascination. Great gulls normally visited the mainland when storms drove them in. Seldom had she had the chance to stand on a fine, clear day and observe them at her leisure.

The three birds perched on the sand, beaks high, catching scents in the breeze. Occasionally they paced, or snapped in irritation at the relatively tiny sea gulls that hovered about, but for the most part they stood still, as if to proclaim their authority over the shore.

The legends said that Persu of the southern kingdom rode a great gull to his cloud city, where he went to dwell with the Queen of the Mists. Other accounts told of daring men or clever sorcerers who caught and rode the creatures. The shipwright's aged uncle even claimed to have witnessed a man ride a gull past the village one stormy afternoon.

Suppose she rode one? That would impress Gan. Furthermore, a great gull could probably fly her out to the Deeps to wave at Ren and have her back before the sun set.

In moments she decided to try.

She had once charmed an owl out of its nest so that she could gather a tail feather. All birds were vulnerable to the same sort of enchantment. She drew off her necklace. Freshly polished, the silver chain and blue quartz pendant gleamed in the sunshine. No gull, large or small, would resist such a lure, given the right prompting.

She advanced boldly, striding in plain sight down the beach. The gulls cocked their heads and eyed her with a caution incongruous to such intimidating creatures. She cast the glamour outward, toward the pure-white bird.

The gull responded to the spell more slowly than owls or household fowl, but gradually it focused one eye on the flashing trinket. It stiffened. Its companions, by contrast, shuffled ever more nervously. As she stepped into the first of the footprints they had left in the sand, both gray-tipped birds launched into the air, screeching. The white one waited placidly.

Kari hesitated at the edge of its shadow, daunted. She waved the necklace in an oval motion. At first, the gull's head circled in synchronization, then it stilled. She let out a pent-up breath and put the jewelry back around her neck. If the spell was true, the gull was completely mesmerized.

She licked dry lips, calmed herself, and took a running leap. She clambered up and settled onto the gull's shoulders. Its rapid, avian pulse beat against her thighs. She gathered a thick knot of feathers in each hand and held tight.

Now the real challenge. In order to fly, she had to release a small part of the glamour. Otherwise the gull would remain immobile.

She weakened the enchantment. The gull waited calmly.

She frowned, and let go of a fraction more. The gull merely blinked.

Kari refused to dilute the spell further. Instead, she slapped it, shouting at the top of her lungs. When that had no effect, she released her leg-lock and kicked its throat with her heels.

Suddenly the bird shot toward the water, wings pumping. Kari barely seized hold in time to avoid somersaulting off. Composure shattered, she lost control of the glamour.

The gull climbed, spurred by updrafts, and let out an ear-splitting screech. Kari hung on in desperation. How could something so big move so fast? She tried to cast her charm again, but the bird was far too agitated to submit to her wiles.

The gull veered inland, bucking. One of Kari's legs slid free. They rose still higher, then suddenly dipped. Feathers tore loose in Kari's hands. She teetered, beginning to slide off.

Fear calmed her. No time to grab hold elsewhere. Instead, she probed within for some bit of sorcery, some inspiration, that would keep her in flight.

Something exploded inside her, a surge of power unlike any she had ever felt before. For a moment she thought she had found her source of rescue.

But her fall continued, outward, off her mount. As she slid completely clear the gull whipped its head around and slashed. The tip of its beak caught her along the side of her abdomen. Blood fanned into the air.

Amid the pain, sparks flew. A burst of eldritch energy converged on the wound, humming furiously, then the sound was buried beneath her scream.

Time held still. Below waited a dense grove of fir trees. Above, the gull was framed against the sky, white on blue, its head thrown back in victory.

Then she was hurtling toward the earth, wind clutching at her singlet. The air sent cold knives into her open flesh, but she no longer felt the pain. She lacked the time to pay attention to it. She needed a particular spell, and she had to remember it correctly on the first try.

She cast it. In response, the branches of the fir trees wove together, forming a series of nets in the path of her fall.

She struck the uppermost branches. They scarcely affected her momentum. The second level held her for an instant, the third a bit longer. The fourth slowed her speed in half. The fifth and lowermost bower accepted her, cradled her, and gently deposited her on a bed of twigs and needles. Her necklace, thrown off during the tumble, landed beside her ear.

The pain returned. She blacked out.

In Kari's dream, a great kraken rose up out of the ocean and captured her. The more she struggled, the tighter the tentacle squeezed, the greater her suffering. *How strange that I can feel pain while I'm dead,* she thought. That told her she was dreaming, and she awoke.

She ached down to her spine. Bandages bound her precisely where the phantom tentacle had been wrapped. Her hair itched as if it had not been washed in many days, and she reeked with the odor of fever sweat. Weak dawn light filtered around the edges of the shutters.

Her father sat beside her bed, head bowed, great lines under his eyes, hair unkempt. When she stirred, he glanced up, displaying bloodshot eyes. She had never seen him look so old.

"You found me," she murmured. "You healed me."

"Yes."

"How long?" she murmured.

"Four days."

He did not have to say more for her to know he had fought battles in that time. She wanted to raise her head, but she lacked the strength.

"Rest," Gan said. For the first time, she noticed the haunted quality in his expression.

"What is it? Did the healing go wrong?"

"No, you're out of danger." He swallowed. "Kari," he began. "Gerryjill . . ."

The latter was her adult name, to be given to her when she came of age. He had never addressed her with it before. She fought off a wave of exhaustion, knowing she needed to listen.

"Life is too short," he said. "Live yours however you will. As a magician, as a fish wife—whatever you choose. I'll not stand in your way."

Three nights later, Kari couldn't quiet the impulse to rise out of her bed, though her body protested every time she twisted or stretched. She dreamed of the beach, of breakers bursting on the rocks and kissing her with salty foam.

A storm was coming. She knew it without question, though magicians usually did not acquire such a sense of the weather until half a century of fog, gales, and humid summers soaked nature's secrets into their bones. Good reason to stay in bed. As if getting well were not justification enough.

But after her father had retired, Kari rose and struggled into her clothing. Pain spread out from her suture in a knifelike wave. She shuddered, held still until the discomfort eased, then surreptitiously glided out the door.

Gray Moon rode at zenith, nearly full, flooding the coastal landscape with its cool beams. Farther west a waxing Pearl Moon added its modest glow, cratered face partly obscured by the incoming clouds. Kari easily picked out the path to the shore.

With each step, her body shook. Not with suffering, though that was there. Rather, her extremities tingled as if she could not contain the energies she held within. Her limbs were buoyed up, the fatigue of convalescence temporarily banished. If she turned and tried to go the other way, the weariness resumed. Slow and painful as her progress might be, she could not refuse the call. There was something waiting for her at the ocean's edge. Mouth dry, wound throbbing, she inched her way around the final bend, bringing the beach into broad view.

The white gull stood on the sand, feathers tufted by the breeze, its form almost luminescent against the backdrop of dark water.

Its gaze locked on her. She had no doubt it was the same one she had tried to ride. She stepped back, intimidated by its awesome, regal stance, but the bird did not move. A gust blew in, and she experienced an avian urge to rise up, to fly, to hasten ahead of the imminent storm.

The emotion felt like her own. Yet it was obviously that of the gull. Her terror doubled. The gull's tongue darted out, as if tasting again the blood it had drawn from her days before.

As before, a subtle message infiltrated her, again very birdlike, vague yet comprehensible. The gull was asking why it was there. She realized then that it had not come by choice. Once the storm had brought it inland, it had been pulled to the beach just as she had.

Kari was at a loss for a response, but the plaintiveness of the request quieted her panic. She hesitated, then held up her necklace. "Hello," she murmured, and tried to project the greeting toward the gull. As an afterthought, she illuminated the pendant with a bit of harmless witchfire.

The bird stepped back, alarm vivid in its deep black eyes. Kari called again, trying to soothe it, but it hurled itself skyward, screeching, and sped down the coast. Mental flickers of fear and confusion lingered long after it had physically vanished.

With it went her preternatural strength. The strain of the walk abruptly caught up with her, buckling her knees. She would have fallen had not a pair of arms caught her.

She turned in surprise. It was her father. He met her glance with the same silent, preoccupied expression that he had worn ever since her accident.

"What are you doing here?" she asked.

"I put a spell on your bed, so that I would be informed if you left it."

Her eyes widened. "You knew this would happen. Why didn't you tell me?"

Supporting her under one arm, he guided her carefully back toward the cottage. "Better that you learn it for yourself first. The event I've waited for all these years has come to pass. You've found a way to tap the core of sorcery I saw within you as a babe." He sighed. "I never considered that you might use it in a spell of Binding."

Her eyes widened. "The fall! When the gull threw me off—"

"You were faced with death," Gan said. "Good reason for your Deep Power to awaken. You tried to bind yourself to the bird. And it worked, though not in the way you intended. I tried when I healed you to cancel the effect, but it was no use. This is magic beyond my ability to influence. The bond will last until death, unless you yourself discover the way to be rid of it."

The wind began to howl in the pines, cold and laden with mist.

Kari mended rapidly, even more quickly than could be accounted for by the healing spells. A transformation was taking place. Sorcery moved through her in strange new ways. Gan reported that he saw vivid webs in her aura. She played with the energy, gradually learning how to organize it. Each day it flowed a little more efficiently, a little more under her control. It might take years before she could manipulate it at will, but in the meantime ordinary magic seemed like child's play, and she felt almost drunk with possibilities for study. It was almost enough to dampen her fear.

She felt the gull's presence, somewhere out beyond the coastal islands. In odd moments she would catch herself dreaming of deep ocean, or of fog banks viewed from above, and recognize them as outside thoughts. Such incidents occurred more often as the days went by.

At the end of a week, her scar began to itch. A storm was coming. With it would come the gull.

She went to her father. "It's time," she said. He nodded, collected his mage bow and arrows, and accompanied her to the shore.

Autumn painted the grasses brown and gray. The rich, fecund aroma of rotting vegetation mingled with the coast's salt air. Kari inhaled deeply. She loved this season. It was on such a day as this, a year ago, that she had first become lovers with Ren.

The memory startled her. She had scarcely thought of Ren since her accident. He would be having an ill time of it, at sea during a storm, the second one the swiftfish fleet had had to endure. She hoped his ship fared well.

All thoughts of him vanished as they arrived at the beach. The gull waited on an offshore rock.

It dipped its beak at her arrival. She regarded it apprehensively, aware of the tendrils of sorcery bridging the gap between them. Gan nocked an arrow.

She resisted an urge to plunge into the surf to join the bird. The emotion was potent, almost a siren call. She tried to temper the flow of magic and failed. Given no choice, she temporarily accepted its existence.

The gull spread its wings and screeched, as if in echo of her decision. He was beautiful, she thought, scanning his sleek white lines, his massive musculature, his bright, intelligent eyes.

His. She realized belatedly that she had stopped thinking of the gull as genderless. Somehow he had let her know that he was male.

Scenes appeared in her head. She saw a large, rocky island many leagues from the mainland, where great gulls wheeled and dived in a chaotic dance. Next she saw two individuals preening each other. Finally came the image of a nest. One of the gulls was laying an egg.

Kari burst into laughter. Gan looked at her quizzically.

"He thinks I'm a girl gull!" she said.

The wizard looked ill. "Then I suggest you correct his impression!"

The poor bird, she thought. He didn't understand the reason they were attracted, so he was trying to relate it to other bonds, such as that with his mate. She carefully formulated her response. A similar image seemed best, so she visualized a woman suckling a baby.

The gull reacted by shaking its head until feathers flew loose. But he seemed to grasp the gist. His reply consisted of a brief glimpse of seal pups nursing at their mother's side. So far so good. He understood that she was a female and a mammal.

What next? Names, of course. Hers meant "wellspring" in the Old Tongue, so she transmitted an image of pure, clear water funneling up out of the earth.

To her delight, his answer followed immediately and quite clearly: his own wing, emphasis on the milky color.

"Pearlwing," she blurted.

"Eh?" Gan asked.

She chuckled. "We've just introduced ourselves." She gestured for him to put away his arrow. Not that Pearlwing had ceased to intimidate her, but it was time to talk, not confrontation.

Ren found Kari on the remnants of an old wharf, the last vestige of a coastal residence that had been burned by mer raiders a decade earlier. Dark clouds hung ominously overhead, but she stood at the final piling, unperturbed, observing the actions of the ten great gulls that meandered through the nearby tidewaters.

"So it's true," he said.

He startled her. The fleet had returned from the Deeps only the night before, and the sound of his voice, unheard for a fortnight, reminded her of events and feelings that seemed long past. She hopped over a rotten plank and hugged him. He squeezed back in a perfunctory fashion.

"What's the matter?" she asked, frowning.

He jerked his chin toward the gulls. "Them. My little brother saw you last week, from the bluff. You *talk* to them!"

She stepped back to arm's length. "To one of them. Sometimes he has interesting things to say." Her lover looked very handsome this morning. She caught sight of the object in his hand. "What's this?"

In his hand was a pelt of gleaming azure fur. The texture was sensuous under Kari's palm. "Blue sea otter," he said. "One got caught in the nets. It will make a good handwarmer or set of gloves for you once it's cured."

"It's beautiful," she said, and was distracted by a mental blurt from Pearlwing. A mottled gray gull had arrived. Apparently Pearlwing approved of its presence.

She caught Ren staring at her. "They're really quite friendly once you get to know them," she explained. "Like dogs." Though in her judgment dogs were not nearly as intelligent.

"They attack boats," Ren said.

"Rarely. If they truly wanted to prey on human beings, we'd never dare set sail."

He pointed up the beach. "Look at them. They're vicious even with one another."

At that moment most of the gulls were occupied picking at debris washed up by the high surf. Three individuals squabbled loudly over a large chunk of driftwood.

"That's how they play," she said. "It's simple enough to stop."

She spoke to Pearlwing. The white gull screeched. The trio ceased arguing, stared at him, and began preening their tousled feathers back into place.

"They're capable of a great deal," she said. "They just don't bother to show it very often." She indicated Pearlwing. "He's been teaching me."

Ren took a step back. He stared at her as if in their many times together he had seen only a young woman, and now he saw only a witch.

"Don't go," she said with alarm.

He gave her body a wistful survey, as if for the last time. "It's going to rain. Come with me back to town."

"The storm won't break for an hour or more. I want to stay."

He sighed, glared with suspicion toward Pearlwing, and turned away. "As you wish."

After he had gone, Kari felt a tentative inquiry from Pearlwing. "It's nothing," she said, and tried not to let her emotions leak quite so strongly. But the pain in her scar sharpened, and remained acute long after the clouds had unleashed their burden.

"I'm going to ride Pearlwing," she said.

Gan trembled, though he was determined to have faith in his daughter's judgment of her own power. "He nearly killed you. Has your rapport grown so strong?"

She frowned. "I'd like more time, but I don't have the luxury. It's the spell of Binding. It keeps me awake nights. It confuses and angers Pearlwing. Unless I ride him, it will evolve beyond my control."

Gan reluctantly nodded. "That agrees with what I've seen. But there is another solution. Kill the gull."

She regarded him coldly.

"Better that than die yourself," he said.

"I have no intention of dying. I'll take as many precautions as I can."

"Such as?"

"I've been reading some of your old books. In Evid's

Heroes there is a story of a man who tamed a gull without any magic whatsoever. Reportedly he was very strong."

"That hardly applies to you."

"No, but he utilized a method I hadn't thought of. He strapped himself to his mount's shoulders, and used a bridle, bit, and reins, as if he were breaking a horse."

A tiny portion of Gan's worry eased.

"Will you help me fashion riding tack large enough for a great gull?" Kari asked.

Kari cast her probes oceanward, oblivious to the stiff breeze that tried to unravel the scarf from her neck. Gan paced the sand nearby, carrying the riding gear.

Pearlwing's characteristic psychic signature came to her, faint and intermittent, from far across the sunlit waves. She focused on the source and called again. It was a test. She had never before tried to summon the gull. If he came now, in clear weather, it would be a sign that he might obey her in other ways.

Pearlwing answered almost immediately, addressing her with her name-image.

"He's coming," she told Gan.

The wizard retreated to a cleft between a pair of boulders, so that she could greet Pearlwing alone. She chose a spot far from the bluff, where the low tide had left the sand dark, spongy, and strewn with segments of kelp.

She raised her pendant as the bird came into sight. He caught the flicker, screeched, and glided to a landing a few yards away, nearly bowling her over with the wind of his passage.

He eyed her curiously. She blanked her mind, hiding her intent. He scratched at the sand, irritated at her withdrawal.

She swallowed, took a deep breath, and waved the necklace once more.

Ironically it was more difficult to cast the glamour this time. She knew now just how powerful Pearlwing was, and just how much it meant to a gull to glide freely, unburdened. He snapped his beak loudly. She trembled, keenly aware how quickly she would die if he chose to strike.

Somehow she found the necessary concentration. His agitated fluttering ceased. The glamour claimed him. She lowered the pendant. Slowly, like an arthritic old man, Pearlwing lowered his body to the sand.

Her father appeared. The gull still towered over his head level, but it was low enough to attach the riding gear. Kari maintained careful control over her spell as the wizard eased bridle over beak and inserted the bit. The reins arced over the giant head.

Kari accepted her father's boost up. He ran the thick safety strap around the gull and handed the ends to her. Sweat popping, she buckled them to her own harness. They had used the strongest leather available, reinforced with potent charms. Her back would break long before the strap would—an unpleasant idea which she forced from her mind.

Cinched tight, she waved Gan away. She was as ready as she was going to be.

Pearlwing's mental protests grew increasingly strident. She had planned to hold him immobile until she could quiet his fears, but she now worried that further delay would make him frenzied. Once her father was safe, she released the enchantment.

Pearlwing screeched and sped into the sky. Kari felt his awesome muscles churn beneath her rump and she lost all composure. The link was gone. All she could read from Pearlwing's mind was outrage. They had scarcely achieved gliding altitude when he twisted and bucked. Her safety strap snapped taut, yanking her savagely back onto her perch.

She tugged desperately at the reins, pulling in the direction of his twist, hoping to steal his initiative. He snapped his head the other way, jerking the reins completely out of her hands. They careened out over the ocean.

Already Kari's arms dangled, half spent. Her scar ached from the strain on her abdominal muscles. Bridle or no bridle, she lacked the brawn to deal with him. Her only recourse was magic.

Pearlwing's wall of fear and anger did not budge. She thrust an image of serenity toward him, at the same time beginning an incantation that might dampen the severity of his reactions.

Pearlwing became even more violent. He dipped left, then right. She managed to seize the reins just as he dived. She pulled with all her strength, boosting the attempt with cords of sorcery. Finally his head came back. He hissed around the bit and leveled off just above the waves.

She gasped. They rode an updraft toward the cloudless heights. Pearlwing veered, wheeled, and shook his body. The reins threatened to cut into her palms despite her thick gloves.

The incantation had no effect. He warded off her attempts at control as if he were a master magician. He was simply too big and powerful for her to affect.

A cold knot of panic seized Kari, centered around her scar. She had not anticipated this. Pearlwing had surrendered to the glamour so easily, she had been certain he would yield to her other spells as well.

Her grip on the reins loosened, fingers no longer able to keep up the tension. She let go and grabbed fistfuls of feathers. She huddled as close to the bird's neck as she could, abandoning all efforts to guide his flight.

Pearlwing reacted to the freedom by speeding out to sea. Kari moaned as the shore faded to a black line. The gull shuddered like a wet dog shaking itself after coming in out of the rain. Kari's teeth crashed together, mauling her tongue. Again, had she not been restrained by the strap, she would have been flung off.

He shook her repeatedly. By the fourth upheaval, her limbs flailed hopelessly. She clutched at feathers, found handholds, lost them again. The impacts knocked the wind from her lungs. Bruises rose on her rump and thighs.

She struggled merely to stay conscious. A vile, bitter tang filled the back of her mouth, the same as she had tasted the day she had fallen, during those seconds when the trees had rushed up at her.

She gave up. She simply hung from her saddle, letting Pearlwing do as he would, barely able to contain her terror. She was sure she was going to die.

Help me. She squeezed the plaintive message out.

Immediately Pearlwing ceased shaking and bucking. Numb, partly in shock, Kari reacted to the smooth glide first with confusion, then with disbelief.

A query came from Pearlwing's mind. She blinked. He was concerned for her.

She cursed. It finally dawned on her—the way to break through Pearlwing's barrier was not by force. Her attempts to command him had been the source of his violent reaction. She should have had faith in him. A great gull was no one's slave. Now that she had ceased to be a threat, he had gladly dropped his defenses.

Images rushed from his mind to hers. In the first scene the two of them were flying to a large island on the horizon, the next showed them gliding over open sea, and the third pictured them returning to the coast. She was staggered. He *wanted* to fly with her. The choice of destinations was hers. Dazed, she told him to head for the mainland.

Pearlwing spun a graceful arc and did exactly that. The ease and clarity of their communication astounded her. But with reflection, she knew why. The spell of Binding had run its course. They were now, dare she say it, like a witch and her familiar.

Gradually she emerged from her daze, stretched forward, and retrieved the reins. The gull did not object. She stared stupidly at the leather in her hands. Finally she tugged toward the right.

Nothing happened. She increased the tension. Pearlwing sent her a mental bark of annoyance.

She corrected herself. She tugged again, but this time she simultaneously projected an image of him veering to the right. Pearlwing did so. Smiling, she leaned back, transmitting a picture of him slowing down. He obeyed. Both times his reactions did not quite synchronize with the movement of the reins, but he had the idea. He warbled excitement toward her. It had become a game to him, this business of carrying a rider. He sent her suggestions of what they might do, given time—images of hunting the waters of the Deep for young kraken to eat, or flying through clouds, mist beading on feathers like drops of dew on spider web.

Kari laughed. Yes, they would do all that, she assured

him. But for now she was exhausted. Now that she knew it could be done, there was plenty of time to practice riding another day. The shore rushed forward. Her father came into view at the top of the bluff. She directed Pearlwing down.

Gan grimaced, noting how stiffly Kari dismounted, but his worry melted seeing triumphant gleam in her eyes. She had a new air about her, an adult demeanor.

"Would you like to ride a gull?" she asked.

"Now?" he blurted, casting a distrustful glance toward Pearlwing.

"No. This is my gull. But if I could ride him, I could help you learn to do it with another. There are the legends. What if we taught a whole group of people how to ride?" The words tumbled out. "We could select the most docile, cooperative, intelligent gulls. Perhaps we could breed them, develop a strain that would accept riders as horses do."

"To what end?"

She swept her hands toward the known lands and the vast sea behind her. "To transport messages from the king's house to the lords of the provinces in only a day. To find floundering ships and fetch them aid. To carry healers to the gravely ill. A thousand things!"

"There are those who would never trust a great gull." Yet even as he said it, Gan's enthusiasm mounted. Here was a challenge worthy of a great mage.

"We'll know better," she said.

Gan smiled. It was kind of Kari to speak in the plural, but he knew very well that history would have only a small place for him. The accounts would speak of Gerryjill the Sorceress, the woman who tamed the gulls. The babe in the snowdrift had grown up. At last it was clear how his prophecy would be fulfilled.

RUNAWAYS
by Josepha Sherman

Now, to use a totally different definition of the word "amateur," here is a story written by an amateur—by which I mean someone who does something for the love of it and not necessarily to make a living. We'd all be amateurs if we could; but when you've done something long enough, you become a professional anyway. Technically, of course, Josepha Sherman is a professional; I bought her story "The Ring of Lifari" for SWORD AND SORCERESS IV. (Is everyone thoroughly confused now? Well, that can happen when you listen to a Gemini.)

Z erah froze, hoe in hand, watching the sudden wild flutterings of the birds, then threw down the hoe and snatched up her bow instead. Someone was struggling up through the thick tangle of forest . . . a girl! A slim, young, fair-skinned thing in silks hardly suited for the wild, a cloud of light hair tossing behind her as she ran. Zerah stared at this apparition in disbelief, wondering if solitude had finally turned her brain.

Nonsense. The young thing was real enough. She was also clearly alone and unarmed, and after a moment Zerah lowered her bow. The girl came stumbling to a halt at the sight of her, wild-eyed. *And have I grown so fearsome, then?* the woman thought dryly. She had no illusions about what the girl was seeing: no great beauty, surely, a lean, strong frame in deerskin, a thick plait of chestnut hair streaked with gray, a fiercely planed, weather-worn face with the intricate blue tattooing still plain on its brow. No one had ever thought her beautiful but Raned, and Raned was . . .

But now the girl was stammering, pleading "Oh please, please, help me! I—Terach—Terach is hurt, I can't get him to move, and I—we— Why are you staring? He's hurt! He needs help! Don't you understand?"

"Well enough." Zerah felt her voice come out rusty, harsh with disuse. "Haven't heard such a rush of words for a long time, that's all." She studied the frantic, lovely face for a moment, bemused at how, for all the girl's terror, she still somehow looked cool and unstained. A lady. "Who are you?"

The girl blinked. "Ailetha, daughter of— Please, it doesn't matter now! Terach's wound opened again, and I don't think he even knows what's happening, and—and he'll die without shelter!" Beautiful blue eyes searched wildly about the little clearing. "Isn't anyone here?"

"Me."

"But—but that cabin?"

"Mine." Zerah hesitated, jealous of her privacy. But . . . "Come. Let me see your Terach."

He lay where he'd fallen, halfway up the mountain, a mound of tattered silk. "Terach," the girl crooned. "Ahh, Terach . . ."

This was a boy, no more, barely bearded, brown hair matted, eyes shut, breath too quick, cheeks too flushed. Wound-fever, no doubt of it, and Zerah carefully pulled aside the ruins of what had been an expensive tunic, wary of what she'd find. So now. A spear wound, she'd seen enough of those to know one, a deep gash slanting up across the ribs, the work of a spear thrown from below and at a distance. Not too serious a wound, all things considered, no sign of poisoning, no smell of death. But Ailetha was right, a night's exposure probably would mean the boy's death.

"Who's chasing you?"

Ailetha glanced up sharply. "What do you mean?"

"Youngsters in silk don't run in the deep woods for fun. Or get spears thrown at them. Who's chasing you?"

The girl set her mouth in a stubborn line. "First get Terach to shelter. Then I'll tell you everything, I promise."

Runaways, no doubt of it. Zerah sighed, picturing angry fathers in pursuit and an end to her peace. Eh, her peace was already ended, at least for now. "I'll not have the boy's death on me. We'll get him inside." She gave Ailetha the grim glance that had once, in another time, another place, quelled foemen. "And then, girl, you *will* tell me everything."

Terach, his wound freshly washed and bandaged, was asleep on Zerah's cot, Ailetha curled protectively about him, murmuring. Zerah snorted. For all Terach's youth, he hadn't been a light burden. She, herself, was still sweaty from it. And yet the girl still seemed as fresh and unstained as before.

"Girl. Ailetha. You can safely leave him for the moment."

The blue eyes stared coldly at her. But then the cold gaze wavered, and Ailetha glanced about the cabin's single room as though seeing it clearly for the first time, its hearth with the sheathed sword and dagger over it, its table and chair and not much else on the hard-packed earthen floor, and a twinge of something that might have been contempt crossed her face.

"Know it's plain!" Zerah's voice was flat. "But it's clean. Won't catch a fever from it."

Ailetha winced. "Forgive me." Carefully she disentangled herself from the restless sleeping boy and moved to Zerah's side, just out of reach like some wary young animal, looking up at her intently. "I promised you our story."

"You did."

"There isn't much to tell. I— Do you know the Lord Ereian? No? I . . . am his daughter. But Terach . . . he's not of high station. We met, though, and—and loved, and . . ." Her eyes pleaded. "My father would kill him if he caught us! We had to flee. He'd kill Terach!"

"Who threw the spear?"

"Oh, I don't know! It's true! I think some farmer saw us running and thought we were bandits, I don't know! Terach—"

"He'll heal."

"Ahh!" The girl flowed quickly back to the cot, leaning over him, fierce possession on her face. "Terach . . ."

Zerah shook his head. All at once the cabin seemed far too small, filled with too many lives, and she went outside, breathing the free air and the clean, wild scents. But the forest birds were rousing again, and the woman tensed at the sound of distant hoofbeats. *Might have known. The angry father.* "Ailetha! Get out here!"

"I—I hear them." Her voice was sharp with terror. "You have to hide us, you must! They'll kill Terach!"

Zerah's hands clenched. Dear gods, not more bloodshed, not here! "Come. Back inside." She moved the table to one side, scuffling a foot in the earth till she'd found . . . "Here."

"A—a trap door."

"My cellar. And back exit. Don't worry, I built it with space for air. You won't suffocate."

"Terach . . ."

"You're both going down there. Eh, don't thank me. Just help me get your boy down there. Ach, he's heavy. There. Now stay where you are and be quiet."

She closed the trap, quickly scuffing earth back to cover it, rubbing it hastily smooth as the rest of the floor, then glanced about the cabin quickly— Ah. She straightened the cot's coverings, then took up her bow and went outside, thoughtfully planting half a dozen arrows point down in the ground, near to hand should she need them in a hurry. And then Zerah settled down to wait, arrow to bow and bow half drawn.

Here they came. Eight . . . nine . . . ten riders on panting, sweat-washed horses; that would have been no easy climb for the animals. Nine well-armed guards, confident men. She knew the type right away, honor-bound loyal to their master. And their master? Past the easy strength of youth, yes, but still strong, wide of shoulder. Black hair and beard as grizzled as her own plait, rugged features and cool dark eyes. Surprised eyes now, because he'd just seen the brow-tattooing Ailetha had overlooked, seen and recognized it.

His men hadn't. One of them was eyeing the ready bow and tightening his hand purposefully on his javelin.

"Do," Zerah told him bluntly. "You'll be dead before I am."

"She means it," the black-haired man said calmly. "Come, man, don't you know a *chenri* warrior when you see one?" He bowed politely in the saddle. "We wouldn't disturb you, lady."

"Then don't."

"Ah. It's been a long, thirsty climb."

She gestured with a jerk of her head. "Spring's there. Keep the horses out of my garden."

He slipped down from the saddle, an unexpected touch of courtesy since it put them almost on a level, handing the reins to a guard, never taking his eyes from Zerah. "We're hunting two youngsters, lady, a boy and a girl—"

"Hunting for the kill?"

"No!" His shock might have been genuine. "Lady, I'm Liern na Serai, brother to Lord Ereian. His boy's the one who's missing, Terach, my nephew."

Ereian's son? Zerah didn't flicker an eyelash, but through her mind raced a startled, *Why would Ailetha lie?* "And the girl?"

Liern hesitated. "Ahh, no one, really," he said at last. "At least I don't think so. A maid, I suppose, or someone's lady-in-waiting. Frankly, I don't recall ever seeing the lass about, but obviously she was at my brother's court, and obviously she met Terach and . . ." He shrugged. "Now they've run off, as romantic young things do." His eyes met hers, inviting her, as another adult, to share his wry humor. "My brother's searching the valleys for them, I, the hills. Lady, there were traces of someone's hurried, awkward passage halfway up the mountain. I doubt they were yours."

"They weren't. Mountain's vast, though."

"You . . . haven't seen them, then? Terach's of medium height, brown of hair and starting a beard, the girl, to all accounts, is a fair blonde lass."

A lass alone, with no family to shield her. Oh, now Ailetha's transparent story made sense! As a lord's daughter she could claim protection. As a nobody, she must go in terror for her own life, for the quick, quiet, final end to potential scandal. *Not on my land!* thought Zerah fiercely. "I don't welcome strangers."

Her eyes bore into his with the old, practiced strength, and after a moment Liern looked away with the ghost of a sigh. "So. Thank you, lady. We'll not disturb you any longer."

But he hesitated, glace going again to the blue brow-tattooing, strong frame suddenly awkward with indecision. "I . . ." He stopped, annoyed at himself, then began again; determined. "Lady, there's something else I'd like to discuss with you. If I may."

"Speak."

He glanced at his waiting men. "With so many ears to overhear? I'd not insult your privacy. Might we speak within?"

Was he trying to learn if she'd tucked Terach away inside? Or was it something else? Zerah realized with wry humor that she hadn't quite discarded curiosity. Eh, the cellar's door was well hidden, she didn't have to worry about him finding it. And she certainly wasn't some silly little slip of a girl afraid to be alone with a strange man! "Enter."

His quick eyes missed nothing, their honest gaze neither condemning nor condescending. After a moment Liern moved to the hearth, looking up at the mounted sword and dagger, then gave a sudden startled little laugh of recognition and reached out a hand to the dagger's hilt.

"Leave it."

"But—a stone dagger? You know the old stories? The ones that say stone knives kill what can't be slain by metal?"

"I know them." Memory unexpectedly flashed an image of Raned, laughing, golden Raned handing her the dagger with a half-joking little bow, saying that now she was well-armed against any harm. . . .

Any harm save grief. "You wished to speak with me. Speak."

"Ah. I know something of the *chenri*-clan, lady, their skill at arms, their honor, how they may be hired only by someone whose cause they judge just."

"Common knowledge."

"Why you've left them is no business of mine. But I know you left without shame; you wouldn't be alive were it otherwise." He paused, uncomfortable beneath the weight of her flat, cold stare. "It's not my business why you've chosen this exile, either. But . . ."

"What are you trying to say? That a *chenri*'s too valuable a tool to let rust? That I should come down the mountain with you? Be a warrior again, this time for you and your brother?" She stopped short, shaken by her own burst of speech. "I left the *chenri*," said Zerah flatly, "because I grew weary of death."

She could have sworn she surprised a flash of sympathy in the dark eyes. "There are other things in life than war, lady! My brother would welcome you in whatever position you chose. Teacher of arms, perhaps, of archery, of healing—whatever. You'd be no one's servant. No one's tool."

"Generous with your brother's welcome, aren't you? Why?"

"I know my brother. He holds the *chenri* in high esteem, as do I. And . . . he hates waste as much as do I." Liern moved a step closer, studying her. Zerah, distractingly, was all at once very much aware of the warmth of him, the healthy man-scent— The pity. "Whomever you're mourning," he murmured, "was worthy of you. But, lady, I don't think he'd want you to give up the living world for him."

"Get out."

"As you will." Liern paused long enough to pull a ring from his hand. "This bears my seal. Keep it. Think about what I've said. And know that should you ever decide to leave your mountain, you'd find an honored place with us." He held out the ring to her, but Zerah, arms rigid at her sides, made no move to take it, and after an awkward moment the man placed it on the table instead. "I must continue my search. Lady, good day."

He bowed and left, just like that. Zerah moved to the doorway, watching, hating him for disturbing the layers of calm she'd so painfully built up, for honing dulled grief, for . . . reminding her of the world. She stood, waiting wearily till the disturbed forest birds had all settled again, telling her that Liern and his men were safely away. Then, forcing herself grimly back under control, Zerah turned to bring Terach and Ailetha back up to daylight.

*   *   *

The boy was recovering poorly. His wound appeared to be healing cleanly enough, but a low, persistent fever remained, and he'd been conscious only now and again, and not quite lucid in those moments, aware only of Ailetha, calling for her. Zerah shook her head, thinking of battlefield fevers and inner infections. If this continued much longer, she'd have to reopen the wound and let it drain anew.

As for the girl . . . eh, look at her, forever curled about the boy like a cat with only one kitten. Zerah spoke her thought aloud.

"Hardly help the boy by smothering him."

That won her a look of sheer loathing. "You don't understand! I love him, I love him so! If he dies, I—I'll die!"

"Who said anything about dying?"

"He can't die! I won't let him!"

"Don't be a fool!" That came out too sharply; Ailetha's obsession was beginning to grate on Zerah's nerve. *Ach, Raned, was I ever like this over you? Was I? Gods, was I ever this . . . young?* Zerah sighed. "Come," she said, almost gently this time. "Leave him for the moment. Rest. Won't do him any good if you collapse."

"I'm not tired."

That looked true enough. Somehow her pale beauty seemed as fresh as ever. Unmussed. Unmarked. And for a moment Zerah jested dourly with herself about blood-drinkers, forever young— Poor taste. Poor taste, with Terach lingering so near death for all Ailetha's pleadings. *Jealous,* Zerah snapped at herself, *you're jealous of her!* "Come, Ailetha, it's late. Eh, come, girl. This isn't helping either of you. Leave Terach for the moment and sit down."

When Ailetha made no sign she'd even heard her, Zerah took the girl by the shoulders, gently enough, but the girl quickly pulled out of her grasp, spitting fiercely, "Leave me alone! Leave us both alone!"

Zerah shrugged. Casting open the cabin's door, she stood in the doorway, looking out into a forest bright with a coldness of moonlight, remembering Raned despite herself, aching.

But then her head came up with a start. Mixed in with memories of Raned had been . . . what? What had there been about the touch of Ailetha's skin? What was there about her clean, cool beauty, too clean, too cool— Oh, no, no. "Ridiculous! I'm letting jealousy turn my brain!"

And yet, and yet . . . Zerah moved quietly back into the cabin, unnoticed by the crooning Ailetha, quietly took down the sheathed dagger from its mountings. The thin, beautiful flint blade glowed warmly in the firelight as she drew it.

"Ailetha."

The blonde head turned sharply to her. And then Ailetha was throwing herself away from Terach, away from Zerah, eyes wide with terror. "What are you doing? Have you gone mad? Get that—that thing away from me!"

"Ahh no," Zerah sighed. "Not mad at all. Not mistaken, either, am I?"

"What do you mean? Terach—"

"No. I'm not letting you near him again."

"You *are* mad! Mad!"

Ailetha darted toward the boy, but Zerah was swifter. The thin stone blade gleamed between them, and Ailetha gave a sharp, wordless little cry and backed away. "Madwoman! Dried up, useless old madwoman! I—I'll kill you!"

"Can't. You've tied up all your strength with Terach. You die, he's free. But if he dies by other than your will—you die. Ha, that's why you were so terrified of the spear wound. Right? Saw your own death in it."

"No! You— Get that away!"

Before Zerah could catch her, she was out into the little clearing, panting in the cool night air. "Let me go. I've done you no harm."

"Me, no. But Terach—"

"I haven't hurt him!"

"Call stealing his will bit by bit not hurting him? That's what you've been doing, isn't it? Feeding from his essence— No wonder he wasn't recovering from the fever! You didn't leave him the strength!"

"That—that's not true!"

"Oh girl, you're not hurting him, you're killing him!"

"No! I—I love him!"

"As the predator loves its prey."

"No!"

"What are you, Ailetha? Not human, that much I know."

"What a ridiculous—"

"Good imitation, though. Fooled me. Easy to fool folk at court, too, where so many are always coming and going. Where ladies don't do any kind of work to raise a sweat."

"That doesn't even make sense!"

"Doesn't it? Think. No muss, not the hint of sweat, not even after helping me lug Terach halfway up a mountain. Didn't dawn on me at first. Why should it? But just now, when I tried to pull you away from the cot, that was the first I really got near you. I've a good sense of smell. Always have. And you know something? You've got no scent, Ailetha, none at all. *Serenin*, aren't you?"

"No!"

"Recognize the word? Odd. They're not common in these parts, the sly, hungry things."

"And—and how would *you* know of them?"

"Ach, the *chenri* see all types of things in their travels." And there'd been one once, long ago, when she was still painfully young, one with the seeming of a man on it, smooth and sleek and quite, quite scentless. Raned had slain it before it had done her any real harm, slain it before her dazed eyes. That had been how they'd first met, and Raned full of anger at a *chenri* who'd let herself be tricked by an essence-stealer. "Eh, come. Am I right?"

All at once Ailetha seemed to sag. "You don't understand," she murmured. "I never thought to love him. But Terach was so sweet, so clean. The lure of him drew me even into his father's court. Ahh, it was so simple to slip in among those folk as one of them, to hunt among all those unsuspecting souls till I found the one I must have!"

"And bewitched the boy into running off with you. Wanted him all to yourself, didn't you? Your sweet prey. Till that farmer and his spear spoiled things for you."

"No, no, you have it wrong! I love him!"

"Tell you what, *serenin*. Here's your chance to prove

it. You claim you love Terach? Make a sacrifice for his sake. Let him go. Leave him."

Ailetha drew a ragged sob of a breath. "No, oh no! Haven't you been listening? Haven't you heard a word? Terach is my own, my own! I love him and I'll never let him go and we'll be happy for ever and ever—"

"Till you kill him."

"No!"

"Face facts, *serenin*. Just by staying with Terach, you're draining him. You'll kill him."

"I won't! I won't!" The blue eyes blazed with pleading. "Give me a chance! Please! Leave me alone!"

How easy to see only a frightened young girl! How easy to forget the truth. Zerah sighed. "You know I can't do that," she said softly. "Give the boy back his life. Leave him."

"No, ahh no! What's wrong with you? Why are you so—so cold? So heartless? You—you hate the thought of love, don't you? Yes, yes, of course that's it! You hate the very thought of love and lovers! All because your own man is dead!"

Zerah froze. "How . . . could you know that?"

"I do, I do, I feel it blazing from you! *That's* why you hate me, not for Terach's sake, Terach is nothing to you! You hate me because—you envy me!"

"Ridiculous."

"You do! Your love is dead, and so you ran away to hide up here! But my love's alive! Alive! And you shan't take him from me!"

The blue eyes caught her, held her. The blue eyes were suddenly very wide, very cold, very, very alien. *Idiot!* Zerah screamed at herself, but it was already too late. All she could see was that blueness, that cold, cold blueness and a hint of the void behind it. . . .

But now. . . .

Raned, ahh Raned! It was a cry no less anguished for being silent. For there he was, conjured in her mind's eye so clearly by memory or *serenin* trickery, as warm, as loving, as *alive* as ever he'd been. *Raned, Raned, the long golden days, the two of us together, laughing through battles, sure of ourselves, invulnerable, invincible.*

Till the sudden arrow and the end of joy. Zerah grimly

forced herself to remember that, too, and came back to reality with a painful jolt. This was no time to go wandering in the past, and damned if she'd let Ailetha use her memories against her! *I lived through the truth of his death. How could anything you might conjure hurt me worse than that?*

But how was it a *serenin* could play with emotions? Sobbing and pleading about Terach—how was it a *serenin* could feel anything at all? Zerah shuddered in sudden comprehension and reluctant pity. An outcast, Ailetha, running from itself, the *serenin* unique of its kind, the only one aware of the emptiness within, terrified, trying so hard to ape the breathing, feeling humans! Trying so hard for what it thought was love. Gods, this was ridiculous! As soon pity a snake! And yet . . .

Aie, but her memory-trance, brief though it had been, had given the *serenin* time to take up her sword! Wary *chenri* instincts making her feign entrancement, Zerah listened to Ailetha muttering nervously:

"Now I have her. I—I'll kill her with her own blade. I'll kill her, and then Terach will be . . . But—but what if she's right? What if he dies, and I with him?" The *serenin* shivered, shifting weight from one foot to the other, licking dry lips. "No, no, I have it! There's a way! I'll take his life myself! I won't kill him, I'll draw his whole essence into me all at once! I'll wrap myself about his soul and make it part of me, Terach a part of me, never to be let go, my love forever and ever!" She swung the sword clumsily back. "Yes!"

"No," said Zerah grimly, and lunged. She heard Ailetha gasp at the bite of the stone blade. She heard her own sword fall. Face to face, Zerah saw the blue eyes go wide and empty, then quickly released the dagger's hilt as the *serenin* sagged slowly to the ground, color bleaching swiftly from hair, eyes, skin, leaving the slight form a cold, lifeless white in the moonlight.

There'd been no odor to the pyre save the smell of flame and wood. And when she'd stirred the cooling ashes with a wary foot, there'd been nothing left of Ailetha but the fire-brittled knife. She'd felt no triumph at the sight, nothing but that sad, unwilling pity.

But when Zerah went to check on Terach, she found the fever broken at last, and the boy quite peacefully asleep, and for the first time that night, she smiled.

"You're sure you won't come with me? My father would be grateful, you know it."

"Ach, you don't need me, boy. You're quite recovered. Go, off with you."

But Terach paused, glancing shyly back. "I . . . thought she loved me."

"So did she."

"We never . . . you know. But I had to follow her, I—I couldn't help it." He stopped, biting his lip. "When I woke up and found her gone, from my mind I mean, when I felt that smothering warmth gone and I could think again— Thank you. I— Thank you."

After a hesitant moment more, the boy started down the mountain path. Zerah, hands on hips, watched him go, then shook her head and entered the cabin. For a long while the woman stood still, glorying in the sudden return of silence.

But something was glinting from the table, catching her eye . . . Liern's ring, still lying where he'd placed it. Zerah hissed in annoyance and swept the ring up, meaning to hurl it away and be done with it. And yet . . . *I don't think he'd want you to give up the living world for him.* Zerah thought of Liern, and Ereian's court, and life, and closed her fingers about the ring instead, thoughtfully.

"Maybe," she said aloud, and smiled.

THE GOLDEN EGG
by Morning Glory Zell

Stories for this anthology, as I think I have mentioned before, tend to run in cycles. The first year, everyone was writing rape and revenge stories; the second year, everyone seemed for some reason to take on the story of the chosen maiden; this year, the fifth we've been doing this, for some reason everyone (and his sisters and his cousins and his aunts) sent me a dragon story.

Now usually I send them back as soon as I identify them; I feel that Anne McCaffrey has done the dragon story up with a ribbon around it, and I don't really want to compete. But I received so many good dragon stories this year, beginning with this one. In a group they seemed to say something about the dragon in fantasy which could be said no other way. And so I present a group of dragon stories; now let's give the dragons a rest for a few years.

T he Witch was very angry. Valla watched her as she approached, silhouetted in the entrance of the small rocky cave. Valla's swordhand, purpled with dried dragon's blood, tightened on the hilt of her rapier as she crouched protectively over the dragon's egg she had stolen. Now Valla could see the Witch's flashing green eyes and the pulsing of the violet colored Fascination Jewel that hung from her neck. In spite of all the terror tales Valla had heard about Witches, the red-haired swordswoman thought this one's head would spring from her fair white neck quite as easily as had the dragon's that she had killed just a while ago with a single clean sweep of her blade. The Swordswoman would have to move fast though, before the Witch's eyes adjusted to the gloom and Valla lost her advantage. Valla sprang to her feet without a sound and, easing around the bulk of the dragon's egg, she raised her rapier and leapt at the Sorceress still poised in the doorway. But somehow the Witch was no longer there and Valla's blade began to pulse in her own hand, then to turn and twist, attacking its owner. As Valla struggled with the writhing weapon, she felt fingers long and cold close on her shoulder at the nape of her neck. After that she felt nothing, nothing at all.

Nothing had finally become a violet hazy pulsing that cleared slowly for Valla. She found that she was sitting with her back to the bole of a giant Blue-Oak tree. Reaching for her blade, she found that her arms were bound to her sides. When she moved her head the world still pulsed, but her vision had resolved to the green and gold of sunlit leaves. She heard the shifting of a large body and turned her head in time to catch sight of a large female dragon advancing toward her and, like the Witch, this dragon was very angry. Plate-sized crimson scales were raised like hackles all down her neck and back. An iridescent throat patch throbbed like a severed artery, and the thin membrane between the ear spines twitched as she lashed her spiky tail and gnashed her gleaming teeth. The Dragon lowered her head (the size of a horse's body) and opened her jaws, making a sound like a hissing teakettle. Then the Witch stepped up beside the angry dragon.

"Tarragon and I know that you are awake now, poacher, and we want information."

"I'm no poacher!" Valla began to answer hotly. "My name is Valla and I am an honored Swordswoman in the bodyguard of the Queen of Lorth."

"Well, 'Valla,' or whoever you are, I don't know what name Her Royal Highness may have for people who trespass onto a wildlife refuge to kill a member of an endangered species and steal its young, but here at Verdeveldt we call such people poachers."

Valla flushed as red as her hair roots. It had never occurred to her, in her desperate need, that what she might be doing was illegal or perhaps immoral; she was just trying to save her own life. "I . . . I . . . never thought about it like that. I had to have a dragon's egg."

The Witch shook back her long salt and pepper hair and laid a hand on the hide of the trembling dragon. "You and everybody else just 'has to have' a dragon's egg. Why do you think they are almost extinct? What will happen when they are all gone? There are only a few dozen left in the whole world, all on Refuges like this one, involved in breeding programs. The Order of Artemet has dozens of loyal guardians and many years invested in trying to save the last of the Mythological Creatures from total extinction and some selfish short-sighted moron always has a 'greater need' and a better excuse. But we've heard them all around here, and a poacher is a poacher. We have our own penalties for your kind."

By now, Valla had begun to feel alarmed and more than a little guilty, yet her voice was sullen and her manner defensive: "What do I care about your rule. Go ahead and do your worst, no penalty could be worse than my fate was already. I caught the Fading Doom from a traveling harper and the royal physician says that the only cure is a dragon's egg. Without one I am a dead woman anyway."

The Witch frowned and blinked, looking at the dragon who lowered its massive head to peer intently at the bound swordswoman. The dragon's eyes were huge and golden with star shaped pupils; something like pity and understanding seemed to float in their depths.

"So go ahead and have your pet eat me, but it will probably catch the Fading Doom from me and then what will you do?" Valla tried to sound belligerent.

The Witch suppressed a smile. "Tarragon is hardly a pet! She is my teacher—and it seems as though you could use some instruction yourself, poacher. No one with half a wit would risk her life on the diagnosis of a single physician, no matter how eminent. Besides, dragons never get sick, they would be virtually immortal if it weren't for humans hunting them to the brink of extinction. Tarragon here, is four hundred years old and still in her prime.

Her mate, Absinthe, that you murdered was over six hundred years old and remembered lore from the time before the Great Comet Swarm changed the seasons." The Sorceress paused for breath. "I'm sorry for you. Self-preservation is the ultimate motivation and can make rogues of even the most decent human beings. However, humanity, decent or otherwise, is not at risk here since humans are not exactly an endangered species, and the stakes are of a higher order than a single life. As pledged Guardian of Verdeveldt Refuge and Servant of Artemet, Our Lady of Beasts, my duty is clear."

"If you would place an animal's life above a human being's," Valla voiced her rage and contempt, "then go ahead, you sanctimonious Witch-Bitch, kill me and be done with it!"

"Kill you?" The Witch's eyes shimmered with the green of butterfly wings and suddenly seemed as huge as the dragon's. "We're not going to kill you; we're going to change you."

The amethyst Fascination Jewel began to glow and pulse in time to Valla's heartbeat and as she felt herself sinking into the violet void once more, she struggled with her will alone. To her amazement and distress her struggles moved to the pulsebeat and became a dance. She heard the echoes of a chant: "She changes everything She touches; Everything She touches changes . . ."

Valla felt as if she were being pulled into a vast black whirlpool with rainbow veils, stars and snowflakes. It felt as if she were being sucked inside out, then turned upside down and spat out again. The Abyss whirled around her, soundlessly screaming, pregnant with meaning just beyond her comprehension. She thought that part of her was being squirted through fragmented space; or perhaps it was she who was fragmented. And then the silent roaring quieted and the crystalline shards of the universe began falling together into strangely glowing patterns. Valla tried to make sense of it and then let go, listening to the sound of her breathing. It sounded harsh in her own ears; she twitched them and membranes rustled. She shivered and felt the rattle of scales. Her vision focused, no longer fragmented, and she saw green grass starred with brilliant glowing purple-white flowers; the sunlight itself seemed to have a new dimension to it. The air was full of strange scents, but overlaying all of them was the musty tang of blood.

The blood dappled a pair of smoothly muscled arms, and spattered the uniformed body of a woman tied to an ancient tree. The blood was dried and much darker than the mop of tousled red curls falling over the woman's sleeping face . . . *it was her own face!* Valla made a strangled cry which came out sounding like a brass horn and put her hands to her face. Her hands still had five fingers but there all resemblance ended. They were covered in fine coppery red scales and the thumbs sported long curving claws. Shorter claws graced the next two fingers which had extra digits and the final two fingers disappeared into scarlet membranes. When she extended her arms, wings unfolded at her side. Valla moaned and her voice still sounded like a brass horn. She saw the Witch staring up at her and she tried to speak, to scream at her: *"What have you done to me?"* Only a brassy squawking resulted from her attempts. Still somehow, the Witch seemed to understand her question.

"I thought you ought to see what it's like to be a dragon for a while. It is our penalty, that the poacher should spend a thrice cycle of moons in the body of the creatures that they would kill in order to experience the lifeforce of the other and to see through their eyes. A species is unique and has irreplaceable contributions to make to the overall web of life. Perhaps you will have the opportunity to contemplate this perspective from a different . . . uh, shall we say, a different point of view."

Valla's thoughts radiated anguished confusion: *"I don't understand."* Her heartbeat sounded like a massive drum.

The Sorceress shook her night crowned head: "I changed you, through the power of the Lady of Beasts, Artemet. All animals are Her children, even humans, though many prefer to forget that kinship. As for you, your spirit will live in the body of the dragon Tarragon, whose mate you killed, for a triple lunation. When three moons have completed their cycle, you must return to this tree and tell me what you have learned."

"But what about my b . . . body?" Valla's heartbeat threatened her ability to hear the Witch's reply, but the words rang silently inside her head:

"Your body contains the sleeping spirit of Tarragon and will be cared for in the temple of the Lady, along with her egg. Go now!"

"But . . . but I don't know how to be a dragon, I don't know how they fly or even what they eat!" Valla's thoughts stuttered and shrank in fear.

"Well, maybe you will learn about the beings you worked to exterminate before it's too late for them . . . and for you." A crow flew down and lit on the witch woman's shoulder and other creatures began to emerge from the woods. The sorceress lifted the body of the swordswoman onto the back of a huge stag. Valla started toward her body, but the crow flew at her shrieking and it was joined by dozens, even hundreds, of others making the air black and raucous. They dove at her head and the dragon woman lumbered away blindly crying like bagpipes.

An ancient Sage once noted: "Time flies when you don't know what you're doing."

The female who had been Valla leaned into the shifting wind, pulling her wings up to land. She brought her heavy body down as light as a butterfly. The wind now brought her messages of sounds for miles around and scents of animals and flowers. But the greatest wonder of all was her augmented vision. Dragon-sight operated in the ultraviolet and infrared ranges, giving all the colors a vibrant glowing depth that seemed almost like movement. *"It was the hardest thing to get used to,"* Valla decided, *"but the one that make it most worthwhile . . . almost."* Valla had lived in the body of the dragon Tarragon while the moon waxed and waned twice and it was in its final waxing quarter before the full. She had almost served her penance and she had learned so much that it was staggering. For instance, she no longer considered her transformation to be such a dreadful disaster, a humiliating reduction in state from a superior human form into that of a brute beast. Instead she now realized from direct comparison that dragons had larger brains for memory storage and that they lived almost forever. They had other senses that human lacked as well. They flew through levitation and could feel the emotions of other beings. They were not true telepaths and could not speak mind to mind except for certain exceptions like the Witch Priestesses of Artemet. Their voices were like musical instruments and their only language was long complex songs carried over far distances. But the most precious knowledge of all had been the secret of the dragon's healing powers.

"The Witch will find that I have a few secrets of my own that she doesn't know about." Valla laughed to herself, for she had long ago forgiven the Sorceress for shape-changing her. It had been a painful lesson though; she remembered the crash landings and hunger spells, until Tarragon's instinctive patterns reasserted their functioning. She had made an uneasy peace with her dragon-self until she begin to meditate and absorb the patterns. Dragons were truly the wisest creatures in the world, she understood that now as well as why they were so precious to preserve.

"I have my own dragons to preserve now," Valla smirked, rubbing an eyeridge with her thumbclaw and settling into the mossy nest she had built inside a ring of tumbled boulders. There were three eggs now—one laid each month—and the ovoid shells had hardened from their gelatinous beginning into a multi-faceted golden treasure hoard. She arranged her bulk fastidiously in place allowing the naked red skinned brooding patch to touch the center egg. She hummed and thrummed in her throat happily. *"The Witch would really be surprised."*

Suddenly, her enormously sensitive ears caught a sound she almost had forgotten; the whisper of a drawn sword-blade. She drew herself rigid and whipped her head around to see the crouched figure of a swordsman creeping toward her. She stood up careful of the nest, crying: *"No!"* in a voice like a trumpet. To her utter horror Valla recognized the man. He was Corvis, her old friend, a fellow in the Queen's bodyguard—and he had obviously come to steal a dragon's eggs. Only now, she was the dragon and the eggs were hers.

Valla's heart pounded with the beat of a dragon-mother, but her humanity strained toward the approaching man. She had to think fast: how could she communicate to him? First, she must draw him away from the eggs. She leapt in his path and he stepped back a pace. She moaned and reached down to trace his name sign in the dust with her claw. She jerked her hand back leaving the severed thumb writhing in the dust as his blade swept down unexpectedly. The dark dragon blood fountained from her wounded hand. She jumped out of his way and used her massive spiked tail to sweep him off the ground. He tumbled and somersaulted to his feet. *"Lady of Beasts protect me,"* she thought, *"he is just too fast and he won't wait while I demonstrate that I can reason."* She swept her bulk away from his renewed assault, but as she gave ground, she realized that he was now between her and the nest. *"What is the use of this vast draconic wisdom I have learned if I can't even save me from this miserable damned eggsnatcher?"* Valla thought in despair, searching her inward dragon memories in frantic appraisal. Then she remembered a bit of a human fairy tale and matched it with a scrap of her dragon experience. *"It might work,"* she prayed, *"It must work."* She thought as she rushed in, avoiding the flashing blade, closing with the man and bearing him down with her weight. She got her injured hand up as he brought his blade around and shoved the spurting stump of her severed thumb into his mouth. He gagged and swallowed by reflex, then his eyes bulged, registering shock and amazement.

"Uh-oo-fth!" he said, dropping his sword on the ground. Valla removed her hand from his mouth. "It's you," he repeated more intelligibly this time.

Valla thought the words again silently: *"Yes, Corvis, it really is me—your friend Valla. A Witch changed me into this dragon shape. Please don't kill me!"*

"How can I be sure it's truly you and not some other Witch-trick?" he asked suspiciously and Valla thought him another thought that drew a blush to his hard-bitten face. "Okay, lass, I believe you now. But why didn't you let me know right away before I hurt you?"

Valla pressed on the artery in her wrist and the blood slowed in the stump of her thumb. Her long yellow forked tongue flicked out and tasted the seeping blood. *"I tried to tell you, but you couldn't understand my language, and then I remembered that the taste of dragon's blood confers the power to understand the speech of all animals, even the dragons themselves."*

"So that's why you shoved your bloody thumb in my mouth." He nodded to her.

"And a bloody smart move it was too . . ." came a voice from behind the rocks, as the Witch woman emerged with her retinue of crows. Smiling at Valla she continued: ". . . so what other little tricks have you learned while in your borrowed shape?"

The dragon-woman showed her the clutch of eggs and watched the Witch's sea green eyes grow misty. *"And that is not even the most important thing."* Valla told her. *"Dragon's healing virtue is so strong that it is in the very egg shells as well as the embryo. When baby dragons hatch, the discarded shells could be ground to powder for healing human ills. Humans need never kill dragons again."*

Corvis interrupted her thought. "Aye, it was for the Queen herself I came in search of the dragon's egg, for she too has the Fading Doom. Won't you bring the shells and come back with me to Lorth?"

Valla's draconic smile was huge and startling, *"No, Corvis. I will send the shells to you when the hatching's done, but I want to stay here after I get my body back."* She looked over toward the Witch. *"That is, if I can apply to become a Guardian of Verdeveldt?"*

The Witch laid a long fingered hand against one of the dragon woman's scarlet belly scales. "Sister," she spoke gently, "you may call me Andred. When you are recovered from the transfer you may begin your training, but you took the first step on the Path of the Wise when you learned that you need not kill the dragon to get the golden egg."

REVISED STANDARD VIRGIN
by Rick Cook

Every now and then, when I reject a story for being too predictable or too much like too many other stories that I have read this year, I quote the old cartoon: a writer gazing despairingly at his typewriter, and a rejection slip which says, "We want fresh original stories which adhere strictly to our formula."

Formula? Yes, I use formula, which, after all, is only the pattern of a good story since prehistory. The first novel in existence, THE ODYSSEY, told the story of "a likable protagonist who overcomes almost insuperable odds to win—by his own efforts—a worthwhile goal."

And if anyone thinks there is nothing new to be said about the ordinary girl-sacrificed-to-the-dragon story, I challenge you to read this one.

I woke up cold and naked on a straw-filled pallet. Outside a cock crowed, trumpeting his concupiscence to the world.

It was too dark to see so I ran my hands over my body. Slim hips, budding breasts, mostly nipple, and a light patch of hair only beginning to curl between my legs. I felt to be about fourteen. *Mother rot them!*

On to more important things. I flexed my arm experimentally and felt the bicep and forearm. There wasn't much muscle there, but what there was was firm and hard. Good. I was neither a starved waif nor some nobleman's pampered daughter—not that the last was too bloody likely.

I swung my feet over the edge of the pallet and stood up. A quick exploration showed I was in a room perhaps two armspans in either direction. The floor was dirt and the walls were peeled logs.

I began exercising, both to test my strength and to get warm. As I stretched and grunted, the tiny barred window above the pallet grew brighter and brighter and the darkness turned to pre-dawn gray.

I heard a scraping sound outside and I dashed back to the pallet as the door began to open. There stood a lean old man with long white hair and beard wearing the white robe and golden torque of a priest of the All-Father.

"Come my child," he said, holding out his hand, "it is time."

He led me gently to the room beyond where three women waited. By the light of smoky, stinking tallow lamps they dressed me in a new gown of white linen embossed with white embroidery. Then the women bowed out and the priest led me out into the chill, fresh dawn.

Everyone was waiting for me. The villagers huddled outside the ring of torchlight the warriors just inside the torches, facing out, the priests and acolytes, the old king who ruled this dungheap, and his son, blond, beefy and vacuously handsome, at his side.

My father was there, inside the ring by special dispensation. His gathered smock and coarse breeks were freshly cleaned and mended and his eyes were red from crying. He embraced me roughly and then stepped back.

Spare me your tears, you old fraud, I thought. *You didn't object when it was someone else's daughter.* But my heart went out to him just the same.

"Come my child," said the old priest. "Be brave." *Bloody old bastard.* I thought. *You don't even know my name.* Warriors grasped my arms. Then we formed a procession behind two men with curved bronze horns slung around their bodies. A man with a drum stepped behind me. Other warriors closed in and the priest and his acolytes stepped in front of the horn players. The priest gestured with his staff and the soldiers cleared a lane through the crowd for us. With a *blat* and a *boom-boom-boom* we moved off. As the great wooden gates in the log wall swung open, I could see the sun peeking blood red over the horizon. I wondered if I would see it set.

Once out the gate we followed a footpath, past fields bedewed and glistening in the wan dawn light, and toward a dark line of trees beyond. The trail wound into a rocky gully and the procession followed the sandy bottom downstream, horns blowing and the drummer behind me banging away for all he was worth.

We came to a place where the gully dropped away. In the wet season there would be a waterfall; now it was only a cliff. Steps were cut in the rock beside the fall, treads worn by time and water.

Mother, I thought as rough hands guided me down the stair. *How long has this been going on? How many girls have come this way?*

The gully deepened and widened into a small, gloomy canyon. Here there were trees along the sides and a shallow stream trickled down among them. The warriors, trying to seem nonchalant, loosed their swords in their scabbards or flipped back their cloaks, exposing the scarlet linings and freeing their arms. The whole party huddled closer and twice the drummer nearly trod on the hem of my gown.

Finally we rounded a bend and came to a place where the canyon's curve formed a natural amphitheater. A spacious sandbank filled most of the space and the rivulet broadened into a pool up against the sheer cliff of rose-red sandstone. The rising sun turned the cliff to flame and the drum and horns echoed metallically off the natural sounding board.

At the base of the other wall, still in deep shadow, was a jumble of boulders. The biggest, central one had iron manacles chained to it by iron staples driven deep into the rock.

Shit. Sometimes they just take the Sacrifice to the

appointed spot and leave her. Mostly they tie her. It would take me time to get out of those cuffs.

Then I got a closer look. The manacles weren't something the village smith had pounded out of soft bog iron. They were steel and fitted with cunning key locks, obviously the work of a specialist. There was no way I could get out of something like that.

Okay, go to Plan B.

I stamped down hard on the foot of the soldier holding my right arm. He howled at the unexpected pain and loosened his grip. I jerked my arm free, twisted my body and snapped the heel of my palm into the jaw of the man to my left. He dropped like a sack of sand and I skipped past him out of the column, grabbing his spear as I went by.

The procession dissolved into confusion. The drummer gaped with his stick in midair. One of the horn blowers nearly choked. The warriors moved toward me and then stopped when I brandished the spear.

"My child . . ." the old priest began, trying to sound kindly but obviously annoyed by the disruption.

"Not your child, you son of a diseased whore," I growled.

His eyes narrowed but he kept the avuncular manner. "Come, this dishonors you in the eyes of the All-Father. It does you no good."

"Neither does being eaten by a dragon," I snapped. From the corner of my eye I saw men moving out to my sides. Before they could rush in, I jabbed at the priest with a quick, full extension, leaning into it and bringing my butt hand next to my extended forward hand. The priest squawked and jumped back. I spun, twirled the spear above my head, and drove the butt into the stomach of the man to my right. He went down retching. Before the rest could react, I feinted a glittering slash at the crowd and closed with the man to my left as he took his first step toward me. A quick upward strike with the haft caught him in the crotch, where his split oxhide skirt offered no protection. He went down and I stamped on his sword hand, feeling the bones crack. I scooped up his sword and skipped backward to open the distance between me and the others.

A couple of the men looked like they wanted to run. The old priest made the sign against the evil eye. "Possession," he breathed. "She is possessed."

"I'm anything you like," I panted. "Now are you going to leave, or do I slice up your miserable carcasses for dragon bait?"

The priest opened his mouth. Farther downstream came a splash, like a big fish jumping in the still morning water.

"Take her. Quickly!" he yelled. Three men moved forward to do his bidding.

From the back of the crowd came two spears, thrown butt-first with the intention of stunning me. I dodged one, fended off the second with my spear and blocked a blow from the lead warrior with the sword.

"Hurry!" shouted the priest, dancing with impatience.

I skipped to the side as the men closed. The nearest one cut at me and then screamed and dropped his sword as my parry and counter sliced his arm open. I ducked under a cut from his fellow and laid him out with the haft.

For an instant I faced the third man. Then his eyes went wide and his face paled.

"THE DRAGON!" someone shouted and the party dissolved into a confused mob, screaming in terror as they fled back up the canyon. The injured ones were limping along at the rear and by the time they rounded the bend old priest was almost at back at the head of the procession, his white robe flapping about his spindly shanks and ancient arse with every stride.

I laughed aloud. Then I turned to the sound of something splashing upstream and all laughter died.

There are dragons and there are dragons. This was a *Dragon*. It was twice my height to the top of its crest and easily four times that long. It wasn't the biggest I'd ever heard of, but it was the biggest I'd ever seen. It wasn't ancient and feeble either. The oily black iridescence of the scales and the springy way it strode onto the sand told me it was in the prime of life. If it lived to grow old, it would be a world record dragon. Just now it was a world record problem.

The trick in this game is surprise. You either ambush the dragon or you do a frightened-maiden imitation until you get close enough to strike. But it was too late for any of that. Now I faced a dragon in a stand-up fight—the thing I had been schooled to avoid at all cost.

The beast paused and cocked its head, almost human in its puzzlement. The tendrils around its great jaws quivered as it tested the air and its eyes narrowed to evil yellow slits. Then it crunched forward onto the beach.

I backed up to get some maneuvering room and the dragon followed a little faster, a little more confident.

No time to get in among the rocks. I grounded my spear, braced the butt against my foot and extended the point toward the dragon's throat. I held the sword behind me, point up. Then I screamed in mock terror—well, half-mock terror anyway.

Despite their reputations, dragons are not very bright. They are mostly creatures of habit. The drum and horns had summoned it and a maiden's scream meant dinner was served. Jaws agape, the dragon charged.

I aimed the spear point into the beast's mouth, but it batted it aside. When I felt the point knocked away, I balled and rolled, passing so close under the swipe of the great clawed foot I felt the wind. The snap of the dragon's jaws echoed off the rock like an explosion.

I came up on one knee as the dragon spun toward me, throwing a great roostertail of sand. Again it charged straight on and again I was looking down that gaping red gullet rimmed by rows of ivory white teeth. I dodged and thrust as the dragon went by, feeling the spear scrape and slide against the dragon's scales.

I avoided the jaws and claws, but not its other weapon. The beast lashed out with its great tail and I went flying.

The soft sand and my training to ball and roll saved me, but I lay stunned and spitting sand as the monster closed once more. With blurred and doubled vision I saw the great bulk block out the daylight, a huge paw come up and the talons spread, and then descend to crush out my life.

By instinct more than planning I thrust up with the sword. The rising point met the descending piledriver paw and my arm was slammed down to the sand. The force of the huge leg drove the point clean through the dragon's foot. With a roar of rage and pain the beast jerked back, raking me up the side with a claw. It rolled over and over, twisting and snapping at its injured member and making the canyon ring with its cries.

I rolled in the other direction, shook my head to clear it and snatched up the spear. I circled cautiously to its blind side as it gave all its attention to trying to bite the sword out of its paw, like a cat beset by a thorn.

It was on its stomach with its head curved toward the injured paw, opening space between the neck scales. I closed almost on tiptoe until I was nearly alongside it and thrust with all my strength down the crevice between the scales and into the neck.

Hot, foul blood sprayed out over me. The dragon's roar became a high, warbling scream and it twisted to me, snapping and flailing, catching my spear and breaking it in two. I skipped back, fell ass over teakettle, and rolled and rolled while the hideous din echoed and rang through my head. Eventually I hit a boulder at the edge of the canyon and lay there without moving, watching its struggles.

The dragon never regained its feet, but it took a long, long time to die.

When it was finally quiet again I rested by the bank of the pool, trying to get my breath as I examined my wounds. Scratches and bruises, but apart from the gash in my side, nothing serious. I stripped off the torn and bloodstained dress and washed the wound in the creek, wincing at the icy chill. Then I used the point of the spear to slice off the hem and bound the wound with it before donning what was left of the garment.

It wasn't even midmorning. The sun was barely halfway across the sand, the dragon's corpse part in shadow. Back at the Temple, my sisters would be explaining to a very frightened would-be sacrifice how she came to be occupying the body of the Chief Combat Instructor of the Mother's Elite Guard instead of the stomach of a dragon. With luck they'd be able to explain a few other things to her and perhaps start her thinking before we were whisked back into our proper bodies.

Sometime tomorrow the Mother's Voice would reach the village and explain what had happened and who they had to thank for their deliverance. I would be gone by then; the transference spell only runs from sunup to sunup.

"You look like Hell," I said to my reflection. But inside I was elated at a job well done—and giddy with relief that I had survived.

How many times had I been led to one of these unholy altars as a virgin sacrifice? Six? Seven? After today my luck was past due to run out.

Well, my replacement was coming along nicely. She'd be ready when the time came.

Meanwhile we were stopping the slaughter of virgins all through the Eight Kingdoms. As word spread and dragons died at the hands of their "victims," fewer of these unholy bargains were struck every year. These dungheap nobles would learn that if they wanted to bribe monsters, they would have to do it with cattle or sheep, not girl children.

I sighed and picked up the spear shaft. Using it as a staff, I started back up the canyon. I had only to show myself at the village with the news the dragon was dead and my job was done.

The Prince met me at the top of the stone stairs.

He was hastily arrayed for battle with no coif under his helm and his shield crooked on his arm.

"The Dragon?" he asked in wide-eyed awe.

"Dead, your highness."

"They said a demon . . ."

"No demon, Only the grace of the Mother."

"Ah," he breathed. Then he smiled.

"You have done your King a great service, and doubtless a fine reward is due you."

"Not I, your highness," I said in a little-girl voice.

"Oh yes," he said, moving closer. "My father will be pleased." His smiled brightened. "As I am pleased. I told my father this morning that it was a great pity for someone as lovely as you to be wasted on a dragon."

Forcefully, he clasped his shield arm around my waist drawing me to him. He ran his right hand down my body, stroking my chin and neck, cupping my breast, tracing the line of my belly and ending with his hand pressing against my loins.

Inwardly I sighed. Well, it *had* been a tough one. I *was* entitled to enjoy myself a little, wasn't I? After all, you can't be *all* duty. So I smiled shyly, blushed modestly and spread my thighs a little under the pressure of his probing hand.

Then I broke his bloody arm.

DRAGON LOVERS
by Cynthia Drolet

And, as usual, I try to find a funny piece to end the anthology—"Always leave them laughing"—and I have yet to come across anyone who read this story and didn't get a good laugh out of it. At least it's different; I never read a kill-that-dragon story before this which suggested that a dragon had anything in common with a black widow spider.

T he trail-weary pony stood patiently at the gate, flicking its tail across its dusty flanks.

A *mountain pony*, the Baron thought with disgust, *not even a proper horse. A* sherka—*like its owner*.

Reluctantly, the Baron returned his attention to the *mesha* standing calmly before him. Her cloak and breeches, like her pony, were dusty from the trail, but they fit her well and were in good repair. Her boots, once the mud was uncaked from them, would be nearly new and her wheat-blonde hair was sensibly tied into two braids to keep it from flying into her face while she rode. *A lady of the lower nobility then,* the Baron guessed. Which was going to make it harder for him to simply dismiss her. She was small, he saw, with the barest outlines of a woman curving her coarsely-woven tunic. But it was to a point above her shoulder that the Baron's eyes kept straying, for flung across her back was a broad-bladed shortsword no longer than the Baron's own arm, yet still looking too large for the *mesha*'s small hands.

"So," and the Baron didn't bother to try to hide the scorn in his voice, "you have come to do battle with Diadom, Eater of Souls."

Ignoring the Baron's tone, the *mesha* said, "If you are still offering a thousand in gold for the dragon's head, then yes, that is why I am here."

The Baron sneered. "And just how do you propose to take its head? With that mouse-pricker of yours?" He gestured rudely toward the sword she carried.

"I wasn't aware that it mattered *how* the dragon was slain." The *mesha*'s voice betrayed nothing in its evenness. "Have you a preference then, Excellency?"

"*Mesha*," the Baron said slowly, angered by her attitude, "have you ever *seen* a dragon? Do you comprehend their size? Diadom has been known to drag fatted bulls from the fields. With no more than a *sherka* for a steed and a carving knife for a blade you will never come within a dozen yards of the beast! If it's suicide you seek, girl, go somewhere else. I'll not have the responsibility of your blood on my lands!" He fought down the impulse to strike the girl, to beat some sense into her. Instead, he turned sharply away on his heel.

"Excellency." Her calm voice stopped him dead. When he turned to face her, there was a dark look building in his eyes. "Which way to Diadom's lair?"

The Baron's voice shook as he strove to master his temper. "Why, I should think a clever dragonslayer like yourself ought to be able to track down her own prey. Shouldn't she?"

He laughed, cruelly.

And the sound died in his throat.

The *mesha*'s face blurred. Her body blurred. The ground and air around her blurred. As the Baron watched, tails and claws appeared, attaching themselves to the frail-looking woman who was a woman no longer but a sizable, and quite formidable, dragon now.

"Shapeshifter!" The word was no more than a breath on the Baron's lips.

The dragon-*mesha* whuffed about a little, getting used to its voice, then let loose with a roar. From the green hills to the north an answering cry came. The dragon-*mesha* lumbered off in that direction.

The little mountain pony watched after her awhile then dropped its head, resigning itself to another long, companionless night.

The little spider stepped gingerly onto the strands of the alien web. Pulled forward step by slow step by an instinct it was powerless to fight, it advanced toward the center of the web where the sleek black female awaited him. The little male hesitated, but the female fell swiftly upon him. She wrapped her legs around him, forcing him to mate with her, moving against him with a fierce and unmistakable joy.

Then, even before the act was finished, the female's legs tightened around the small body between them, stilling the male's violent struggles.

Calmly she began to munch on his head.

The Baron woke, sweating. In the distance he could hear the roars and moans and squeals of dragons and the strange and eerie sounds, coupled with his repulsive dream, made him shiver.

Toward daybreak he heard a loud and angry roar, cut off abruptly just as the sun's first rays touched the greening hills. Last night's dream-image of the female spider with the male's nearly severed head stuck in her mouth flitted through the Baron's mind.

Later, the Baron found the *mesha* standing in his courtyard. On the ground beside her rested Diadom's great bloody head.

The Baron pressed a pouch of coins gratefully into her small hand. "My Lady, forgive me for what I spoke earlier. I heard the dragon's cries the whole night through. It . . . it must have been horrible!"

"No, Excellency," the *mesha* said, a contented smile on her lips. "I think you misunderstand entirely. The pleasure has been all mine. Truly. In fact, I spent a *most* satisfying night." Her eyes momentarily lost their focus. "Aye, a most satisfying night indeed. And, confidentially," she leaned toward the Baron to whisper, "it takes a *lot* to satisfy me."

Grinning, she mounted her *sherka*. "Oh, you were

right about one thing, Excellency," she called over her shoulder. "I *didn't* realize how *big* a dragon could get." With her knees she urged her pony forward. "But I do now. Ah, sweet and blessed goddesses yes, I truly do now."

The contentment in her smile deepened as the *mesha* rode off into the morning.

DAW

DAW PRESENTS THESE BESTSELLERS BY
MARION ZIMMER BRADLEY

NON-DARKOVER NOVELS

☐ **HUNTERS OF THE RED MOON**   (UE1968—$2.95)

☐ **THE SURVIVORS**   (UE1861—$2.95)
  (With Paul Edwin Zimmer)

☐ **WARRIOR WOMAN**   (UE2253—$3.50)

NON-DARKOVER ANTHOLOGIES

☐ **GREYHAVEN**   (UE1985—$2.75)

☐ **SWORD AND SORCERESS**   (UE1928—$2.95)

☐ **SWORD AND SORCERESS II**   (UE2041—$2.95)

☐ **SWORD AND SORCERESS III**   (UE2141—$3.50)

☐ **SWORD AND SORCERESS IV**   (UE2210—$3.50)

☐ **SWORD AND SORCERESS V**   (UE2288—$3.95)

COLLECTIONS

☐ **LYTHANDE** (with Vonda N. McIntyre)   (UE2291—$3.95)

☐ **THE BEST OF MARION ZIMMER BRADLEY** (edited
by Martin H. Greenberg)   (UE2268—$3.95)

DAW

DAW PRESENTS THESE BESTSELLERS BY
MARION ZIMMER BRADLEY

THE DARKOVER NOVELS

The Founding

☐ DARKOVER LANDFALL   UE2234—$3.95

The Ages of Chaos

☐ HAWKMISTRESS!   UE2239—$3.95
☐ STORMQUEEN!   UE2092—$3.95

The Hundred Kingdoms

☐ TWO TO CONQUER   UE2174—$3.50

The Renunciates (Free Amazons)

☐ THE SHATTERED CHAIN   UE1961—$3.50
☐ THENDARA HOUSE   UE2240—$3.95
☐ CITY OF SORCERY   UE2122—$3.95

Against the Terrans: The First Age

☐ THE SPELL SWORD   UE2237—$3.95
☐ THE FORBIDDEN TOWER   UE2235—$3.95

Against the Terrans: The Second Age

☐ THE HERITAGE OF HASTUR   UE2238—$3.95
☐ SHARRA'S EXILE   UE1988—$3.95

THE DARKOVER ANTHOLOGIES
with The Friends of Darkover

☐ THE KEEPER'S PRICE   UE2236—$3.95
☐ SWORD OF CHAOS   UE2172—$3.50
☐ FREE AMAZONS OF DARKOVER   UE2096—$3.50
☐ THE OTHER SIDE OF THE MIRROR   UE2185—$3.50
☐ RED SUN OF DARKOVER   UE2230—$3.95

DAW

Don't Miss These Exciting DAW Anthologies

DAW

Attention:

DAW BOOK COLLECTORS

"A Bibliographic Retrospective of DAW Books, 1972-1987" entitled:

FUTURE AND FANTASTIC WORLDS

by Sheldon Jaffery

is now available from Starmont House and certain selected bookshops.

It contains a complete coverage of every DAW Book, its logo and order number, number of pages, cover artist, and date of publication, as well as descriptive material about the book. Also included are three indexes: an Author-Title Index, an Artist-Title Index, and a Title Index.

The book is available by mail from:

STARMONT HOUSE
P.O. Box 851
Mercer Island, WA 98040

and costs $29.95 for the hardcover edition, $19.95 paperbound. DAW Books will not be selling this title directly—please do not order it from us.

This notice is for the benefit of our readers and is not a paid advertisement.

—*D.A.W.*